The Forgotten Duke

Diamonds in the Rough

SOPHIE BARNES

THE FORGOTTEN DUKE
Diamonds in the Rough

Copyright © 2020 by Sophie Barnes

Printed in the USA.

Cover Design and Interior Format

©

ALSO BY SOPHIE BARNES

CHAPTER ONE

London
September, 1820

EVERYTHING IN REGINA'S LIFE HAD always gone according to plan. She'd been born on March fourteenth, exactly as the physician and midwife had predicted. Since then, her sole purpose had been to become an accomplished lady. She'd been educated in a manner befitting the daughter of a British peer. And so, it was not surprising that she could play the pianoforte, embroider monograms on handkerchiefs, converse in French, and dance as if floating on air.

Her life was as it should be, as it had been designed to be, and she had no illusions about the duty that would one day be required of her. As a female, she would have to make the best possible match. Love would not factor into this eventuality since her marriage would without doubt be one of convenience.

Her parents had spent the last eighteen years preparing her for this. And yet her father, Charles Berkly, Earl of Hedgewick, still managed to surprise her when he interrupted tea one afternoon to inform her that she and the Marquess of Stokes were to be married.

The very next day.

By special license.

Apprehensive and slightly dazed, Regina told herself that all would be well. Her father had made a magnificent match – one that would elevate not only her but her entire family. She trusted him to have her best interests at heart, so she did not think to protest the hasty union or to remind her father that she and Stokes had never met. Instead, she breathed a sigh of relief when he described the marquess as a handsome youth with a fondness for poetry and music. She imagined herself enjoying his company, of entertaining him in the evenings with music and song, and of giving him children as duty required. She convinced herself that in time, love would blossom between them and that they would be happy together.

But when Stokes arrived that same evening for an introductory dinner, and was shown into the parlor by Plath, the butler, Regina realized that everything she'd imagined was but an illusion. Instead, she was expected to walk into hell and live there.

The resolve required to maintain her composure as Stokes approached her, to drop into an elegant curtsey and not run screaming from the room, was extraordinarily difficult. Like sitting still while a swarm of bees tried to sting you. But she now understood why she'd never met the marquess before and why she had to marry him faster than she could blink. Most likely, her father hoped to complete the task before she realized she was marrying a child.

Even though it was rather difficult not to notice such a thing, considering Stokes's appearance. He had the typical rounded features of a young adolescent with a lanky body to match. Regina supposed he could be fifteen, if she were lucky, but rather feared he might be much younger than that. His face was regrettably covered in pimples of varying sizes, though this was the least problematic aspect since he would likely be rid of those within a few years. Of greater concern was his difficult gait, which suited an aging old man much better. And when he extended his hand to Regina, the stiff rigidity forcing his fingers to curl at odd angles was more than she could bear.

With a gasp, she looked up, only to be met by pain in his eyes. The heartbeats thumping fast inside her slowed, easing a path toward sympathetic understanding. He did not want this marriage any more than she did.

So Regina smiled. Not because she was pleased on either of their behalves, but because it was what Stokes deserved. However difficult this situation was for her, surely it must be worse for him, not only because he was so much younger but because he probably thought she would spurn him.

"It is a pleasure to finally meet you, my lord," she said as she placed her hand in his.

Behind him, his parents, the Duke and Duchess of Windham, looked on with a mixture of hopefulness and concern.

"The pleasure is entirely mine," Stokes told her politely. He gave her hand a gentle pull and she let him create the appearance of helping her rise.

"Perhaps the two of us can take a turn about the room together before we're called in for dinner?"

"I'd like that," Regina said. She deliberately avoided looking over at her brother Marcus, whose glower she could feel as acutely as the heat emanating from the fireplace. He would undoubtedly have some choice words with their parents later, but for now, Regina believed the best policy would be to make the most of an already difficult situation.

So she placed her hand lightly on the arm Stokes offered and forced her steps to match his as they moved toward the far end of the room.

They reached the bay window looking out on the dusky garden and drew to a halt. Giving her a sideways glance, Stokes spoke in a low whisper. "I am sorry about all of this. When my parents told me of their intention to see me wed, I did my best to dissuade them. But Papa is determined to secure the lineage of his title and with the undeniable progression of my illness, he sees Hedgewick's offer as the only hope of doing so."

His comment caused numerous issues to poke and prod at Regina's mind, like how her father had apparently started all of this by approaching Windham. And the idea that she would have to lie with him tomorrow after the wedding.

Forcing all her aversions to this aside, she chose to get to know this boy whose life must be unbearably difficult, and asked, "Do the physicians know what it is that ails you?"

He inhaled deeply, as if this subject required additional strength. "They say it is primary asthenic gout." He looked at her directly. "Incurable, by all accounts."

"I am sorry." It was all she could think to say even though she knew it was not enough.

"Apparently, it is rare in children, which makes me special according to some physicians." He gave a low snort. "I must say I've never felt so myself."

Regina winced. The physicians were idiots if they believed that Stokes would find comfort in such a notion. "How long have you suffered like this?"

"The symptoms began five years ago and have been progressing since."

Hoping he wouldn't detect the pity she felt for him, she casually asked, "And how old are you now, if you do not mind my asking."

"Fourteen." The edge of his mouth lifted and for a second she caught a glimpse of the fun-loving boy he might have been if he'd been granted good health. "It is the age of consent for a boy, provided his parents approve."

Regina nodded. The duke and duchess were hoping to marry him off as expediently as possible before he got worse and lost his chance completely.

Determined to put a positive spin on the situation, Regina said, "You're probably the most eligible bachelor I've ever met. A pity you're going to be squandered on an old woman like me."

He grinned with what appeared to be genuine amusement. "I doubt there's a woman in all of England as beautiful as you."

She nudged him slightly while giving him a sly smile. "Top points for charm and for not inquiring about my age."

Affecting a debonair look, he said, "No proper

gentleman would ever think to do so."

"I am eighteen," Regina confessed with a chuckle.

"And entirely wasted on me."

Regret flickered in his eyes and Regina's heart squeezed painfully in response. "Don't say that. You and I—"

"Have no hope of happiness." His blunt statement, as obviously simple as it was, jarred Regina's soul.

"Don't say that," she whispered.

"Why not?" He gave her a quizzical look. "It is the truth, when you think of it." When she said nothing in response to this, he added, "My illness will not kill me for at least a couple of decades."

With a gulp, she met his gaze head on. "I should hope not."

"You say that now, but as I deteriorate with time, you will regret being my wife, just as much as I will regret ruining your life."

Regina stared at him and as she did so, it occurred to her that she had to find a way to save them both. Perhaps they could have the marriage annulled immediately after? It was an option, though not a very good one when she considered the vicar who would be conducting the ceremony. He ought not be able to do so unless she and Stokes gave their consent. And yet, it was becoming increasingly clear that they would be pronounced husband and wife no matter what they said or did. Their parents were powerful people. What chance did she and a child stand against their determined wills?

Fear started to drip through Regina like freezing rain. "I'll find a way out of this," she assured him.

He raised an eyebrow. "How?"

"I don't know." Short of running away...

Her nerves tightened in response to that thought. It went against the obligation instilled in her since childhood. It felt wrong and disobedient and... wonderfully freeing, all things considered.

Swallowing, she glanced sideways. Assembled on the sofa and in the armchairs were their family members, all watching with syrupy smiles painted on their faces.

Except for Marcus, who looked rather grim. His eyebrows were drawn together, one partially obscured by a dark blonde lock of hair. Jaw tight, he appeared to be holding a great deal of anger in check. If she were to flee, she would miss him the most, which was something she contemplated a great deal as the evening wore on.

When the time eventually came for Stokes and his parents to depart, he stepped close enough to Regina so he could whisper next to her ear, "Time is running out." He leaned back and gave her the sort of sad smile that quickened her pulse with the knowledge that only she had the power to act.

"We shall see you again in the morning," Lord Windham said as if they were preparing to start a joint venture together, which Regina supposed they were, in a way.

Hedgewick smiled with the satisfaction of a lion who'd just caught a fat gazelle. "Eight o'clock sharp." He smiled again and bowed toward Lady Windham. A few more parting words were spoken and then Stokes was helped down the front steps of Hedgewick House and into the awaiting carriage. The front door closed with a deep thud and Regina expelled a long breath.

"Well," Hedgewick said, turning about so he could regard his family. "That went rather splendidly I'd say."

"The Windhams are delightful people," Louise said in support of her husband. "Very proper and most elegantly attired."

Marcus stared at them both as if they'd just performed a series of cartwheels. "Are you serious?" Apparently he'd decided the time had come to speak up. "That is all you have to say?"

"What else is there?" Louise asked her son in that timid voice that had always been so comforting and soothing. Now it just sounded weak and devoid of character. Like tepid tea.

"I don't know," Marcus clipped in an acrid tone that warned Regina of the argument to come. "How about the fact that you're planning to foist Regina off on a decrepit child?"

Hedgewick's eyes darkened to storm cloud grey. "Your sister is going to be a duchess one day."

"At what cost?" Marcus asked. He swung around to face Regina. "You cannot go through with this. I won't permit it."

"You. Won't. Permit. It?" Hedgewick's voice trembled while fine flecks of spittle flew from his mouth. His face had turned beet red. Leaning forward, he glared at his son. "Perhaps if you were head of this family you'd have a say in the matter. But you don't." He turned his attention on Regina whose skin began to prick in response to his anger. She'd never seen him like this. He'd always been loving and kind. "Everything has been arranged, so the wedding will proceed as planned." Leaning back, he puffed out an agitated breath through his nose. "I suggest you get some sleep now so you can be well-rested and ready."

"Yes, Papa," she obediently murmured while Marcus gave her a stupefied look of concern. Pretending to be agreeable seemed like the simplest option while coming to terms with the fact that not even her brother was able to sway her father's decision.

"I do not understand you," Marcus told her moments later when both of their parents had retired. "You cannot seriously want this for yourself."

"Stokes isn't so terrible." She started up the stairs while Marcus trailed behind. "He and I will get along well with each other, I think."

"But he's…I mean…how will you…" His words were blown away on a heavy sigh of frustration.

"I have always known that I would marry for convenience. This isn't much different than the women who have to marry men thrice their age."

"It's different in the sense that Stokes might stay alive for some time yet."

"Good God," Regina gasped as she halted halfway up the steps and glanced back at her brother. "I should certainly hope so."

Marcus lifted one shoulder. "Forgive me. That comment was in bad taste. I just wish you could marry the man of your choosing and not be a pawn in whatever it is Papa's trying to achieve."

"You think there's more to his wanting this marriage than social status alone?"

"Considering how angered he was by my mere suggestion that you not go through with the wedding, I'd say so. But I cannot imagine what it might be."

Regina pondered this as she resumed her progress. When she reached her bedchamber, she paused. "I love you dearly, Marcus. You know that, right?"

Tilting his head, he gave her an odd look. "Of course."

She forced a smile. "Good." She pressed down the handle and opened the door. Telling her brother she might not be there by morning would be a mistake. He'd only want to help her escape and thus implicate himself in her disappearance, which was something she could not allow. Besides, she still wasn't sure she'd go through with it.

"I love you too," he told her gently, and she was glad for the darkness because it stopped him from seeing the tears in her eyes. "Sleep well."

Echoing his parting words, she entered her bedchamber, closed the door and leaned against it. Could she really run away? Her parents would not expect it, which would make the task so much easier. This was a benefit to being the dutiful daughter, the proper young lady who never strayed from protocol and always behaved with decorum. She could simply walk out the front door and vanish.

Glancing at the white lace gown hanging from a hook on the wall, Regina allowed the idea of running away to capture her imagination more fully. She'd worn the dress when she'd made her debut at the Coventry ball three months earlier. It had been altered slightly this afternoon by a maid tasked with turning it into her wedding dress. In Regina's opinion, too much lace and silk netting had been added, but she supposed it would do. She stepped forward and touched the fabric, letting it slide between her fingers. The bonnet she would wear sat on her dressing table, with additional silk netting sewn onto the brim to create a frothy ruffle that descended toward the back where it fell away in a big voluminous tail.

Regina allowed a sad chuckle. She would look like a cake in this.

Her brow puckered even as she pulled the gown into her arms and pressed it against her chest. What would life be like for her if she married Stokes? It wasn't as if she loved some other man. And yet, the realization that they wouldn't dance with each other or ride together or enjoy the sort of active life that was meant for people their age was a blow. Instead, they would live like old people, imprisoned in some large manor somewhere.

She laughed bitterly. What good would her title do her then? What solace would she find in having done her duty when even Stokes had made it clear that he had no desire to marry? Indeed his features had softened with gratitude when she'd said she would find a solution. But could she go through with it? She clutched her dress tighter. If she sought refuge with friends her father would find her. The inevitable would only be delayed. So where would she go?

She pondered these questions for hours while pacing her bedchamber floor, until she was sure she must have worn out the sheen. Each question left her more indecisive and unsure than the last. At some point during the night, she'd put on her wedding gown and matching bonnet for no other purpose than to confirm how ridiculous she would look. She still wore it now as the darkness began to recede to the corners of her room. Dawn was breaking and she'd soon lose her chance to leave.

Could she be brave and do the unexpected? Could she face the unknown alone?

"I have to," she murmured. It was time to put herself first for a change. Only then would she stand a chance of building the sort of future she wished for – a future she hadn't even known she wanted until today. But the truth was that she dreamed of falling in love and of being loved in return. She longed for compatibility with a man strong and healthy enough to be her partner for life.

Glancing at her cheval glass, she considered the woman reflected back and made her decision. "I have to save myself and Stokes from misery."

But first, she had to get changed.

So she reached for the end of the ribbons that held her bonnet in place and prepared to give them a pull when the sound of an upstairs door closing caused her to pause. The servants were already rising. There wasn't any more time.

Giving a resolute nod, she abandoned the thought of putting on a more practical dress, eased her bedchamber door open and stopped to listen. The clock in the hall chimed five. Soon the maids would start cleaning the downstairs rooms.

With this in mind, Regina stepped into the

hallway and headed toward the stairs. Descending them on her tiptoes, she made her way into the foyer. No one was about yet. The front door was right there. Unguarded.

Regina moved toward it, unbolted the lock, and opened the door to cool morning air. Mist sat low in the street, concealing most of the buildings. Heart pounding, she glanced back over her shoulder once before stepping outside, closing the door behind her, and breaking into a run.

She wasn't sure where she was going exactly, but she had to get out of Mayfair before someone saw her and forced her to go back home. The wrath she would face there would likely surpass what her father had shown toward Marcus last night.

Turning onto Piccadilly, she raced toward a side street and almost skidded into it in her haste to escape the clatter of hooves from a carriage somewhere behind her. This was madness. Good God, what was she thinking? Perhaps she ought to go back before anyone realized she was missing. But her feet didn't slow, they just kept going as if propelled by the part of her brain that refused to accept what her parents were doing. Why would they force such a hasty wedding upon her or Stokes? Why was her father so unrelenting? It was almost as if this match mattered more to him than she did.

Regina's chest tightened against the air being forced in and out of her lungs. She had no idea where she was now, she reflected as her slippers struck the pavement with increasing speed. The streets and buildings were unfamiliar, though still somewhat respectable.

Something clanged behind her, causing her to dart down a street to her left where she almost smashed into a man. He staggered sideways, his hand briefly touching her elbow as she swerved around him.

"Looking for a groom?" His drunken voice turned to lewd laughter. "I'll help you out!"

Ignoring him, Regina continued on her way with increased determination. The silk netting and lace billowing out around her merged with the thickening fog in a ghostly effect. Three streets later, her toe caught an uneven spot on the ground and she tripped, stumbling forward with a gasp. Her arms cartwheeled as she made a desperate attempt to maintain her balance. But her body was angled too far forward, and her speed only added momentum to the fall that now seemed inevitable.

Until her entire front connected with something warm and wonderfully solid that instantly stopped her descent. An arm came around her, bracing her against the person who'd caught her, and Regina instinctively started to struggle.

"What the devil?" a masculine voice muttered. "Be still, damn it!

Regina gasped and looked up at the man who now held her.

A pair of coffee-colored eyes stared down into hers with mesmerizing intensity. Raven locks protruded at haphazard angles from beneath the brim of a velvet top hat. Expressive eyebrows drew together in wonder, puckering a prominent forehead and drawing Regina's attention toward the man's nose. It was elegantly shaped in a chiseled straight line that slanted toward a neatly trimmed moustache. The dense hair hovered above a wide mouth that presently smirked at her with what could only be described as lethal amusement.

Recognizing him from all the sketches she'd seen in the newspapers over the years, she blurted the first thing that came to her mind. "I know who you are." Carlton Guthrie's notoriety was such that not knowing who he was would have been impossible. His smirk became more pronounced as the edge of his mouth curled upward. "You're the Scoundrel of St. Giles."

CHAPTER TWO

"AT YER SERVICE," CARLTON SAID while continuing to hold the young woman who'd hurled herself into his arms. Not because he'd quit being a gentleman the day his father died, or because he wished to exert his power over her, but because there were very few pleasures to be had in this life and he'd decided to savor each one. "And who, might I ask, are ye?"

She tilted her chin up a notch. To some, she might have seemed confident, but Carlton didn't miss the tremor in her jawline or the pulse vibrating at her neck. "Lady Regina Berkly, if you please." Even her voice was strained and a notch too high. "And since you are here, I would," she glanced around quickly before returning her gaze to him and raising her chin even higher, "like to enlist your help."

He bristled in response to her name, which was all too familiar. If she was somehow related to the man who'd haunted his nightmares for two long decades, he'd bloody well use her to take his revenge. Already a cool sweat had broken out at the nape of his neck. Clenching his fingers in the mass of fabric surrounding her, he attempted to slow the blood rushing through his veins.

Forcing a bland expression even as his heart thumped, he released her and casually asked, "With what?"

She squared her shoulders and tried to adjust the layers of billowing white around her. A pointless attempt at pretending that strolling around St. Giles and asking criminals for help was a normal everyday occurrence for her. "With avoiding my wedding."

"You're—" he gave her a full perusal and acknowledged that the silk netting now made sense— "a bride."

A firm nod confirmed this. "Forced into unhappy matrimony with the Marquess of Stokes."

His muscles tensed so much they started to tremble. Effecting indifference became an immediate challenge. *The Marquess of Stokes.* He knew the title well, though he did not know the face of the man who currently held it.

With the fierceness of a general warding off an enemy on the attack, Carlton kept the past at bay so he could think. He considered his options carefully for a moment and eventually asked. "Who are ye related to, exactly?"

"The Earl of Hedgewick is my father. My brother is—"

"Viscount Seabrook. Yes, I know."

She looked at him with some surprise but Carlton didn't bother explaining. He only smiled and offered his arm. "I'd be delighted to give ye sanctuary fer as long as ye need it, me lady. 'Tis the least I can do to ensure yer safety."

Instead of accepting his offer however, she took

a step back. "You want me to come with you?"

"How else do ye propose I help ye?"

"I…" She glanced around again and it became clear her courage was finally starting to fail. "I'm not sure. Perhaps…perhaps coming here was a mistake." She stepped back even further.

Carlton dropped his arm and did his best to appear as non-threatening as possible. "Of course it was," he agreed. "St. Giles is no place fer a lady." Deliberately, he tipped the brim of his hat. "I wish ye luck with yer wedding."

Without making another move, he watched as doubt crept into her eyes, but her fear also seemed to have grown as she'd taken stock of her surroundings, which included a one-legged man with an eye-patch who stared at them from a doorway, and a ragged old woman hobbling past. So instead of accepting his help after all, Lady Regina turned on her heels and strode away.

Carlton deliberately let her go. St. Giles was a complex maze of alleyways filled with people who made their living from preying on others. It was just a matter of time before she discovered that she was lost or found herself in dire straits. The edge of his mouth curved upward. When he'd offered to take her home with him, she'd panicked, and rightfully so he supposed, given his reputation. But if he helped her…

His smile widened as he went in pursuit. Lady Regina could prove a useful asset if he could convince her to stay, but doing so would require her trust. He turned a corner, half expecting to spot some hint of her billowing gown through the now receding fog.

When he didn't, he frowned and quickened his pace. Until an undignified shriek pierced the air and alerted him to her location. Breaking into a run that almost sent his top hat flying, he raced to her rescue.

Her voice quivered through the air with panic. "Get your filthy hands off of me!"

Carlton rounded a corner and took quick stock of the situation. Pinned against a wall, Lady Regina wriggled and kicked as she tried to evade the man who held her. A brawny fellow dressed in drab clothes was pushing up against her with vile menace while his friend slid the tip of a knife up the length of her throat.

"Not a chance," the brawny man said with a low chuckle. "It's not every day we find ourselves in such splendid company."

Fists clenched, Carlton stepped forward with every intention of doing bodily harm to these men if they hurt her. "I'd recommend that ye do as the lady demands," he drawled.

The men froze at the sound of his voice and the brawny man looked over his shoulder. The moment his eyes met Carlton's, he sprang back as if propelled by a spring. His friend dropped the knife and slid sideways along the wall.

"Our apologies, Mr. Guthrie," the brawny man muttered. "We meant no disrespect."

Carlton glared back at them. "I dare say ye didn't." He moved toward the spot where Lady Regina still stood, trembling from head to toe while the two men retreated. "Apologize to the lady, lads, or I'll punish ye fer yer inconsideration."

The brawny man gulped, nodded three times

and sputtered, "I'm sorry."

"So am I," his friend blurted.

"Won't happen again. We'll just...thank you kindly and be on our way."

The pair took off down the alley like a pair of terrified boys who believed the devil was out to get them.

Carlton waited until they were out of sight before turning toward Lady Regina. Wide-eyed, she stared at him as he took a few cautious steps toward her. "Are ye all right?"

She nodded.

"Ye're not hurt in any way?"

"No. Not really," she managed, in a voice much weaker than the one she'd used when they'd first met. "Just a bit bruised, I suspect."

Muttering a curse beneath his breath, Carlton chastised himself for not acting sooner. If he'd stayed closer to her, he could have stopped the men before they grabbed her. But it was too late for regrets now. So he offered his arm once again. "I know ye don't wish to come with me, but this is no place fer a lady."

Still, she hesitated. "Where will you take me?"

"Somewhere safe where ye can get yer bearings and decide what ye want to do next." Spotting a hint of red at her neck he tamped down the anger that rose up. Instead, he jutted his chin toward her. "Ye've been nicked. Might be wise to 'ave that wound tended to."

Apprehension captured her features. "I—"

"Ye'll not be harmed while ye're with me." At least not as long as she served a purpose. "Ye've me word on that."

She seemed to consider and then, with the greatest degree of hesitation he'd ever seen, she stepped forward, accepting his escort like a lamb agreeing to accompany the wolf.

Her shoulder bumped against him as he drew her close to his side, the added contact jostling something inside his chest. She smelled like springtime, like a breeze infused with the scents of blossoms and honey. It was rather enchanting in this dismal part of town where the stench from the gutters tended to overwhelm.

It's just a touch of soap and perfume. Nothing magical. Don't let it distract you.

And yet, in spite of the fact that he meant to use her to his advantage, he could not help but ask, "Are ye sure ye trust me?"

She gave him a startled look. "You saved me. And besides, it seems like you're my best option at the moment." She said the last part so quietly he almost missed the remark.

An odd sensation swept through him, causing a tightening of his heart and a general sense of unease. No. He would not pity her. She was the daughter of the one person in this Godforsaken world whom he wanted to torture until he begged for death to save him. Years of planning and two failed attempts had made him realize that bringing a peer to his knees was no simple task. It required endless amounts of patience, planning, and waiting for just the right moment to strike. And that moment was now. He could not allow a beautiful face and a haunted pair of dazzling blue eyes to make him second guess his resolve.

Not after everything he'd gone through in order

to get to this point.

So he decided to hold his tongue and not ask her to elaborate further. The less he knew about her, the better. To sympathize with her would be disastrous.

"This way, me lady." With a firm tug, he steered her forward, further into St. Giles and toward the street leading back to The Black Swan. The occasional cripple held out a scrawny hand as they passed. Further along, they encountered a filthy youth with a hollow gaze who was pushing a cart full of rags.

"I wish I had a few coins with me," Lady Regina said when they'd gone a few additional paces.

Don't take the bait. Do not let her lure you into conversation.

"Why?" he asked, the word springing from his lips like a foxhound giving chase.

From the corner of his eye, he saw her tilt back her head and look at him from beneath the brim of her bonnet, and try as he might, he could not help but turn his gaze more fully toward her. Which was a mistake, of course. Her eyes, devoid of cynicism and hardship, were like a pair of lighthouses in the lilac shades of dawn. And he was but a sailor caught in a violent storm, helplessly drawn to the welcoming glow they emitted.

"There are people here who appear to have more use for them than I." The blueness in her eyes deepened and shimmered like pools of water reflecting the heavens. "It would be nice to help them."

Carlton cleared his throat and forced his gaze away. Clenching his jaw, he told himself that this was the sort of thing any young woman would say upon spotting a beggar. He told himself that Lady Regina was simply doing the expected. Not because she was kind or considerate but because a few coins given away would make little difference to her. In fact, it would only improve her self-worth by making her feel like she'd done a good deed. Which in turn would allow her to sleep well at night. It was *not* because she genuinely cared.

Except he knew from the pure serenity in her gaze that she did care rather a lot and that he was now trying to tell himself otherwise.

God damn it.

"We're almost there," he grumbled, his mood darkening on account of the danger she posed to his carefully crafted persona. Carlton Guthrie was supposed to be a crime lord, a hardened criminal without any scruples. The sort of man people feared.

"Did I say something wrong?" she asked.

"No."

He would not engage her further. Not when The Black Swan loomed ahead, its crooked wall slanting outward as if it might fall right into the street at any second. The timbered framework held it in place, supporting the brick and plaster. Thick rippling glass windows set in black lead dotted the façade. A sign, suspended by wrought iron swirls, depicted a black swan against a tarnished background. The script beneath was a perfect match for the artwork, the bold letters calling out to men in need of drink, a night of gambling, or the thrill of a fight. The prize to be won by those who managed to best one of Carlton's fighters was always tempting, though it remained unclaimed.

"What is that?" Regina asked, pulling away from him slightly so she could get a better view of something that must have caught her interest.

Since he'd yet to get her inside and doing so would be simpler if she went willingly, he decided to humor her by answering her question with one of his own. "What is what, me dear?"

She pointed one finger at the building next door. "Amourette's." Her nose twitched as she spoke the word. "I find it a very interesting name for a business."

Carlton bit back a surge of involuntary laughter and schooled his features. "I take it ye've never seen a brothel before," he remarked as if he believed she should have done so at some point in her life.

Her lips parted and her eyes almost looked like they might fall out of her head. A delightful shade of pink swept upward from her neckline before disappearing beneath her bonnet.

"So there are courtesans in there?" The question contained a pinch of nervousness, a spoonful of embarrassment, a cup of condemnation, and a gallon of genuine curiosity.

Knowing she might reconsider accepting his help, he smiled and drew her away from the shocking edifice and escorted her up the two steps leading into his tavern. "Not to worry, luv. The women who work there are perfectly nice. Now what say ye that we find ye somethin' to eat?"

Wariness caused her brow to pucker. Leaning back ever so slightly, she resisted his escort just enough to convey a renewed degree of hesitance. "You won't make demands in exchange?"

Seeing where her line of thought had headed, Carlton shook his head and made every effort to look as non-threatening as possible. Having her cooperation would be so much simpler than the alternative. And he really didn't feel like chasing after her again.

"I don't mistreat those under me protection. Ye understand?" When she still looked uncertain, as if the enormity of her decision to let him help her was finally sinking in, he sighed. "It would seem ye've had a rough mornin'. The fact that ye, a lady of the peerage, was runnin' through St. Giles, would attest to that. Now as ye already know, there are worse men out there than me and since it would be a shame to see any real harm come to ye, I'll offer ye shelter as long as ye need it."

"But…why? Why would you want a woman like me on your hands?" She swung her arm out beside her in a helpless gesture. "I have no means of paying you for your hospitality."

"Consider it an attempt on me part to cleanse me soul with a good deed." Spotting his right hand man, a towering Scotsman with dense auburn hair, coming toward them, Carlton folded Regina's hand into the crook of his arm. "Now 'ere's someone I must introduce ye to right away since he practically runs this establishment fer me. Lady Regina, allow me to present to ye Mr. Blayne MacNeil."

Without even thinking, Regina tightened her

grip on Guthrie's arm, anchoring herself to him like a capsizing ship in need of mooring. She was forced to tilt her head back in order to stare up at the giant of a man who stood before her. He was huge, like a monolith filling her vision.

Determined to hide her fear, she forced a smile and said, "Delighted."

MacNeil's eyes narrowed, creasing at the corners as if not trusting her sincerity. His mouth was set in a firm line, though it did appear to twitch slightly as if he attempted not to smile. "Likewise."

He spoke more gruffly than Guthrie and with less finesse. For although Guthrie's voice was uncultured, there was a flamboyant element to him that made him seem like a character from some fantastical tale. Of course, his attire, cut from vibrant velvet and silk, accentuated this aspect of him. And while most men would have looked comical dressed as he was, the clothes suited Guthrie, adding a larger than life appeal to him that intrigued Regina more than it ought to.

Had he been a sculpture, there would have been no doubt about the love and skill the artist had applied when he'd made him. By comparison, MacNeil resembled the work of a novice. His features completely lacked Guthrie's elegance.

Eyeing Guthrie's profile, she saw that even his cheekbones were perfect, which was probably an odd observation to make of a man. But if she were honest - truly honest - she had to concede that Guthrie was not only handsome, but lovely to look at. With the exception of his moustache. That part of him was downright hideous and she could not help but wonder what he might look like without it.

Not that she'd ever find out. She'd definitely never acquire the courage required to ask him to remove it. And he would never bow to such a request anyway. And why on earth did she suddenly wish that he would?

She had no idea how to answer that question.

She also wasn't the least bit sure she'd made the right decision in coming here with him. For the fact of the matter was that she was a lady. She didn't belong amid riffraff. And yet she was standing in the middle of a tavern with a man suspected of thieving, blackmail, and possibly murder. Come to think of it, she ought to be terrified. Yet she wasn't. Not anymore. Which might be incredibly naïve, but the fact that he'd come to her rescue had eased her mind and encouraged her to trust him. If only a little.

Guthrie glanced down at her, frowned, and returned his attention to MacNeil. "Her ladyship's 'ungry," Guthrie murmured, and to Regina's mortification, her belly answered with a low rumble. "Can ye arrange fer a breakfast plate?"

"Of course." MacNeil's expression remained somber. "Where should I bring it?"

Guthrie was silent a moment as if considering. After giving Regina another quick look, he said, "To me office." Grabbing her hand, he strode toward a doorway on the opposite side of the room, pulling her along.

"Mr. Guthrie, perhaps we could simply remain here?" Years of perfect upbringing rooted in etiquette and the need to preserve her virtue, not to mention the apprehension of being alone with this man, revolted against his intention to spirit her away to his lair.

"Not a chance."

"May I ask why?" She tried to dig in her heels but that just made her feet skid across the hardwood planking of the floor.

He came to a halt so abruptly she almost slammed into his broad back. A whiff of something wonderfully pleasant drifted toward her: a smoky aroma infused with a hint of sandalwood and coffee. Curiously, she was tempted to press her nose into his plush velvet jacket for a deeper inhalation.

Thankfully, he prevented her from doing something as foolishly improper as that by tersely telling her, "Because putting ye on display an' lettin' the world know ye're here would be unwise. Seein' as ye're tryin' to hide."

Contrition forced her back a step. "Of course."

He held her gaze, allowing her to lose herself in the fathomless depths of his dark brown eyes. When people considered the neutral color of brown, they often thought of it as flat and dull, lacking depth and vibrancy. But that simply wasn't the case where Guthrie's eyes were concerned. An almost-black umber ring surrounded the pupil. It turned to rich mahogany as it fanned outward and was overlaid by flecks of gold.

He turned away, breaking the spell even as he left her shaken to her core. She didn't approve of the life he led or of the things he'd reputedly done. By all accounts he belonged in prison. To trust him would probably prove her a fool. And yet, the alternative was unthinkable. After having a knife pressed to her throat only half an hour ago, she had no wish to venture back into the streets of St. Giles on her own. And returning home so she and Stokes could be married was equally unsettling. Which left her with only one option, even if it was far from perfect.

They reached Guthrie's office and he gestured toward a green velvet armchair, inviting Regina to sit. Without comment, he then went to pour himself a drink. Or so it seemed until he produced a handkerchief from his pocket, dipped it in the liquid and pressed it to the side of her neck where she'd been cut. She inhaled sharply, in part because of the sting, but mostly because of the unexpected touch. It was gentle and warm, even soothing and…over much too soon.

Regina blinked, heart pounding as she watched him retreat.

"Now then," he said once he'd claimed the chair opposite hers and set the glass of brandy aside. "Do ye have a plan beyond runnin' away?"

"Not really." Ignoring the discomfort of his penetrating gaze, she sank into the cushiony plushness of her chair and instantly felt as if she'd received a loving embrace. How absurd. She allowed herself a moment to glance around the room. Every item had a rich texture, from the glossy surface of Guthrie's desk, to the heavy satin drapes framing the only window, and the thick, silky pile of the carpets covering the floor.

After smoothing her skirts so they would not crease too much, she raised her hands to the ribbon securing her bonnet and began to untie it.

The silk netting on the brim had been tucked and stitched into place to create a plump pleat. It was thicker on the sides where the ends had been turned back behind the bonnet ribbons and this caused the fabric to chafe at her skin.

"Ye've not considered what will happen once yer family finds ye missing?"

"Of course I have," she said while she worked. "My father will be furious."

"And you fear his wrath," Guthrie observed. Removing his hat, he set it on his desk and raked his fingers through his shaggy locks.

Regina paused to stare, mesmerized for a moment before she managed to collect herself and avert her gaze. "I cannot deny it. But even if I didn't, going through" —the bonnet ribbon came loose and slid between her fingers— "with the proceedings would have been a terrible mistake." Carefully, so as not to catch any strands of hair, she lifted the bonnet off her head and placed it in her lap.

When Guthrie didn't comment on what she'd said, she hazarded a glance in his direction. His eyes were fixed upon her with even greater intensity than before, his expression tight with some indefinable emotion that caused her stomach to flutter and tiny sparks of heat to creep over her skin. Reflexively, she sucked in a breath and quickly returned her gaze to her bonnet. She could not possibly be attracted to him, could she?

Her throat dried up on that thought. Of course not. He was a St. Giles criminal for goodness sake. And even if he weren't, he wasn't well-groomed enough for her to consider in such a light. His debonair messiness ought to discourage her interest while his moustache should make her recoil from the idea of him possibly kissing her.

She forced herself to swallow past the thickness of her tongue. Where in blazes had the notion of his mouth meeting hers come from? As she glanced at him from beneath her lashes, the quickening of her pulse answered that question: the texture of those layered hairs and the need to discover what they might feel like against her lips was shockingly alluring. It awoke the same kind of impulse inside her that always prevailed whenever she entered a modiste's shop. She never could stop from touching the fabrics, the urge to feel the grain slide against her fingers impossible to resist.

"Why?"

Regina blinked. "What?" Heavens, her voice sounded breathless.

Guthrie smiled, eyes gleaming as if he knew precisely what she'd been thinking. He leaned forward, bringing his rich fragrance closer. "Why would marryin' a marquess be a mistake?"

Aware that her body was heating by several degrees, Regina struggled to face this self-possessed man without coming across as a timid nitwit. "Because I want more for myself than to be a pawn in my father's plans," she blurted, only to snap her mouth shut and stare back at Guthrie in shock. She couldn't believe she'd just said that. She also couldn't believe how good it felt to do so.

The edge of Guthrie's mouth lifted, slanting his moustache. "Ye've had enough of being the dutiful daughter, have ye?"

Regina sat up straighter, tamped down her

rioting nerves, and looked Guthrie squarely in the eye. "I'm tired of having to sacrifice my own happiness to satisfy others." She pursed her lips in thought. "Do you know, I've never been allowed to eat cake or go swimming?"

He frowned back at her. "Why on earth not?"

"According to Mama, cake ruins the figure while swimming exposes ones skin to the sun."

"That's not entirely untrue."

"Perhaps not," she agreed, "but to deny a child the joy of such things completely is unreasonable." They were also just two examples of all the things she'd been deprived of through the years for some absurd reason or other. Somehow, she'd managed to convince herself that her parents were always right and that they only had her best interests at heart.

"In that case," Guthrie was saying, "I'll have to ask the cook to prepare a cake for ye while ye're here. As fer the swimmin'—"

"There's no need for that. Since Mama wouldn't let me take lessons I..." She swallowed while trying to push through the wave of riotous panic the thought of submerging herself in water instilled. "I never learned, so I actually prefer to remain on land."

"A good thing too since I'd rather not go fer a splash in the Thames." He crossed his arms. "I was only goin' to say that swimmin' won't be as easy."

"Oh."

When he continued to watch her, she wondered whether she ought to say more on the matter but was stopped from doing so when MacNeil arrived with a tray. On it, she glimpsed a plate from which steam was rising in slow and inviting swirls. "When Cook learned this was for a lassie, he decided to outdo his usual efforts." Clearing a space on Guthrie's desk, he set the tray down. "Best eat it while it's hot."

Regina hesitated until Guthrie said, "Go on. I know ye're itchin' to taste it."

"Do you have a minute?" MacNeil asked Guthrie while Regina began to sample the food. Her mouth had started to water the moment she'd smelled the bacon.

"Certainly." Guthrie stood and followed Mac-Neil to the door. He paused there. "I'll be back in a trice, me lady."

Having just bitten into a slice of toast slathered in cherry preserves, Regina could only answer with a nod. Guthrie grinned and turned away, shutting the door behind him and leaving her to one of the tastiest breakfasts she'd ever had the pleasure of enjoying.

"Who is she and what do you plan on doing with her?" Blayne asked as soon as he and Carlton were alone. Arms crossed, his friend looked mighty intimidating.

Undaunted, Carlton leaned back against the wood paneled wall of the hallway. "She's Hedgewick's daughter." He savored the impact of this information, the way Blayne's eyes widened with surprise. "As to what I intend to do with 'er...I'd say that's obvious now, ain't it?"

"I should caution you, Val. That—"

"Ye know better than to use that name," Carlton snapped. No longer relaxed, he pushed away from the wall and gave Blayne his most condemning gaze. "I'll not have ye ruin things fer me last minute by bein' careless." The thought of being banished from the place he called home was a fear that he lived with daily.

"Nobody here would turn on you if they learned who you really are. They like you too well."

"Only because they think I'm one of them."

Blayne held his gaze until he eventually bowed his head and said, "My apologies, Guthrie. I misspoke, which willnae happen again. But you cannot seriously want to use an innocent lass in your quest for vengeance. It's downright diabolical, if you ask me."

Carlton glared at him. "As much as I value yer opinion, it's unwanted where Lady Regina's concerned."

"But keeping her here, surrounded by men and whores, will ruin her completely. She'll never be able to return to Society."

"As unfortunate as that may be, I cannot ignore this chance I've been given," Guthrie growled. "It's the only way I can think of fer Hedgewick to experience the sort of dread an' loss he put me through. An' as the person of greatest value to him, she—"

"Has he no son?"

"Indeed he does. But he's just the heir." Carlton smiled smugly. "That lady in there, she's 'is ladder, an' knowin' what I do about the bastard, he'll be carin' more about that than anythin' else in the world."

"Maybe," Blayne conceded, "but does she deserve what's coming?"

"I 'ave no intention of findin' out." Christ, the woman had already caused doubt to hook itself in his conscience. Irritated, he tightened his jaw. "The last thing I need is to learn that I have a heart this late in the game."

"That would be an inconvenience," Blayne told him acerbically.

Carlton narrowed his gaze. "Ye're not goin' soft with age are ye?"

Blayne flattened his mouth. "I woulnae dare to."

"Good to know." Inhaling deeply and pushing the air back out slowly, Carlton forced the tension in his body to subside. "Ready me bedchamber for her." Noting the horrified look on Blayne's face, Carlton rolled his eyes. "Fer Christ's sake, man, I'm not plannin' to swive her. But me room is bigger than the rest, the furniture more in line with what she's accustomed to. She'll be most comfortable there and...why are ye smiling?"

"'Cause it's starting to look like you may have a heart after all."

"I'm just tryin' to make her stay more comfortable. The happier she is with her accommodations, the less trouble she'll be."

Blayne snorted. "You can tell yourself that if you like, but it doesnae make it true." He turned away, leaving Carlton with a muttered, "I'll have the room sorted. Shouldnae take more than an hour."

Agitated, Carlton pinched the bridge of his nose and squeezed his eyes shut for a moment.

Blayne was wrong about him having an ounce of goodness in him. Only an empty space remained where his heart had once been.

Lowering his hand, he raised his chin and straightened his spine. He then returned to his office where he found Regina licking the last remains of her breakfast from her fingers.

Something inside him unfurled, curling outward with promises of warmth, companionship, happiness...

Everything he'd lost when he was a boy.

And he didn't like it one bit.

CHAPTER THREE

REGINA GLANCED AROUND THE CLUT-
TERED space she'd just been ushered into.
A bright yellow velvet sofa stood to her left with
a burgundy divan directly opposite and two chairs
upholstered in turquoise silk in between. A low
table stood at the center of the arrangement, its
surface occupied by playing cards, a chess set, and
a half filled decanter. Two bookcases stuffed to
capacity reached toward the ceiling, their shelves
bowing beneath the weight they carried. On the
floor, pushed up against the walls, were hundreds
of additional books all stacked in uneven piles. On
top of one such pile sat a misplaced teacup while a
candlestick stood on another.

Directly across from Regina, next to a blackened fireplace in which a low fire burned, was
a large wooden chest, the lid propped open by
the mountain of clothes inside. To the right was
a desk, the surface barely visible beneath a melee
of papers, trinkets, and various other items. The
accompanying chair held an ivy-green top hat on
which a tabby cat had decided to take a nap with
its legs dangling over each side.

Clearly, this room belonged to a man without a

valet or maid to offer assistance.

"It's very...eclectic," Regina said, settling on the most apt description she could think of. "I hardly know where to focus my attention." Noticing Guthrie's tight expression, she added, "There's so much to look at."

"I've collected a lot of things over the years." When he passed her, the brush of his arm against hers caused a dip in the middle of her belly. She instantly dismissed it as nothing more than a normal response to feeling out of place.

Stepping further into the room, Regina considered the stacks of books.

"Ye're welcome to read whichever ones strike yer fancy," Guthrie told her.

Spotting a copy of *Nicomachean Ethics*, she picked it up and stood for a moment just savoring the solid feel of the thick leather volume. "This is my brother's favorite." She opened the book and read the first page. "'Every art and every scientific system, and in like manner every course of action and deliberate preference, seems to aim at some good; and consequently the good has been well defined as that which all things aim at.'" A wistful smile caught her lips and she prepared to set the book aside, until the one that had been lying beneath it caught her attention. *The Mysterie of* –

Regina caught herself before she uttered the blasphemous word that followed. She stared at it, completely mesmerized and confounded by the fact that she found herself mere inches away from such an immoral book.

"That one's probably not as suitable," Guthrie said, jolting her slightly with the sound of his voice. Flushing, she hastily covered it up with Aristotle's far more appropriate tome. "I'll wager there are those who'd insist that only the devil himself would tempt someone to open it."

Regina believed he was right. While the need to pretend utter outrage and distance herself from the book was strong, the desire to take a peek and discover its secrets whispered through her. She took a step back. It was like the Tree of Knowledge in the Garden of Eden, there to open her eyes to a subject on which she lacked education.

Turning away, she found Guthrie watching her closely. His expression offered no hint of what he was thinking, and yet the shiver his dark gaze evoked informed her that she should be careful where he was concerned.

"If ye'll forgive me," he murmured, "I'm not used to entertainin' young ladies as fine as yerself." He crossed to a door that Regina had not yet noticed. "This is where ye'll be stayin'."

He disappeared through the doorway and Regina followed, arriving in what had to be the most garish bedchamber in existence.

A gilded four poster canopy bed draped in swaths of burgundy velvet crowded the space. Half of it had been filled with an overwhelming abundance of silk clad cushions in various colors, shapes and sizes. The prospect of diving right into the middle of them was incredibly tempting.

But since doing so would be improper, Regina resisted the urge and explored the rest of the room with her gaze. There was a tall cheval glass mirror, a dresser, a wardrobe, and a wash stand. Black bombazine curtains hung in heavy pleats on either side of the room's only window.

"Is this" —Regina's breath shuddered, causing the words to stick in her throat— "*your* bedchamber?"

"Aye."

She almost leapt high enough to hit her head on the ceiling. Guthrie was closer than she'd realized. So close in fact that she'd felt his breath on the back of her neck when he'd spoken. She wasn't sure what startled her more, the fact that this was what her brain was choosing to focus on at the moment or that she now wished she'd been able to stay still and savor the experience properly.

Embarrassed that she was allowing such thoughts to form, that her body seemed to enjoy his proximity, Regina stepped sideways, adding distance.

"I cannot stay in your room." She pretended to find great interest in a landscape painting that hung on the wall. "I mean, you're a man. A bachelor, I believe?"

Guthrie raised an eyebrow. "This is the most comfortable bedchamber available. The sheets are clean an' ye'll have whatever privacy ye require. That door over there leads out onto a walkway that'll take ye back to the stairs so ye won't have to go through me parlor. Where I'll be stayin'."

"You..." Words finally failed her at the idea of sleeping just a few feet away from this extraordinary man. To say the situation she found herself in was scandalous didn't quite cut it. Another word would have to be found, quite possibly one that had not yet been invented.

Exasperated, Regina dropped onto the edge of the bed with a sigh.

"Havin' second thoughts about yer escape plan?" Guthrie asked. Arms crossed, he stood in the doorway between the two rooms with one shoulder leaning against the frame. The question was light and blasé, with no indication that he cared one way or the other about her response. But his eyes gave him away. The intensity there suggested that he was extremely curious to know her answer.

"Of course I am," Regina told him honestly. For what was the point in lying? She'd gain nothing from it. "I have done the unthinkable. The only way my situation could possibly be any worse would be if I'd run off to Gretna Green with a chimney sweep."

"Chimney sweeps can be nice enough."

She glared at him. "You know what I mean."

He pursed his lips. "Instead, you ran away to St. Giles with a criminal. I'm not so sure things can get much worse than that."

"Dear God, I'll be utterly ruined."

"And ye're just now realizin' this?"

Every muscle in her face went slack beneath the weight of acceptance. "No. I considered it before I left the house. It just didn't seem as real to me then as it does now."

"You could still go back." His voice was low and soothing, like a balm to her strangled nerves. "The repercussions won't be as bad as they will be later."

She shook her head. "How will they even explain my absence?"

"Who? Yer parents?"

When she nodded, Guthrie pushed away from

the door frame with a shrug. Striding to the window, he drew the veil behind the black curtain aside just enough for him to look out onto the street. "The Season has ended, so yer absence will not be noticeable right away. Most likely, yer mother will soon leave town. If anyone asks, it will be said that the two of ye have decided to travel."

Struck by the trouble she was putting her family through, not to mention the shame they might have to endure if anyone learned the truth, Regina experienced a brief moment of regret. But then she thought of Stokes and how both their parents were trying to direct their futures against their wills. She'd run away just as much for him as she had for herself and to go back now would ruin all of that. The only thing she could hope was that Guthrie was right and that Windham had been provided with an explanation plausible enough to prevent him from ever suspecting the truth.

"I cannot go back," Regina said, more as a reminder to herself than anything else. She would have to find another solution instead, even if she couldn't think of one at the moment.

"Then ye may remain here as long as ye wish, or at least until ye figure out what to do next."

Guthrie's hand caught beneath the veil curtain as he turned, sweeping it aside just enough to allow Regina a better view through the window. Her palms turned clammy and she swallowed audibly in response to what she saw. "Are those bars on the window?" The thought of being trapped here in this room caused all the tiny hairs at the nape of her neck to stand on end. She'd thought he was trying to help her, but perhaps she'd been wrong. Swallowing, she forced herself to ask, "Am I your prisoner?"

Guthrie answered her question with a chuckle that seemed to suggest she was being silly. "Not at all. Ye're free to leave whenever ye wish to, luv. But this ain't Mayfair. The bars are there for yer protection. Or mine, mostly, seein' as that there bed tends to be where I lay me head."

"Of course." The words scarcely whispered past her lips. All she could see now was him laid out on the bed where she presently sat. She vaulted to her feet as if someone had pinched her.

"I've got some things to attend to now, so I'll leave ye to settle in a bit." He studied her a moment and God help her if her body didn't grow hot from his stare. She crossed her arms and hoped he couldn't tell. "Would ye like to get out of that gown?"

Regina's mouth fell open. A garbled, "Wha..er.. ugh?" was all that came out.

Guthrie glanced up at the ceiling as if he hoped for divine intervention to save him. On a sigh, he waved one hand in her general direction and said, "It doesn't look very comfortable, so if ye want somethin' else to wear, I can 'ave a few items delivered." He slid his gaze down the length of her body before returning it to her face. "Last I checked, weddin' gowns tend to attract attention. Disguisin' ye as lower class will help ye blend in. One of the servin' wenches can help ye change."

"Oh. Um." Once again, Regina wondered why he was being so thoughtful and nice, but realized she was too tired to question his motives right now. There would be time to figure that out later. So she tried to smile. "Thank you."

The edge of his mouth quirked and for a second, a youthfulness that was generally hidden behind his somber expressions and ugly moustache, revealed itself to her. Regina stared. She'd thought he was well into his forties, but perhaps he was younger. As in five to ten years younger. Intrigued, she decided she'd have to learn more about this man who had yet to show her the callous side he was so renowned for. As of yet, he'd been nothing but kind and helpful. To a woman to whom he owed nothing.

As if sensing her interest in learning his secrets, Guthrie backed away slowly, retreating into his parlor. "If there's anythin' ye need, just give a holler an' someone will come to assist ye." And with that, he departed, leaving Regina alone to ponder her fate.

Carlton was fleeing. It was really the only way to describe the haste with which he'd left her – the loveliest woman he'd ever encountered in all his damned life. How the hell was he going to use her without getting sidetracked? Hell, when she'd found that book about sexual pleasure and he'd seen curiosity light up her eyes, he'd had thoughts... Thoughts he'd no business having where she was concerned.

Returning to his office, he shut the door and expelled a deep breath. "Christ have mercy." Crossing to the sideboard, he poured himself a glass of brandy and downed it, even though it was only nine in the morning. "Damn!"

She was different from any other woman he'd ever met, sophisticated and cultured, yet somehow incredibly normal without being ordinary. Instead she was daring and brave.

She was everything he was not. Innocent and beautiful.

The need to reach out and touch her hair, the golden tresses tinged with copper, was almost paralyzing.

And her skin…

He'd never seen anything quite so smooth or unblemished. The creamy complexion was a stark contrast to his own darker coloring, which was something he'd thought on a great deal while watching her sit on his bed. It had taken carefully honed control not to let the effect of her presence there show in his actions or his expression. She was like a siren, tempting him with perfection.

Topping up his glass, he took another sip of brandy.

Perhaps he ought to visit Amouratte's later and work through some of the tension Lady Regina had caused him. When he'd suggested getting her out of her dress, he'd pictured himself unbuttoning the row of buttons at her back and sliding the sleeves down over her shoulders. Muttering an oath, he went to his desk and retrieved a fresh piece of paper. She was both an inconvenience and a blessing. Certainly not a woman that he could have. No matter what. He wasn't quite that cruel.

Picking up his quill, he dipped it in the inkwell and proceeded to write.

My Lord Hedgewick,

I wish to inform you of your daughter's wellbeing. She is in excellent health and perfectly safe in my care. For now. As you have probably deduced, your intention to ruin her life through marriage has greatly upset her. But you need not worry. She will find comfort with me in my bed.

Sincerely,

V.S.

Satisfied, Carlton folded the letter and sealed it with crimson wax. A smile teased his lips. He doubted the bastard would figure out who the initials belonged to, which ought to increase his distress. Summoning one of his lads, a young man by the name of Claus Schmidt, Carlton told him to go to Bromley and post the letter from there. Just in case Hedgewick tried to track its point of origin.

"I saw her come in earlier," Claus said. Having tucked the letter into an inside pocket of his jacket, he stood facing Carlton who'd just given him a pound for his troubles. "She's a real looker, she is. There's quality about her."

"She's a lady," Carlton explained, aware that Claus would not have seen many of those up close. "I expect ye an' everyone else here to treat her with the respect she deserves."

"Of course."

Carlton had taken Claus under his wing just a couple of years ago when he'd tried to win against one of Carlton's fighters. Impressed by the youth's perseverance, he'd offered him a spot on his crew, which now consisted of twenty souls.

Since then he'd proven his worth and worked his way up, becoming one of Carlton's most trusted men. Only two other people held higher ranks, and they were Patrick Donovan, who'd been with Carlton for over five years, and Blayne, who'd once saved his life.

Claus took his leave with the assurance that he'd return as soon as possible. Carlton then called for Patrick and Blayne to join him. "I want increased surveillance on number two Hanover Square. Make it discreet."

"We'll enlist a couple of boys looking to earn some easy blunt," Blayne said.

Carlton nodded. "Good. Make sure they know what to look fer. I'm especially interested about the comin's an' goin's. If they can gather information on Hedgewick's reaction to his daughter's disappearance, ye may give the lads a bonus."

Patrick knew not to question an order, but Blayne had known Carlton far too long to keep his mouth shut. "The only way to learn that much would be to interrogate the servants and that could make them suspicious."

"Ye're right," Carlton agreed. "Make sure the boys know they're only to observe from a distance."

"We'll see to it immediately," Blayne said. He followed Patrick to the door and waited until he'd disappeared through it before turning back to Carlton. "How is she faring?"

"Well enough after that abundant meal ye served her."

Blayne frowned. "It's not like we can't afford it."

Carlton nodded. "True. But I don't want ye

takin' a likin' to her. She's a weapon to be wielded. Nothin' more."

"Duly noted," Blayne clipped before quitting the room. The door closed behind him more loudly than usual.

Staring at it for a long moment, Carlton fought the urge to return upstairs and see how Regina was doing. He would not seek her out like some smitten swain eager for her smiles. But he *had* promised her a change of clothes and should probably make sure she got them sooner rather than later. Yes. She could hardly continue wearing a wedding gown for God's sake when she had no wedding to get to.

"I need a couple of day dresses," Carlton told Philipa Harding ten minutes later. "They're fer a lady I'm helpin'." The owner of Amourette's, a bawd in her early forties, did not appear to be the least bit pleased by his visit. Wrapped in a silk fuchsia dressing gown and with her red curly hair like a puffy cloud surrounding her plump face, she could not have looked more unprepared to offer assistance.

"Do you have any idea what time it is?"

"Almost ten?"

"Which might as well be the crack of dawn for someone in my line of work."

Carlton nodded. "My apologies, but this is rather urgent."

She puffed out a breath and glanced at the pot he'd brought with him. "Please tell me that's coffee."

"Hot and ready to be served," he assured her with the most dashing smile he could muster.

She chuckled lightly and nodded toward a nearby sofa on which a collection of silk scarves, garters, and ostrich plume fans served as reminders of the sin that transpired within these walls. "Then let us enjoy a cup or two while I get my bearings."

Half an hour later, Carlton returned to The Black Swan with the garments he had acquired, no questions asked. It was one of the things he loved about Philipa. She never poked her nose into his business, and if he chose to volunteer information, he knew he could trust her to keep a secret.

Climbing the stairs, Carlton reached the landing swiftly and without stopping to consider the eager heartbeats spurring him on. He had no particular desire to see Regina again. After all, he'd just left her company a little over an hour ago. But he had said that he'd give her dresses and... He opened the door to his parlor and froze. Because there she was, sprawled out on his yellow velvet sofa, fast asleep. A book rested on her breast, rising and falling in accordance with her breaths.

Carlton set the clothes he'd brought for her on a vacant chair and moved closer. Her head was turned at a slight angle so it rested upon her left arm. Too tall to stretch out completely, she'd bent her knees to one side. The pose pulled the hem of her gown up around the middle of her calves, revealing the most delicate feet and ankles he'd ever seen.

His chest tightened and he deliberately slid his gaze up to her face where black lashes lay undisturbed against her pink cheeks. Seeing her made vulnerable in sleep, Carlton felt a fresh surge of anger. What had her parents been thinking, insisting she marry Stokes when she clearly didn't want him? Certainly, there was the obvious explanation about the match being a lucrative one, but since he wasn't the only eligible peer available for marriage, Carlton worried there might be another reason behind it. Especially when considering Hedgewick's connection to the previous duke of Windham.

"I'll figure it out," he murmured.

"Carlton, I—" Blayne's voice broke through the silence with the force of a plough. "Ach, I'm sorry." Having fully entered the room now, he'd lowered his voice upon spotting Regina. Guthrie narrowed his gaze at his friend and was instantly met by a broad smile. "She hasnae even been here a full day and you're already watching her sleep."

"I was merely curious to know which book she decided to read," Carlton grumbled. Making a show of prying it carefully out from beneath her hand, he glanced at the cover and nodded. "*Pride an' Prejudice.* No surprise there."

"No," Blayne agreed. "What's surprising is that you would happen to own that particular novel."

Feeling unstable, like a new foal attempting to find its legs and not caring for the experience one bit, Carlton frowned. "The women who visit me here need somethin' that suits their tastes as well. It can't all be history an' philosophy."

Blayne gave a low snort. "I hardly think the women who frequent your rooms are coming here to read. Now," he changed the subject with the swiftness of a buzzard catching a mouse, "we've gotten a couple of lads to do as you asked. They've been told not to lurk, so I'm hoping they'll manage to look inconspicuous. I'll check back with them tomorrow and—"

A rap at the open door interrupted the conversation. "Begging your pardon," Patrick said as he leaned forward to address them. But rather than keep on speaking, his eyes went straight to Regina.

Bothered by the interest he saw in the younger man's face, Carlton stepped directly in front of her, blocking her from his view. "Ye were sayin'?" He asked in a voice too tight to sound nonchalant. Hell, he could almost hear Blayne grinning at his protective behavior.

Patrick's eyebrows shot upward. "Right. Err. Mrs. Harding's waiting for you in your office. She seems agitated."

"Tell her I'll be right there." He waited for Patrick to leave before turning to Blayne. "Get out."

"Must I?" Blayne made a show of skulking toward the door. "I'd so much rather stay and watch you fall in love."

"I. Am. Not. Falling. In..." It was too late. Blayne was already gone, no doubt laughing all the way to wherever his hulking body would take him next. Annoyed by the teasing, Carlton raked his fingers through his hair. He then went to collect a blanket and tucked it carefully around Regina's slender body.

Love indeed.

What a ridiculous notion.

He barely knew the woman. Had only met her that morning. He shook his head and turned away from her with a curse. Trust Blayne to take what little kindness he was willing to give and turn it into something that would never exist. Why couldn't he show a young lady some sympathy without being accused of wanting her in some way?

But you do want her, you scoundrel.

Of course he bloody well did. He was a man in his prime after all and she…she was a gorgeous young woman with curves that made his fingers itch with the need to explore her. But he wouldn't, because he wasn't a bloody animal.

Annoyed, he forced his thoughts away from Regina and descended the stairs.

Curious to know what Philipa wanted, Carlton entered his office and instantly knew that the world must be ending if her stricken expression was anything to go by. "What's happened?" he asked, getting straight to the point. "When we parted ways twenty minutes ago ye looked well."

"That was before I discovered that one of my girls has gone missing."

CHAPTER FOUR

AN ODD PRESS AND RELEASE of her belly woke Regina from her nap. Squinting, she saw that the strange sensation was caused by Guthrie's cat. The feline had decided to take a walk on her and was now pawing and circling as if preparing to settle down.

"You should have joined me earlier." She allowed her hand to slide slowly across the creature's back, chuckling in response to the deep purr that followed. "I probably ought to get up though."

Opening her eyes more fully, Regina noticed the fluffy wool blanket in which she had been cocooned. Frowning, she pushed herself into a sitting position. Was it possible Guthrie had done this? She could hardly credit it. And yet she could not imagine that anyone else here would treat her with such consideration. An odd blend of pleasure and wariness assailed her, so she rose from the sofa and quickly spotted the clothes he'd brought her. Relieved by the distraction they offered, she picked each garment up one by one and held it out to gauge its shape and size. Everything would do, except one of the day dresses which looked as though it was meant to contain a much larger bosom.

Biting her lip, Regina wondered if she might be able to remove her wedding gown by herself. She twisted one arm behind her, but quickly realized the buttons ran too high for her to reach. Forcing out a breath, she swept a stray lock behind her ear and went to the door. When she opened it she almost collided with MacNeil, who materialized before her like a wall that could not be scaled.

"May I help you with something, my lady?"

In spite of the soft, gentle manner in which he addressed her, he still made her take a step back. She raised her chin since speaking to his chest felt both silly and cowardly. "Mr. Guthrie mentioned a maid who might be able to assist me."

MacNeil nodded. "Wait here while I find her for you." He turned to go, then paused and turned back to face her. "Is there anything else I can get for you while I'm downstairs? More food or perhaps some tea?"

"Some tea would be lovely. Thank you."

He smiled – an odd grimace that didn't suit him at all – then disappeared in the direction of the stairs.

A shrill meow and the feel of something pressing against her legs caused Regina to drop her gaze to Guthrie's cat. Green eyes met hers and the cat meowed again as it curled itself around her, seeking attention. Regina scooped it up in her arms and gave it a loving scratch behind one of its ears. She then turned back into the room and shut the door.

By now, her father would likely be tearing his

hair out in frustration while cursing her to perdition. Her breath trembled on that thought, of risking her family's reputation and of being a disappointment. And poor Marcus. He would worry over her endlessly until he knew she was safe, which meant that she had to get word to him somehow.

And then once that was done, she would have to think of some way to get out of this mess. She certainly couldn't remain here forever, no matter how hospitable Guthrie might be. In fact, the sooner she left, the better, since every second spent here increased the chance of the most calamitous scandal befalling her family.

Perhaps…

She returned to the sofa with the beginnings of an idea only to have it interrupted by a loud rap on the door.

MacNeil entered, bringing with him a young woman with a slender build whose eyes expanded to the size of scones when she spotted Regina. In her hands, she held a welcoming tea tray.

"Blimey," the woman muttered, then promptly bowed her head and attempted an awkward curtsey. "I mean, I beg yer pardon yer lovely ladyship."

MacNeil stared at her for a brief second as if she'd recited Shakespeare in Latin. He then turned his serious gaze on Regina. "This is Laura. She won't be what you're used to and you may need to teach her a thing or two about ladies things, but she'll get the job done."

Having risen during this exchange, Regina thanked MacNeil and waited until he was gone before moving closer to Laura. She'd set the tray on the sofa table and was now fidgeting with her apron. She seemed incapable of focusing her gaze on one fixed point.

"You must call me Regina."

That got Laura's attention. "I couldn't possibly. I mean, ye look like a princess an' I—"

"Will hardly look much different than me once I get out of this increasingly uncomfortable gown and put on a plain dress."

Laura smiled with the sort of shyness that suggested she wasn't sure how much she could say before causing offense. "Beggin' yer pardon, but ye could likely wear a coarse brown sack an' ye'd still look lovely. Yer face alone is like that of an angel."

"Thank you. It's very kind of you to say so. But how I look and who I am doesn't matter so much right now." Circling around Laura, Regina retrieved one of the gowns Guthrie had brought her. "What I need most of all is a friend who can help me fit in. So please, call me Regina and I'll call you Laura. If you permit."

"Oh, indeed. I'd be honored, me lady. I mean Regina," Laura amended when Regina raised an eyebrow.

"Excellent. Now what do you think of this dress? Will the dove grey suit or should I put on the rust colored one instead?"

Laura appeared to consider the question most seriously before recommending the dove grey option. She then helped Regina out of the wedding gown and into her new dress.

"He's not as bad as people think him to be, is he?" Regina asked a bit later while Laura did up the buttons on her back.

"Do you mean Guthrie?" Laura's cheerful tone conveyed her eagerness to chat.

Regina nodded. "Considering all the things I've read in the papers about him, how he's suspected of blackmail, causing people to disappear, thievery...I expected him to be..."

"Less nice?"

A laugh forced its way past Regina's lips. "I suppose so."

"Well, if there's one thing I can tell ye, it's that I've not met a man more just or 'onorable than Mr. Guthrie. He's good to the people who work for 'im but he's also harsh on those who deserve it." She patted Regina on the back to inform her that she was finished with her task.

Regina turned. "Is he also known for being charitable?" she asked in an effort to understand his treatment of her more fully.

Laura frowned. "Not exactly. I mean, he'll give a coin 'ere or there to a beggar in need, but for the most part, he believes in encouragin' people to earn their way. He'll rather offer a job than a handout." As if made cautious by something she saw in Regina's expression, Laura smiled brightly and hastened to add, "But he's not the sort to turn 'is back on a woman in need either. Now, I hope ye don't mind me saying this, um...Regina...but if there's nothin' else ye need help with right now, I've a few things to do downstairs."

"Of course," Regina muttered. "You mustn't let me keep you."

Laura needed no further urging and promptly departed.

Regina remained where she stood for a long moment. The respect Laura had for Guthrie increased Regina's curiosity. It was clear that the papers had striven to turn him into a monster when he appeared to be anything but. But why would they do that unless they'd been given a reason?

A frown tightened her brow as a more pressing thought presented itself. If Guthrie wasn't known for being charitable, then there was a chance he'd been lying when he'd told her he was trying to make amends for past misdeeds. Which made her wonder what he really wanted from her and why he was willing to let her disturb his life.

Shivering, she decided to figure that out, if for no other reason than to satisfy her own curiosity.

Carlton's shoes played an even beat upon the pavement as he made his way back toward The Black Swan. His gait was slow, his steps measured, and his gaze constantly searching so he wouldn't miss anything. All day he'd been out making inquiries, hoping that when he returned, he'd have some news for Philipa.

He knew the girl who'd gone missing well since he'd paid for her company on a few occasions over the years. Her name was Scarlet, and like all of Philipa's girls, she was more than a skilled courtesan. She also had a mind for business and was simply doing whatever she had to until she saved enough blunt to open a florist shop of her own. In the meantime, Philipa kept her safe. As with all her girls, she made sure they ate well, were properly clothed, slept in comfortable beds, and received monthly checkups at the St. Giles clinic. To think something tragic might have happened to any of these women gutted him. But as he'd explained to Philipa, it was possible Scarlet had simply decided to walk away. It happened. Didn't it? Regina was proof that even the least likely person could do the unexpected, given the right reason.

Spotting a hunched woman huddled against a doorway, he approached her as he'd approached so many others already. "I don't suppose ye saw a young woman last night. Brown hair, about this tall an' wearin' a crimson dress?" She'd been out acquiring clients, as the women so often did, and hadn't returned.

"Nah. But there were a carriage. Came clattering through here like it were trying to win a race or something."

Carlton bent closer and peered into the woman's creased face. "Which way did it go?"

Raising one hand, she pointed in the direction of Drury Lane. "Turned right at the end of the street. Toward Holborn."

Straightening, Carlton wondered if there could be a connection between the carriage and Scarlet's disappearance. If so, she might simply have struck a deal with a toff who wanted his rendezvous with her to be discreet. Some of these men had peculiar needs, and if one found the right woman willing to satisfy them, he might choose to keep her a while before letting her go.

Or perhaps the carriage meant nothing. Either way, it gave Carlton no indication of where to look next or if continuing his search was reasonable. At least he'd be able to tell Philipa that Bow Street hadn't been alerted to the death of a woman matching Scarlet's description. Neither had the coroner's office or the nearest hospitals or clinics. The last person he knew of who'd seen her alive was a boy who'd been on his way home for supper last night. He claimed to have passed her on Monmouth Street and had told Carlton that she'd been alone at the time.

Reaching into his jacket pocket, Carlton retrieved a sovereign and handed it to the old woman. "Thank ye fer the information." Doffing his hat, he continued toward Parker's Lane where The Black Swan was located.

It would be good to get home to a hot meal. After he'd walked about for most of the day, his shoes were starting to squeeze his toes. Carlton looked forward to getting them off and putting his feet up. Perhaps he'd ask Regina for a wee foot rub. He grinned at the thought of how she would respond to such an outrageous suggestion. Her entire face would turn a deep shade of pink and then she'd probably storm from the room. Or maybe she'd give him the set down that he deserved.

Not that he actually cared.

Deliberately, he schooled his features. He wasn't walking faster now than before and if he was, it certainly wasn't because of any desire he had to see her again. He would not wonder how she'd spent her day or if she could be happy while under his roof. None of that mattered.

She didn't matter.

Except in one regard.

So then why did his skin grow warmer as he approached The Black Swan's entrance? And why had his belly turned into something that felt more like jelly than stone? Yes, she was pretty and desirable, but he'd met his fair share of such women before. Hell, he'd taken most of them to his bed. As far as his sexual appetites went, they were sated, so it wasn't because he needed a woman and Regina just happened to be there that he was feeling unstable around her.

So then what?

Her purity certainly appealed. As a man with a blackened soul, it was only natural that he'd be drawn to that. Wasn't it? An unpleasant smell of rot and sewage climbed up his nose and he winced. Would she even welcome his advances if he were to make them? And why the bloody hell was he even wondering about that?

By the time he entered The Black Swan he'd thrust the thought from his mind, only to have it resurface with a vengeance the moment he saw her. The emotions that banged against him, like the clapper hitting the dome of a bell, were so numerous he found it impossible to focus on a singular one alone.

What he did know was that he might strangle Blayne, Patrick, and Claus for letting her come downstairs to the taproom. Because while they were all busy playing cards, they'd failed to notice the interest all the men in the damned place had taken in her.

Carlton clenched his fists, ready to beat every one of them to a mangled mess. She was just a means to an end, he reminded himself. And yet he could not stop from feeling like a pirate who'd stolen her away from her gilded tower to claim her as his own.

A muscle twitched deep in his belly and heat flashed against his skin, and in that instant, he realized the danger he was facing. Because he'd never wanted a woman as much as he wanted her. He wanted to bask in her beauty, surround himself with her goodness, savor the wanton gasps he knew she'd emit as he gave her pleasure.

But it could never be. His soul was too corrupt, his heart completely lacking, and she too perfect for a man like him. He'd resist her even if it killed him, because that was the least he could do after what he was going to put her through.

She laughed and Carlton watched as several men eyed her like boys receiving a sweetmeat for the first time. Muscles flexing, he strode forward until he reached the table at which she sat, her eyes bright with the victory she'd just won over his men.

"What do ye think ye're doin?" His voice was dangerously low.

She looked up, surprise evident in her expression. And then she smiled, the most glorious smile he'd ever seen, and it was directed at him. "Learning how to gamble," she said, offering him a glimpse of her perfectly white teeth as the smile transformed to a grin. "Apparently I'm rather good at it."

Feeling as if the floor tilted beneath his feet, Guthrie grabbed the back of the chair on which Blayne sat and prayed he wouldn't fall over. Wasn't the whole weak-kneed thing supposed to be reserved for women?

He clenched his jaw and gave them all his most disapproving glower. "Ye shouldn't be down here, me lady. 'Tis not safe."

Her eyes widened in response to his tone. "But I'm not—"

"There's a table full o' toffs just over there in that corner behind ye an' ye're not exactly keepin' a low profile," he told her tersely.

"We didnae think there'd be much harm in showing her a good time," Blayne said.

The way he phrased *that*, almost earned him a fist to his face. Carlton bristled. By God he was almost shaking he was so damn angry. And worried, he realized. On her behalf, actually.

"She's been cooped up in your parlor all day, Guthrie," Patrick said, joining in to protect the lady's decision to be reckless. "Anyone would be itching for a change of scene."

"Not if they're tryin' to avoid gettin' recognized," Carlton gritted. He swung his gaze back to Regina. "Or do ye wish to return home now? 'Cause if anyone finds out who ye really are, it'll be hard fer me to stop them from notifyin' yer father of yer location."

Regina froze for a second, then she dropped her cards on the table and pushed her chair back. "Thank you for entertaining me," she told Carlton's men, "but I fear the hour has come for me to retire."

Carlton moved close to her as she stood, shielding her from prying eyes as best he could. Before leading her away, he met Claus's gaze. "Did ye manage to post the letter all right?"

"Aye. It wasn't any trouble at all. Should arrive by tomorrow." Carlton nodded and then addressed Blayne. "I wasn't able to learn anythin' about Scarlet, although an unmarked carriage did barrel through St. Giles last night. Can ye look into that a bit more? Maybe ask some of the men here if they know anythin' about that? And please let Philipa know that we're doin' what we can. We'll keep our eyes an' ears open, but as of yet, there's no reason to believe any harm has come to the girl."

"I'll tell her right away," Blayne assured him.

"And Claus and I will start inquiring about that carriage," Patrick promised.

"You're upset with me," Regina stated when they returned upstairs to his parlor.

"Can ye blame me?" When she only stared at him, he added, "Decidin' to go downstairs was incredibly foolish."

Her jaw tightened. "I needed a change of scene."

"Then I would suggest ye read a book."

Her eyes widened while the color in her cheeks deepened. "You are being..." She drew in a breath. "Overbearing and insufferable."

He placed one palm upon his chest. "Oh, how ye wound me."

"Sarcasm doesn't suit you."

"Well I dare say it's better than yer prim tone!"

Her eyes hardened. "You of all people have no right to criticize someone else's speech."

"Oh, has me uncivilized way begun to offend yer haughtiness?"

She looked as though she might start sputtering. Or hit him over the head with her clenched fists.

Which could be interesting.

Instead, she simply stood there for a long moment, until the rising tension between them fizzled away into nothing. And then, to his utter astonishment, she started to smile. "I've never engaged in a fight before."

He stared at her. "That wasn't a fight."

"Well, whatever it was, it felt invigorating." She suddenly looked uncertain and hastily added, "I hope I didn't offend you too much with what I said. It just popped out and—"

"It's fine. I'm fine. And to be fair, I owe ye an apology too fer the way I just spoke. But me point remains," he told her firmly before he forgot what they'd been arguing about in the first place. "I cannot ensure yer safety unless ye're willin' to be more careful." Damned if he wasn't tempted to lock her in this room until he achieved his goal. But since his plan would be easier to accomplish with her cooperation, he couldn't afford to lose her trust. Being friendly and showing concern for her was far more likely to meet with success. So he softened his tone and added, "It's not just the risk of you bein' recognized and forced to return home. It's also the threat of some blackguard takin' an interest in ye an' causin' ye harm."

She swallowed and gave a small nod. "You're right, and I'm sorry. I just wasn't thinking."

Her willingness to accept her mistake and apologize for it reduced the strain Carlton had felt in every muscle and tendon since spotting her in the taproom. He exhaled slowly and offered a conciliatory smile. "I suppose I can understand yer reasonin' though. It must have been borin' fer ye to be stuck in 'ere all day by yerself."

There was a hint of a smile on her lips. "Just a bit." She tilted her head. "Who are Scarlet and Philipa?"

Sighing, Carlton removed his hat, set it aside on a chair, and proceeded to peel off his gloves. "Scarlet's a prostitute," he told her plainly. "Philipa owns Amourette's." Tossing his gloves aside, he raised his gaze to hers. The fierce curiosity in her eyes stirred something deep in his chest. Briefly, he considered closing the distance between them so he could reach out and touch her.

"And Scarlet is missing?" Regina inquired. She spoke the words slowly, as if adjusting herself to a topic she'd never imagined she'd ever address. But there was something else in her voice too – an indication of grave concern.

"Since last night." Because touching her would be unwise, Carlton went to collect the half-filled decanter he'd left on the sofa table.

"And you've been trying to discover what happened to her?" When he nodded, her eyes seemed to sharpen. "I hope you find her soon."

"As do I," he murmured.

"No. You do not understand. I…I had a friend once who was taken and…and she suffered terribly before she was found." Regina shivered. "To this day Katarina remains reclusive and utterly silent. It's almost as if she's dead inside." A shudder went through her, compounding her distress on Scarlet's behalf. "Promise me that you won't give up on this woman."

Holding her gaze, he stared back at her, losing himself for a few blessed seconds in pools of infinite blue. "To do so would be unthinkable."

A look of relief washed over her features. "Thank you."

He nodded. "Have ye eaten supper?"

"No." When he turned to her in surprise she said, "I had a snack around three and didn't feel very hungry after that."

"And now?"

She watched him pour the brandy into a pair of glasses. "Is one of those for me?"

He gave her his most innocuous smile. "If ye like?" There was no comprehending the thrill racing through him as she stepped forward to collect her glass. She reached for the tumbler and her fingers brushed his.

The contact was so brief it barely happened. And yet a dart of awareness sped through his veins like wildfire.

Regina sucked in a breath and retreated a step. She took a quick sip of her drink and winced, but not even that could distract Carlton from her troubled expression. Whatever it was that had just passed between them, she'd felt it too. The deep rosy hue coloring her cheeks, the flutter of her lashes as she turned her gaze away from him and the increased pitch to her voice when she spoke next, confirmed it.

"I believe you'd just mentioned supper when I changed the subject." The wave of her hand, like a nervous breeze swirling around her, only made her look more out of control.

It also made him want to pounce on her, to capture some of that energy for himself.

He coughed to mask his response. "I can 'ave

somethin' brought up from the kitchen. Some roast, a mince meat pie or perhaps some stew?"

"What sort of stew?"

He shrugged. "I don't know."

A slow smile curled her lips. Christ, how he wanted to kiss her. "Let's try it."

"Feelin' adventurous are ye?"

"As a matter of fact, I am."

Carlton turned away and went to put in the order. If he kept himself busy, then perhaps he wouldn't wonder just how adventurous she might be willing to be.

"I've been thinking," Regina told Guthrie when she was half way through eating her stew. It was wonderfully delicious. Much better than she had expected.

A crease above the bridge of his nose drew his eyebrows together in a sharp V. "About what?"

"Freedom." Trapped in the depths of Guthrie's captivating gaze, Regina wondered if she would ever be free again, though she was determined to try. "This is the only place where I'm sure my father won't find me, but—"

"Unless ye're careless." Guthrie set his tray on the sofa table and reached for Regina's. "Finished?" When she nodded, he removed her tray as well and went to the door. "Can ye please return these to the kitchen?"

MacNeil entered, collected the trays and was just about to leave when he caught Guthrie's eye and told him, just loud enough for Regina to hear, "Be careful, my friend."

Guthrie nodded and shut the door behind Mac-Neil as he left. Returning to the armchair he'd been occupying all evening, he leaned back and stretched out his legs, crossing them at the ankles. Propping one elbow on the armrest, he stroked the edge of his moustache while studying Regina. "Ye're welcome to stay as long as ye like."

His voice was a low murmur that vibrated through her. Earlier, when his fingers had grazed hers, her entire body had hummed with awareness. It was almost as if she'd been sleeping her whole life and he'd jolted her awake. The entire experience had shocked her, not only because it was unlike anything she'd experienced before, but because she'd experienced it with *him*. Could anything else have been more inappropriate? But even as her mind resisted and the guilt over her reaction to him assailed her, there was no denying that her body wanted. For the first time in her young life, she'd met a man who filled her with questions, a man whose secrets she longed to discover.

"That's a very generous offer, but one I cannot possibly accept."

A flicker of something dark and dangerous flashed in his eyes so briefly she almost missed it. "Did ye not just say that this is the only place where yer father won't find ye?"

While his voice was pleasant enough, his penetrating gaze unsettled her. For some peculiar reason, she sensed that he didn't want her to leave, and this caused the tiny hairs at the nape of her neck to rise with concern. "Yes," she told him carefully, "and it will work well as a temporary solution, but in the long run, I need a more permanent plan."

He nodded. "I understand."

A little surprised by his shift in demeanor, Regina instinctively grinned. "To begin with, I'll need to write my brother to let him know I'm all right." When Guthrie raised one eyebrow, she added, "I love him too much to let him worry."

He inclined his head. "Of course. I'll provide ye with some writin' materials an' make sure the letter gets posted."

"Thank you." She considered the amicable smile with which he responded and decided she must have imagined his angry reaction to her comment about leaving. Encouraged by his willingness to help, she added, "There's another letter I plan on writing."

"Oh?" He sipped his drink while watching her over the rim of the glass.

Regina shifted in her seat. "It will be addressed to the Earl of Fielding." When Guthrie said nothing in response to this, she went on, "He's a respectable gentleman in need of a wife and I...I am not the worst match for him if he'll have me."

"Yer reputation would be secured if the marriage took place before word of yer disappearance got out," Guthrie murmured.

"If it works, it will also prevent potential scandal from befalling my family." Not exactly the romantic solution she'd hoped to find, but one that would have to do. For practical reasons. And who knew? Perhaps in time, love could grow between her and Fielding. At least he'd be able to dance and go riding and boating and play hide and seek with their children.

Guthrie nodded. "It's certainly an interesting idea. Clever, even, I dare say." He leaned forward in his seat. "But how will ye convince him without yer father's support?"

Regina hadn't gotten quite that far with her plan so this was a question she'd not yet considered. "I'll be perfectly honest with him," she said.

"And if he says no?"

"Then I'll ask someone else." A nervous smile pulled at the edge of her mouth. "Eventually I'll find an eligible gentleman willing to marry an earl's daughter." A man whom she hoped she could turn to for friendship and guidance as well. "I'm sure of it."

His flat smile convinced her that he didn't share her optimism. But even if he thought her the silliest and most naïve girl in the world, he didn't say so. Instead, he said, "When ye're ready, I'll 'ave a messenger drop yer letter to Fieldin' off at his home so ye can receive an immediate response."

Pleased to have found a temporary solution to work on, Regina thanked Guthrie for his assistance.

A couple of seconds ticked by and then he said, "It's gettin' late. If ye'd like a bath, me men an' I can 'ave a tub brought up so ye can bathe before ye retire."

Instinctively, Regina tensed. "No. Thank you, but I'd rather use a wash basin. If that's all right." When he gave her an odd look, she said, "I told you I don't wish to swim but it's more than just that. In fact, I never submerge myself in water at all. Not since I almost drowned as a child."

Instead of telling her she was a fool, that it was impossible for her to drown in a small tub of water unless she was very determined to do so, he nodded. "Very well. I'll make sure a towel, wash cloth, basin and decanter filled with fresh water are brought up."

Sensing an opportunity to learn a bit more about him, she said, "Your hospitality is surprising, given your reputation." His eyes glinted in response to the light from one of the four oil lamps brightening the room. "Why are you being so nice to me?"

"Ye're a lady." He spoke pensively and with great care, as if making an effort not to say the wrong thing. "It would 'ave been wrong to leave ye to yer own devices in this part o' town. Any number o' thievin' villains could 'ave taken advantage. As ye well know, based on experience."

She shivered as she recalled the men who'd accosted her in the alley. But then she pushed that unpleasant memory aside and said, "You're supposed to be the worst of the lot though."

Tipping his head back, he held her gaze. "Are ye afraid?"

Regina's pulse quickened. There were times when she felt she could trust him completely and others when she feared he was trying to use her somehow. "I haven't decided yet."

His eyes darkened and she felt her skin tighten in response. "Per'aps ye should be. Just a little." He dropped his gaze and leaned forward, resting his elbows on his thighs. Behind him, flames danced in the open fireplace offering warmth to the room. "A healthy dose o' fear is never amiss, me lady. It keeps ye on yer toes."

She considered him, this enigma of a man who could wear a plum jacket, plaid trousers, and an unfashionable moustache with more confidence than she'd ever managed wearing a smart gown. He oozed self-assurance in a way that made her jealous, for although she'd been taught to look like she owned a room, she'd always longed to retreat to the corners.

"How did you end up here?" she asked. She longed to learn more about him, to discover why she was torn between wanting to flee him and wanting to stay. Even his men had treated her well. She'd laughed with them while playing cards, and that alone, along with what Laura had told her, was enough to make her suspect that there was more to Carlton Guthrie and his crew than met the eye.

She leaned forward in her seat, pinning him with an intense need for answers. "How did you become the Scoundrel of St. Giles?"

He held himself utterly still, like a statue frozen in time. Finally, when she thought he might never move again, he stood and went to add a log to the fire. It crackled in response to the dry wood, sparking a larger flame than before. "I left 'ome when I was thirteen, after me father died."

"And your mother?"

He picked up a poker and gave the log a nudge. "Consumption took her when I was eight."

Regina drew a sharp breath. "I'm so sorry." She wanted to go to him, to put her arms around him and hold him close. She wanted to ease away the pain he'd suffered when he was a boy. But she didn't, partly because she knew it would cross a line and also because she knew the last thing he'd want was a hint of pity. Not him. Not this slum king whose power was known and yet quite impossible to prove.

"She was the best mother there was." Still giving Regina his back, he spoke to the fire. "Her embrace could put everythin' to rights. I never doubted her love, fer it was vaster than everythin' the eye can behold."

"And your father?"

He stiffened and when he spoke again his voice was measured. "I miss 'im every day." The confession stunned her with its surprising display of vulnerability. "One of me favorite memories is of 'im and I buildin' a tree 'ouse together behind our home. I'd been beggin' him fer it fer years, but it wasn't until I turned eleven that he felt I was ready to do me part with the project." He chuckled lightly, lifting the melancholic air that blanketed the room. "He taught me how to use the necessary tools so that I could take pride in knowin' I'd helped."

"If only all children were as fortunate as you, to have a father who's willing to play with them and teach them things."

Rising from his crouched position, he turned to face her. "My father was taken from me, Regina. There's nothin' fortunate about that."

The vehemence in his voice made her stomach contract. Wild fury tempered solely by whatever self-control he possessed, burned violently in his eyes, reminding Regina that this was no placid man. If unleashed in all its fullness, his wrath would likely be lethal. A thought that caused an unpleasant dip in her belly. "Forgive me. I only meant that—"

"What of ye? Did ye have a happy childhood in yer fine ivory tower? Did yer father buy ye a pony when ye asked fer one an' tickets to the theatre when ye got bored?"

He was stalking toward her now, prowling like a cat on the hunt. All pleasantries about him had vanished, and she saw for the first time the man who deserved to be feared.

Reaching her, he bent forward, bracing his hands on the armrests of her chair as he loomed over her retreating form. Except there was nowhere for her to go. His face was level with hers and so very close she was able to spot the faint imperfection of a scar beneath his moustache.

"Tell, me, Regina." Her name dripped with contempt and yet she still liked the way he said it. Which surely meant she was crazy. "Do ye think yer father loves ye?"

"Of course."

"Even though he would 'ave pushed ye into an unwanted marriage if ye hadn't run away?" His eyes bored into hers with unrelenting ruthlessness.

Regina's heart drummed frantically against her ribs. Every muscle in her body strained in response to his anger. She wanted to flee it while standing her ground and pushing it back until he returned to the man he had been just a short while earlier.

"As misguided as his intentions were, my father was only trying to do what he believed would be best for me. Women have so little to hope for unless they marry well. Papa gave me the chance to become a marchioness and a duchess in waiting." It occurred to her that she was defending her father for something she didn't agree with, but Guthrie's anger made it impossible for her to act differently. "As Stokes's wife, I would have been welcomed everywhere. My future would have been secured both financially and socially."

"An' in exchange ye would 'ave been miserable."

"Without a doubt. But happiness isn't what most peers strive to obtain. At least not in marriage." Relaxing now that the worst of the storm seemed to have passed, she sighed. "I proved myself to be a disappointment. My parents will never forgive me for that."

"No. They probably won't."

Startled by his lack of sympathy, Regina struggled to understand what it was that caused him to act this way when he'd been so pleasant before. It had happened when she'd mentioned his father, but—

"It's late an' I need to rest," he told her bluntly. "Ye ought to retire too fer the night."

"Of course." She winced at how weak she sounded when all she wanted was to prove her strength. She cleared her throat. "Thank you for helping me today." She headed toward the bedchamber door.

"One moment."

She froze, her skin heating as if it were caught in the sun when she sensed him step up behind her. "What is it?" Her voice was merely a hesitant whisper.

"I don't think ye can undo all those buttons on

yer own."

And before she could fathom his meaning, she felt his fingers at the nape of her neck. He worked swiftly and with the skill of a man accustomed to undressing women. This thought caused an unpleasant knot to form right beneath her ribs even as her stays seemed to shrink against the swell of her breasts. Good lord, she wanted to lean back into him and…and what? She wasn't exactly sure what she wanted next and before she was able to figure it out he gave her a gentle nudge forward.

"There. Ye should be able to manage the rest on yer own."

Speechless. Regina muttered an incoherent, "Thank you," and entered the room where she would be sleeping, in a bed that was so very his.

"Make sure ye lock the door," he told her gruffly. When she turned back to stare at him, he added. "It's fer yer own safety."

CHAPTER FIVE

WHEN REGINA WOKE THE NEXT day, she completed her toilette then dressed as well as she was able to do on her own, twisting and contorting until she managed to close most of the buttons at the back of her gown. Locating a comb, she used it to smooth out her hair and then pinned it in a simple knot.

With this accomplished and feeling as though she was better prepared to tackle the day, she went to the window, drew the curtain aside, and looked out. A grim exterior greeted her. It was as if all color had been sucked from this part of town and deposited elsewhere. Everything was painted in brown, black, or grey, from the building across the alley, to the laundry hanging from the clotheslines between them, to the three-legged dog scampering after a man dragging a cart.

Turning away from the dismal scenery, Regina considered the door leading into the parlor. She'd locked it as Guthrie had told her to. Last night, she'd puzzled over what he had meant when he'd said, "It's fer yer own safety," until she'd fallen asleep. The words returned to her now and made her wonder once more if he'd meant he might pay

her a midnight visit if she left the door unlocked
– if he'd take it as an invitation to join her in bed
– or if there were some other danger from which
she needed protecting.

The first option caused a flutter to rise up from
deep in her belly while the latter sent icy chills
down her spine. She reached for the shawl Laura
had kindly offered to lend her and wrapped it
around her shoulders. The fire Guthrie had built
last night had burned out, allowing the cool
autumn air seeping into the room to replace the
comforting heat.

She craved a cup of hot tea. But would Guthrie
be awake by now or would he be lounging on
the sofa, stretched out with his legs resting on the
armrest? If so, she had no wish to disturb him.
Especially if he'd removed some articles of cloth-
ing for the sake of comfort. Not that she would
fault him for doing so, but considering how grand
he looked when fully attired, she wasn't sure she
was ready to see him in only his shirt and trousers.

So she gave her attention to the other door in
the bedroom. U-shaped, The Black Swan had a
central courtyard with direct access to the street.
Overlooking it was a walkway onto which all the
upstairs rooms exited. While playing cards yesterday, Regina had learned that these rooms were
occupied by MacNeil, Claus, Patrick and Gareth,
the cook.

Guthrie had told her not to return downstairs
because it increased the chance of her being
found. She'd promised him she wouldn't leave the
upstairs rooms. But it was morning, which meant
there would be no customers yet. And besides, she

needed Laura's help with the rest of her buttons and was now getting really hungry as well. So she made her decision and exited onto the walkway only to have her path cut off by MacNeil, who'd apparently been sitting on a chair right outside her room.

She frowned up at him. "Are you guarding me?"

"Good morning, my lady. I trust you slept well?"

His politeness forced her to reevaluate the way she'd greeted him. She felt herself relax a smidgen. "Good morning." Her breath misted slightly in the cool morning air. "I slept very well. Thank you."

"Would you like a breakfast tray brought up?"

Regina took a deep breath and straightened her spine. "I need Laura's help with my dress, and after that, I was actually hoping to have my breakfast in the dining hall instead of up here by myself."

MacNeil glanced toward the courtyard. "I'm afraid Guthrie wouldnae like that. I'm sorry."

Following his gaze, Regina spotted the man on whose goodwill she now depended and noted that he was very much awake. Instinctively, she took a step closer to the walkway railing so she could get a better look. His plum colored jacket from yesterday had been exchanged for a burgundy frock coat. The trousers he wore were once again plaid, this time with red lines running through them to match the coat and the satin band wrapped around the crown of his black top hat.

With him were a pair of boys no older than twelve, one with tawny hair, the other with brown. Positioned across from each other, they stood with arms raised and their hands curled into tight fists.

"Is he teaching them how to fight?" Incredulous, she'd asked a question to which the answer was obvious. These were children for heaven's sake. They ought to be taught how to settle disputes without the need for violence.

"Just watch," MacNeil murmured.

Huffing out a breath of distinct disapproval, Regina did as MacNeil asked. She watched Guthrie take hold of one boy's hand and slowly move it forward to indicate where it would make the best impact against the other boy's face. Regina bristled. If this was how children were raised in this part of town, it was little wonder that the crime was so high here.

"Now ye raise this arm 'ere to block," Guthrie said as he showed the other lad how to stave off the blow.

They continued like this, moving slowly and without either boy actually hitting the other. And as she watched, Regina forgot that she disapproved. She became more and more engrossed in Guthrie's method of teaching. With the kind of extraordinary patience that deserved to be admired, he explained different steps, thrusts and counter-attacks, and then worked to correct the mistakes the boys made. He even tousled their hair and laughed with them when they got something right.

It was mesmerizing to see, this mentoring side of Guthrie that made room for laughter. Clearly he took pride in teaching these boys how to fight. That he cared for them and that they cared for him in return was evident in how they interacted. Swallowing, Regina felt a sharp pang in her breast. She and Marcus had shared a similar bond, and she realized now how much she missed him. Today, she'd write him that letter.

"He'd make an excellent father," MacNeil said, interrupting her thoughts.

"Perhaps. But I think it a pity to bring more children into a place such as this," she said, her eyes fixed on Guthrie who'd now taken off his hat and was urging the boys to try and take it from him. Practice was apparently at an end and it was time to engage in some playful fun.

"They look happy enough, those two," he told her gruffly. "The way I see it, there are more important things in life than being born into wealth and privilege."

"Forgive me. I meant no offense. It is just that—"

"A child has no say in the matter, and you wouldnae wish to force upon them a life of hardship surrounded by crime." Regina nodded and was somewhat surprised when MacNeil chuckled. "That's his reasoning as well. For the most part."

Astonished that a man like Guthrie would think in those terms, Regina cast her gaze back at the courtyard where one of the boys was now pulling on his coattails in an effort to hold him still while the other tried pulling his raised arm down so he could grab at the hat. It was difficult to figure Guthrie out. On one hand, he was this protective individual who seemed to care about others, but on the other, there was the threatening element she'd witnessed last night.

Realizing she had a chance to question MacNeil about him, she said, "I once read that he was suspected of being involved in a smuggling operation involving the illegal selling of champagne from France. Is that true?"

"He's had his hands in a lot of endeavors," Mac-Neil told her vaguely. His lips curled into a sly smile and he leaned a bit closer, lowering his head until it was level with hers so he could look her straight in the eye. "But he's never killed anyone unless he had to."

With a gasp, Regina recoiled and instinctively looked back at the man whom they'd been discussing. "He..." She forgot her words when he looked up at the same moment, his dark gaze colliding with hers and washing the smile from his face. Was Guthrie truly capable of being so violent? She wouldn't have thought it, based on what she'd seen of him so far. And yet...she could not forget the angry look in his eyes last night when she'd mentioned his father.

"Time for you to return to your room, my lady." MacNeil held his hand out toward her bedchamber door. "I'll make sure Laura comes to assist you and that your breakfast is brought up soon."

Numb and unsure if remaining here one more day was wise, Regina went back inside and closed the door.

"I'll get ye both somethin' to eat," Carlton told Sam and Jacob as he watched Regina turn away from the railing and disappear inside. The boys were progressing well, which was good since their mothers and sisters would have to rely on them for protection now that their fathers had passed.

Carlton strode into the kitchen where bacon already sputtered and sizzled on the saucepan Gareth was wielding. Blayne was there too, his large frame propped against the wall as if he supported the building. From the oven came the sweet and wholesome scent of freshly baked bread.

"I see ye're outdoin' yerself fer the second day in a row, Gareth." Carlton went to stand next to Blayne while the cook cracked some eggs into a bowl and whisked them. "I take it that's fer her ladyship since the rest of us tend to make do with porridge fer breakfast." Not because he couldn't afford to feed his men better, but because he'd always believed that porridge gave the stomach a solid foundation on which to start the day.

"Aye. I told her I'd send up a tray," Blayne explained. "And I didnae want her to be disappointed after yesterday's meals."

Carlton nodded. "I suppose the standard's been set."

Gareth's brow folded in a number of creases. He was a stocky fellow who looked like he took great pleasure in his own cooking. "I'll not serve gruel to a well-bred lady, Guthrie."

"Of course not. An' ye shouldn't." He crossed his arms and watched as Gareth began melting butter on a second pan. "In fact, the more hospitable we are, the more likely she is to enjoy her stay. Which is why I'd like fer ye to make her a cake."

A clatter of cooking utensils conveyed what Gareth thought about that. "I'm not some fancy pastry chef you brought here from France."

"An' what? They're the only ones who know how to make such delicacies?"

"You know what I mean." Gareth stared in exasperation at the food he was cooking. "I don't know the first thing about baking cakes."

"Then I suggest ye learn," Carlton told him wryly. He glanced at Blayne, who appeared to be following the conversation with rapt interest. "Her ladyship mentioned that she's never had the chance to try one and that she would like to do so, so—"

"She's never had cake?" Blayne asked in disbelief.

Carlton sighed. "Somethin' to do with her mother insisting that it would ruin her figure."

Gareth scratched the back of his head. "I bought a cookbook once, out of interest. There might be something in there I can try." When Carlton prepared to thank him he hastily added, "But I'm not promising you that she'll like my efforts."

Accepting this eventuality, Carlton stole a small piece of bacon from the plate his cook was preparing and turned to Blayne. "Did ye learn anythin' more about that carriage I had ye look into?"

Blayne pushed away from the wall and straightened himself to his full height of six feet five inches. He shook his head. "I'm sorry." He watched Carlton for a moment, glanced briefly at Gareth and then back at Carlton. "How did it go last night?"

"I woke up tryin' to strangle the bookcase," Carlton confessed. Talking about his father, thinking about what had happened, had made the man he hated most return to his dreams.

"When I spoke to Lady Regina earlier," Blayne murmured, "she showed no sign of concern, so you must not have been very loud."

Carlton expelled a breath he'd not even realized he had been holding.

The thought of her learning how dangerous he could actually be was cause for real concern. Hell, he ought to send her away before he hurt her. Or did something monumentally foolish like kiss her.

Last night he'd been tempted.

Christ, when he'd helped her undo the buttons of her gown, he'd had to fight the urge to pull her into his arms. Which had left him in a state of severe discomfort for a good while after.

Shaking off his awareness of the attraction he felt toward her, he said, "There's a good chance things will get worse the longer she stays, so I hope I can count on ye to keep an eye on me, Blayne."

"I'll do my best," Blayne promised as he took the tray that Gareth had prepared for Regina. When he was gone, Guthrie addressed his cook. "Can ye please get food fer Sam and Jacob as well? I told them I'd get them somethin' to eat."

"Of course." Gareth cleared his throat. "About that cake you want me to make…"

"Just add some cream an' I'm sure it'll be well received." When Gareth looked hesitant, Guthrie said, "The important thing is fer ye to try yer best." Gareth muttered something that made Carlton grin as he left the kitchen. Stopping by his office briefly, he leafed through his notebook, reminding himself of some unfinished business he had to take care of. Just because he'd been given the chance to go after his greatest foe didn't mean there weren't other men for him to deal with.

Satisfied with the goals he had set for himself,

Carlton locked his notebook away in his desk drawer, returned to the front of the tavern, and headed toward the stairs. It was time for him to check on his guest.

"Guthrie?"

He turned in response to Philipa's voice and was slightly startled by how haggard she looked, as if she hadn't slept in years. "Any news about Scarlet?" he asked.

She shook her head. "She still hasn't returned. And I've not received any message from her either." Her eyes took on a watery shimmer. "Something's not right. I can feel it, but I can't think of what to do."

"I'll conduct another search," he promised. When she nodded tightly and thanked him, he asked, "Would ye like a cup of tea or perhaps somethin' stronger to calm yer nerves?"

"No. I must get back and check on the rest of my girls. They're all distraught by Scarlet's disappearance, so I'd like to be there to help them through it."

"Ye're a good woman, Philipa." He could see that she made an effort to smile in response to the compliment, even though it looked more like a grimace. When she was gone, he took the stairs two at a time and strode toward his parlor door.

Blayne had resumed his post on the chair outside, keeping guard just as Carlton had ordered. Blayne tipped back his head to better address him. "Word just arrived from one of the lads keeping watch over Hedgewick's home. There was a lot of activity yesterday with several carriages coming and going."

"Did the boy say who was in them?"

"Mostly men. But an unmarked carriage with loads of luggage on top did depart with a middle aged woman of quality in it. Could have been the countess."

"Good work, Blayne." Hedgewick was doing as Carlton had expected him to. He was getting his wife out of town to better explain his daughter's absence. "Tell the lad to stay at his post fer now."

"Will do."

Recalling his notebook, Carlton said, "We also need to get back to the matter regarding Mr. Reynolds."

"The gentleman who—"

"I'd rather ye call 'im a blackguard, fer surely he's nothin' else."

"We don't know that yet. Not for certain."

"No. But I can feel it. Somethin's rotten about that man. I'm sure that Rembrandt he sold to the Duke of Coventry was—" A thud on the opposite side of the door made Carlton stop mid-sentence. He stared at the door that stood between him and Regina, then reached for the handle.

The door opened and he was immediately faced with Regina's stunning blue eyes. Her rosy lips parted as if in surprise. "I...um..." She stopped herself when he frowned, and took a step back, moving to grant him entrance.

He dropped a look at MacNeil, who was watching him with a smirk.

"What?" Guthrie asked.

"Ah, nothing." Blayne's lips twitched. "But you should have seen your face just now when she opened the door. It looked like you were being granted a view of heaven."

"Ye're imaginin' things that aren't there." But the need to enter the room now so he and Regina could be alone was impossible to ignore. So he took a deep breath and stepped into his parlor, and shut the door.

Having finished eating a moment before she'd heard voices in the hallway, Regina had risen and gone to the door. When she'd realized the voices belonged to Guthrie and MacNeil, she'd intended to open the door and ask for writing materials in order to pen her letters. But then she'd heard Guthrie mention Mr. Reynolds.

It wasn't so much the name itself that had caused a chill to seep into her bones but rather the way he'd said it. And then, because she'd been stupid enough to knock her elbow against the door, she'd now been caught eavesdropping.

Briefly, she thought of coming up with an excuse for standing right on the opposite side of the door, but the sharp accusation in his eyes deterred her from making such a pointless attempt. So she crossed her arms instead and glared back. "Mr. Reynolds is a longtime friend of my family's. Whatever you think he may have done, I can assure you you're wrong."

The sharpness of his gaze pinned her in place as the edge of his mouth curled upward. "Is that so?"

His voice, low and smooth and extremely intimidating, caused a shiver to scrape down her spine. It made her forget his interaction with the two boys he'd been teaching to fight and how ready he was to help find a missing prostitute and even the fact that he'd shown her nothing but kindness since her arrival. All she could think of now were the words MacNeil had spoken earlier, prompting her to carelessly ask, "How many men have you killed?"

His eyes darkened to black. "Five."

She sucked in a breath. When he said nothing more, she backed away and lowered herself to the sofa. "You…" Stupidly, she'd not expected him to answer. And certainly not so precisely. In fact, she'd rather imagined – or hoped – that he would deny having taken another man's life. But he didn't, which meant he was just as dangerous as the papers had always suggested. Even if the authorities had never managed to prove it.

Slowly he crossed the room to where she sat, his gaze intense and unwavering as it held hers. "You don't want to know why?"

She shook her head and clasped her hands together to keep them from trembling.

He stared at her like the devil himself come to haul her back down to hell. "The reasonin' doesn't matter to ye?"

"How can it?" Her voice was but a faint whisper. "You've taken a life, Guthrie. Several, if you're being honest. There's no forgiving that."

Leaning forward, he lifted her legs and sat. A rush of warmth flooded her veins and she hated herself in that moment for responding to him as she did – to a man who had just admitted that he had blood on his hands.

Twisting toward her so he could trap her with his attention, he settled her legs in his lap and placed one hand firmly upon them. Regina's heart pulsed with quickening beats as she felt his heat permeate her flesh. She hadn't feared him before because she'd believed all the awful things she'd heard to be exaggerations. She'd thought him incapable of the actions he'd been accused of.

But she'd been wrong. And she was now here with him. Completely alone. If he chose to hurt her, then no one would come to her rescue. No one would even know what had happened since nobody knew where she was. Oh God, she'd been foolish and—

"Calm yerself, luv." His voice was softer now, like velvet, and heaven help her if it didn't soothe something deep inside her. She opened her mouth to speak, to protest or at least say something, but all her thoughts tangled together and jammed in her head. "Let me explain somethin' to ye, me lady. The world is not a nice place. Most people are selfish an' cruel." He raised his hand and pressed it against her cheek, and even though her brain urged her to push him away, she could not make herself move and thus allowed the caress. "Ye've been protected yer entire life. Ye've not seen the things I've seen, an' thank God fer that. But if ye think fer one second that I'll let any 'arm come to a woman or child an' not rid the world o' the scourge who caused it, then ye're mistaken."

Regina blinked as if trying to awaken from a daze. Her heart was flapping around inside her, and yet his words also tugged at her soul. "Are you saying that the men you killed were causing deliberate harm to others?" The anguished fury that burned in his eyes informed her that this was the case. "Tell me," she murmured. "Explain it to me."

"Ye just said the reason fer killin' someone doesn't matter an' that there can be no forgiveness, so what difference will anythin' I say make?"

She drew a deep breath. "I think I may have spoken too quickly. Without considering all the possible factors."

He stared at her and she knew what she saw in his eyes was respect. And something else as well, though she wasn't entirely sure what. "The truth ain't pretty, me lady, an' if I describe it to ye, ye'll know it ferever. Ye won't be able to un-think it again."

A shudder went through her, but rather than shy away, she gazed back into his stormy eyes. "I want to know." She wanted to understand him, to figure out what it was about him that drew her – why, when he'd just confessed to committing the worst sort of crime, she wasn't trying to escape him but rather encouraging him to tell her about it.

His thumb brushed her skin as he caught a loose strand of her hair. He tucked it behind her ear, and she shivered in response to the unexpected tenderness. The compulsion to reach out and touch his face in return was agonizingly strong. But she resisted the urge and waited for him to speak.

"I took a life fer the very first time while tryin' to defend me own. The man in question, Will Maher, was a member of Bartholomew's crew."

His comment only presented her with more questions. Bartholomew had been another renowned criminal and, as it had turned out, the

Duke of Redding's father. Taken down by his own son, he'd been hanged for murder last year. "How did you end up with Bartholomew in the first place?"

Guthrie dropped his hand from her cheek, leaving a cold spot in its place. "Bartholomew recruited me when I was a lad. Both me parents were dead an' he took me in – gave me a roof o'er me head and put food in me belly. He also taught me 'ow to pick pockets, cheat at cards in order to con people out o' their money, an' a bunch of other things." He shrugged as if this was a minor detail. "Later, when I realized how 'e was makin' most of his blunt, I ran away an' he sent Maher to kill me."

Regina gasped and Guthrie chuckled mildly. "No one leaves Bartholomew alive. That was the rule o' thumb that was meant to ensure the loyalty of 'is men."

"How old were you when you escaped?"

"Eighteen." His expression had tightened in response to the memories rising up from the past. "Maher found me, came at me with a blade, an' actually caught me close to me ribs. But I had youth an' dexterity on me side, an' so I managed to twist away an' counter attack with a knife of me own. Got him right in the throat."

An icy chill wrapped itself around her as she thought of what that would have been like for him. "You must have been terrified," she murmured.

He shook his head. "There was no time fer that." A pause followed and then, "That's 'ow I met MacNeil, by the way. He found me bleedin' from the stab wound and made sure I got patched up."

"I'm glad to know he was there to help you." The gold in his eyes shimmered and she quietly asked, "What was Bartholomew doing that you disagreed with so vehemently?" Considering all the things he must have seen during his time with the man, it would have taken something truly awful to make him leave.

Guthrie inhaled through his nose and sank deeper into the sofa. Propping one elbow on the backrest, he leaned his head against his hand. "He was in the whorin' business, an' I'm not talkin' about the sort o' business that Philipa's runnin' next door. *That*, I can support, but Bartholomew…" His jaw clenched, causing his moustache to stretch at an odd angle. When he spoke again, there was a hollowness to his voice that rattled Regina's bones. "There are sick people out there with very particular tastes when it comes to sex; men who like fer it to be violent, who want to know that their partner's unwillin'. And then there are those so depraved that they want to do it with children."

"And Bartholomew…" Dear God it was too abhorrent to think of.

"He made every twisted fantasy possible."

"Good lord." Not even in her worst nightmares would she have imagined that something so awful was possible. That there were people out there who would do such vile and despicable things – who would harm the innocent to fill their own pockets.

"The other four men that I killed were 'is clients." He made the confession without any hint of remorse. "Bartholomew 'ated me fer it. And fer takin' o'er part of 'is territory here in St. Giles. Came after me in all sorts of creative ways o'er the years, but never quite managed to catch me."

"Did you ever go after him?"

"I tried, but he was always heavily guarded – especially after 'e learned I was out to get 'im."

He fell silent, allowing Regina to process all of this new information. The life he had led had not been easy. She could not imagine what it must have been like for him, an orphaned child all alone on the streets of London. No wonder his life had turned out as it had. He'd been exposed to crime since a very young age, but even though the opportunity for him to become truly rotten had been there, he'd turned away from that path. Instead, he'd sought justice on behalf of those who were too weak to seek it for themselves. And this was something that she could admire and respect.

Although…

"I know Reynolds well. His sister is married to one of Mama's good friends and—"

"He's not as nice as ye think."

"In what sense?"

Guthrie answered without hesitation. "He produces counterfeit art and sells it as the genuine work, and in doin' so he's taken advantage of a lot of good people."

Regina considered that comment for a second. Earlier she would have insisted that he was wrong. But now, after everything he'd revealed about himself, she wasn't so sure. He sounded very convincing and yet…it also felt as though he was trying to hide something from her.

His cat leapt into her lap, halting her thoughts. Regina smiled in response to the loud meow and instinctively stroked its back. "What's his name?" she asked while considering the feline's clumpy fur. The poor thing could do with a fair bit of grooming.

"Ralph."

She nodded. "I like that name. It suits him."

Guthrie snorted. "Just as well since it's the only one he's got." He pushed her legs from his lap and stood. "I've got to go out fer a while and probably won't be back until late."

Unsure of what to say, she watched as he strode to the door. Reaching it, he turned back to face her. "There are writin' materials in that box over there – the one on the bottom shelf of the bookcase. Feel free to use them fer the letters ye want to write yer brother an' Fielding." He paused, then added, "I'm leavin' Patrick outside this room, so if ye need anythin' else, just let 'im know and he'll fetch it fer ye. All right?"

"All right." He opened the door and she hastened to say, "Thank you for sharing your past with me. It means a great deal."

Without responding, he left her.

CHAPTER SIX

CARLTON WOKE THE NEXT DAY to the sound of furniture scraping across the floor. He opened one eye and stared at the room. Belly down on the sofa with his left cheek pressed into a pillow, his right arm dangled over the side so his knuckles rested against the floor. Ralph, who'd sensed his wakefulness, leapt up onto his back and began a slow march along the length of his spine. A loud squeak pierced the air and Carlton groaned. He'd returned at four in the morning without discovering anything new about Scarlet. It was almost as if she'd been swallowed up by the ground itself.

Screaaaaaaaaach. Thump, thump.

He muttered a curse, swatted Ralph away with a backward swipe, and stood. Christ almighty! It felt like he'd jammed his head straight into the ceiling it hurt so bad. He cursed again, strode to his bedchamber door and gave it an angry knock.

Silence took over.

Then the door opened to Regina's bright and beautiful face. Her eyes were sparkling and her cheeks were a rosy hue that compounded her youth and vitality. Stray locks hung around her face in haphazard disarray that only made her more stunning.

She cleared her throat and averted her gaze for a moment before looking back at him more directly. "You're up," she said.

"An excellent observation," he muttered. The color in her cheeks deepened, and she stared at him as if she'd never seen a man before in her life, which was something of an odd experience.

But then it occurred to him that in his annoyance over the noise, he'd gone straight to the source without stopping to think of how he was dressed. Since sleeping in his waistcoat, jacket, and cravat would be deuced uncomfortable, he'd removed all those articles and left them on a chair. Which meant that he only wore his shirt, which gaped open to the middle of his chest, and the trousers he'd had on last night.

"Why are ye makin' such a ruckus?" he asked. If she wanted to look her fill, he'd let her. And savor her interest in the process.

"I um…I was trying to clean up a bit." Her eyes were fixed on the spot right beneath his collarbones and it took every ounce of restraint Carlton had not to reach out and grab her and…what? She was a lady. Too good for the likes of him, no matter her father's transgressions. He squared his shoulders on that thought. She was first and foremost a means to an end, not a woman with whom he could have a liaison.

The fact that she chose to lick her lips next did not help in the slightest. On the contrary, his body began responding in ways that he very much doubted she'd find appropriate.

"An' to do so ye needed to make more noise

than a regiment out on the march?" Speaking was the only solution – the only way for him to distract his brain from what he wanted.

"I thought it best to be thorough, which meant moving some things about."

The pitch of her voice and the speed with which she spoke made him question her honesty. Something was up, and that caused unease to settle like rocks in the pit of his belly. "Let me see."

She sniffed and then promptly sneezed, forcing him back a step. "Pardon me, but I doubt this room has been properly dusted since you moved in. Not that I'm surprised. It's not easy to clean when you have as many things as you do." She shoved a stray lock of hair behind her ear, leaving a smudge next to her eye. "But I've made good progress and…" Her eyes widened as he leaned in to try and get a better look of the room. "You really don't have to come in here right now. I promise to be more quiet and—"

Carlton pushed his way past her and almost tripped over a box that wasn't where it was supposed to be. Recovering his footing, he regained his balance and straightened his posture. "Good God." He stared at the mountain she'd built on the bed. There were pictures that he'd never gotten around to hanging, a lap desk he hadn't used in years, papers of varying importance, three clocks, a couple of music boxes, an extraordinary amount of knickknacks, and at the very top, a crimson garter with black lace trimming.

As if she knew precisely what he was looking at, Regina said, "I wasn't aware that such scandalous underthings existed."

"Weren't ye?" The question sounded raspy to his own ears, which wasn't surprising when the next thing he noticed was a pile of newspaper clippings spread out on his dresser. Those had not been lying about but carefully hidden away in the bottom of a drawer.

"I found it under the bed," she said, in reference to the garter. "Which is probably a good thing since it looks quite pricey and will no doubt be missed by its owner."

Carlton gritted his teeth. "You went through me things."

"I had to in order to clean. But don't worry. I promise to put it all back where I found it."

He turned to her then and she must have noticed that he wasn't the least bit pleased, for her smile disappeared as if slapped from her face. "Explain to me how this," he reached out and snatched up the clippings, "includes cleanin'?"

"Well um…" Her eyes seemed to dart around frantically in her head. "I was looking for a cravat to tie around my mouth and nose so the dust—"

"Don't lie to me."

Her eyes settled on his face and for a long moment he watched her brain work to conjure up other excuses. His annoyance continued to grow, not only because she'd invaded his privacy but because of what she had found.

"Very well," she suddenly said. "The truth is that our conversation last night made me want to know more about you, to understand you better, that is. I mean, you're known as a fearful villain and yet you fight for justice and—"

"Don't turn me into a hero." His fingers tightened around the clippings. If she'd read them all, she'd know who he was, but nothing in her expression suggested she'd made such a shocking discovery.

"But—"

"Stay out of me things." He shoved the clippings into his pocket and turned, intending to put some distance between them before he lost his temper. But as he stepped toward the door, something cracked beneath his weight.

"I just wanted to get to know you better," she said while he moved his foot to reveal the porcelain miniature of his father. "Your kindness toward me is so at odds with...oh dear...I must have dropped that when I—"

"Get out." A sharp ringing in his ears was accompanied by a pounding headache. His vision started to blur.

"But this is—"

"Just go!"

The force of his words pushed her back toward the door. He heard her sharp intake of breath, could tell that his outburst had hurt her, but blood was rushing too fast through his veins and he could not seem to regain his composure. All he could think of right now was the ruined portrait. Crouching, he scooped the miniature up in his hand and considered the hairline cracks that traversed it, like tiny tributaries splitting off from a large river.

With a sigh, he closed his fingers around the image and stood. Why the hell did she have to stick her nose where it didn't belong? *Because you made her curious. Because you told her just enough to*

make her believe there was more to you than met the eye.
And so there was. But he didn't want her or anyone else to learn about that. Not when he'd spent
the last twenty years reinventing himself.

Raking his fingers through his hair, he set his
father's portrait aside on the dresser and put his
mind to clearing the bed. The mindless task would
help ease the tension still gripping his body. So
he pocketed the garter with the intention of seeing it returned to Amourette's and placed his lap
desk on the floor before finding spots for the rest
of his things. When he was done, he felt calmer
and more able to confront Regina again without
losing his temper. But when he returned to his
parlor, she wasn't there. Only Ralph gave life to
the room, which had to mean that Regina had
taken his words more literally than he'd intended.

He grabbed his hose and began to dress while
unease pushed its ragged claws under his ribs.
Dear God. If she'd left him… He jammed his feet
into his shoes, flung his jacket over his shoulders,
and exited the room. Why wasn't anyone out here
keeping watch? Damn! If she vanished, or worse,
returned home, he wouldn't be able to use her
to taunt her father. He'd lose his best chance of
making Hedgewick experience the fear and the
pain he'd put Carlton through all those years ago.

"Why isn't someone upstairs keepin' watch?"
he called out to Blayne as he passed him on his
way to the front door.

"Her ladyship asked me to fetch her some food.
Is everything all right?"

"No, it bloody well isn't." Carlton didn't stop
to explain. She must have used the request as a

means to give Blayne the slip. Which meant security would have to be strengthened when he got her back. And by all that was holy, he would get her back. If he could find her.

But the street offered no indication of her existence at all.

A fresh wash of panic spilled over his skin, causing the hair to rise at the nape of his neck. His heart was thumping loudly while blood churned through his veins to create a deafening roar in his ears. No. He would not think the worst. She wouldn't be foolish enough to attempt navigating St. Giles on her own. Not after her last experience with the men who'd attacked her. Which meant she was still nearby.

Expelling a slow breath, he felt the panic recede as soothing air rushed into his straining lungs. Right. Only a few options availed themselves: a cobbler, some private homes, a gin shop, and Amourette's.

A smirk tugged at the corner of his mouth as he started toward the brothel. If she'd sought refuge there, he'd respect her all the more. Not because there was anything admirable about it per se, but because it would prove once again that she wasn't a typical lady of breeding. Indeed, Regina was likely too kind to judge a woman for her choice of work. Which was confirmed moments later when he walked through Amourette's front door, entered the parlor, and found her. Comfortably seated on a mauve velvet sofa, she was keeping company with Philipa and two of Amourette's other residents.

"Ah," Philipa said. "I was wondering how long

it would take for you to show up. Came in a rush, did you?" She tutted like he was a misbehaving boy. "Why, you're not even wearing a cravat. How very unlike you, Guthrie."

She was right. He never left his rooms without being properly dressed. "I see you've met me houseguest," he muttered right before offering a hasty greeting to the two other women present. Only Nicolette was a prostitute. The other, whose name was Ida, was something else entirely – a secret that Philipa guarded with her life.

Without asking if he could join them, Carlton pulled up a chair and sat.

"Indeed we have," Philipa said with a glint of amusement in her eyes. "And we've taken quite a liking to her, haven't we girls?"

"In less than 'alf an hour?" Carlton asked when Nicolette and Ida both murmured their agreement. Regina, he noted, kept her gaze averted, and for some peculiar reason, that rankled. He wanted to be the center of her focus, just as he'd been when she'd opened the bedchamber door. He wanted to make her blush.

"It doesn't take more than that to judge someone's character, Guthrie. You know that."

Indeed he did. Noting the glass set before Regina, he said, "A bit early in the day to imbibe, is it not?"

She gave him a hesitant glance that allowed him to see the pain in her eyes, before turning her gaze away from his once again.

"The poor girl needed it," Philipa told him sternly. "Lord help me, I cannot imagine what you might have said or done to her, Guthrie, but she was in a state when she came here."

Carlton bristled. "I did not do anythin', Philipa." With one retort, she'd riled him. "She's the one who decided to meddle with me things. If it weren't fer her, me father's miniature wouldn't be broken."

"Ah." It was a simple remark. Just one syllable. But it let Carlton know that Philipa realized how much this upset him.

"I'm very sorry," Regina said. She'd turned to face him, and in her gaze he could see the full extent of her torment. Liquid blue shimmered with regret as tears threatened to spill on her lashes. "I shouldn't have gone through your things. It was wrong and I...." She swallowed as if she was struggling to speak. "You've been so kind to me and I abused that and now your father's portrait is ruined and it's all my fault." She dropped her gaze and gave her eyes a quick swipe. "I can only hope that you can forgive me."

Forgive her? She looked as if her heart was breaking, and that alone caused his own to stutter a little. "Of course." Even though she'd crossed a line, he could not resent her or remain angry with her for long. Not when she looked as miserable as she did. If anything, he wanted to pull her onto his lap and wrap his arms around her. He wanted to hold her close and fill her with endless assurance. "I'm the one who actually broke it."

She looked back up. "Yes, but you wouldn't have done so if I hadn't dropped it on the floor for you to step on." An unhappy smile touched her lips. "I went looking for answers and—"

"Just promise me ye'll leave me things alone

from now on, and we'll put the matter behind us."

Her entire face lit up with gratitude. "I prom- ise."

Guthrie's breath caught and it took him a moment to find the right words. "I ought to ask yer forgiveness too fer the way I yelled at ye," he said with a sudden need to make peace. "I was angry." Glancing at Philipa, he jerked his chin discreetly in the direction of the door.

With a nod, Philipa stood. "It was lovely to meet you, my lady. I hope we'll have a chance to further our acquaintance in the future. But right now there's a matter that I must attend to, and I need Nicolette and Ida to help me with it. If you'll please excuse us."

Regina wanted to beg them to stay. She wasn't quite ready to be alone with Guthrie again. Not after violating his trust and then realizing the true significance of the miniature. It was very likely the only thing he had left of his father. Knowing that she'd played a part in ruining it made her feel like her insides were being ripped from her body and trampled on.

The door closed behind the three women who'd welcomed her into their place of business, and a very uncomfortable silence filled the room. Acutely aware of Guthrie's presence, Regina reached for her glass and took another quick sip of her sherry. The sweet heat warmed her throat and eased her overly agitated nerves.

"I was worried about ye." The low murmur stroked its way across her shoulders until it reached the top of her spine. There, it burst apart in a series of shivers that sank deep into her flesh. "Ye cannot run off like that, luv. Not in this part o' town."

"I know. But you told me to go."

"I meant to the parlor, not into the street." He'd risen and was now moving toward her.

"I just wanted to get away," she confessed. "From you."

Lowering himself to the spot beside her, he reached for her hand and turned it over between his own as if it were some rare gem that he wished to study in greater detail. "I hurt ye, Regina, an' I'm sorry fer it. But ye also went an' scared me 'alf to death." Curling her fingers into her palm, he raised her hand to his lips and placed a kiss upon each of her knuckles.

"What does that mean?" The question just sprang from between her lips without warning. Was that even her voice? It sounded so breathy, like the words had been spoken on a sigh of pure pleasure.

No touch she'd ever received had felt as lovely as this. Her stomach sucked itself inside out at the feel of his lips. Accompanied by the slight tickling of his moustache stroking her skin, the effect was rather...something she wasn't quite able to describe, except to say that it sent hot shivers scurrying through her.

"I'm not entirely sure." The low timbre with which he spoke was like velvet. It wrapped her in comfort while filling her soul with a deep, innate yearning. "Would ye like to find out?"

The promise of decadent sin burned bright in his eyes as his gaze held hers. Slowly, and without looking away, he pressed a kiss to the back of her wrist. The effect was immediate. A gasp went through her as tingles darted up through her arm to fill the rest of her body.

She sucked in a breath. "I don't know." It was the most honest answer she could give him since it was the truth. She had no experience with this sort of thing, was completely unfamiliar with the myriad of new sensations he stirred in her. And she feared…she feared that if she said yes, he'd own part of her forever. Because while she might like him and perhaps even want him in ways that surprised her, her future could not be with him. As a lady, she would either have to marry a proper gentleman, or choose the life of a spinster.

But since she lacked the will to pull away, she remained where she was and allowed him to close the distance between them.

His mouth met hers, carefully and with far more tenderness than she had expected. Sensation rushed through her: his moustache softly tickling her skin, the sensual press of his lips against hers and the touch of his nose as the tip of it brushed her cheek.

The entire experience lasted no more than a couple of seconds. It was over before she was ready, before she was able to fully enjoy it.

"Fergive me," he murmured, "but I could not resist." Heat burned in his eyes, leaving her scorched. "Shall we return to The Black Swan now?"

Somewhat dazed from the kiss they'd just

shared, she nodded. For although she was sure that Philipa would give her sanctuary if she asked, Regina wanted to stay close to Guthrie. He'd reached inside her somehow and claimed a part of her heart that had not belonged to anyone else. Within only three days, she'd learned that she could rely on him more than she could on her own parents. That she mattered to him and that he would do all he could in order to keep her safe.

And she craved that safety and the way that it made her feel, the way *he* made her feel, as if she was more than simply a pawn.

CHAPTER SEVEN

A WEEK.

That was how long it had been since Marcus had woken to the shocking realization that his sister, who'd always followed the rules, had fled the demands of their parents and run away from home. Which would have been fine with him if he'd known where she'd gone. But the thought of Regina out there in the world on her own had made him queasy. She was a proper young lady. How would she manage without a maid? Had she even thought to take any money with her and if so, how would she cope once her funds were depleted?

These questions had plagued him day and night. He'd been sure she'd return the next day, not because she wished to, but out of necessity. When she hadn't, he'd thwarted his father's demand for discretion and had gone to call on her friends, Lady Teresa Bradshaw and Miss Livinia Kingsley. Both were surprised by his visit and claimed they hadn't seen Regina since meeting with her for tea a few days earlier.

But when he'd returned home, there had been a progression. A letter, written in an unfamiliar hand, had been delivered. His father had handed it to Marcus, who'd read it with rising dread. "At least she's alive," he'd said for no other purpose than to grasp at something optimistic.

"She should have married Stokes." Hedgewick had met with numerous Bow Street runners since Regina's disappearance. None had delivered a solid lead yet.

"This is all your fault," Marcus had said. "You drove her to this by demanding too much."

"All I asked was for her to do her duty. She knew it would come to this. Your mother and I made sure of it."

"Your mistake was in thinking she'd throw herself off a cliff for you," Marcus had shot back.

"Don't be so bloody dramatic. Stokes was an excellent choice for her."

Unwilling to argue with stubborn blindness, Marcus had walked away from that conversation and hadn't spoken to his father since. The Windhams had been extremely displeased when they'd learned that Regina had changed her mind and refused to leave her room, which was what they'd been told. They had even threatened to tell the world that Regina had jilted their son, until Stokes himself had calmly reminded them both that doing so wouldn't look good for him either. Reluctantly, they'd seemed to agree to this point and had promptly left the Hedgewick home with tight expressions and clipped words of parting.

Marcus had spent every day since then prowling the streets and making inquiries. He'd visited every hospital and coroner in London proper. But there was no sign of her. Not one single clue as to where she might be. And if his father had learned anything new, he'd chosen not to share it with Marcus, which was why he'd enlisted the butler's help. Keeping apprised of the situation was critical to gaining results, and Plath was a man of integrity whom Marcus knew he could trust. He wasn't as confident when it came to the rest of the servants, which was why he'd promised them all ten pounds each if Regina returned without the truth getting out.

Exhausted, he went home so he could eat, sleep and be ready to continue his investigation the next morning. "Good evening, Plath" Marcus said when the butler opened the front door for him.

"Another letter has arrived." Plath took Marcus's hat and gloves from him and set them on a nearby table. Discreetly, he produced the letter from his jacket pocket and handed it to Marcus.

"Thank you." There were benefits to treating a servant well. Years of helping Plath pay for his widowed sister's rent had earned him the old man's loyalty. Of course, there was also the fact that Plath was particularly fond of Regina and would do whatever he could to help her. So when Marcus had asked for the next unmarked letter that arrived to be delivered to him first, Plath had agreed. "Where is my father now?"

"In his study, my lord."

Thanking him again, Marcus stepped into the parlor. A fire had been lit to heat the room for the evening and Marcus strode toward it. Withdrawing the pocketknife he always carried on his person, he heated the blade over the flames. Then, with great care so as not to damage the seal in any way, he used the hot blade to lift it.

The page crackled between his fingers as he unfolded it and read.

My Lord,

Your daughter is a remarkable woman. It stuns me to know that someone as lovely and kind as she can have you for a father. The time has come for you to reflect on your past, Hedgewick. And then you must ask yourself if you think you deserve to see your darling daughter again, or if I should keep her as payment for your sins.

One way or another, justice will find you.

V.S.

Marcus re-read the lines multiple times. Perhaps there was some hidden clue in the phrasing or in the words themselves that would lead him closer to finding his sister. But nothing stuck out, except for the fact that she lived. Closing his eyes for a moment, he breathed a sigh of relief. He then heated his blade again and used it to melt the underside of the seal so it would reattach to the paper.

"You should deliver this to my father," he told Plath when he found him waiting outside the parlor door. "He won't know I read it."

Plath nodded and turned to leave, then paused and glanced back at Marcus. "Did it help you in any way?"

"Not with finding Regina. But it has assured me that she is presently well." It had also made it clear that the man who held her was seeking vengeance against Hedgewick.

Returning to the parlor, Marcus poured a measure of brandy into a tumbler and set it to his lips. The amber liquid provided a welcome bite to his throat as he swallowed. What might Hedgewick have done to warrant the hostage taking of his daughter? He thought on that for a while and came up blank, so he decided to ask himself who could be behind it instead. Surely it must be someone of rank. Hedgewick didn't associate with anyone else. Which meant that he must have a powerful enemy among the peerage. Perhaps a handsome young gentleman with the means to lure Regina into his carriage with the pretext of trying to help her? But if the villain was young, then that meant Hedgewick would have crossed him in recent years, which didn't seem likely. Unless he'd been dealing in things that Marcus had not been aware of.

Downing the remainder of his drink, Marcus went to find his father. When he knocked on the study door and received no answer, he entered the room uninvited. Hedgewick didn't seem to notice the impropriety. He just stared off into the distance, his unfocused gaze suggesting that he was caught in deep thought. In one hand was the letter Plath had brought him twenty minutes earlier. In the other was a half empty glass of brandy.

Marcus closed the door and moved toward a vacant armchair. Lowering himself into it, he considered his father a moment; the hollowness of his cheeks and how his hair had thinned in recent years. "Have you received additional news about Regina?" he asked.

Hedgewick blinked and dropped his gaze to the

paper he held. He stared at it for a second, then hastily folded it and placed it in his desk drawer. "No. Just a note from your mother informing me that she has arrived in Paris and that all is well."

"I see." The urge to reach across his father's desk and haul him to his feet by his cravat so he could shake him was rampant. Gripping the armrest, Marcus forced himself to overcome it. "Do you know how long she'll be away?"

"Until Regina is found."

"And what if that never happens?"

Hedgewick stared back at Marcus. "She will be."

"You are certain of this?" He wanted to ask his father what he had done. If it wasn't terrible then surely he would have shared it with Marcus and they would have worked together on figuring out who'd sent the letters. Instead Hedgewick had lied, confirming that there was something he was ashamed of or possibly even afraid of. And this made Marcus nervous.

"Bow Street is looking into her disappearance and—"

"Ha!" Marcus leaned forward in his seat and pinned Hedgewick with an incredulous glare. "She's been gone a week now. Hell, she could be in Scotland at this point for all we know."

"She isn't in Scotland, Marcus. The letters were posted in England."

"Letters?" Marcus tilted his head in question and watched as Hedgewick drew back.

"Forgive me. I've not been sleeping well lately. I'm afraid I misspoke."

"So you've had no other word from the man

who's holding Regina? No indication at all of her whereabouts or why he's letting you know that he has her?"

Incredulity shaped Hedgewick's features. "Of course not, Marcus. I would have told you about it immediately if there were."

Marcus's heart gave a dull thump of disappointment. "Good to know," he forced himself to say. Because if he revealed that he'd read the letter and knew his father was somehow connected to Regina's prolonged absence, Hedgewick would be more careful about concealing the truth and prevent Marcus from discovering anything more.

So Marcus wished him a pleasant evening instead and went to eat his dinner in his bedchamber. If additional letters arrived, Plath would help him discover their contents. And until then, Marcus would start looking into every peer with a strong connection to his father, because taking a man's daughter hostage – that was personal. Whatever Hedgewick had done, it likely involved a severe breach of trust and perhaps some sort of betrayal.

Regina stood in the middle of Guthrie's parlor and glanced around. After their argument six days earlier, she'd told herself that she wouldn't touch any of his things ever again. She'd also told herself that the kiss they'd shared had been a mistake. After all, she was a young lady, and in spite of her current situation, she hoped to return to Society one day and marry a man of her own social class. To pursue a romantic relationship with Guthrie was utterly unthinkable. Which was why it was so unfortunate that she hadn't yet heard back from Fielding.

According to the messenger who'd delivered her letter to him, the earl was not in Town at the moment and there was no indication as to when he would return either.

Sighing, Regina contemplated making a list of other potential candidates for marriage. She could also write another letter to Marcus, although she supposed the one was enough since she didn't really have anything left to tell him.

Restless and with a depressing sense of helpless passivity creeping through her, she wandered into the bedchamber and crossed to the dresser. The miniature depicting Guthrie's father was still there, a constant reminder of Regina's foolishness. It made her heart ache, just looking at it. The main crack ran right below the man's chin, traversing what appeared to be a pearl–tipped cravat pin.

Frowning, Regina bent closer. The cream colored waistcoat peeking out from behind the jacket had been painted to represent a shimmering type of fabric that seemed to resemble silk. And there was some sort of red ribbon around the neck, like that belonging to a medal perhaps, though she couldn't be sure since only part of it was visible. It wasn't something Regina had noticed before because looking too closely had filled her with guilt.

But studying the image now, there was no doubt in her mind that Guthrie's father must have been gentry. Which made her wonder why no one had stepped in as guardian after he died. It seemed rather odd. Especially since there must have been an inheritance of some sort. At the very least, a solicitor should have been able to help a child in such a position even if no one else could.

Befuddled, Regina made a mental note to inquire about this when Guthrie returned.

He wouldn't like her prying, but she figured the best way to get some answers was to ask him for them directly.

With this in mind, she returned to the parlor, flopped onto the sofa, reached for the deck of cards sitting on the table, and prepared to wait. Guthrie had taught her to play casino a couple of nights ago, and she'd finally managed to beat him yesterday evening. She smiled at the memory of it, at how excited he'd been on her behalf when they'd tallied the scores and hers had been higher than his.

Selecting a couple of cards, she set them upright on the table and leaned them carefully against each other until they no longer required her support. Adding cards slowly, she built outward and upward until she'd completed three levels. She was just beginning on the fourth when she heard the door open.

Startled by the sound, she looked up and inadvertently budged the card house with her wrist. The entire thing quivered back and forth and then promptly collapsed in a heap.

"Sorry," Guthrie said. "I didn't mean to distract ye."

Regina gathered the fallen cards and returned them to the stack. "It's all right. I can always build another." She scooted back on the sofa, folded her hands in her lap, and tried to think of how best to address the subject regarding the miniature. But her thoughts on the matter scattered the moment she saw the plate he was holding.

His lips quirked. "I realize the cake Gareth baked fer ye the other day didn't quite meet yer expectations."

"It was tasty enough," she said, not wanting to sound ungrateful or critical of the cook's attempts, "and certainly better than anything I'd have been able to make myself."

Guthrie laughed. "Seein' ye knead dough with yer sleeves rolled up to yer elbows and flour dustin' yer hair would be a lovely sight." He set the plate before her with a flourish. "Behold, a mille-feuille, courtesy of Patisserie Amelie."

Regina stared at the confection and at the strawberry placed on top. "You went to Bond Street to buy me a cake?"

"It only seemed fair that I get ye a proper one after watchin' ye force Gareth's efforts down."

The edge of her mouth lifted. "I think he used too much sugar."

"I'm sure ye're right. Now give this one a go and let me know what ye think."

She felt his gaze on her as she reached for the silver fork on her plate. Carefully, so she wouldn't tip the cake onto its side, she scooped up a corner and put it in her mouth. And almost groaned with pure satisfaction. The puff pastry layered with jam and cream was rich but not too sweet. It filled her mouth with decadent boldness, leaving behind a taste of vanilla that made her hungry for more.

"This is excellent," she said as she took another bite and then yet another. "The best thing I've ever had." Glancing up when Guthrie said nothing, she noted the satisfied look in his eyes. "Thank you. Truly."

"Ye're welcome." Removing the forest green silk top hat he'd chosen to wear that day, he took a seat in the armchair furthest from her. "Now, there's another matter I'd like to address." He watched her pensively while she continued to eat, completely undeterred by his perusal since savoring this delicious treat was far more important than being subject to his observations.

"Ye're obviously bored," he remarked after a moment while giving his lapels a quick brush with his fingers. Finding her gaze, he stretched out his legs and leaned back. "Perhaps I should take ye out fer the evenin'?"

Regina stilled, and for a second she held her breath so she wouldn't disturb the joy his suggestion instilled in her veins. Her fork remained suspended in mid-air. "Really?" He merely inclined his head. "What about the risk of me being discovered?"

"It still exists. There's a good chance yer father has men posted all over London just waitin' fer ye to resurface. But if ye do wish to get away from this place fer a bit, I believe it can be accomplished without detection. If ye'll trust me, that is."

He'd given her no reason not to. In fact, it impressed her how hospitable he was being toward her. So much so that he'd gone to the trouble of making her dream to try cake come true.

And since she couldn't leave until she had somewhere better to go, she remained, hoping each morning that this was the day when she'd finally hear from Fielding.

"I do," she said in answer to Guthrie's comment. Adjusting to the excitement that suddenly filled her, she gave him her brightest smile. "So where are we going, how will we get there, and what am I going to wear?"

Sitting across from Regina in the hackney carriage that would take them to the Strand, Carlton told himself for the hundredth time that the only reason he was taking her out was to keep her happy. As long as she was happy, she'd be more likely to stay with him of her own free will. Which meant he would have no cause to restrain her, and that made everything so much simpler.

But the truth was that the kiss they'd shared had changed things between them. While they hadn't discussed it and no other kisses had followed, the brief caress had forged an intimate bond that he longed to nurture. It made him want to be more than Carlton Guthrie in her eyes. It made him want to pretend, if only for a brief moment in time, that things were different between them – that he was in a position to court her and…

He sighed. A man didn't court a woman like her unless he intended to marry, which was something he couldn't allow himself to consider. Not only because he wasn't respectable, but because of what he intended to do. Regina would loathe him forever for killing her father. Which meant that pursuing a romantic attachment with her would be pointless.

But for just one evening, he'd allow himself to

treat her to some amusement. Already the smile she'd given him when he'd made the suggestion had made his heart triple in size. He wanted to hold that smile in his hands forever or keep it in a box so he could look at it when his grey life needed the sun.

He studied her profile as she peered out the window at the darkened streets beyond. The hood of the cobalt blue cloak she'd borrowed from Nicolette hid most of her hair. But that didn't matter. He knew precisely what it looked like, how each lock curled against her head, and the way the red strands conquered the blonde when the light of an oil lamp cast its glow upon her. During the last couple of days, he'd gotten to know her better. She'd told him that while she was skilled at playing the pianoforte, she actually loathed having to do so.

"I would so much rather have learned how to play the viola," she'd confessed. "But all young ladies must be adept at the pianoforte." She'd affected a deep commanding tone that must have been meant to mimic her father's.

"Ye could still learn to play the viola," Carlton had suggested. He'd smiled, because for some odd reason, he'd envisioned her playing a jaunty tune instead of some peaceful melody. And in this vision of his, she was also barefoot and dancing, like a fairy, skipping along the edge of a moonbeam.

"Perhaps." She'd frowned for a moment but then the creases upon her brow had faded and she'd asked, "Is there anything you wish you could do if you had the chance?"

Kiss you again, had been his immediate thought. "I'd like to travel."

"Where to?" Her eyes had held his with the most sincere interest he'd ever been subjected to. And in that moment he'd realized something shocking. That this woman, who'd burst into his life in a flurry of netting and lace, had chiseled away at the ugly remains of his heart and burrowed her way deep inside it.

By then of course it had been too late. He'd already fallen for her in ways that were hard to describe. But knowing that she would leave him one day, most likely with hatred burning in her eyes, threatened to shatter his soul.

The carriage rocked to one side, bringing him out of his reverie. "Tell me about yer parents," he encouraged even as guilt began to gnaw at his conscience. "Was theirs a love match, do ye think?"

She turned to face him more directly, which caused her cloak to part just enough to reveal a sliver of purple taffeta beneath. The gown was also Nicolette's and offered a far more daring neckline and a much tighter fit across Regina's breasts than anything else he'd seen her in yet. The black lace trim contrasted against her pale skin in the most provocative way imaginable. Indeed, he'd been half tempted to tell her she had to change back into her day dress before they left. But the sparkle in her eyes when she'd stepped from the bedroom and seen his mouth open in utter dismay had kept him silent.

Here was her chance to be wild and free, if only for one evening, and he could not make himself ruin her fun. His motivation had nothing to do with the lovely view that he'd be allowed for the rest of the evening. Or so he kept telling himself.

"No," was her response to his question. "I have never seen any hint of affection between my parents. And while they are always civil, it never felt as though they liked each other very much." She dropped her gaze and fiddled with the skirt of her gown. "The atmosphere at home has always been cold and reserved whenever Mama was present. I think she regrets marrying Papa, though I'm not sure why."

The carriage drew to a halt and Carlton moved to open the door. But before he did so, he addressed Regina with genuine sympathy. "Children ought to be raised in happy homes filled with love and affection. I'm sorry you weren't."

She stared at him until he grew uncomfortable. Eager to rid himself of the feeling, he stepped down onto the pavement and offered his hand to help her alight. But the shock that went through him when she placed her palm against his almost caused him to lose his footing. Heat rushed up his arm and caused sparks to dart over his skin. The degree to which she affected him was…well, rather terrifying, really.

"The way you just said that," she muttered while studying him with intense curiosity. "You sounded different."

All heat evaporated from his body. "How do ye mean?" he carefully asked.

She looked him square in the eye with more boldness than even his men ever dared. "You sounded well-spoken."

"As opposed to what?" Feigning ignorance would be the only way to make her second guess what she'd heard.

"You know." He gave her a blank stare. "You don't pronounce all your words correctly. They're often cut off at the ends."

Tilting his head, he decided to push for embarrassment. "I didn't realize ye were so 'igh in the instep as to take issue with me speech?"

"Oh for heaven's sake, Guthrie. Stop spinning my words." They'd left the carriage and were now making their way to the theatre's back entrance. His arm was securely linked with hers so he could keep her close to his side as they walked. "I have no issue at all with the way you speak. In fact, I find it rather charming, if you want my honest opinion. But for a second there it was almost as if you belonged in a Mayfair ballroom. And then of course there's the miniature of your father. I've been meaning to ask you about it since yesterday but the moment never felt right."

"An' it does now, does it?"

"Not exactly, but since we're addressing the issue, I'm curious to know who he was. I mean, that cravat pin he's wearing suggests he was upper class and there's also a ribbon around his neck that looks like it could be part of a medal." She glanced up at him through the darkness. "Did he fight against Napoleon by any chance?"

Carlton tried not to panic even as he felt every muscle in his body grow tight in response to the threat Regina posed to his carefully crafted persona. If the truth about him got out, then he might as well pack his bags and flee London forever. Because he wouldn't belong in St. Giles anymore. The people there would turn on him in a heartbeat if they discovered who he actually was. Not only because he'd lied, but because of what he'd deliberately hidden from them.

Only Blayne knew the truth about Carlton's past. Carlton had unwittingly disclosed it to him in a fevered haze when that wound Maher had dealt him had gotten infected. It had taken a week for Carlton to recover – a time Blayne still referred to as the fight he'd once had with the devil.

"Me father was an artist," he told Regina smoothly. "Nothin' more."

Her shoulders slumped as if in defeat. "I see." Her voice, filled with disappointment, made him wish he could trust her with the truth. The trouble with that, however, was that trust often made a fool of even the wisest of men. He'd seen it happen to his father first hand. Which was why he always lived with the keen awareness that even those closest to you could betray you.

Tightening his jaw, Guthrie greeted some of the theatre workers, actors and actresses as they passed them. He didn't come here often, but when he did, he knew he could count on being welcomed because of the high tips he gave them all after each performance. And because of the handsome fee he paid for the private box he kept there. It was located directly next to the stage and had its own separate entrance, allowing Carlton to avoid the rest of the theatre goers.

Leading Regina toward it, he ushered her into the box and closed the door behind them. A velvet drape hanging to the left meant that they could remain completely hidden from the audience while still enjoying a perfect view of the stage.

Having pushed back her hood, Regina undid the ties that held her cloak in place. Without even thinking, Carlton stepped forward and placed his hands on her shoulders. A tightening deep in his belly the moment he heard her sharp intake of air and felt her heat permeate his skin made him freeze for a second. He drew a deep breath to steady himself, but instead he felt more undone than ever by the sweet scent of honey and chamomile clinging to her hair. Swallowing, he buried his fingers deep in the folds of the cloak, clutching the garment while seeking the strength he required to resist the temptation she offered.

She cannot be yours.

He took a step back and hung the cloak on a hook near the door.

"This is so strange," Regina said as she took a seat next to the drape. Her voice was soft, with a dreamy quality to it. "We're in a theatre surrounded by hundreds of people and yet we're completely alone. Like we're tucked away in our own private world."

Smiling with more pleasure than he'd felt in years, he took a seat beside her. He loved the joy she was able to find in the simplest of things. He'd not done much, but he'd given her a different experience. And she was enthralled, as evidenced by her wide smile and the light that danced in her eyes. Within the confines of his chest, in a dark place behind his ribs, his heart beat harder than ever before. It beat for her and for the purity of her soul.

With difficulty, he resisted the urge to place his hand over hers and chose to rest it on his knee instead. "Few aristocrats come here, so it is unlikely that you will be recognized," he murmured next to her ear. "Most of the Adelphi Theatre's patrons are clerks, barristers, and solicitors, but you should probably stay behind the curtain anyway. Just in case."

She turned her head and her eyes met his, like inky-blue water reflecting the stars. "Thank you for bringing me here."

He merely inclined his head and waited for her to return her attention to the stage.

CHAPTER EIGHT

THE LOUD CHATTER OF VOICES and rustling of people moving about was muted by the low hum of a bow sliding over a cello's strings. A vibrating murmur of violins joined with the tooting of trumpets and flutes until all the instruments sounded like they were arguing with each other. And then they fell silent, leaving the theater completely devoid of all sound, as if all ears waited to hear what would happen next.

Regina held her breath. And then the sweetest, most melodious piece of music she'd ever heard sifted through the air like a moonbeam carefully casting its light through a window at night. The instruments that had seemed so disjointed during their tuning joined in perfect harmony now as they welcomed the performers to the stage.

A man and a woman dressed in bright sixteenth century clothes proceeded to sing a jaunty duet filled with humorous phrases resulting in bursts of laughter.

With a grin of her own, Regina allowed the musical play to distract her. But she could never quite ignore the man who sat by her side. Her awareness of him caused ripples of warmth to caress her skin whenever he moved. To think that he'd come to affect her so completely during the short time she'd known him was both confusing and frightening.

Deep inside, she'd hoped that he would confirm her suspicions when she'd asked about his father. She'd hoped that Guthrie would turn out to be the sort of man a woman like her might marry.

Which was almost too silly to think of. He was everything she ought to avoid. Besides, even if he had been some prominent lord, his history made him completely unsuitable for her. The fact that she would forget that proved how easily she'd been influenced by his kiss. But the truth was that if she was going to save her reputation, she would need to make a respectable match.

"How do ye like it so far?" Guthrie's voice traced the lobe of her ear and a shiver sailed down her spine.

How many women have you kissed? How many have you bedded? Who were they? What were their names and did they matter?

"Very much," she told him while burying all of the questions she wanted to ask him. He had no reason to share such intimate information with her just as she had no reason to care about any of the answers that he might give.

And yet she did. More so with each passing second she spent in his company.

She also wanted to know why he'd really been forced to leave home when his parents had died. She wanted to figure him out and understand him – to learn all she could about Carlton Guthrie, the notorious crime lord, Scoundrel of St. Giles, protector of prostitutes, mentor to children, and her very own savior.

"Thank you for a lovely outing," she said when they left the theatre later. "The performance was excellent and so very different from the opera, which is the extent of my theatrical experience. Being allowed to catch a glimpse of what goes on behind the stage was especially interesting. I never imagined so many ropes, rolled up sceneries, props, curtains, or people, all to offer a bit of amusement to a crowd of spectators. It just—"

"Ye are very welcome," Guthrie said with a grin.

Heat rose to her cheeks, making the cool evening air a welcome relief as they stepped out through the back entrance. Regina took Guthrie's arm without even thinking. It just felt natural now. "I hope you can forgive me for nattering on. I'm just so excited about everything I've experienced this evening."

He frowned at her even as he smiled. "I get the sense that ye crave an insight into the simpler facets of life. Takin' ye to the Theatre Royale, while appropriate, would not have made the same impression. Would it?"

How could he possibly know her so well? "I would have enjoyed it and found it nice. But it would also have been a theatre experience like any other while this...this was a welcome departure from what I am used to."

He hailed a hackney and helped her climb in before issuing orders to the driver. "It won't be yer only experience this evenin', luv," he said once he'd sat down opposite her and the carriage had taken off. "Have ye ever been to Vauxhall Garden?"

A flutter of excitement swept through her. "No. Not yet. My Season was filled with dinner parties, balls, and musicales. I dare say there wasn't the time." Which wasn't entirely true. When she'd asked her parents if they would take her to the pleasure garden one evening, they'd told her it wasn't an appropriate place for young ladies to venture.

"The most scandalous things happen there in the dark," her mother had said.

"But surely if I am with you and Papa it will be all right," Regina had tried. "Several of my friends have been and their reputations have not suffered from it."

"Then they are most fortunate. But I'm not prepared to take the risk. Going to Vauxhall is out of the question." Hedgewick's words had been final and the subject had not been brought up again.

"Then it's a good thing we've nothin' but time at the moment," Guthrie told her. A heavy pause followed. Through the dark interior of the carriage she could see him tilting his head as if in speculation. "Unless of course ye'd rather return to The Black Swan. I don't want to press ye into any—"

"No." The word shot past her lips in an almost desperate plea. Taking a breath, Regina relaxed her shoulders and settled more comfortably against the squabs. "I would love to visit Vauxhall with you."

"Excellent." His voice was low, almost a purr, and it hummed through her body, increasing her anticipation. Tonight's experiences were only made possible thanks to Guthrie. Without him, she wasn't sure what might have become of her after she'd run away. Most likely, she would have returned home that very same day, provided she'd managed to find her way and avoided getting hurt by those thugs she'd run into. She would have married Stokes once her father had managed to explain the delay, and her life would have gone on much as before. Albeit with a husband she didn't want and who did not want her.

"I'll have someone stop by Fielding House tomorrow," Guthrie said as he led her along one of Vauxhall's walkways a short while later. All around them, hundreds of gas lights painted the air with an ethereal glow. Soft lyrical music performed by a string quartet near the entrance followed behind them like tiptoeing fairies. "While his butler did say he would let me know when he returned, I don't really trust him to do so."

Regina tightened her hold on Guthrie's arm, drawing closer to him. Nearby, a group of young men out for a bit of fun laughed uproariously in response to a joke one of them had made. "You want me to leave?"

"I want ye to do what makes ye happy." He paused before saying, "I thought ye were hopin' to make him an offer."

"I suppose…"

Guthrie snorted. "Well I dare say Fieldin's a fortunate man. The joy in yer voice when ye speak of him is so overwhelmin' it just might inspire Byron to write a poem."

Without even thinking, she slapped his arm and

grinned. "You're terrible."

"Ye'll not hear me argue that fact," he muttered.

Sobering, she tried to consider his comments more seriously and finally said, "I cannot stay with you forever."

"Not even if I tell ye that ye're welcome to do so?"

He'd pulled her to a halt, a little off to one side so they stood near a thick line of trees. The lights were further apart here, the yellow haze not quite reaching his face. And yet, when Regina looked up, she could still see the need he subjected her to. Perhaps because it was also in his voice.

"Why?" It was all she could think to ask.

Why?

It was an excellent question that Carlton didn't know how to answer. Least of all when she was staring at him as if he'd lost his mind. Which he probably had.

In no time at all, he'd allowed this Society woman – a debutante, no less – to sneak past his defenses. She'd caused him to want in a way he'd not wanted before. And she'd made him wonder what it might be like to simply forget his whole reason for being, to abandon his need for revenge and pursue a life of normalcy for a change. With her, he might find genuine happiness and contentment.

But she was like a diamond that sparkled in a world filled with soot. She didn't belong in St. Giles, and she also deserved far better than anything he was able to offer. Not to mention that it was unlikely she would ever love a man like him. At least not once she realized how ill he'd used her and how much he'd lied.

"Guthrie?"

Her expression had changed into that of perplexed curiosity and he realized he'd taken too long to answer. "I've taken a likin' to ye," he said with a careless shrug. Determined to treat the comment as though it held no great significance, he prepared to recommence walking.

Except the smile she gave him was so incredibly blinding he found himself rooted to the ground. Indeed, it was like the sun had just made a surprise appearance right there in the middle of the night. And her eyes...they sparkled like pieces of silver caught in the moonlight. Carlton held his breath for no other reason than that he was starting to think inhaling might actually kill him. After all, nothing else was as it should be. He ought to be indifferent to Regina, not smitten by her. He should be plotting Hedgewick's demise, not trying to romance his daughter with theatre visits and intimate walks. So then, since the world as he knew it was obviously flipped upside down, why not presume that drawing air into his lungs would result in death?

"I like you too."

Carlton blinked. "I'm sorry?"

She grinned and it was as if an angel had blessed him with a heavenly glow. "You just said that you'd let me stay because you've taken a liking to me, and I'm telling you that I like you as well. Quite a lot, actually. "

And then, as if she hadn't just punched him

straight in the gut, she rose up onto her toes and pressed her lips against his.

His heart shuddered and for a brief moment, when his astonishment had passed, he feared he might weep. Because unlike the previous kiss they'd shared, this one had been incited by her in a way that confirmed the truth in her words. But then his muscles flexed and the masculine need she'd instilled at his core broke free from the tethers he'd used to bind it.

Without even thinking, he grabbed her wrist and pulled her between the trees, away from the revelers filling the path and into their own wooded world.

"Guthrie! What are—"

He spun her around, pinning her roughly against the nearest tree. Her breaths grew rapid, though not from fear. No. Her response was entirely born from excitement so keen he could practically smell it.

"Why did ye do that?"

She raised her chin and stared back at him through the darkness. "Because it felt right." Swallowing, she asked with the sort of hesitance that might break him, "Do you mind?"

Undone by her innocence and the wonder with which she experienced life, he told her honestly, "No. Minding isn't the problem. "

"Then what is?"

It was a dangerous question he ought not answer. But he couldn't resist. Not any longer. And certainly not where she was concerned. He simply didn't want to.

Moving closer, he placed one hand at her waist

while using the other to trace a path over her cheek. "The problem, luv, is that it isn't enough. I want more." And with that declaration, he lowered his mouth to hers like a madman seeking his sanity.

For a moment, he sensed the uncertainty building within her, questioning whether to push him away or yield to his expert command. But then he felt her surrender, like an anxious bird willing to trust the fox. A sigh of relief swept through him, transforming into a groan of pleasure the moment she parted her lips beneath his and granted him entrance.

Dear merciful God in heaven, she tasted exquisite, like dewdrops clinging to rose petals in the morning, or sunbeams falling on poppy fields during the summer. And she was arching into him now in her quest for additional friction in just the right places.

His own body responded. How could it not when she was a dream come true – the most perfect creature he'd ever encountered? Gripping her firmly, he pressed up against her and deepened the kiss. She gasped but didn't retreat. Instead, she met him every step of the way until he was left completely breathless and suffering from discomfort.

Pulling back before he found some excuse to explore her more fully with his hands, he considered apologizing for his advance, but then changed his mind. Because he wasn't sorry. This kiss was perhaps the best thing he'd ever experienced in his life, and he would not let her think he regretted it in any way. And considering how she was gripping his jacket as if reluctant to let him go, he didn't think she regretted it either. Which only made him want to kiss her again.

A firework burst overhead, showering the sky with bright flashes of color. The sounds of chatter and music drifted toward them, reminding Carlton of time and place. If he kissed her again he would only want more, and the last thing Regina deserved was to be ravished against a tree in a public setting.

Christ!

He'd had countless women over the years, all experienced lovers. But Regina's innocence slayed him. Her novice approach, so tentative at first, followed by her increased eagerness as she learned what to do, was so fresh and compelling and unlike anything else he'd experienced before. It was also bloody erotic and made him eager to take her to bed. He wanted to strip her naked and give her pleasure, to feel her quiver in his arms and to witness her ultimate surrender.

Mine.

The word shot to the front of his mind, attacking what remained of his reasoning. She was his now whether she knew it or not, and as that fact sank in, his world righted to a state of normalcy once again.

Slowly, he unhooked her fingers from his lapels and took her by the hand. "Come." He guided her back to the path, and she came with him carefully, as if in a daze.

Arms linked, they continued on in silence. Carlton wondered if he should say something to spark a conversation, but he rather liked just being with her without the need for either of them to speak. And since she seemed to be processing what had occurred between them, he thought it best not to distract her.

It wasn't until they were coming back on the central walkway that she chose to say, "Your moustache is very soft."

He couldn't help but laugh. "Really?"

"It surprised me the first time you kissed me as well, since I thought it was going to be rough and bristly."

"Does that mean ye like it?"

She was quiet a moment. "I cannot claim to *dis*-like it, but I would like to kiss you one day without it being in the way."

Carlton tightened his hold on her arm. "Is that so?"

"Unless of course you meant for that kiss to be a onetime experience. A lapse in judgment on your part perhaps?"

"I can assure ye that there was no lapse in judgment, Regina." He placed his free hand over hers and deliberately drew a circle against her skin with his thumb. "What happened back there was my capitulation – a helpless surrender to yer irresistible charm."

"Oh."

"Oh?" He wasn't so sure that he liked such a simple response to his open confession. His masculinity would certainly have preferred it if she'd rejoiced with vocal exuberance over him finally giving her what she'd been longing for too.

"Does that mean you'll kiss me again?"

He hesitated on the cusp of blurting out yes.

Instead he asked, "Would ye like me to?"

She was quiet so long he started to fear she'd say no. Because he would respect that and stay away from her if she insisted upon it. But then, when he was about to lose hope, she fanned it to life with one simple statement. "Yes, Carlton. I would like that a lot."

CHAPTER NINE

FOR THE NEXT TWO DAYS, Regina's mind was occupied by the memory of her second kiss with Guthrie. *Carlton*. She scrunched her nose. That name didn't quite suit him. Much like the mustache, it seemed out of place. But both were a part of the man she'd come to care for, and all it had taken was a couple of weeks in his company.

If only he would turn out to be more than the son of an artist – the sort of man with whom she might consider sharing her future. She pursed her lips and considered. The pearl-tipped pin, the silk waistcoat, and the red ribbon bearing some unseen honor didn't quite square with the low-ranking man Carlton claimed his father to be.

She'd promised him that she'd refrain from going through his things, but he had allowed her to use his desk, so a quick peek inside the drawers wouldn't exactly be prying. Would it?

Crossing to the piece of furniture, she hesitated briefly before taking a seat and opening the first drawer. It was filled with scraps of paper, some tobacco, a broken quill, and a couple of note-books. Selecting one, she leafed through it quickly. When she saw that it was unused, she picked up the other, her expectations of making some sort of intriguing discovery almost depleted. Until she opened the book.

An elegant hand comprised of bold letters filled the first page, drawing Regina's gaze in and compelling her to read.

The heavens rage
While angels weep
A young boy's world forever changed.
Once safe from harm
No longer so
His heart once whole exists no more.
And he who dared
To cause such pain
Shall one day face that boy again.

"What do ye think ye're doin?"

Startled by Guthrie's voice, Regina dropped the notebook and stood. "I…" She hadn't heard him come in, she'd been so caught up in the poem and what it might mean. Swallowing, she tried to ignore the knot in her belly and how her hands started to tremble. He didn't exactly look angry, but he certainly didn't look happy either.

His gaze dropped to the notebook now lying on the floor near her feet. "I thought ye agreed to stay out of me things."

"Yes. Of course. I'm sorry." She bent to retrieve the book and when she rose, he was there, much closer than before and with his hand held out. Regretting her choice to intrude on his privacy once again, she handed him the book. "But you did say that I could use the desk and—"

"And that gave ye reason to think that ye could just riffle through me drawers? Read things that aren't yers to read?"

"I'm sorry."

"So ye've said before." Leaning past her, he returned the book to the drawer and closed it. When he straightened himself, his eyebrows were drawn together with what appeared to be deep concern. "If this is how ye were taught to repay hospitality, I dare say yer education was sorely lackin'"

His remark cut her to the quick and made her feel underserving of his generosity. "I just...I want to know more about you."

He inhaled deeply and a tick at the edge of his eye informed her that he was struggling to keep his composure – that she'd angered him more than he was willing to show. "Perhaps you'd prefer to return to yer home, me lady?"

Regina stared at him while the thought of doing so settled in her mind. She shook her head. "No. I...I cannot do that. At least not until I am married to the man of my choosing."

He held her gaze until she was forced to shift with discomfort. "In that case, I'd suggest that ye treat yer host with a bit more respect." And on that note, he located a key and locked the drawer. "One more chance. That's all I'll give ye."

Regina nodded and waited for him to leave the room before lowering herself to the chair once more. The man she'd kissed at Vauxhall had vanished, for which she had only herself to blame. Heavy hearted, she glanced at the door through which he'd made his exit and decided

that she would have to do better. Carlton Guthrie deserved her compliance and thanks. If he
was hiding something important about himself,
she would simply have to accept that she'd never
know what that something might be.

Sitting on the yellow velvet sofa in Carlton's
parlor the following day with her feet tucked
up underneath her, Regina pushed a needle and
thread through a piece of fine linen. A message
from Fielding had arrived the previous evening,
declining her proposal to meet and discuss a
potential union between them. Apparently, he
was already engaged in a courtship with someone
else. Disappointed, Regina had written the Earl
of Yates that morning, not because she actually
wanted to marry him, but because she wasn't sure
what else to do and was starting to feel slightly
desperate.

When she'd handed the letter to Carlton and
asked if he would make sure that it reached its
destination, she'd done so with the awareness that
he owed her nothing. And because of this and the
need she'd felt to get back in his good graces, she'd
asked him if he had any mending with which she
could busy herself.

"Mendin'?" He'd stared at her, incredulous.
"Ye're a lady, Regina, not a maid. I'll not 'ave ye
doin' chores fer me, luv."

Oh, how she loved that endearment. It lifted
her spirits even though she was well aware it was
no more than a turn of phrase commonly used to
address a woman. Any woman. Not only her.

"I'm not a porcelain doll to be placed on a shelf. There's no reason why I can't be useful to you in some way."

The look he'd given her in response had turned her blood to molten lava. "Ye're useful to me in every way that matters." This statement had been followed by a kiss, milder than the one at Vauxhall and far more deliberate. By contrast, it had been a slow exploration filled with endless tenderness. The sort that told her she'd been forgiven, the kind that could easily fill her head with dreams of things that would never be.

When it ended, she had lowered her voice to a sensual whisper and said, "Letting me help you in some small way would make me feel better." Like she was actively doing something to earn back his trust and appreciation. "I need to busy myself, Carlton. I cannot just sit in this room, always waiting for you."

"And if I say no?"

She'd smiled at him with a touch of mischief. "Then I'll probably start organizing your books by color."

"The devil ye will," he'd muttered, upon which he'd kissed her again. But he'd accepted her need to pass the time in some way besides reading and had given her a couple of shirts.

Careful to keep her stitches small, neat, and close together, Regina worked on the torn seam of a sleeve. It pleased her to know that she could do this small task for a man who had done so much for her. He'd told her that she was welcome to stay at The Black Swan as long as she wished, and so she would. At least until she received an offer of marriage compelling enough to make her leave.

The door opened and Regina glanced up. "There's still no hint of what 'appened to 'er," Carlton said as he entered the room. Slumping into the nearest armchair, he removed his hat and set it aside on the floor. Every day and night since Scarlet's disappearance, he'd gone out searching for her and making inquiries, but it was as if the young woman had never existed in the first place.

"Do you think she might be dead?" It was a reasonable conclusion at this point, however much Regina regretted having to think it. But she knew from what Katarina had suffered when she'd been kidnapped that there were fates worse than death. Although no one had ever told her exactly what her friend had gone through, she'd been able to guess. A young outgoing woman about to make her debut did not become reclusive without good reason. At the time, Regina had imagined that Katarina had been locked away in some miserable place and beaten, but after learning what some men were capable of, she believed her friend had also been raped.

"I don't know." He raked his fingers through his hair in obvious frustration. "People sometimes disappear without explanation. It's startin' to look like this is such an instance."

Setting her mending aside, Regina crossed to where he sat and placed her hand against his cheek. "I'm sorry." She could see the toll Scarlet's disappearance was having on him and wished there were more she could do to ease the burden he carried – this feeling that he was responsible for the welfare of everyone who lived in St. Giles.

He placed his hand against hers and leaned his face into it. His eyes closed and he took a deep breath as if shedding some great weight from his body. And then, faster than the lash of a whip, he wound his arm around her waist and pulled her into his lap.

She let out a squeal of surprise as her bottom connected with his thighs. Hugging her close, he chuckled in response before seeking her mouth with his own. This kiss was hungry, and far more demanding than any of the others. It told her that he hoped to escape, to forget the defeat he suffered from not finding Scarlet alive or succeeding in bringing her home. So Regina allowed him to take what he wanted. She pushed her fingers through his hair and pressed herself closer, showing him without words that she needed him just as much as he needed her.

"Regina." Her name whispered across her neck as he kissed his way down to her shoulder. It made her wish for the hundredth time that they could somehow find a way to be together.

If only...

He nipped at her skin, producing a lovely shudder that tickled her spine, before planting a kiss on her forehead and easing her out of his lap. "I appreciate the comfort of yer arms," he said, rising as well, "but it's probably wise fer us to stop now before things get out of hand."

He always did this, pushing her away when she started longing for more. In a way, it was yet another reason for her to trust him, and yet the end result was increased frustration on her part. For even though common sense and a good solid

upbringing told her she ought to protect her innocence at all cost, she couldn't help but wonder if
losing it to Carlton wouldn't be worth every wonderful moment.

So she said the only thing she could think of.
The only thing that made sense in her current
state of rejection. "You don't really want me, do
you?"

He was silent for a moment and then he moved.
One second later, she was back in his arms with
her face pressed against his chest. Sturdy arms surrounded her, keeping her safe while the rich scent
of brandy, coffee, and sandalwood toyed with her
senses.

"I've 'ad whores, widows, actresses…ye name it.
Women by the 'undreds. Most of whom I don't
remember."

Hating what he was telling her, Regina tried to
pull away and to somehow escape the truth and
the gnawing jealousy it evoked deep inside her.
But he held her fast, without mercy as he continued. "None of them mattered. They were just a
necessary tup 'ere an' there to keep me from losin'
me mind. A man needs that, ye know. But ye…

"Ah, Regina, me luv, ye're more to me than
all of them put together. Ye're the light that was
once snuffed out in me life, the fresh air I long to
breathe. The more I'm with ye, the more unwillin' I am to see ye go."

Clutching at him, she looked up into his hungry
gaze. "What exactly does that mean?"

He smiled as though she meant more to him
than all the treasure in the world. "It means that I
won't be the man who ruins ye fer another. Ye've

a future that cannot include me, luv, and I'd hate to be yer biggest regret."

Closing her eyes, she fought the disappointment that wanted to claim her and tried to appreciate his honesty. While other men in his position might have whispered sweet promises in her ear until she climbed into their beds, Carlton was trying to protect her.

Reluctantly, she released her hold on his jacket and withdrew from his embrace. "I'll never regret anything you and I choose to do together. You mean too much to me for that."

He stared at her intently, then turned and strode to the door. Pausing there with his hand on the handle, he glanced at her over his shoulder. "I beg to differ." When she remained silent, he exited the room with the assurance that he would have food sent up to her soon.

Feeling numb, Regina returned to the sofa on wooden legs and dropped heavily onto the plush velvet seat. Had she really just propositioned Carlton Guthrie, renowned criminal – a man who'd confessed to murder – and been turned down?

Flopping back against a cushion, she eyed the shirt she'd been working on earlier and pulled it into her lap. If things went according to plan, she'd end up marrying Yates or whoever was on her list after him. Not for love, but out of necessity. Which was why she wanted Carlton to be the man who showed her where kisses could lead. Because he meant more to her than the man she married would.

She was choosing him with her heart.

Every muscle in Carlton's body quivered and flexed with pent up tension as he strode into his study after ordering Laura to take a dinner tray up to Regina. Blayne, who'd been chatting with Patrick and Claus at a nearby table, had frowned in response to his brusque tone and was now in the process of pouring two glasses of brandy. He set one on the desk in front of Carlton before claiming the chair that stood opposite his.

Carlton stared at the amber liquid for a long-drawn-out moment before capitulating and setting the glass to his lips. He downed the contents, satisfied with the low burn in his throat and the heat now filling his chest. "Are the men ready fer this evenin's match?"

Blayne nodded. "Finnegan's already growing restless."

Carlton wasn't surprised. His fighters were used to throwing punches at least three times a week, but with Regina's arrival and Scarlet's disappearance, Carlton hadn't had the time to arrange or host the events.

"I was goin' to 'ave 'im go up against Hunter before lettin' volunteers try an' best 'im. Make a show of it as we always do. But I think I'd rather face 'im meself."

Blayne raised an eyebrow. "I see." When Carlton stared back, the Scotsman gave a low chuckle. "She's starting to get to you, isn't she?"

"I've no idea what ye mean."

"Ah, come off it." Carlton glared and Blayne threw up his hands. Rising, he went to fetch the decanter so he could refill his friend's glass. "That lovely little skirt upstairs has you wound up tighter than a hangman's noose."

Anger pulsed through Carlton's veins. "Ye'll speak of 'er with respect, man, or not at all. Is that understood?"

Blayne sank back into his chair with a sigh. "You've broken your own bloody rule, haven't you? You've taken a liking to the chit you're supposed to feel cool detachment toward." When Carlton said nothing, Blayne started to laugh. "For Christ's sake, I was only teasing when I said you were falling for her. I didnae think you would actually go and do it."

"I'll admit that my resilience is being tested," Carlton grumbled.

Blayne narrowed his gaze. "Is that so?"

"She...affects me and..." He reached for his glass.

"And you want her in your bed now, don't you?" When Carlton merely proceeded to drink his brandy, Blayne leaned forward in his seat. "You cannae do that to her, Guthrie. It wouldnae be fair."

"Not even in light of who she is?" Blayne's eyes darkened with understanding. "Imagine the satisfaction of telling her father I've robbed his daughter of her most precious asset. Of letting him know that she gave herself to me willingly. I can just envision him going white with rage. He'll—"

"Stop." Blayne's curt word of command cut Carlton off. "You're frustrated, in the worst possible way a man can be frustrated, and as a result you're saying things you don't really mean. You care for Lady Regina. Admit it! You'd never treat her so callously as to use her only to cast her aside. I've seen the way you look at her, damn you. It's not ideal 'cause it doesnae work in your favor and certainly not according to your plan, but that doesnae make it less true."

Carlton stared at Blayne's outraged expression. His face was red, his mouth firmly set. "Ye're right," Carlton muttered after a pause. He raked his fingers through his hair and sighed. "I'll not treat her ill. If anythin', I'll care fer her an' protect her as long as she'll let me."

"And?"

Glowering, Carlton gritted, "I'll not discuss any intimacies with ye."

"Understood. Just…promise me that you'll think things through so you don't do something you'll both regret."

Carlton's lips twisted. "Why the hell do ye think I'm sittin' here tellin' ye I'm gonna be the one fightin' Finnegan, instead of upstairs enjoyin' a tasty meal with the woman I want?"

"Point taken." Blayne leaned forward in his seat. "How are you sleeping these days?"

"I've not had any bad dreams since the last one I mentioned, which was what? A week ago or more? An' if it's Regina ye're worried about, ye may rest assured that she locks her bedchamber door every night. I've checked."

Blayne stood. "You're a good man, Guthrie. Better than most on account of your moral compass. But you've some ghosts to put to rest before you can think of living happily ever after."

Carlton snorted in response. "Happily ever afters are fer children an' dreamers, Blayne. I learned early on that it would be foolish to have such high expectations."

Blayne went to the door. "I'll see you in the courtyard then?"

When Carlton nodded, Blayne let himself out of the study and shut the door behind him. Carlton closed his eyes and attempted to clear his mind. He did not want to think of Regina or the fact that she was Charles Berkly's daughter. He did not want to consider how she would react when she learned that he'd meant to use her to punish her father and lure him to his death.

For twenty years he'd been praying for just the right moment to arise – a moment when he would be strong and powerful enough to win against the man who haunted his nightmares.

He'd made his first attempt at ridding the world of the Earl of Hedgewick when he was fourteen and he'd managed to sneak his way into the mews behind Hedgewick House. While the stable hand collected water from a nearby pump, Carlton had cut the leather strap that secured the saddle to the horse Hedgewick rode. Unfortunately, the fall Hedgewick had taken later that morning while riding in the park had not broken his neck as Carlton had hoped. It had only damaged his leg.

The incident had led to heightened security at Hedgewick House and caused the earl to hire a new team of brawny footmen who accompanied him everywhere for a long time after. It was not until Carlton turned twenty that another opportunity had arisen.

Sensing that Hedgewick's bodyguards had grown lax in their duties and that the earl himself no longer feared a threat, he'd entered the Berkly garden through the gate at the back and had finally found the earl alone for the first time in years. Or at least that was what he had thought when he'd spied him walking along a paved path and peering between the rhododendron bushes as if he was looking for something.

Eager to enact his revenge, Carlton had withdrawn the pistol he always carried in his pocket and had been about to take his aim when the squeaky voice of a child had asked, "Who are you and what are you doing in my garden?"

Hedgewick had instantly turned in Guthrie's direction and for a brief second their eyes had locked from between the foliage. He still could have shot him, but instead he'd turned away and fled the same way that he'd come. But before the gate had closed behind him, he'd glanced back over his shoulder and been met by the petulant glare from the girl who'd just stopped him from killing her father.

Regina.

She would likely stop him again if he wasn't careful. Whatever happened, he could not afford getting too attached to her or he'd have to live with regret for the rest of his life.

Absently, he glanced at a blank piece of paper that sat on his desk. He'd been meaning to write another letter to Hedgewick today – taunt him a little bit more with the hint of causing his daughter bodily harm. Instead, he swallowed the remains of his brandy and stood. The letter could wait. He'd much rather face a bare-knuckle boxer.

The roar of voices chanting in unison broke past the parlor walls and piqued Regina's curiosity. What on earth was going on? It sounded as if The Black Swan was being invaded by pirates. Abandoning the rest of her dinner, Regina padded across the floor to the parlor door and pressed her ear to it. The shouting grew louder and she could now make out a few of the words, most notably, "Come on," accompanied by some creative expletives involving duck tits and Zeus's bare-arsed army of whores. When it came to swearing, it clearly didn't have to make any sense.

Regina stepped back and stared at the door. She wasn't supposed to leave the parlor alone. Especially not in the evenings when The Black Swan was filled to the brim by drunken patrons. And yet, it was clear that all the excitement was happening out there and that she was being excluded. Perhaps a quick peek would suffice? Just enough to gauge what was happening.

She opened the door a crack and looked out to check if MacNeil, Patrick, or Claus was there. None was present, which meant that whatever was happening must have made them forget about guarding her.

A cacophony of voices swept toward her on a wave of applause and hooting. And then they were back to shouting. "Punch him until he groans like a whore! Jab the bugger right under the chin! Aim for his bloody throat!"

Crikey.

She ought to have stepped back into the parlor and shut the door firmly behind her. Instead, the bloodthirsty instructions increased Regina's curiosity. She moved forward steadily, until she was able to glance down into the courtyard below. And as she did so, her heart almost leapt up into her throat. Because there was Carlton, dressed in nothing but a pair of tight breeches as he faced a man who was just as scantily clad. Their arms were raised, muscles strained as they circled, dodged, and attacked.

A gasp escaped Regina's lungs as she watched Carlton take a hit to his left cheek. But the punch barely nudged him, and he quickly responded with a blow to the other man's chest. The crowd around them thickened as more people came to watch. They seemed to spill from the taproom with keen curiosity, pushing and shoving to better see what was going on.

Carlton's opponent dodged a blow and then counter attacked with a hit that cut a deep gash on Carlton's brow. Regina stared in horror as blood trickled into his eye and dripped onto his cheek. The spectacle was barbaric and yet she could not look away. Instead, she found herself riveted, not only by the match but by the man on whom she'd come to rely. He moved with the skill and grace of a warrior prince who'd done this countless times before. He wasn't a stranger to being hit or to dealing blows in return – a fact he proved when he knocked his opponent's nose sideways so hard she was certain she heard the bone crack.

And yet the fight continued even though both men now showed obvious signs of fatigue. Sweat

dripped from their hair, dampening their fore-
heads, and sheens of perspiration sparkled upon
their backs. Their movements slowed and Regina
could tell by the labored rise and fall of their chests
that catching their breath was becoming increasingly difficult.

How long would they continue? Until one of
them fell to the ground unconscious? She did not
like that idea at all, was tempted to turn away and
return to the parlor, and yet, the masculine display
of power Carlton exuded called to her feminine
instincts. She wanted to run her hands over his
body and feel those muscles flex beneath her fingers. She wanted his skin against hers with no
barriers between them, to feel his weight pressing
against her and...

"You know..."

Caught by surprise, she gasped and spun to find
MacNeil watching her intently. A blush rushed to
her cheeks at the chance of him having discerned
the wayward direction her thoughts had taken.
"I..." Embarrassed, she could think of nothing
else to say, so she glanced back at the fight instead.
Carlton was now pummeling his opponent, who
was hunched slightly forward while he protected
his face with his arms.

"He won't like spotting you out here," MacNeil
continued. His tall broad shouldered frame filled
the space beside her as he stepped closer to the
railing.

Regina stared down into the courtyard. "I suppose you want me to go back inside then?"

MacNeil was silent for a second, as if distracted
by the sudden break in rhythm that allowed

Carlton's opponent to fight back with swift and exacting motions. A jab caught Carlton's chin, sending him into the crowd. They caught him but showed no mercy and shoved him back out to the other fighter.

"He's too riled up to focus on his technique," he muttered, not answering her question. "Look now. If he would have sidestepped, he could have swung round behind Finnegan and caught him by surprise. Instead, he's left with no choice but to keep his guard up again."

Regina frowned. "I thought he was doing quite well."

MacNeil scoffed slightly, then smiled with the sort of kindness she wouldn't have expected from a man as fierce looking as him. "He's too distracted by a certain houseguest to focus. So yes, I probably should get you back inside. Before he sees you and has my head for not keeping you in his parlor."

Regina stared up at MacNeil in surprise. Carlton was fighting poorly because of her? She blinked. His recent rejection had made her believe that she didn't affect him as much as he did her. But maybe that wasn't true. Perhaps if she really set her mind to it, she could have the night she wanted with him after all. Scrambling to put a quick plan into place, she nodded. "Of course. We should go. But if it's not too much trouble, I'd like a word with Mrs. Harding." His eyebrows lifted with obvious surprise at the mention of Amourette's owner, so Regina hastened to add, "It pertains to a female matter."

Her words seemed to cut the hulking man

down by a couple of inches. He glanced sideways and cleared his throat. "Is it...um...urgent?"

"Yes." If she was going to seduce an experienced man like Carlton, she'd need to know a thing or two about lovemaking first.

"Then you may expect her visit shortly."

"And Guthrie?" Regina nodded toward the courtyard where Carlton's arm was being raised to convey his victory. Focused or not, he'd still managed to win the fight, but exhaustion was evident in his slumped posture. Regina's every instinct made her want to take care of him, to wash the dirt from his body and soothe his bruises with cool compresses.

"You mustn't worry about him. I'll tend to his wounds after calling on Mrs. Harding."

CHAPTER TEN

FROM AN ORDERLY LIFE THAT always went according to plan, to this. Regina almost laughed as she poured a measure of sherry into a pair of glasses. She handed one to Mrs. Harding, who thanked her before taking a sip. Who would have thought that she, the dutiful daughter of an earl, would be entertaining a bawd in a crime lord's parlor? It was so bizarre she almost wondered if it were a dream from which she would soon awaken.

"What can I help you with, dear?" Mrs. Harding's expression was both welcoming and kind. Her eyes were a dark shade of green, like the color of moss that hid in a forest's shadows, her hair a bright, curly red. "I brought some cotton pads in case it's your time of the month and you need them."

"Thank you." Regina accepted the parcel Mrs. Harding gave her. She hadn't considered how she would handle her menses, but she would probably have to figure that out in about one week, so having the pads handy was welcome. Setting the parcel aside, Regina took a sip of her drink. "There's actually something else on my mind – a matter on which I hope you'll be able to advise me."

Mrs. Harding's eyes widened with interest. "I shall certainly strive to do my best."

Regina nodded. Her awareness of Carlton and the unfamiliar desire he stirred in her, the need she felt for something more between them, compelled her to educate herself on a matter she wasn't supposed to know anything about until her wedding day. She'd always been told that a lady had to preserve her innocence at all cost. It must not be offered to any other man than her husband. The very idea that she would consider doing so could lead to scandal and ruin and eternal damnation.

And yet, nothing had ever felt more right than being wrapped in Carlton's embrace or feeling his lips upon hers. So she hoped Mrs. Harding could help enlighten her a little on a subject she knew next to nothing about. The lady in question stared at her expectantly, though not with any indication of wishing to rush her.

"I was wondering if you might explain something to me. Something of a...um...delicate nature." When Mrs. Harding didn't blink, Regina groaned and reached for her glass again. She took another sip to bolster her courage and then blurted, "I would like for you to teach me about the intimacies that can occur between men and women who like each other. You should know that I haven't a clue about any of it." She frowned. "Besides kissing, that is."

To her utmost relief, Mrs. Harding looked neither shocked nor perplexed. She merely tilted her head a little and smiled. "Would it be presumptuous of me to assume that your interest is connected to Mr. Guthrie?"

Regina swallowed. She was probably as red as a lobster by now. "It would appear that he and I share a mutual attraction to each other." Her words were not as confident as she had hoped they would be. Instead they conveyed the uncertainty of someone about to traverse unknown territory without a map to guide them.

"And he's kissed you, you say?" When Regina didn't answer, Mrs. Harding said, "Or did you learn about that with someone else?"

Regina shook her head. Nervously, she clutched the fabric of her skirt. "No. There has been no one else."

Mrs. Harding sank back against her seat with a satisfied smile. "And now you're curious to know why your body responds as it does to his touch and whether or not you should give yourself to him more fully. Is that it?"

A squeak was all Regina could manage by way of answer.

"I see." The older woman nodded while studying Regina with great consideration. "Has he made an attempt to seduce you into his bed?"

"No. I mean, I sleep in it every night but he stays in here on the sofa."

"Which means that he cares enough about you to put you ahead of his own needs. Which is rather remarkable when considering his sexual appetite." She blinked upon seeing Regina's startled expression. "Forgive me. I know you do not wish to hear about that. It is just that I've known Guthrie such a long time."

"Please. You mustn't apologize. I..." Regina

pressed her lips together and forced her shaky voice under control. "I don't just want to learn about the…um…sexual act itself and what it entails. Part of the reason I asked you here was also because of the vast experience Guthrie has with women who know what they're doing. And if he and I were to…um…you know…" She took a deep breath and then said, "Well, I'd hate for him to be disappointed."

"My dear. That would be quite impossible."

"How do you know?"

"Because no meaningless tumble with a courtesan will ever be better for a man than making love to the woman he's emotionally attached to."

"Even so, I would like to be as prepared as possible."

"And so you shall be." Mrs. Harding rose and proceeded to pace the room while studying the various books that were stacked on the floor. She selected a few before moving to the book case where she picked out an additional one. "These will be helpful," she said as she sat down beside Regina and opened one of the books to the most shocking picture Regina had ever seen.

"Now then," Mrs. Harding proceeded, as matter of factly as a seasoned school teacher, "As you can see from these pictures, a man's body is very different from that of a woman's." She turned a page. "As such, they're made to fit together, like so." The technical detachment with which she went on to describe the sexual act itself, allowed Regina to consider the subject as if it was nothing more than a mathematical equation or a new scientific discovery.

"What about that," Regina asked, pointing to another image later in the book. "It looks rather awkward."

"Oh, most of it is, but that doesn't mean it can't be enjoyable."

With a sigh, Regina slumped back against the sofa cushions. "I thought all of this would help me. Instead, I'm even more confused and uncertain of what to do."

"It's a big decision. Your parents would probably have me flogged if they learned what I've told you this evening." She closed the three books they'd been using and placed them on the sofa table. "My advice to you would be to refrain from rushing into something so permanent unless you're prepared to live with the consequences."

"You're right," Regina agreed even though she'd already made her decision. After everything she'd just learned, there was no man in the world to whom she'd rather lose her innocence than Carlton Guthrie. He was like a magnate, drawing her to him with unforgiving force. With him, she had no doubt that the experience would be glorious.

"I'd also hate to see your heart broken," Mrs. Harding said as she stood.

The door opened before Regina was able to come to terms with such a possibility. She stared at Carlton, whose own surprise showed when he spotted Regina's guest. While his breeches hinted at his recent activity, his shirt was neat, his cravat perfectly tied and his face completely clean. The only evidence he'd been struck was the cut on his brow and a bruise on the left side of his jaw. His hair, however, was wet, suggesting he'd just come from a bath.

"Good evenin,' Philipa. I didn't expect to find ye here."

"I asked MacNeil to send for her," Regina told him. She gestured toward the parcel Mrs. Harding had given her earlier. "There are certain eventualities for which I must prepare. When Mrs. Harding and I last met, she told me to let her know if there was ever anything I needed, and so I have."

"I see." Carlton stepped further into the room and away from the door. "If ye'll excuse me, I need a change of clothes." He strode toward the bedroom but stopped before entering it. Glancing back at Regina, he asked, "Ye don't mind me goin' in there, do ye?"

The fact that he would ask if it was all right for him to enter his own bedchamber made something warm and fuzzy bloom inside her. She shook her head. "Of course not."

With a curt nod, he continued forward and shut the door firmly behind him.

"I must be off," Mrs. Harding said. She hesitated briefly, then quietly said, "I hope I've been helpful."

Regina rose and went toward her so she could clasp the woman's hands between her own as a sign of appreciation. "Most assuredly so."

Mrs. Harding smiled. "Well then. If there's anything else you need, you know where to find me."

Thanking her, Regina saw her out the door and waited until she'd started down the stairs. Turning, she prepared to close the door when a

movement caught the corner of her eye. Glancing sideways, she spotted Patrick who was leaning
back against the walkway railing while watching
her with a lopsided smirk and a gleam in his eyes.

He tipped the brim of his hat. "Good evening,
my lady."

Regina swallowed. There was something about
him she didn't quite like. She'd felt it when she'd
played cards with him too, but had chosen to dismiss the feeling as a natural response to the then
unfamiliar surroundings and people.

"I'm used to finding MacNeil out here," she
said, forcing a smile.

Patrick gave her a head to toe look before meeting her gaze. "He's busy right now, so I've been
given the honor of seeing to your safety."

"Well, Guthrie's here now so, um…"

"My orders are clear."

"Right." She forced another smile and he
touched the brim of his hat once more, upon
which she shut the door. For a second, all she
could do was stare at it. And then she shook her
head. Patrick was one of Carlton's most trusted
men. There was no reason whatsoever for him to
make her uneasy since harming her in any way
would mean crossing Carlton, and that was something that only a fool would do.

With that settled, she returned to the sofa where
she quickly pushed the books she and Mrs. Harding had been studying underneath it so Carlton
wouldn't see them. Partly because she was rather
embarrassed by her interest in the subject the
books addressed, but also because she didn't want
him to know what she hoped to achieve.

But when he returned to the parlor wearing a robe that opened in a V to reveal a hint of dark hair, Regina's mind went blank. All she knew was the pull he had on her body, the way he commanded her with no more than a look, compelling her to rise and to go to him as if he would be her salvation. Her hand cupped his cheek and the coarse, unshaven bristles there scraped her skin. Gently, so as not to hurt him, she slid her thumb carefully over his cut. It was too high up for her to kiss it, even though that was suddenly what she wanted to do.

"You've been hurt," she said instead and let her hand drop.

The edge of his mouth quirked. "I had a bit of a run-in with an Irishman's fist."

"I know," she whispered while holding his gaze. "I saw it happen. Repeatedly."

His eyebrows dipped. "Ye watched the fight?"

"It was more of a brawl if you ask me, but yes, I did. You're quite good."

"I'm usually better," he muttered in a low tone that vibrated through her. "But me mind was preoccupied an' I couldn't focus properly."

"I see." She sounded breathless but it couldn't be helped. The scent of him, of soap and bergamot right after seeing him caked in blood and dirt, was intoxicating. Clean or filthy, flamboyant or scruffy, Carlton Guthrie exuded virile masculinity in a way that threatened to overwhelm her. His close proximity, dressed as he was –the knowledge that she could part the robe with her hands and have instant access to his bare chest – caused heat to flare up inside her.

Her fingertips itched to explore the torso she'd seen just an hour earlier. She wanted to trail them slowly across each rise and dip, to make his heart race as hers did whenever he was near.

But she wasn't given the chance to do any of that as he dropped a chaste kiss to her forehead and moved around her. "I'm ravenously hungry," he said. "I don't suppose ye've left a bit of food fer me?"

Regina blinked. "N-no." She coughed to mask the tremor in her voice. His dismissal of her was disappointing. She'd not expected him to be so standoffish, but at least kiss her as he had done on four previous occasions already. Saddened by the distance he seemed to be putting between them, she padded across to the door and began to push down the handle, her intention being to ask if Patrick could fetch some more food. But before she was able to open the door she was pressed up against it with almost violent force. With a yelp of surprise, her body went rigid, on instant alert while her brain tried to process what had happened and if she might be in danger.

But then awareness settled, alerting her to the hands that now covered hers. Roughened and with raw knuckles fresh from a fight, the familiarity of them eased the tension that had briefly assailed her and allowed her to relax. At her back, solid warmth permeated her clothes and sank into her flesh. And then she felt the rough scrape of stubble against the side of her neck. A ragged breath brushed her skin and her body answered with a welcome shiver.

"Where do ye think ye're going?" His voice was

like the velvet he so often wore: soft and smooth.

A flare of excitement swept through her as heat pooled low in her belly. "To order a meal so you can eat." She barely recognized her own voice, the sultriness like a purr in response to the headiness of his touch.

He did not answer, but she could feel his chest rising and falling against her back with unsteady movement. His breaths grew increasingly labored as though he struggled to keep some magnificent beast in its cage. And as he pressed closer, sandwiching her more firmly between himself and the door, she experienced a desperate longing for him to touch her. Everywhere.

It was so elemental and raw that it forced an unbidden whimper from deep in her throat.

Without even thinking, she arched her back and pushed her hips back. A groan rumbled through him, the sound more erotic than any of the scandalous images in the books she'd been studying earlier. She knew what she could expect now and this resulted in eager anticipation. It freed her mind from worry and concern by filling her with desire.

His hand went to her thigh, gripping her there and holding her to him with unrelenting force. And then, as quickly as he had grabbed her, he pushed her aside and opened the door himself. "Patrick. Can ye please bring me a plate of food?"

A muffled response came from the hallway and then the door closed again. Carlton turned to face her, his expression hard and unyielding. Gone were all hints of the passion she'd felt seconds earlier, replaced by forced control. "Fergive me," he told her crisply. "I didn't intend to be so rough. I just wanted to stop ye from goin' downstairs since the taproom is currently half-filled by drunkards."

"I…" Regina stared at him in baffled confusion. The way he was speaking, so curtly and precise, made it seem like the heated embrace they'd just shared had been but a figment of her imagination. Even though she knew it wasn't.

Her heartbeats stuttered as she stared back at him, this man who'd held her and kissed her as if she mattered – as if he might actually care for her as deeply as she cared for him. Hurt that he'd push her away as if she were some inconvenience he must avoid, she felt a lump rise in her throat. Her eyes started to prick and she turned away swiftly so he wouldn't see the devastation he'd caused.

"I wouldn't be so foolish," she managed to say in a tone far lighter than she'd believed herself capable of. "Not after all the warnings you've given me."

A knock at the door prevented him from responding. It was Patrick with a bowl of stew and a large chunk of bread which Carlton proceeded to devour with gusto the moment Patrick was gone and the two of them were alone once more.

"What's yer relationship like with yer father?" Carlton asked out of nowhere a few minutes later when he seemed to have appeased the worst of his hunger. "Do ye generally get on when he's not tryin' to marry ye off against yer will?"

The question caught Regina by surprise. She was still attempting to come to terms with what had just happened – his heated response to her followed by swift rejection. And the way he was speaking to her now, as if nothing of consequence had happened between them, made something shrivel and die inside her.

Feeling numb, she did her best to force the pain away by focusing on his question. "Why do you ask?"

He shrugged. "Just curious."

Regina watched him for a moment. If only she hadn't developed feeling for this man so her heart would not be so vulnerable.

Intent on appearing as calm and collected as possible, she folded her hands in her lap. "Hedge-wick has always been very attentive toward me," she began. "More so than most aristocratic fathers, from what I understand." Spotting a momentary crease on his forehead, she hesitated briefly. But then it vanished and she continued. "When I was little and the weather was good, he and I would play hide and seek in the garden. Sometimes Marcus, my brother, would join in, but for the most part it was just me and Papa."

"What about yer mother?"

"She's always been very soft and delicate. Not the sort of woman who would ever wade between bushes in search of a hiding child."

"More of the 'sit on a sofa with perfect poise' sort of woman?"

Regina smiled even though it saddened her to know that her mother had only ever tried to live up to the image she'd been raised to believe was expected of her. "I suppose so," she agreed.

"That must be awful," he said, echoing her thoughts. She wondered if her mother had ever been truly happy. She'd always behaved so carefully, as if afraid one misstep would send her plummeting from the pedestal on which her strict upbringing had placed her. "Why do ye think she married yer father?"

Startled, Regina blinked. What an odd question to ask. "For convenience. As most aristocrats do."

"So then it really shouldn't 'ave surprised ye that yer parents expected the same of ye."

"It didn't. But I never imagined the husband they'd choose for me would be no more than fourteen years old or that he would be frail and—" She stopped herself abruptly because she'd actually liked Stokes. He did not deserve her criticism. Not after he'd encouraged her to find a way out of their wedding.

"Stokes is a child?" The disbelief in Carlton's voice was so tangible she felt it like a lash to the back of her spine.

"Yes."

A dangerous glint in Carlton's eyes caused a tremor to dart through her breast. He looked more furious than she'd ever seen him before. And when he spoke again, his voice was sharp enough to cut through bone. "Seems to me that yer father doesn't care about ye as much as ye think."

Instinctively, Regina opened her mouth to argue. But she couldn't. Not when she shared Carlton's opinion. And yet, she could not agree with a man who was glaring at her as if she'd committed some sort of crime.

"I've always known him to be loving and caring."

Carlton snorted. "It's in a man's best interest to nurture 'is investments. Seems to me ye were nothin' more."

Discomforted by the subject they were discussing and the loathing with which Carlton spoke, it came as a relief when another knock interrupted their conversation. Setting his fork aside, Carlton went to see who it was.

He opened the door and MacNeil filled the frame. "Philipa needs you," he told Carlton gruffly.

"Has Scarlet been found?" Hope tinged Carlton's words and Regina's heart trembled as she wished that this was the case.

"Nay. It's not that." An uneven shake of the Scotsman's voice suggested that something must be terribly wrong. And then he said, "Ida's been taken."

Carlton's stomach dropped like a cannonball. In his veins he could feel his blood chilling, turning to ice. "Dear God."

"Taken?" he heard Regina ask while a hollow noise roared in his ears. "What on earth do you mean? Taken where?"

"I donae know," McNeil grumbled with the annoyance of a man about to lose his patience. "Philipa found her gone when she returned from here. The door to her room was wide open and a shattered vase could indicate a struggle."

"But what about the other women? Surely they would have heard if—"

Guthrie didn't wait for Regina to finish her panicked question. He marched straight into his bedchamber without bothering to ask for permission this time. If going in there bothered her ladyship somehow, then so be it. Furious, Carlton flung his robe on the bed before going in search of some clean clothes. Rushing to dress, he yanked on a shirt, a charcoal grey waistcoat with flowers embroidered on the front and a burnt umber jacquard silk jacket. Whoever had dared to encroach on his territory like this was either a fool or incredibly brave. Either way, he'd find the bastard, and when he did, he'd bloody well kill him for taking Ida.

Returning to the parlor, he went to join Mac-Neil by the door before addressing Regina. "Stay in this room," he told her tersely. "I'm lockin' the door behind me."

"Carlton, I—"

"If there's a lady snatcher out there, ye could be in danger."

"But—"

"Don't argue with me now, woman. I haven't the time."

"Romantic troubles?" Blayne queried as they left The Black Swan together.

Carlton glared at him. "No." He would not discuss Regina with him again. Doing so only led to severe discomfort and unfulfilled need. Along with a heavy dose of guilt. "And there's more important concerns right now don't ye think?"

"You're right. Ida going missing is disastrous."

Carlton wasn't quite sure if disastrous cut it. Was there even a word that could aptly describe the failure to protect a woman who'd been placed in your care? Even though she'd initially been Philipa's responsibility, Carlton had taken on the role of secondary protector years ago when he'd learned of Ida's circumstances.

Stalking into the slate grey night, Carlton headed straight for Amourette's so he could figure out how, when, and why Ida might have been taken. If her disappearance was somehow connected to Scarlet's, other women in St. Giles would be in danger. Including Regina.

CHAPTER ELEVEN

WORRIED AND WITH A SENSE of helplessness she'd never had to face before, Regina paced Carlton's parlor with mounting concern. She couldn't imagine why someone might want to kidnap Ida, and she feared that whoever had done it might also be linked to Scarlet's disappearance.

Clutching her hands, she tried not to fret over how easily they'd been taken from a place where they were supposed to be safe. A shudder raked her spine as she glanced at the door. She dared not imagine what they might be going through now at the hands of their abductor. All she could do was hope that Guthrie would find them as quickly as possible and bring them home.

The thought of him put an unpleasant strain on her heart. His curt tone when he'd spoken to her on his way out the door made it feel as if a snowdrift had fallen between them. She understood that Carlton was angry on her behalf, and she appreciated that, but she sensed there was more to it – a reason for the deep resentment he'd shown for her father in particular that she couldn't quite figure out.

In spite of everything, Papa was kind. She might

disagree with him when it came to her future, but he'd always been generous and supportive in other areas. Like when she was struggling to learn her sums. He'd dismissed her governess and taught her himself with exceptional patience. She wished she'd thought to explain this to Carlton. To make him see that he wasn't in a position to judge when he didn't have all the facts.

A knot formed in her throat as she thought of how much she loved her father. She loved her mother too and Marcus, of course. And she'd treated them all abominably by running away, by forcing them to explain things to the Windhams and to put up a façade.

It was selfish of her and totally thoughtless. But it had felt like her only option.

Hoping to distract her mind, she retrieved *Pride and Prejudice* and settled herself on the sofa to read. Mr. Darcy was also a difficult man to deal with, she thought when she reached the scene at the ball. In fact, he was downright rude and too high in the instep for her liking. She could only hope that would change as the novel progressed because if it didn't, she wasn't so sure that she wanted him paired off with Elizabeth Bennet.

Occasionally, she'd pause her reading to glance at the door. What if the building caught fire and she needed to get out? Carlton might have locked her in to protect her, but what if he'd put her in danger instead. Swallowing, she tried not to think about such a possibility. She also tried not to think of all the awful things that might have befallen Ida and Scarlet. Instead, she tried to hope for a positive outcome. Scarlet and Ida both lived and worked at Amourette's, so perhaps their disappearances were linked to a client.

Making a mental note to mention this to Carlton when he returned, Regina kept reading until she heard the key scrape in the lock. The door opened and Carlton strode in, the tension in his features impossible to ignore.

"Any luck?" Regina asked as she sat up straighter, closed the book, and set it aside. His bleak expression was answer enough. "I'm sorry."

He shut the door and turned the key in the lock. "It's dark and foggy out there. I'll continue searchin' fer her in the mornin'."

"That makes sense." Regina stood and just watched him a moment as he removed his hat and jacket with weary movements. "I don't like the way we parted earlier. All I wanted was to wish you well but you wouldn't let me."

"I was in a hurry," he grumbled.

"And angry."

"Not at ye." His voice was getting rougher, his movements jerkier as he pushed his arms free from the sleeves of his jacket and flung the garment aside.

She raised her chin. "No. It seems to me that you hate my father, though I can't quite understand why."

His jaw tightened. "The man's a bastard." The word, spoken as vehemently as it was, made Regina blink. As if sensing her shock, he closed his eyes briefly and drew a deep breath before saying, "I don't like the fact that he tried to use ye fer personal gain."

"He didn't do anything other men of rank haven't done for centuries, marrying their daughters off for alliances and wealth. It's expected."

"Marryin' a lady as lovely as ye to a crippled infant is not expected, Regina." He almost shouted the words. "It's bloody callous, is what it is and…"

"And what?" she carefully asked when he failed to continue.

"Nothin'." He stared at her. "I'm tired and eager to end this discussion, so if ye don't mind removin' yerself to the bedchamber there, I'd be mighty grateful."

He was dismissing her. And as much as that stung, Regina sensed they'd make no progress with this discussion tonight. So she crossed to the bedchamber door and turned back to face him. "Good night, Carlton. I hope you sleep well."

He merely watched her in silence while she closed the door between them and turned the lock.

With thoughts of Carlton, the argument they'd had, and the missing women still tumbling through her head, it took a while to fall asleep. But eventually, Regina did sink into oblivion. She even managed to have a nice dream that lasted until she was startled awake by a bone-jarring banging which felt as though someone was beating her head with a mallet. Still mostly asleep, she rolled onto her stomach and pulled her pillow over her head in an effort to block out the sound. But it was relentless and as it brought her more awake, she realized that it was accompanied by shouting, though this seemed to come from a different direction.

Groggily, Regina opened one eye and squinted into the darkness. It was still night, she judged, based on the deep purple hue cloaking the room. More banging and shouting had her tossing the covers aside and rising to wobbly legs. She took a second to regain her balance while growing increasingly confused. It almost sounded like a group of wild animals had been let loose in Carlton's parlor.

Yawning, she rubbed her eyes and then crossed to the door. All had gone silent now, except for the shouting which still continued, albeit with less force than before. It sounded as if MacNeil was trying to get Carlton to open his door from the hallway. Which seemed strange. She pressed her ear to her own door and listened. There was nothing now. No indication of what had been going on in the parlor. Briefly, she wondered if she ought to check. Perhaps Carlton needed her help? But then surely he would have opened his door to MacNeil. The fact that he wouldn't was perhaps the oddest thing of all.

She knit her brow and stared at the key that stuck out of the lock. Hesitantly, she reached for it, then leapt back with a start when the door handle suddenly moved. A jarring bang followed, and then another.

"Let me in damn ye!"

Regina edged backward, away from the door and the man who stood on the opposite side. He sounded nothing like the one she had gotten to know, but cruel and demanding. Swallowing, she glanced at the other door to her room. The one leading out onto the walkway.

Another yell sounded from Carlton. "Ye'll not get away with it, ye bastard. I'll cut yer bloody throat if it's the last thing I do!"

Regina's heart thumped rapidly against her ribs, like a trapped animal trying to escape its cage. Her stomach twisted and her hands began to tremble as panic set in and confusion twisted her brain. Was the door strong enough to keep him at bay? More banging followed. More shouting. What would happen if he broke into her room? Would seeing her make him snap out of his madness or would he do to her what he intended to do to the person he believed he was chasing?

Perspiration dampened her skin. She shivered and cast her gaze about for something to use as a weapon – something to at least hold between him and her body. But there was nothing and the banging was only getting louder, drowning out the sound of MacNeil's voice. It caused dread to sink deeper into Regina's bones, which in turn prompted her to make a decision.

She ran to the other door and unlocked it. "Mac-Neil," she shouted, not caring that she only wore her nightgown or that MacNeil wasn't alone. Patrick and Claus stood behind him.

MacNeil turned in response to her call and began coming toward her. "I'm sorry for the noise, my lady, but it canae be helped."

"He's trying to break down my door and threatening to commit murder." She met Mac-Neil's gaze as boldly as she could and demanded, "Why?"

"He's having a nightmare," MacNeil explained.

Regina's eyes widened. "That," she pointed in the direction of Carlton's parlor, "is a bit more dramatic than a nightmare."

MacNeil frowned. "I'll agree that I've never seen anyone experience episodes as severe as the ones Guthrie's prone to, but that's what's happening. If you'll grant me access, I can get to him through your bedchamber and try to wake him from it."

Stepping aside, she let the Scotsman into the room. Patrick and Claus followed but only Patrick made eye contact with her, causing a wave of unease to wash through her. There was just something about him that put her on edge.

Claus kept his gaze trained on where he was going as he went to stand at MacNeil's left shoulder. Patrick set the oil lamp he'd brought along on top of the dresser and positioned himself across from MacNeil. Once the men had made sure Regina was as far away from the door as possible, MacNeil turned the key. The click that followed seemed louder than usual. Regina pressed herself into the wall. Her heart trembled as she sucked in a breath and held it, unsure of what was to come.

MacNeil eased the door open and peered into the parlor. All Regina could see was his back. It filled the opening and with both Claus and Patrick standing close by, they blocked her entire view. But then a roar sounded – guttural and fierce and not at all human. And before Regina knew what was happening, MacNeil was staggering back as Carlton barreled into him head first.

MacNeil grunted as air was pushed from his

lungs. His body was thrown off balance by the force of Carlton's attack, so in spite of his greater size, it took him a moment to regain his footing. Which it seemed he was only able to do thanks to Claus and Patrick, who immediately stepped in to help. They pulled at Carlton's arms, trying to restrain him, but Carlton just beat them away with a blind blow to Patrick's head and a swipe that caught Claus in the throat. The young man sputtered and coughed, backing away before Carlton could hit him again.

Regina was tempted to go and make sure Claus was all right, but that would mean passing dangerously close to Carlton and in the state he was presently in, she'd rather not do so.

"Wake up," MacNeil shouted. He gave Carlton a solid shove that propelled him toward Patrick. He caught him and held him, allowing MacNeil to land a resounding slap against Carlton's cheek.

Regina flinched and averted her gaze, hating the sight of the man she...

The man she what?

Cared for? Respected? Enjoyed spending time with?

The man whose kisses she'd started to crave and with whom she'd begun contemplating a great deal more?

The way her heart ached at the thought of him suffering like this, of wanting to physically harm whoever it was that made him endure this, suggested that there were stronger emotions at play. Feelings she didn't dare recognize yet. For she knew that the moment she did, they would bind her to him forever.

So she focused on all the things she had yet to tell him – parts of herself that she wanted to share when he was more able to listen. Like the fact that she wished she could live by the sea so she'd always hear waves rushing to shore, that she had an almost obsessive fascination with other countries and cultures, and that she would love to travel in order to explore them.

"Come on," MacNeil's voice broke through her thoughts and caused her to glance back in his direction. The Scotsman had somehow managed to maneuver Carlton onto the bed where he held him down with the weight of his body. Carlton wore only breaches and a loose shirt that hadn't been tucked in, the fabric billowing and bunching as he struggled against MacNeil's grasp.

"Ye'll not win. Do ye hear?" Carlton said as he tried to shove him away.

"Do you know who he's fighting?" Regina asked. Sensing the worst of the danger had passed and that Carlton would not be getting back on his own feet until he was fully awake, she moved toward the bed.

"No." MacNeil grunted. "Patrick, hold his legs will you? And Claus, try slapping his face to see if that will bring him out of it."

"Perhaps a gentler approach would be better," Regina suggested. She lowered herself to the edge of the mattress. "If he's fighting someone, you could be making things worse by responding with violence."

"Please go back to where you were before, my lady," MacNeil implored with a strained voice. "Guthrie's not himself right now. There's a chance he might hurt you."

Regina was well aware of that. She'd seen what he'd done to his men. Nevertheless, she ignored the advice MacNeil offered and climbed further onto the bed until she was lying down on her side with her face next to Carlton's.

"Stubborn woman," MacNeil muttered. "Restrain his arms, Claus. Don't let him hit her."

Inhaling deeply, Regina tried to calm her breathing. It was so strange, the thought of Carlton being asleep, for in spite of the darkness, she saw that his eyes were open. He bared his teeth and began moving furiously from side to side in an effort to push MacNeil off him. But the Scotsman held fast, allowing Regina to place her hand against Carlton's cheek.

She brushed her thumb gently against his temple. "Shhh..." she whispered next to his ear. "Relax. It's just me. Regina." When he panted out a series of hard breaths, she added, "You're safe. There's no danger, no one to hurt you, no reason for you to be angry."

He flinched and she realized too late that she'd said the wrong thing. MacNeil cursed in response to Carlton's renewed effort to obtain his freedom. But Regina would not be deterred. She'd seen the calming affect her voice had had, if only for a brief moment. So she slid her fingers into Carlton's hair, stroking and caressing while speaking in soothing tones, much as she imagined she'd do to a wild and terrified animal.

"I'm here, Carlton." Shifting closer, she reached for his hand, curled her fingers around his and sensed some of the tension leaving his body. "I'm not going anywhere. Not ever." She'd made her decision, she realized. It no longer mattered if Yates responded to her letter. A life without Carlton just wasn't an option. "There's no walking away. No future for me that does not include you. Please. Wake up so I can kiss you."

"I'd like that," he murmured. His voice was slightly slurry, as if part of him still slept.

Leaning in, she pressed her lips to his cheek. And was roughly pushed aside when he suddenly jerked to full awareness and tried to sit up, only he couldn't because he was partially trapped beneath MacNeil's chest.

"What the hell?" Carlton blurted. "Get off me, ye brute."

"What's my name?" MacNeil asked.

"Oh Christ. Did I have one of me episodes?" Appearing to register where he was, he glanced about until he found Regina. "What did I do? Did I hurt ye somehow?"

"Ach, he's all right," MacNeil muttered and withdrew his weight from Carlton's torso. "You were hollering like a lunatic, Guthrie, and making a hell of a lot of noise too. I wouldnae be surprised if you destroyed half your parlor."

Carlton scrubbed his hand across his face and muttered something Regina couldn't make out. A curse, no doubt. He expelled a deep breath and sat up. The glow from the oil lamp Patrick had set on the dresser barely reached Carlton's face. The lack of light added a harshness to his features which was further enhanced when he looked at her with the blackest stare she'd ever been subjected to. A shiver raced through her and she instinctively edged back, adding distance with the intention to stand.

Swiftly, he reached out and snagged her wrist. His eyes hardened as he slid his gaze over her, hovering briefly on her breasts before lowering it to her belly and legs. "Don't ye dare move." The command in his voice stayed her actions.

"Guthrie," MacNeil said, "We should probably—"

"Get out." Guthrie's words sliced the air with uncanny precision as he turned his attention toward his men. "Get out right now!"

"You're welcome," MacNeil grumbled as he herded the other men out of the room and closed the door behind him.

"That was both unnecessary and rude after everything they just did to help you."

"Rude, I'll agree. But unnecessary? No." He tugged her roughly toward him and pressed his mouth to hers, kissing her hard and deep and with the possessiveness of a man who was trying to stake his claim.

Her body responded without hesitation, as if it had been in deep hibernation and he'd just roused it from its wintery slumber. Heat poured through her and all she could do was surrender, giving as he gave in equal measure until she grew desperate for more. His hand found her waist and curved into her flesh, rumpling the nightgown she now wished he'd tear from her body. But just as abruptly as he'd grabbed her, he released her and stood.

Regina's mind whirled. She felt dizzy and…and unfulfilled.

"Ye need to think before ye act," Carlton told her.

She blinked. "What?"

He glared at her as if she'd just committed some horrible sin. Jaw tight, his lips drawn into an angry line and with shadows obscuring his brow, he looked like the menacing scoundrel that he was reputed to be. Even so, Regina did not fear him. She just wasn't sure she completely understood why he was so upset.

Until he said, "I'll not have ye showin' other men yer body." Disapproval tightened his words. "Fer Christ sake, Regina, I can see yer tits through that sheer fabric."

Fire erupted all over her face, burning her skin as she hurried to find some means of covering herself. It wasn't so much the crassness with which he'd just spoken, or even the fact that he'd seen more of her than he should have, that bothered her. It was realizing how much MacNeil, Patrick, and Claus must have seen that embarrassed her most. How on earth was she going to face them again?

As for Carlton, he just continued to glare at her censoriously as she pulled the blanket off the bed and wrapped it around her body. He raised an eyebrow. "A bit late fer modesty, wouldn't ye say?"

Swallowing, she raised her chin a notch. "Perhaps. But I cannot have a proper discussion with you if I feel like I'm standing before you naked."

"Discussion about what?" Irritation dripped from his voice. "I'm goin' to get some more rest an' I suggest ye do the same."

"Not until you explain this to me." When he

didn't respond, she softened her voice and said, "I'd like to know what just happened."

"It was nothing."

"Nothing?"

He crossed his arms. "Just a bad dream. I get them from time to time. Which is why I've been tellin' ye to lock the door at night. So I can't get in here an' cause ye harm."

A fresh wash of shivers puckered her skin. "Are these dreams the real reason for the bars on the windows?"

Glancing away, he made a gruff noise before looking at her once more. "I jumped out of it once an' hurt meself badly. Woke up mid fall."

Regina's hands flew to her mouth. "You could have been paralyzed or…or killed. All it would have taken was an unlucky landing and…" She took a step in his direction.

"Hence, the bars an' the locks." He frowned and it looked like he might say something else. But he didn't.

"Do you think something could have triggered it?"

Meeting her gaze, he stared into her eyes for what felt like endless minutes. "No," he eventually told her. "Now go to bed."

He turned away, but she wasn't quite ready for him to leave. "Who were you trying to kill, Carlton?"

He froze and she could see by the way his shoulders and back went completely rigid that her question displeased him. "A demon," he muttered. Then he crossed over the threshold to the parlor and shut the adjoining door.

CHAPTER TWELVE

"**A** YOUNG LAD JUST TOLD ME he saw Ida being carried out of Amourette's the night before last by a man of medium height whose appearance he likened to that of a dockyard worker," Blayne told Carlton two days later.

"Why the devil did it take him so long to come forward?" Had he not made it clear that time was of the essence?

"The lad is but ten years old. He wasn't here when you made your announcement about the disappearances. It was his older brother who mentioned it to him last night."

"I see." They were in Carlton's study downstairs at the back of the tavern. Yesterday morning, after seeing Regina and being reminded of what she'd looked like with a lot fewer clothes on, he'd felt his desire flare up and had instantly fled the parlor.

"He also said that...Guthrie? Are you listening?"

Carlton blinked and muttered a swift, "Of course." It shook him to think that Regina could distract him so easily. He forced himself to focus.

Blayne frowned but did not question him further. Instead he said, "He described the same sort of unmarked black carriage."

"A hackney perhaps?"

"That's what I'm thinking. According to the boy, it headed south. He managed to follow it all the way to Seven Dials, after which it disappeared."

Carlton considered this new information. "I didn't think to investigate there."

"Perhaps we ought to head back out," Blayne prompted.

Carlton nodded. "There isn't a moment to lose." He strode from behind his desk and collected his hat from a nearby chair. He opened the door and proceeded to make his way through The Black Swan. As he went, he signaled for Patrick and Claus to follow, demanding that they bring their knives with them just in case.

"What's happening?" he heard Patrick ask Blayne as they walked toward Broad Street.

Reaching the wider road, Carlton raised his hand to hail a hackney. "We're goin' to comb every street between Holborn and the Thames."

But as with the previous occasions when Guthrie had gone out looking for Scarlet and Ida, the trail went cold. While some of the people they questioned had seen a black unmarked carriage and confirmed that it was indeed a hackney, no one could say for certain which way it had gone. One man scratched the back of his head and said he believed it was bound for the east end while a couple of women insisted it was heading for the docks.

"We'll have to split up," Carlton said. It was the only way to cover so much ground.

"I can check the docks," Patrick told him. "I grew up in that area so I'll know where to look." When Carlton hesitated, Patrick said, "The people there also trust me. If the women are there, I'll find them."

"Very well," Carlton agreed. "Claus can go with you."

"That…" Patrick began, paused, then finally said, "sounds good."

Carlton frowned in response to an odd bit of doubt creeping over his shoulders, but then Blayne said, "I'll come with you, Guthrie."

Agreeing to meet back at The Black Swan, the groups parted ways, each consisting of five additional men. But as darkness settled upon the streets, Carlton had to accept defeat once again. He could only hope that Patrick and Claus had been more successful in their search and was encouraged when they mentioned a warehouse that appeared to have been recently vacated.

"A beggar I spoke with said that he saw a man leaving the place with a woman who matches Ida's description," Claus said. He hesitated, then added, "He said we missed them by about ten minutes."

"Was he able to tell ye what the man looked like?" Guthrie asked as he clenched his fists.

"About my height," Claus said, "with brown hair sticking out from underneath the cap he was wearing. He didn't get a good look of his face, but he did say he walked like a young man rather than an older one."

"I want eyes on that building," Carlton told his men darkly. "And the surroundin' area."

"I don't think that will help us much," Patrick

argued. "Ida's obviously not there anymore."

Carlton knew he was right, but with no other clues to her whereabouts, keeping watch on the place where she'd been was better than doing nothing at all. "There's always the chance that the man will come back."

Patrick gave him a look of apology. "I understand."

Carlton sighed and addressed Blayne. "Any additional news about Hedgewick?"

"Not really," Blayne answered with a glance toward Claus.

"He's keeping to himself," Claus said. "Rarely leaves the house. His son, however, has been going out a lot lately. Ever since your most recent letter was sent."

"Do ye think there could be a connection?" Carlton asked with interest. "That Seabrook might be doin' his own investigation?"

"I don't know," Claus said. "One of the boys watching the place followed him yesterday. Seabrook didn't seem to have a destination. He just walked around for about five hours, going all the way to Tower Hill before heading back."

"Hmm…"

"On a different note," Patrick muttered, "It looks like you were right about Mr. Reynolds. He is selling counterfeit art to his peers."

Carlton straightened. He'd made it his business to keep a close eye on the aristocrats and gentry with London addresses. Only those who behaved honorably were allowed to escape his wrath. Greedy men who sought to take advantage of others and those who were cruel to their servants did not deserve to live without concern.

"Set up a meeting with him, Patrick. I'm sure the gentleman in question would like to donate to my coffers as long as I promise to keep his secret." Once he'd received a decent payment, he would of course tip off one of the Mayfair Chronicle reporters so they could investigate further and hopefully ruin the man's reputation.

He sighed. There really wasn't anything worse than those who lied and cheated their way through life, taking advantage of others as they went. As far as Carlton was concerned, they deserved no compassion. Certainly not from him.

"Thank ye fer lettin' me know."

Patrick nodded, shared a look with Claus and said, "If that's all for now, we'd like to go and have some supper."

"Of course," Carlton agreed. He waited until they reached the door of his office before adding, "I trust ye'll keep me informed about the watch on that warehouse, Patrick?"

Patrick turned, "Of course, Mr. Guthrie."

Carlton waited for the door to close, then turned to Blayne. "I'm not sure I can trust him," he muttered.

"Who? Patrick?"

"I've this gut feeling that isn't to my liking."

"Are you sure you're not just imagining things 'cause you're tired and worried?" Blayne asked. "Patrick's proven his loyalty to you repeatedly over the years. I doubt there's cause for concern.

"You're probably right." What he ought to be focusing on now that he'd returned home was Regina. He ought to go and check on her. Instead he asked Laura to take a dinner tray up.

"Do you plan on avoiding her from now on?" Blayne asked as they ate together in Carlton's study.

"A bit of distance will do us both some good, I should think," Carlton said as he stuck some fried fish in his mouth. He followed it with a piece of potato. "I can't afford the distraction she poses. Not if I'm still to go through with my plan." Alone, with the door firmly shut and no one to overhear him, he allowed his voice to relax and spoke as he'd been raised to do by his parents.

"You could make a different plan." Blayne watched him closely and with great consideration. "One that includes a future with her?"

"I can't live a lie with her forever," Carlton confessed. "I won't." He hadn't meant to discuss something so personal with anyone, but it was also a relief to share the weight of the burden he carried with someone else. And Blayne was the only person he knew he could trust without question – the only man with enough information to offer proper advice.

"Because you're developing feelings for her?"

"She is…" He tried to find the right words and ended up taking another few bites of his food while Blayne watched. Eventually, he dropped his knife and fork on his plate and pushed it aside. "She's the dream I dare not allow myself to have."

"It's not unheard of for dreams to come true," Blayne murmured.

"Not for men like me. And once she discovers the truth – once she learns who I am and why I invited her into my home in the first place, she'll hate me forever. There will be no forgiveness on her part, Blayne, of that I assure you."

His longtime friend did not look convinced. "She might be hurt at first – angry even – but if she cares for you, Val, I'm sure she'll get past it."

Carlton shook his head. "She'll feel as though I betrayed her and she'll be right. Our interactions with each other, our emotional attachment, and the unrelenting desire we both have for more has forged a bond between us, Blayne. The idea of having to cause her pain makes me ill."

"Then don't."

"And what? Abandon the one goal I've had for the last twenty years?"

Blayne shrugged. "I was thinking more along the lines of exchanging it for something better."

Carlton stared at him. "Seeing justice served on behalf of my father is everything to me." His voice was hoarse but the words were solid.

"Then your purpose is clear." Blayne took a sip of his drink. "Don't worry about Regina. Your feelings for her aren't as strong as you think. With time you'll find a way to move on."

This should have been reassuring. Instead, it filled Carlton with doubt. A doubt that only increased when he went upstairs later and found her asleep on the sofa. She was lying on her side with Ralph curled up next to her belly. One hand was tucked under her cheek and a few strands of hair curled against her brow.

Carlton felt his heart squeeze with tremendous fondness, then ache with the thought of her absence. She'd become such a huge presence in his life, he could not imagine what it would be like without her. Already, in the space of only two weeks, she'd managed to make him laugh and smile for the first time in years. She'd unburdened his soul and brought happiness into his life.

To give her up…

His throat worked as he stood there, as helpless as he had been as a boy when Hedgewick had come to call on his father. Since then he'd fought for control, always seeking to gain the upper hand. But with Regina there was no control. He might as well be caught in a whirlwind, unable to choose which way it would blow him.

But knowing that she'd walk away with only disdain for him – that she'd never grant him a smile again – sent a piercing pain through his chest that caused him to wince. Ralph opened one eye and shifted. Regina moved her arm but kept her eyes shut. Carlton picked up the blanket he used at night and took a step forward. He prepared to place it over her when his gaze inadvertently dropped to the floor beside the sofa and he spotted an open book.

Ordinarily, this wouldn't have struck him as odd. He had no issue with leaving books on the floor, and Regina was certainly welcome to read whichever ones struck her fancy. He just never thought it would be the lewdest one that he owned. Surprised, he finished tucking the blanket around her, then gathered up the book and sat down in one of the armchairs with it.

The page it was opened to featured an image of a woman straddling a man along with a detailed description of how the act was performed. Carlton raised an eyebrow and glanced across at the seemingly innocent woman still peacefully sleeping. Apparently she had a curious nature that leaned toward the improper. He gave a low chuckle. Oh, how he wished he could have seen her expression the first time she opened this book and discovered its contents. Had it made her blush and feel wary? Or had it produced the same sort of thrill inside her that he'd felt when he'd first been made aware of the wonderful possibilities of lovemaking?

A surge of excitement rushed through him. Their most recent kiss had left no doubt about her desire. And he longed to take it further – to show her how good things could be between them. Resisting her was no easy task. In fact, it was becoming increasingly difficult. But surrendering to his baser need…

If they made love, there was a chance she'd give him more than her body, and he wasn't sure he was ready to safeguard her heart. There was also the issue of causing her pain when he got arrested. As he would be when he was done with his plan. Going to jail and hanging for the crime he meant to commit was acceptable. Hurting Regina more than necessary was not.

It was almost ten o'clock when Regina woke from her nap. She stretched and slowly opened her eyes. A hot shiver raked her skin when she found Carlton studying her. He was lounging in one of the armchairs, his long legs stretched out before him and his elbow propped on the armrest so that his hand could support his head. In his lap was a book. *That* book. Her cheeks grew instantly hot and warmed by a few more degrees when he gave her a lopsided smile.

"Did ye have a good rest, luv?" His voice was low and intimate – the sort that could lure the chastest woman straight into sin.

Regina nodded. Still somewhat sleepy, she sat up slowly and reached for the glass of water she'd had on her tray. "Have you discovered anything new about Ida or Scarlet?"

"Not as much as I'd hoped." His chest rose and fell with strenuous movements.

A tendon moved at his throat where his absent cravat and open shirt front allowed her to see more than she ought. Fascinated, it took her a moment to avert her gaze, only to find her eyes locked with his. She swallowed and his eyes seemed to grow a shade darker.

"But something?" she pressed, hoping to keep his mind on the missing women instead of on her and the book he must surely know she'd been reading.

He broke eye contact, allowing her a reprieve from the flustered state he'd put her in simply by being in the same room. His presence alone was enough to make every cell in her body cry out in yearning. The feeling was exacerbated by his lack of a jacket and waistcoat. Instead, fine white cotton draped his broad shoulders, hinting at their more than perfect shape. The sleeves were rolled up, offering a casual view of his forearms. She wasn't sure why the dark dusting of hair there appealed as much as it did or why she had a sudden compulsion to touch it.

"We found where Ida was, but she's not there

anymore."

His comment caused her to stop admiring his body. "And Scarlet?"

"There's still no trace of her."

Regina's heart sank, until she thought of something and said, "If Ida's been moved, perhaps the man who took her knew you were coming to find him?"

Carlton stilled. "I'd not thought of that, but it's definitely a possibility."

"And if that's the case, he might start making mistakes on account of sheer panic." She straightened herself on the sofa. "Just think back on how this villain could have learned of your search, and you should be able to find him and get Ida back."

He eyed her thoughtfully. "It's not quite that simple, luv." When she gave him a stupefied look he explained. "I'm sure most of London knows I'm lookin' fer Ida. The man who took her probably learned of it in me very own taproom. But I'll agree with ye that the chance of findin' her has improved, which is more than I was able to say this mornin'."

Regina was glad. Immensely so. She could not stand the thought of something bad befalling Ida. Even though she'd only met her once and didn't really know her, she'd liked the young woman immediately. "Is there anything I can do to help?"

Something flickered in the depth of his dark brown gaze. "Aye." He shifted in his seat, leaned forward slightly, and held up the book. "Ye can offer me an excellent distraction by tellin' me why ye were readin' this."

Was it possible to radiate more heat than the

sun?

Judging from the way her entire face burned, Regina was quite convinced that it was. She took another sip of her water which wasn't nearly as cold as she wished it would be. "I… um…"

Carlton raised a black eyebrow and she took yet another sip. Her heart was trembling as much as her body right now, the nervousness coursing through her threatening to upset her stomach.

"Yes?" he prompted.

Fine!

She set her glass aside and clasped her hands together in her lap. "I was curious and that book along with a couple of others seemed highly educational."

He stared at her. "Educational?"

"Well, yes." She met his stare with one of her own. "Young ladies aren't taught about such things, in case you were wondering. They're kept in the dark, their minds preserved in the purest form possible. God forbid they might have an inkling of what to expect when they one day marry. Or how they might please their husbands so the men won't feel the need to acquire mistresses. It would also be nice to know that there's nothing to fear about procreation and that if it's done right, the man and the woman involved can both enjoy it. Not to mention the added benefit of preventing the birth of unwanted children by letting women know of the various safe measures that can be taken. Why should men have all the information? Why…" She stopped abruptly, aware she'd been babbling. And he… His eyes were suddenly brighter and his moustache appeared to be twitching until she realized… "Are you laughing?"

A sputter emerged from his mouth followed by a most unexpected guffaw. His head was now tilted back against the headrest of his chair as he let his mirth show with carefree abandon. Regina stared. His entire body shook as he continued to laugh. Eventually, when he managed to regain some control, he wiped one hand across his eyes and returned his attention to her. "Good God, woman! Had I known ye were so passionate about this particular subject, I'd have brought it up sooner."

The flush she'd been feeling spread to the tips of her ears. "As I said," she mumbled, a little put out by how humorous he found this, "I was interested."

"Which is only natural, I suppose." He smiled. "If ye have any questions, I'd be happy to answer them fer ye."

"No thank you," she clipped.

He pressed his lips together as if attempting to keep his humor at bay. "Some of these pictures can be confusing. Perhaps I should point out exactly how—"

A growl of irritation rose from her throat, and he started laughing once more, which was when she realized that he was deliberately trying to tease her. Not in a mean way, but as someone who liked her company and considered her a friend. It was a playful side she'd not thought him capable of, but one that she realized with sudden force that she rather liked, even though it was making her uncomfortable at the moment.

He sobered, his eyes sharpening to arrow points. "Ye must know that I desire ye, Regina, fer I've made no attempt to hide it. I just…" He blew out a breath and raked his hair with his fingers, mussing the thick locks. "I cannot be the man who takes yer innocence. Ye do realize that, don't ye?"

She wasn't sure where that comment had come from. It caused her spine to straighten with rigidity. Her skin felt suddenly tight and prickly. But before she was able to gather her thoughts and form a response that wasn't, "how dare you", "who do you think you are", or worse, "but why?" he'd risen, snapped the book shut, and returned it to the spot where Mrs. Harding had initially found it.

"How about a game of cards?" he suggested as if all were normal and her nerves weren't dancing a jig.

She inhaled deeply through her nose, hoping to still the pulsing sensation his comments had caused in the pit of her belly. "That would be nice," she said as she pasted a smile on her face. What she would not allow him to see were the unsteady beats of her heart. She wanted him so desperately she'd sought guidance from a bawd, for heaven's sake! But that didn't matter because Carlton had decided he would never be with her in such an intimate way. The question was why? She didn't want the obvious reason, because she was quite sure that didn't matter. She wanted to know the real one.

With her mind fixated on this, her concentration failed and she lost every round of vingt-et-un that they played but one. "Ye're not ready fer the gamin' hells just yet," Carlton told her when they packed away the cards later.

Another attempt at humor?

She frowned, unsure of what it meant or how best to respond. Deciding to be herself, she gave him a smirk. "Maybe I'm playing a longer game. One in which I'm just trying to make you think I'm a terrible player."

He actually grinned, which made all the stupid feelings she'd started having for him swirl up inside her like autumn leaves caught in a storm. Nitwit. That's what she was. She was falling for a man she had no hope of ever, *ever*, sharing her life with permanently. A renowned criminal who'd actually told her he'd killed people.

Good God, she had to be mad.

He eyed her as he went to collect a bottle and a couple of glasses. "Sherry?" he inquired.

"Yes, please." She desperately needed something to numb her senses and lull her brain so she could stop thinking about what he'd said. After all the times he'd kissed her as if he wanted to rip the clothes from her body and claim her, now he'd taken a giant step back and put up a wall.

"If ye could have crafted the life of yer choosin' when ye were little," he said while filling their glasses, "where would ye be right now?"

He placed her glass on the table before her, right next to the tray that contained the remains of her dinner. Regina frowned at it while considering her answer. The question was without a doubt the most interesting one he'd ever asked her. Biting her lip, she reached for her glass and sipped her sherry while Carlton went back to his armchair. This time he sat leaning forward, his knees slightly bent as he cradled his own glass between them. Genuine curiosity brought a sparkle to his eyes.

"Does it have to be realistic?"

He shook his head, then set his glass to his lips and drank. "Yer perfect life can be as fantastical as ye want it to be."

"In that case, I'd be living in a house with a view of the sea. Outside, there would be a wide terrace and beyond that, lavender." A wistful smile played on her lips. "Bees and butterflies would be the only insects. And ladybirds. I like them too. And the sun would shine each day. Not too hot, but warm enough to make the outdoors pleasant. There would be a cat, perhaps two. Freshly baked scones would be waiting for me each morning along with clotted cream and raspberry jam. The beach between the house and the sea would have the whitest sand, so fine it would feel like silk between my toes..." She trailed off, allowing herself to be swept away for a moment.

"Who else would be livin' there with ye?"

"My children. Two boys and two girls."

"And their father?"

Silence filled her as she tried to picture the man of her choosing. When only Carlton came to mind, she shook her head. "I don't know," she lied, unwilling to let him see how important he was to her life after he'd all but told her they'd never be together. So she met his gaze with defiance and shrugged off the sadness that slid toward her like water licking its way onto shore. "Perhaps they won't have one."

His lips quirked even as a dark shadow fell over his eyes. "An immaculate conception?"

"You said yourself that it is my dream and that it can be as fantastical as I want." She smiled in an effort to hide every trace of what she was really thinking – the longing that pulled at her soul and made her wish things were different. "Your turn."

He hesitated briefly, then said, "I'd travel the world with me wife and children." He gave her a knowing look and she sucked in a breath. It was almost as if he knew this was her dream as well, even though she had not said it. "We'd swim in the bluest lagoons an' explore places other people only read of in books. Our experiences would be just as vast as the love we would feel fer each other." Eyes, so intense that they pierced her and held her captive, warmed with emotion. The edge of his mouth drew upward. "We'd dine beneath the stars and…there would always be a home fer us to return to whenever we'd want to experience dry land. It would be warm an' cozy an'…safe."

Something about the way he said that made her heart twist with pain. She wasn't sure if she could speak without the uncomfortable lump now lodged in her throat destroying the words. So she nodded, took a sip of her drink and allowed a moment to pass.

When she finally whispered, "That sounds perfect," her voice didn't crack as she feared it might.

He inhaled deeply, his eyes still riveted upon her in a way that made her feel slightly self-conscious. "I've seen ye read romance an' more provocative forms of literature." Fire erupted in her cheeks and she briefly averted her gaze. "Are there any other types of books ye enjoy? Poetry perhaps?"

She shook her head, relaxing a little. "I've never been able to appreciate it much. Accounts written by explorers or biographies of people who've led remarkable lives are far more intriguing. Benjamin Franklin's memoir is just one example of such a book. It was most compelling."

An almost incredulous look captured his gaze. "Just when I think I know what to expect from ye, ye surprise me again."

"How so?"

He lifted one shoulder in a lazy gesture. "Ye're more complex than the average romantic. Ye enjoy tales of happily ever afters and dream of a life that's perfect without complications or challenges. But ye also strive to enrich yer mind in a way I believe to be rare among ladies of yer age and rank."

"My entire upbringing has been centered around my becoming as accomplished as possible. My parents hired a piano instructor when I was three. They also hired French, Latin, and German tutors, an artist who showed me how to paint, and a music teacher to help me develop my voice. I have been taking lessons ever since, eight hours a day every day without fail so that when I eventually made my debut, I would be able to make the best match. Because men don't want wives who think and who speak their minds and who might interfere with their opinions. They want one who can entertain, who will carry herself with perfect poise, and not cause embarrassment. But becoming such a person was never enough for me. I wanted to expand my horizons and discover the world, even if I could only do so from the comfort of my home."

Carlton's chest rose and fell with even movements, but his gaze was intense. "Ye're perhaps the most impressive woman I've ever 'ad the pleasure of knowin'." His gentle tone dove to the bottom of her soul and lifted it up. "It's a shame that yer life is bein' wasted by the few choices ye have been given, fer ye could have been so much more than a step up the ladder fer yer father." His expression hardened and his fingers curled into his palms. "I'm sorry, Regina."

She forced a smile that didn't feel genuine. "It's nothing less than I expected. And there are people in this world who are much worse off than I." She thought back on some of the people they'd passed the first day she had come here, of how desperate they'd looked. "I have no reason to complain."

His eyes widened for the briefest of moments before hiding whatever response he'd just had. She wasn't sure she could pinpoint it exactly. "Would ye sing fer me if I asked ye to?"

"Maybe." Performing in front of others had never disturbed her before, so why did it suddenly make her feel shy and uncertain?

Because his opinion of you matters more than any other ever has.

She gripped the edge of the sofa with one hand to steady herself. How had this happened? How on earth had this man she'd just recently met impacted her so?

Drawing a ragged breath, she let it out slowly while knots began forming deep in her belly.

"Please?"

One word, so softly spoken it could barely be heard, drifted toward her. And the tender sincerity of his plea undid her completely. "Very well." With her hands clasped together in her lap, she opened her mouth to the first notes of "Robin Adair" with an increased pace to compensate for the lack of a pianoforte.

Carlton watched, his expression so serious she was forced to look over his shoulder in order to calm her nerves and slow her racing heart. When she finished, it was with the utmost relief. Silence followed, so thick and resounding she started to speak just to fill it.

But Carlton cut her off. "I've never heard anythin' so exquisite," he murmured. "Thank ye, Regina, fer bringin' heaven to earth."

Her throat closed completely and all she could do was nod. Because if she tried to speak, she feared she might choke and that the hot burn that now pressed at the back of her eyes might evolve into tears. Nobody had ever complimented her on her singing, or on any of her other achievements for that matter. She'd been expected to do everything well so when she did, it was simply the norm.

But Carlton's appreciation for her and his willingness to get to know the person she was behind the façade her parents had crafted meant more than she'd ever be able to put into words. All she could do was feel. And what she felt the next morning when she entered the parlor and found him already gone could only be described as deep disappointment. Until she spotted the tray that waited for her on the table in front of the yellow velvet sofa.

It contained a plate on which two hot scones awaited, along with a small pot of clotted cream and…raspberry jam. Regina's mouth stretched until her smile grew so wide that it almost hurt. She covered it with one hand as she took a step closer. There was also a cup of tea covered with a lid in order to keep it warm. And next to the plate were three sprigs of lavender tied with a silver bow and a note which she picked up with trembling fingers.

Women like you are few and far between. You deserve the breakfast of your dreams.
C.G.

Rounding the table on shaky legs, Regina lowered herself to the sofa and swiped the dampness from her eyes. Dear God in heaven, what was she to do? Staring at the food he'd so thoughtfully prepared and the lavender which wasn't even in season any longer, Regina surrendered to the myriad of feelings expanding her heart and acknowledged the truth.

She was no longer falling for Carlton Guthrie. She already loved him. More than she'd ever imagined she would ever be able to love another person. He was everything to her.

CHAPTER THIRTEEN

TWO WEEKS. MARCUS LET THE reality of time settle heavily at the front of his mind. If Regina had been all right, then surely she would have written to him by now. But all he had were letters written by an unknown hand.

Frustrated and angry, Marcus swiped his forearm across his desk, scattering paper and books and making a mess of the ink when it spilled from the inkwell. With heavy-lidded eyes burning from lack of sleep, he hung his head and took a stuttering breath. They'd received no word about her for the last week. Not from the man who held her or from the runners. She hadn't turned up dead yet. He'd checked. But that didn't mean she was still alive.

Emitting a rough sound of utter despair, he scrubbed his hand across his jaw and was met by the beard he'd let grow. Shaving and looking his best was not a priority right now. Nor did he have the energy for it. Even though his valet continued insisting he make the effort.

For what, Marcus wasn't sure. The only places he frequented right now were White's and Gentleman Jackson's. And he couldn't care less about what anyone there might think about his appearance. They could all sod off if it bothered them.

His fingers flexed. None of the men he'd spoken to since discovering his father was hiding something had offered any clue as to what it might be.

"He's always been a good friend," most would say. "I cannot imagine him not being liked," was another frequent comment. "He's one of the most respectable peers there is."

What Marcus *had* learned was that his father and the previous Duke of Windham had been like brothers. Right up until the duke's tragic death in that fire that had burned down most of his home. It had also taken the life of a maid and of Windham's son, who'd only been thirteen years old at the time. Marcus wasn't surprised that his father had never mentioned the attachment. It was probably still a difficult thing for him to discuss.

Grumbling beneath his breath, Marcus stood and went to the sideboard where a pot of hot coffee awaited. He poured himself a cup and drank it as it was, savoring the bitter flavor. His father's connection to Windham wasn't going to help Marcus find Regina. Neither was walking the streets every day, aimlessly searching for her.

He added a splash of brandy to his coffee and took another sip. There was something he was missing – something the runners were missing too. He could feel it like some elusive presence creeping up behind him. If he could just grasp it and…

Voices echoed from the front of the house and Marcus groaned. His father's nerves were more frayed than his, his irritation growing from day to day, making him impossible to be around, never mind talk to.

Easing his door open, Marcus glanced toward the foyer where Hedgewick stood. His rigid body leaned forward, as if he was getting ready to lunge at the man to whom he was speaking.

"Find her!" Hedgewick bellowed. "It's what I'm paying you for!"

The man he addressed muttered something and departed. Hedgewick cursed him to perdition before retreating to the stairs. Marcus waited until he was gone before crossing the hallway and stepping inside his father's study. He'd not searched it yet, but decided to do so now, dismissing the breach of trust as a necessary one since he'd exhausted all other efforts of figuring out what his father was hiding. And if he discovered something that might help him save Regina, he'd have no regrets.

But rather than finding hints of Hedgewick wronging someone, Marcus was stunned to discover the opposite – a collection of letters suggesting that Hedgweick was the one who'd been crossed. Apparently, his wife had once had an affair. With none other than the previous Duke of Windham.

Marcus quickly returned the letters to where he'd found them and left the room. Infidelity wasn't uncommon among the aristocracy, but it did make Marcus wonder why Hedgewick was so eager to tie himself to the Windham title. It made more sense that he'd want to distance himself from it as much as possible. Not that any of this was very helpful. When it came to finding Regina, a decade's old love affair wasn't the answer.

Widening his search for her, though, might be. He stopped to think. Regina had run away in her wedding gown. Marcus reflected on that for a moment. A bride racing through London would have been noticed. Unless she'd climbed into a carriage or…

He drew a sharp breath as a new possibility struck him. In all the areas of London where he'd looked and questioned people since she'd gone missing, he'd dismissed one location because it had seemed impossible that she'd be there. And yet it was close enough for a woman travelling on foot to quickly conceal herself if that was her aim.

St. Giles.

Marcus shuddered at the thought of Regina being there. But if she was, he would find her. It was certainly worth a look.

Having called a meeting in the taproom, Carlton faced his men with renewed determination. The information Patrick had given him twenty minutes earlier could prove invaluable. It pertained to a house near Hackney Meadows where Patrick said he'd spotted Ida after following a tip.

Carlton had listened to Patrick's account with relief. It seemed Blayne was right and whatever mistrust he himself had had of Patrick had been unfounded. Ever since discovering the warehouse, Patrick had striven to find other clues that could help with Ida's rescue. Locating the coachman who'd driven the hackney and interrogating him had been a smart move.

"There's more than the one man we were expecting though," Carlton said, repeating what Patrick had told him. "At least ten are guarding the house, so ye'll have to be ready to fight."

"We're ready," Blayne said with a fierceness that seemed to rile the others. "Especially if it means bringing the wee lass home."

It took almost an hour to get there.

"We'll approach from both sides," Carlton said once the house was in sight. They'd exited the carriages before they'd reached their destination, paid the drivers, and walked the rest of the way. Only the light from a single window would guide them through the thick blanket of darkness.

Waving Blayne off, Carlton gave him and the men he took with him enough time to find their positions, then signaled to them with a whistle. Everything was still. Almost eerily so.

He frowned and began moving forward, unsettled by the lack of activity outside the house. It didn't fit with what Patrick had told him. A niggling feeling in the pit of his belly informed him that something was wrong. He glanced around, searching for Patrick so he could ask him for his opinion. But he wasn't part of his group, so he must be with MacNeil.

Reaching inside his jacket pocket, Carlton pulled out one of his pistols as they drew closer. If the men guarding Ida had gotten wind of their rescue plan, they might be lying in wait, ready to attack. Carlton's heart beat low and steady. This wasn't so different from some of the raids he'd participated in in the past. First on behalf of Bartholomew and later on his own. The difference was that Bartholomew'd never cared who they attacked or who got killed in the process while Carlton only went after those who were harmful to others.

There'd been a shop with a cellar full of children who'd been forced to rinse out old wine bottles and fill them with gin. When Carlton had found them he'd given the man and woman in charge of the operation a thrashing until they were barely alive. When he was done, he'd tied them both to a couple of chairs and dropped a note off at Bow Street.

Many more cases existed and while Carlton knew that his way of handling them usually involved breaking the law, he had no regrets. Those who preyed on the weak deserved the punishment he gave them.

A fence came into view and Carlton drew his men to a halt. He tilted his head and listened. Still nothing. Not even the croak of a frog or the hoot of an owl. He narrowed his gaze and peered through the blackness of night in an effort to make out the dark shapes surrounding the house. It would be easy for someone to hide in the shadows from bushes and trees and to spot Carlton as he approached from the road. But for ten men to make no noise at all was unlikely.

He gritted his teeth. "There's no one here," he muttered.

"What?" one of his men asked close to his shoulder.

Carlton paused for a second to check on his

instincts before striding forward more swiftly. He reached the gate in the fence and eased it open. Blayne's shadow, tall and wide, moved to the far right of his peripheral vision. Carlton glanced toward it without concern and briefly considered approaching so he could tell Blayne and Patrick that the man who'd taken Ida must have given them the slip. Instead he went to the front door and knocked. Just to be certain.

An old man opened the door. His wary gaze met Carlton's and held it for a moment before he asked, "Can I help you with something?"

Carlton glanced beyond the man's shoulder at the neat foyer with landscape paintings hanging on the walls and a vase that stood on a narrow entrance table. The flowers in it didn't look like they'd come from a hothouse but most likely from the man's garden.

"I'm lookin' fer a young lady with blonde hair, about this height." He held his hand up to his shoulder.

The old man frowned. "I'm sorry, but I haven't seen anyone matching that description. Few people come to call on me and my wife. Except our oldest son, on occasion. He's got a good position as a clerk. Works for the barrister who helped Mrs. Lowell a while back. If you ask me, she deserved to win that case against her stepson. William thinks the judge was paid off or something." He shook his head. "Who can you trust if not the hand of the law?"

"I'm not sure," Carlton muttered, his body absorbing the chill in the air like a sponge soaking up icy water. "Sorry to have troubled ye."

"I hope you find her. This woman you're look-ing for."

"So do I." Carlton tipped his hat and stepped back. The door closed. He turned to Blayne. "Where's Patrick?"

Blayne moved toward him until Carlton man-aged to make out parts of his face even though his large body was still slightly fuzzy around the edges. "I thought he was with you."

Every muscle in Carlton's body tightened like the string of a newly crafted bow. His hands clenched at his sides so his nails dug into his palms. He barely registered the discomfort as his mind tried to make sense of this information. "Scarlet was easily snatched up. She could have been taken by anyone. But Ida... The man who took her knew exactly where to find her. He knew when the rest of the girls would be occupied with their clients so they wouldn't notice her disappearance. He knew Philipa wasn't there and he knew which room belonged to Ida."

A sick feeling started to grow in Carlton's chest as the only possible explanation began to sink in. The man who'd been seen leaving Amourette's fit Patrick's height and appearance. And at the docks, Patrick could have whisked Ida away to a different location before Claus spoke with the beggar and found the warehouse where she had been.

Christ!

Why the hell had he not considered all of this sooner? He'd sensed that something was wrong with Patrick and yet he'd dismissed his suspicions. How could he have been so bloody careless? He shook his head. An uncomfortable shiver raked over his skin.

Because of Regina.

Because you were too damned distracted.

Because…

Regina.

Time slowed as it had that day long ago when his father had fallen to the ground right before him. "Be quiet," he'd whispered. "Don't make a sound."

Every bone in Carlton's body had been on the verge of collapse back then – like twigs that would surely topple in the face of a storm. Just like then, he could feel blood rushing through his veins with increasing speed, pushing his heart to pump a faster, more painful rhythm. He blinked and acknowledged the fear trickling through him, gradually building until it became a cascade. His mouth was dry, the nerves in the tips of his fingers vibrating as if preparing for him to do violence. And he would. By God he would murder that traitorous boy when he found him.

"We have to get back!" He was already running toward the road, not caring if anyone else came with him – not bothering to waste any time with explanations. Because if his instinct was as good as it tended to be, Regina was in terrible danger – danger he'd put her in when he'd taken most of his men with him on this wild goose chase Patrick had sent him on.

Increasing his pace, Carlton ran faster, only mildly aware that Blayne was with him. They ran until they spotted a carriage. Carlton didn't bloody care if it was occupied or not, he'd toss the passengers out at gunpoint if he had to. Right now, nothing would stop him from getting back to The Black Swan and checking on the woman who captured his every thought. If anything happened to her… If someone took her, threatened her, hurt her…

The carriage slowed when Blayne stepped into its path. The horses nickered as they reared back and trotted from side to side while the driver pulled on the reins.

"What in blazes is wrong with you, man?" he shouted.

"We need a ride," Carlton told him while Blayne brought the horses under control with a firm grasp of their bridles. He flung the carriage door open and peered inside the compartment, happy to find a friendly face. "Yer Grace. I regret to be an inconvenience to ye, but me associate an' I must return to St. Giles at once an' yer carriage is the most efficient way to do so."

The Duke of Coventry didn't look remotely amused, and for a second Carlton thought he'd have no choice but to threaten the man as he was prepared to do. Only this was someone he knew quite well – someone he respected and liked, which was something that couldn't be said of most people.

"I suppose I can spare a couple of spots since I'm heading that way myself," Coventry said. His voice was stern and utterly fearless as he glared back at Carlton.

"Come on, Blayne. Let's go," Carlton called. He climbed up into the carriage while Blayne told the driver where they were headed. A few of Carlton's other men had caught up and Blayne gave them some coins so they could pay for a hackney if they found one.

"You're stopping by the school?" Carlton asked Coventry after a while, mostly for the purpose of thinking of something besides all the terrible things that might have happened to Regina during his absence. Driving himself mad wouldn't help. He needed a clear head to think and to act as rationally as he could. For her sake.

"The duchess often stays late. I thought I'd check if she's still there before continuing home."

Coventry's wife was Amelia Heathmore, sister to Raphe Mathews, the Duke of Huntley and Juliette Lowell, the Duchess of Redding. Carlton knew the siblings well. He'd taken them in when they'd been little and facing a similar fate to the one he'd faced when he'd fled the scene of his father's murder. But they'd always resented him for turning Raphe into a fighter, for forcing him into tough matches and taking part of his winnings.

As far as Carlton was concerned, he'd done the man a favor by teaching him how to survive.

He glanced across at Coventry's stony face. He and Amelia had done a great deal of good for St. Giles. She in particular, since it had been her idea to open a school for the children there that offered education on par with what upper class children received.

"I heard about what you did for Mrs. Lowell," Coventry said. He paused and for a moment Carlton thought that was it, that he wouldn't say anything else. The carriage turned a sharp corner, and the duke reached for the strap beside his window. "If you continue being so helpful and generous with your blunt, people might start thinking you're a good man."

"God forbid," Carlton muttered. He stared back at Coventry through the darkness.

"Any chance you'll tell me what you were doing all the way out by Hackney Meadow or why you're in such a rush to get back to St. Giles?" When Carlton didn't answer Coventry leaned back into his corner, melding with the darkness. Neither said anything more for the rest of the journey, but when they arrived at the corner of Gerrard Street and Carlton followed Blayne out onto the pavement, he turned back and said, "Thank you, Yer Grace. I owe ye a favor."

He didn't know if Coventry responded or not as he raced away with Blayne right behind him. "Where's Patrick?" he shouted when he entered The Black Swan. A couple of men who'd been left behind to 'hold up the fort' as it were, appeared from the taproom.

"Thought he was with you," one of them said while Carlton dashed up the stairs. He took the steps two at a time and almost leapt onto the landing. Sweat dampened the back of his neck, causing a chill to wash over his skin. It intensified when he spotted the open door to his parlor and sank its teeth into his flesh when he stepped over the threshold and glanced around.

Everything was exactly as it should be. Nothing looked out of place or different. But there was a lifelessness about the room now – a lack of presence – that told him Regina was gone.

Even so, Carlton crossed to his bedchamber and

peered inside. The bed was neatly made and the lavender he'd given her lay on her pillow, infusing the air with its rich scent. Carlton struggled to breathe. It felt as if he'd been buried alive and the weight of the world would soon crush his chest. For the first time in twenty years, a painful knot formed in his throat and threatened to choke him. He turned and went back to the parlor where Blayne's incredulous gaze met his.

"I'll hunt him down and rip his eyes from his skull." The words were forced out from somewhere deep inside him. His hands shook. Hell, his whole damn body felt as if it was wracked by some sort of crippling disease. "I'll drown him in his own spit!"

"We'll find Lady Regina," Blayne said, his voice eerily quiet and pensive. Jaw set, Carlton saw that in spite of the calm he exuded, he was tightly wound and ready to fight.

Carlton inhaled deeply, hoping to clear his mind and rid himself of the anxiety clutching his body. "How?"

"Patrick obviously thinks he stands to gain something from what he's doing."

"I recruited him. I fucking recruited that bastard, put a roof over his head and fed him, made sure he received the care he needed when he took ill, and this is the thanks I get?" Heat pooled behind his brow, pulsing there until his head felt ready to explode.

"Let's take a moment," Blayne said.

"I don't need a moment." Carlton heard his teeth gnash as he clenched his jaw. "I need to do something. I need to—"

"Let's have a drink, gather our thoughts, and make a plan."

Carlton shifted his gaze and it landed on the tray on which the remains of Regina's dinner still stood. It was as if she'd just set it aside for a moment and would soon return. "I can't stand the idea of him touching her. Of her being cold or scared or…or possibly hurt."

"I know," Blayne told him gently. "And I promise you that I will help you get her back. But rushing about without aim in the state you're in won't help. And neither will staying in this room."

There was wisdom in Blayne's words – the sort that Carlton currently lacked. With a nod, he followed his friend downstairs. The men he'd had to leave behind at Hackney Meadows were now returning, and he made sure to offer his thanks along with an apology for the haste with which he'd left them. When Blayne explained the situation, their brows furrowed and their mouths tightened and it was clear that they understood.

"Patrick betrayed you," one of them said without any finesse. "He deserves whatever comes next."

The rest of the group agreed and Carlton felt his throat tighten again on account of their loyal support. He cleared it with a cough and accepted the glass of brandy Blayne handed to him. Its soothing warmth helped him gather his wits and focus on what must be done.

"I need ye out there patrollin' the streets an'…I 'ope ye'll fergive me fer this, but I want all of ye in pairs. No one goes alone." A quiet murmur was the first response followed by a series of concrete nods. His men seemed to accept the lack of trust he was willing to place in them now. "We need to find out where Ida an' Regina are bein' held and if Scarlet is with them. The fact that Patrick took these women tells me it's no random snatch. He's plannin' somethin', which means we may be short on time." He downed the rest of his brandy to wash away the dread that resurfaced as he spoke those words. Holding the glass out, he let Blayne re-fill it. "Call in the children who were posted in front of Hedgewick House. The more eyes we've got, the better."

The look Blayne gave him was not lost on Carlton. Yes, he'd abandon all surveillance of Hedgewick in order to get Regina back. Nothing was more important right now. And although he told himself that his reasons were tied to his plans for revenge, he knew better. Regina mattered to him. More than anyone else ever had.

CHAPTER FOURTEEN

A SHIVER WRACKED REGINA'S BODY AS she sat across from Patrick in the carriage he'd acquisitioned. Not because she was cold but because she was starting to fear that he'd lied to her. Having fallen asleep on the sofa in Guthrie's parlor, she'd been groggy and confused when he'd roused her.

"You must come quickly," he'd urgently told her. "Here. Put this on." He'd flung a cloak over her shoulders and pulled up the hood.

"Where…where are we going?"

"Somewhere safer than here. Guthrie insists."

She'd yawned and done as he'd asked without further question. It wasn't until now that she wondered why he'd been in the parlor instead of outside, knocking on the door. And what place could possibly be safer for her than at The Black Swan?

As disturbed as she was, Regina tried to stay calm. Perhaps her concerns were unfounded. And yet, she needed more information than what he'd provided. "Why would I be in danger at The Black Swan, Patrick?"

"Because you've been seen there, my lady."

Regina frowned. "Not in over a week. I've remained upstairs."

"Nevertheless. Guthrie doesn't want to take the risk of the man who took Ida and Scarlet kidnapping you as well."

Regina stared at him while her insides started to quiver. "I didn't think Guthrie was sure of their disappearances being connected." She watched him closely, her unease growing as he clamped down his mouth and glared at her through the darkness. Swallowing, she reached for the door handle only to have him grab her wrist in a painful grip that twisted her skin.

"I wouldn't do that if I were you," he warned. "Best if you keep calm and do as I ask."

A tremor licked her spine. "You ought to let me go." The calmness of her voice surprised her.

Patrick yanked her across the space between them and locked her in a tight hold. "Not when you're worth so damn much, my lady." He chuckled lightly. "You'll make me a wealthy man once I auction you off."

"What?" Surely she had misheard him.

"Some men will pay a high sum to keep a woman like you as their pet."

"I'd rather die first," she hissed and promptly yanked him sideways. Patrick pulled her back hard and tightened his hold, but when she continued to struggle, wriggling around in his arms, he lost his grip for a second and gave her the chance to leap for the door.

"Damn you," she heard him shout, then something hard hit the back of her head and she collapsed, hitting the floor of the carriage with a thud that ended in darkness.

"I trust you're still a virgin?" Patrick asked as soon as she was conscious again. They were in a small room and he was now standing in front of the chair in which she had been restrained. Slowly, he raked her body with a horrible gleam in his eyes. When Regina refused to answer, he said, "Perhaps you'd rather I tie you to that bed over there and inspect you myself?"

Swallowing the fear the idea of such a forced violation brought on, she shook her head and quietly told him, "My innocence is intact."

Patrick smiled with satisfaction. "Good. For a while there I feared that Guthrie might have ruined you completely. Not that you wouldn't be worth anything if that'd been the case, but it's better this way." He turned away. "I'll get you some water so you can freshen up. Perhaps you're hungry?"

"No." She wouldn't eat anything he gave her. Not willingly at least.

Patrick went to the door and turned back to face her. "Don't worry, my lady. You won't be here very long."

Trembling, Regina watched him disappear into the hallway beyond. The door closed and Regina let out the breath she'd been holding while struggling for some sense of calm so she wouldn't panic. Carlton would come. He had to. She would not think of the fact that he had no clues to go on and that Patrick could have, as far as Carlton knew, taken her anywhere.

"We've got something," Blayne said as he strode into Carlton's study. "One of the boys we sent out has come back. Claims he saw a man fitting Patrick's description shoving a woman into a carriage behind that brothel the magistrate shut down last month."

A touch of ice chilled the space between Carlton's shoulder blades as he recalled the place. When he'd learned what went on there, he'd informed the authorities right away, and thankfully they'd done their job for once so he hadn't been forced to interfere further.

Leaning forward, Carlton gripped his armrest so tightly he heard the wood crack. "Did he say where the carriage was headed?"

"He hitched a ride on the back and followed it to the docks."

Carlton was already on his feet. "Let's round up the men then and head out."

Blayne nodded and stepped aside so he could follow Carlton through the door. "The lad brought a hackney back with him. It's waiting outside and ready to go."

Carlton strode forward with increased purpose. Something was finally going right. He'd have to reward the boy later. For now, there was business to attend to – women to be rescued and a traitor to punish. He chose to leave two men behind in case Patrick was foolish enough to return. Three, including Claus, accompanied him and Blayne in the hackney while the rest were asked to make their own way to the docks.

Carlton's mood was somewhat dulled though when they arrived and there was no indication of where Patrick and Regina might be. He wasn't sure what he'd been expecting, but some sort of sign would have been nice.

Refusing to be discouraged, Carlton told the hackney to wait and then glanced around. He walked along the wharf searching for clues that could lead to Regina's whereabouts. All was quiet. Except… He tilted his head. Was that clopping? The sound grew louder and then a carriage rounded the corner. It slowed to an immediate halt as soon as the coachman saw him and clearly tried to turn. But Blayne was there, both quick and strong. He grabbed the horses by the reins and forced them to stay.

"You'd best let us go," the coachman said. He'd reached for a pistol, but Carlton had one of his own.

He aimed it at the man and watched as his eyes went wide with fear. "An ye'd best do as we say." He jutted his chin at the spot the coachman had been trying to reach. "Kindly hand over yer weapon and I just might spare ye."

Shaking, the man did as was asked. He gave his pistol to Blayne, who remained there with it now aimed directly at the coachman's head.

Carlton opened the door to the carriage and climbed up inside.

"What the devil?"

There was no mistaking the man's identity. It was Mr. Reynolds, the very same upstanding fraudster Patrick had told him about. Without explaining or offering an apology, Carlton took the opposite bench and aimed his pistol directly at Reynolds's chest.

"If I'm not mistaken," Reynolds said, "my meeting with you is supposed to take place tomorrow."

"Best not leave fer tomorrow what one can accomplish today," Carlton sneered. "Now, ye'll tell me what ye're doin' here, Reynolds. And ye'll do so now."

Reynolds glanced at the window as if the foolish man imagined escape lay in that direction. "I'm supposed to meet with a business associate of mine. He's interested in getting a good deal on some textiles that I'll be importing from India."

Carlton narrowed his gaze and pulled back the hammer on his pistol. "I don't have patience fer lies."

"I...I'm not lying!"

Faster than Reynolds could blink, Carlton reached for the man's fluffy cravat and yanked him closer so he could grab him securely by his throat. "Are ye sure about that?" Carlton asked as he pressed his pistol against Reynold's head.

The man trembled and Carlton tightened his hold, squeezing the trachea until he cried out in fear. Eyes wide, he stared at Carlton in horror while gasping for breath. "Now then. Would ye like to give me a different answer?" He leaned slightly forward and arched an eyebrow.

"I don't...I don't..." Reynolds gasped. Carlton pressed the pistol more firmly against Reynolds head. "All right. All right," Reynolds wheezed and Carlton loosened his hold to let the man speak. "There's an auction tonight. It's exclusive. Invitation only."

"Art?" Carlton asked on account of the forged paintings he knew Reynolds sold. It did not explain Regina's or Ida's whereabouts though.

"No. It's something else – something special that can't be gotten anywhere else."

Carlton curled his hand more securely around Reynolds's neck. "I suggest ye tell me about it quickly."

"Yes. Yes of course," Reynolds stammered. "It's women. That is…I mean…there are men with particular tastes and I…it's been difficult since Bartholomew died. I don't like visiting filthy brothels and he understood that. He got that there was a need for something exclusive – a place where people like me can do the things that most of the whores won't allow."

Disgust began boiling inside Carlton's stomach. He moved the pistol and pushed it up under Reynolds's chin. "Such as?"

"I…I…I…"

"Spit it out, Man, before I blow yer head clean off yer shoulders."

Reynolds whimpered and for a second, Guthrie feared he might start crying. But then he muttered, "I like to…to hurt them."

"Jaysus!" Reynolds gasped as Carlton gripped his throat tighter. His eyes bulged and began to water. Deliberately, Carlton forced himself to relax his fingers. "Explain."

When it took Reynolds a moment to speak, Carlton narrowed his gaze. "I'll make ye suffer unspeakable pain unless ye come clean this instant."

Reynolds gulped and gave a quick nod. "When Patrick came to set up the meeting with you, I learned that he's offering something much better than the tired whores Bartholomew always supplied." Carlton felt as though his heart had stopped beating. "Virgins. Expensive as hell but—"

The cracking sound of the pistol connecting with bone as Carlton used it to punch Reynolds in the face cut the bastard off. Carlton hit him again, and again, until blood smeared his pistol and parts of his hand, until Reynolds fell silent and slumped back against the squabs.

Carlton drew a deep breath. "Where?" He'd barely stopped from killing him.

A hoarse throaty crackling sound rose from Reynolds's throat. "On the barge."

Carlton took just one second to consider what to do. He could finish Reynolds off as he would have done before, but part of him wanted to be better than that. Part of him wanted to go to Regina without more blood on his hands.

"Damn!" Time was ticking by fast and he had to be off. So he quit the carriage and tried not to regret the decision he'd made to let Reynolds go. There were more important things for him to focus on now, like making sure a lecherous reprobate didn't acquire Regina before he showed up. "She's out there somewhere," he told Blayne while trying not to think of how scared Regina would be on the water. "Reynolds mentioned a barge."

"Let's have a closer look." Blayne turned his back on the carriage and went to address the rest of the men. The entire crew had now shown up and was ready to help. Carlton followed and after a couple of steps the whinnying of horses and clatter of hooves informed him that Reynolds's carriage was taking off fast.

Nets were heaped together on the side of the wharf. Three massive ships were docked, obstructing the view of the river. Their gangplanks were raised, which suggested their crews had already retired for the night. A pungent smell of decay filled the air, but it wasn't any worse than what Carlton was used to in St. Giles.

"I sent Mitch and Rupert that way," Blayne said as two men split from the larger group and disappeared into the darkness.

Carlton nodded. "Then the rest of us can continue toward the other end of the wharf." He started walking and everyone else fell into step behind him. But they hadn't gone far before Mitch came back at a run.

"There's a jetty over there." He pointed behind him. "With rowboats we can use."

"Were ye able to see anythin' from it?" Carlton asked. He was already following Mitch at a clipped pace. The jetty would be close to where they'd initially arrived and to where Reynolds's carriage had been heading, but they must have missed it because of the darkness.

"Aye," Mitch murmured. "Lights on the water. Just enough to guide the way."

Carlton's muscles began to strain with the anticipation of what was to come. He stopped when they reached the spot where Rupert waited, immediately aware of the fact that several other boats appeared to be missing. "We'll approach the stern of the barge in complete silence. If all goes well, we'll manage to board without anyone bein' the wiser. Just follow me lead and don't attack unless it becomes necessary. Our main concern is to get the women Patrick's holdin' to safety." They could deal with Patrick later, but the last thing Carlton wanted was to give him more reason to hurt Regina.

Which he just might do if he felt cornered.

Regina's wrists and ankles were tied so the coarse rope dug painfully into her skin every time she moved. Cut from white gauzy muslin, the gown she'd been told to put on was without a doubt the most scandalous creation she'd ever seen. The neckline was at least an inch lower than any dress she'd worn before and barely held her bosom in place. And since she hadn't received any undergarments, she felt as naked as she would have if she'd worn nothing at all.

She glanced sideways at where Ida was sitting with her chin held high at a stubborn angle that bolstered Regina's own courage. Similarly attired, the young woman hadn't said much since Regina had met her on the barge. But when Regina had quietly told her that Carlton had been out looking for her, she'd smiled.

"He'll come for us," she'd said.

Her gaze had been firm and without any hint of the doubt that Regina felt. After all, they were on a barge in the middle of the Thames (as if that wasn't terrifying enough), about to be auctioned off to a group of men. And Patrick wasn't alone. Somehow, he'd formed his own band of unsavory miscreants. A group of men with leery grins and sinister gleams in their beady eyes.

Regina shuddered. What chance did Carlton have of getting to them in time? What information could he have learned to aid in her rescue? She already knew that Patrick had sent him to Hackney Meadows. The odds of him returning and figuring out where she was in time were so slim they barely existed at all.

She swallowed as she looked toward the other girls being held captive. They were so young. One did not look more than eight years of age. Her stomach curdled at that thought – at what their fates would be when they left with their owners.

"Stop worrying," Ida hissed beneath her breath. "They'll smell your fear and use it against you."

As if on cue, Patrick appeared. He walked the length of the area where they all sat, considering each girl in turn until his focus went to a girl who was practically trembling with fright while tears streaked over her cheeks. A smirk appeared on Patricks's lips, removing all lingering traces of the agreeable man he'd appeared to be at The Black Swan. "Bring her," he commanded the man who'd followed him to the stern of the ship where they waited.

"No. Please…" The girl shook her shoulders in a futile attempt to push the man away. He lifted her effortlessly into his arms and carried her toward the bow where the auction was set to take place.

Patrick smirked. "A pity Reynolds didn't show. He did say he liked them young and feisty."

Reynolds? Was he really involved in all this?

Regina swallowed the bile rising up her throat and shuddered. She glared after Patrick as he strolled away casually, cursing him to perdition and beyond. But Ida was right. Panicking wouldn't help and neither would getting riled up. The only hope she had of escape was if she stayed calm. So she closed her eyes and took a deep breath, tried not to think of the dark water all around her or how deep it was.

The creaking of timber caused her to flinch. Could a barge splinter and break apart? And if it suddenly filled with water, how long would it take for the boat to sink? How long would it take her to drown? Her heart started pounding with furious vigor and air rushed in and out of her lungs with increasingly short breaths. Her limbs began to shake and her skin felt like it might suffocate her if she didn't escape it.

"Stop," Ida gritted. "Pull yourself together."

Regina could only marvel over the younger woman's ability to maintain her composure, but she might not suffer the same debilitating phobia Regina had struggled against for most of her life. And if it weren't for the water, the truth was that being held captive like this wouldn't be quite as bad. She'd keep her mind sharp and focused. She'd think of some way to get out of this mess, even if it meant killing someone.

But it was as if her brain was filled with an all-consuming darkness that threatened to swallow her up any second. "I can't," she gasped, hating how weak and defeated she sounded. "I'm afraid."

"We all are," Ida told her quietly. "You're not alone in this."

"It's the water," Regina muttered. "I have to get off the water."

Ida turned her head and looked straight at her with the clearest blue eyes she'd ever seen. "There's nothing to fear from the water." She held Regina's gaze until Regina relaxed with sudden understanding. Whatever the water might do to her, it would never be as bad as what she would face at the hands of the man who bought her. So if Carlton didn't come, the river might be the only thing that would save her.

Footsteps approached once more, bringing Patrick with them. He considered the girls before nodding at Ida. A different man than before hauled Ida to her feet, lifted her into his arms and carried her off. Patrick followed, leaving Regina behind with two other girls, both of whom looked just as frightened as she felt.

The procedure for auctioning off the women repeated until only Regina remained. When the same man who'd come to fetch Ida came to collect her as well, she waited until he bent to pick her up, then knocked her head hard against his. He stumbled sideways with a groan and Regina scrambled away, banging one knee against the deck as she stumbled toward the side of the barge. But the railing remained a distant goal as she felt a thick arm reach around her, pulling her forcefully back in the arms of the man she'd tried to escape.

"Little bitch," he spat. "You're lucky I'm not allowed to hit you or I'd have given you several bruises by now." He hoisted her high in his arms and held on tight as he started to walk. "But you'll fetch more blunt if your skin is unblemished. No doubt the man who buys you will want to know he's the only one ever to mark you."

Instinctively, she pressed her thighs together and turned her face away in a pointless attempt at hiding as much of herself as possible. Before she was ready he set her down, and when she straightened, she saw that she was standing on a dais in front of a half dozen well-dressed men. All appeared to be members of the gentry or... Her gaze shifted and her entire body convulsed when she recognized one as someone she'd actually danced with a few weeks earlier. Baron Naughton, Viscount Islington's son, was watching her with cool interest.

"This lovely creature is quite the rarity," Patrick began as he slid one finger along the length of Regina's arm. When she flinched in response, Patrick grinned, right before pushing one hand into her spine while pulling her shoulders back sharply. With a gasp of surprise, Regina did as Patrick intended and arched, pushing her breasts up until they threatened to spill from her bodice.

The men who were watching leaned forward, their hungry eyes fixed upon her like vultures eagerly admiring a carcass that they could devour. Naughton smirked and Regina deliberately looked away from him and the rest of the men. Ida and the other girls who'd been sold were now seated directly behind them, awaiting their departure.

"She's the Earl of Hedgewick's daughter," Patrick continued, "so she won't come cheap and you'll have to make sure that no one finds out that you have her, but I dare say it will be worth it for a taste of her virgin body. We'll start the bidding at one thousand pounds."

Regina froze in response to the staggering sum.

"Two thousand," an older man said.

"Two thousand five hundred," the one sitting next to him muttered.

The numbers increased to five thousand without Naughton saying a word, until the first man's offer of five thousand one hundred seemed to go uncontested.

At which point Naughton casually stated, "Ten thousand pounds." His eyes were pinned on Regina like needles piercing her flesh. A murmur rose from the rest of the men but when none of them chose to counter, Patrick announced that Regina was sold.

Naughton stood and approached, and because she was scared, because she was frightened of what he would do and of what would happen to her if she ended up locked away in his home, she almost missed the thud that came from the stern and the muffled voices that followed. She barely registered the gesture Patrick made to one of his men before Carlton strolled forward, as casually as if he was walking down Bond Street.

He cast a quick glance in Regina's direction, and she saw that he wasn't nearly as composed as he was letting on. The muscles in his face were tense, the smile on his lips completely disingenuous and his eyes as hard as steel.

"What are you doing here?" Patrick asked, his cool façade cracking to reveal his alarm over being found.

"Lookin' fer ye," Carlton murmured. He stared at Patrick and eventually asked, "What the hell are ye thinkin'?"

"That I'm tired of always being third in command with no hope of advancement."

"Are ye stupid?"

Patrick balled his hands into fists. "It's time for me to make it on my own, Guthrie. I want to be a leader, not a follower, and after all the years I've given you, it's clear that the only way to achieve that is to set off on my own."

"And ye decided to do so by causin' harm to young women, did ye?" Carlton cursed under his breath and when he spoke again, his voice was harsh. "Ida is yer friend. And Scarlet…" He glanced around, his gaze lingering only briefly on Regina before moving back to Patrick. "Where's she?"

"I've no idea," Patrick muttered.

Carlton's posture stiffened. "If ye know what's good fer ye, ye'll step back and let me return these girls to their rightful homes."

"Now hold on one moment," one of the buyers began. "You can't just—"

Carlton held up a hand, silencing him without having to utter a word. "Ye know what I'm capable of, Patrick."

Incredibly, Patrick raised his chin. "Yes, I do, but I have you outnumbered. And in any case, you've arrived too late. The girls have already been sold."

"Includin' her ladyship?"

Patrick smiled like the cocky young fool he apparently was. "She was just bought for a grand sum of ten thousand pounds."

"By whom?" Carlton asked, his voice low but clear.

"By me," Naughton said as he came to grab Regina by her arm. She winced in response to the hard grip.

"Let her go," Carlton said, again without any force behind the words, which only made them sound even more threatening.

"So you can have her?"

"Now *there's* a thought," Carlton agreed. He tilted his head to one side, seemingly oblivious to Patrick's men moving in around him. Where were MacNeil and the rest of Carlton's crew? Surely he hadn't come alone?

Naughton laughed. "I'll see you in hell first, Guthrie."

The edge of Carlton's mouth lifted. "I'm more than happy to help ye on yer way."

It was then that Regina spotted the pistol he held at his side, partly concealed by his jacket. He raised it now without any hesitation and fired. Upon which everything descended into chaos.

CHAPTER FIFTEEN

NAUGHTON DROPPED TO HIS KNEES, taking Regina down with him. She landed on her hip with her legs twisted underneath her. All around, men were fighting. She couldn't tell which ones were loyal to Patrick or who Carlton had brought with him, but she did know that she had to move out of the way if she didn't want to get trampled on.

Naughton groaned. His fingers curled into Regina's arm, digging deep until she cried out in pain. "You're mine," he sneered in her ear. Scooting back, he began dragging her across the planking toward the side of the barge, heedless of the wound he'd sustained to his leg.

"Carlton!" Regina screamed for the man who'd come for her as loud as she could.

"Shut up," Naughton warned. Sweat beaded his forehead, and his eyes had taken on a wild look that made Regina's heart tremble in fear.

She chose not to heed him and called out to Carlton again.

A flash of vibrant purple, illuminated by the light from the nearest torches, caught her eye right before something hard struck her forehead.

She fell back only to be jerked forward again and hauled to her feet.

"Let's get her into the dingy," someone – a man who wasn't Naughton – was saying.

A sharp pulsing pain erupted right beneath Regina's brow. Her arm was yanked roughly to one side as she was pushed closer to the railing. She groaned in response to the deep twisting ache and tried to look over her shoulder, tried to shove the man who held her aside, but it was to no avail. He was much stronger than her. And he wasn't alone. A second man was with him and he was helping Naughton.

Beyond the railing was nothing but endless blackness, shimmering like ink in the moonlight. Regina shivered and her heart ricocheted with violent apprehension. "No." She dug in her heels and bent her knees, making her body heavy.

"You don't get a say," Naughton told her with menace. He steadied himself against the man who helped him and glared into her eyes. "Best get used to following orders, darling."

Sickness churned in her stomach, threatening to make its way up her throat. A shout sounded, followed by thuds and then, while Regina watched in utter dismay, a blade, long and wide, flashed in the torchlight.

The man helping Naughton opened his mouth, his eyes widened and started to bulge. A choked sound ground its way over his lips as crimson blood pooled there, trickling over his chin where it started to drip. Regina stared at him in horrified silence until his knees buckled and he sank to a heap on the deck. Right behind where he'd stood was Carlton, the dangerous gleam in his eyes and predatory quirk of his lips the only warning Naughton received before Carlton grabbed him by the back of his neck and slammed his head into the railing.

It happened so quickly the man who held Regina only managed to take one step back before Carlton was on him next, the blade in his hand moving swifter than Regina's eyes were able to follow. The man ground out a curse and started to stagger, but rather than loosen his grip on her arm, he held on tighter.

Carlton reached out toward her, but her assailant managed one rallying blow to Carlton's face right before he lost his balance and fell. Regina went with him, over the railing and into the freezing depths of the Thames.

Ice, like a thousand knives piercing her skin, enveloped her body as it was dragged downward. Panic, the likes of which she hadn't felt since she was a child and the boat she'd been in had tipped over, seized her in its claw. Her gown had caught on the rowlock back then, holding her in a downward position beneath the boat until Marcus had managed to save her. The fact that they'd both survived the incident was something of a miracle, considering the anxious despair with which she'd grabbed at him while he'd been trying to free her.

Responding with mindless terror would not help now either. And yet, with her wrists and ankles bound, Regina could not stop from twisting and turning and tangling herself in her gown. The billowing cotton swirled around her like ghostly seaweed, impairing her movements even further. Her chest tightened and she knew she would soon be forced to inhale. And when she did so, the Thames would claim her forever.

Renewed fear set in and she tried to yank her arms back, every instinct inside her insisting she had to escape the hand that gripped her. But the man with whom she was sinking held on, dragging her further away from safety and straight down to where only death awaited.

There was no time to think, only to act. Driven by reflex and incomprehensible fear, Carlton followed Regina into the water. Dear Mother of God, if she died… His life would be over. It would no longer be worth living.

All rational thought had fled when he'd seen her and the other women on blatant display. The rage that had filled him had been like a poison. It had eaten away at the part of him that might have shown some mercy until he no longer cared who lived or who died. The only thing that mattered was making sure Regina was safe.

But when he'd shot Naughton, the fighting that had commenced had stopped him from reaching her right away. MacNeil, he knew, had managed to get hold of Ida while Claus had helped a young girl make her way to the stern. Meanwhile, the rest of Carlton's crew had fought Patrick's men like marauding pirates attacking a merchant ship. They'd gotten in Carlton's way and now Regina might die because of it – because of a rash decision he'd made in anger.

No.

That wouldn't happen.

He wouldn't allow it to happen.

He'd save her, damn it, or he would die trying.

The water pressed hard against his fingers, resisting his movements as he dove deeper, searching with his hands for something resembling a person. Just knowing how terrified she would be prompted him to force himself forward, even though his lungs were starting to burn. The chance she had of saving herself would be limited when her hands and legs were both tied. This would be a hindrance to even the best swimmer, but detrimental to someone like Regina who couldn't swim at all. Hell, she wouldn't even be able to use her legs as a means of staying afloat.

He reached out blindly and felt something swirl between his fingers. There, then gone. His arms stroked through the water, propelling his body downward until he was able to grab long tendrils of hair and use them to guide himself closer to her body. He caught her, but she was still being pulled down by the man who held her, so Carlton worked on the fingers that clasped her arm, bending them back until they released. With his last remaining strength, he held on tight to her body and pushed himself upward, hoping it wasn't too late.

"Help her," he begged Blayne when the big man had managed to get them both back on the barge. Things had quieted down and Carlton fleetingly noticed that Patrick was tied to a chair while most of his men were lying on the deck, either dead or wounded. The rest had been gagged and bound like him.

Cursing the traitorous bastard, he returned his attention to Regina and hastily removed his jacket so he could throw it over her exposed body. Blayne had her belly down on the deck and was pushing against her back while Carlton struggled to catch his breath.

He'd never been a religious man, had never set foot in a church or put much stock in the power of prayer. So he wasn't sure how to ask an invisible force for assistance. Yet somehow, driven by desperation, he managed a silent plea that he hoped to God would save her.

Please. Don't take her from me just yet.

Scooting closer to her, he placed his hand on her head and carefully stroked her hair back while Blayne kept trying to push the water she'd swallowed out of her body. A knot tightened his throat and his eyes began to sting.

Please. She's the most important part of my miserable life

"We need to tilt her," Blayne said.

Disregarding his own weakened state, Carlton helped him hold her just so.

Please. Let her live so I can tell her how much she means to me. So I can—

A sputter and a cough caused her body to quake. She pushed up onto her forearm but lost the strength quickly and collapsed back onto the deck. A rush of relief swept through Carlton. He blew out the breath he'd been holding and grinned as he pulled her toward him.

He looked up at Blayne. "Thank ye."

Blayne muttered something low and inaudible, then said more loudly. "We should get her back to

The Black Swan so she can warm up."

"Give me yer jacket," Carlton told him. It was dry while the one he'd draped over Regina was wet and cold.

Blayne didn't even blink. He just did as Carlton asked and soon Regina was bundled up in the Scotsman's large woolen garment. Carlton made sure that she was as comfortable as she could be under the circumstances before getting up and going to where Patrick sat. Water dripped from Carlton's hair and ran over his face. His clothes were pasted to his skin and a chattering chill was beginning to attack his bones, but answers were needed and he would get them before he left here this night.

"Why'd ye do this?" he asked.

Patrick glared at him and Carlton saw both contempt and regret in the young man's eyes. "It seemed like a good way to get ahead."

"Have I not treated ye well then?" Carlton stared back at him. "If ye were unhappy, why the hell did ye not come and talk to me, Patrick? I'd 'ave listened."

"Maybe. But you would always have been my superior."

Sighing with the realization that he'd tried to do what he himself had once done to Bartholomew, Carlton chose to ask a different question. "Where's Scarlet?"

Patrick's jaw twitched and anger rose up in Carlton once more as he realized the lad had lied to him earlier and that he actually knew the answer. Stepping forward, he prepared to grab Patrick by his throat, but the fury in his eyes must have warned Patrick not to keep silent.

"Reynolds has her," he blurted.

Carlton stared into Patrick's terrified eyes. "I'd like to kill ye for what ye've done."

"Please. I'll do anything you ask." Patrick no longer looked like the coldhearted villain who'd sold young girls to a fate worse than death, but like the helpless boy he'd once found in an alley, shivering cold and starving.

Carlton reached for the dagger he kept in his boot and held it to Patrick's throat. "Ye know what I think of those who abuse women and children."

Patrick gulped. "I didn't do anything myself. I just...I just..."

"Ye facilitated rape, Patrick. That's not somethin' I can ever fergive." Carlton pressed the dagger into his flesh until blood began pooling around the blade.

"Wait. Please. I—"

"Carlton." Regina's voice was faint, but firm. His name, a desperate plea drifting through the night air, stilled his movements. "Don't do this."

"He doesn't deserve to live," Carlton gritted.

"Perhaps not. But if you kill him, you risk your own life." She was silent a moment, then added, "What sense is there in that?"

She was right. If he died now before killing Hedgewick, everything he'd worked for most of his life would be for nothing. Frustrated by this knowledge, Carlton turned away in disgust so he could address Claus. "I'm goin' to send Blayne to Bow Street as soon as we get back to The Black Swan. He'll make sure some runners, per'aps even the chief magistrate himself, come out here to handle this mess. Can ye and the rest of the men manage until then?"

Claus nodded. "Aye." He glanced sideways for a second. "What about the rest of the girls and young women – the ones we don't know?"

"Philipa can put them up at Amourette's until their families are found. I know it's not ideal, but it's goin' to be a hell of a lot better than what they've recently gone through."

"I agree." Claus called out instructions and turned back to Carlton. "We won't let you down."

Satisfied with this piece of knowledge, Carlton went to gather Regina in his arms. He might be wet and exhausted and close to getting seriously ill, but he would be damned if he'd let another man near her right now. Somehow he'd find that extra bit of strength required to see her safely back to The Black Swan himself.

CHAPTER SIXTEEN

SHE WAS SUBMERGED IN SOMETHING so wonderfully warm that it soothed every limb and made blood flow more easily through all her veins. Inhaling, Regina breathed in what felt like hot steam and then sighed, expelling it slowly. Perhaps she was dreaming? Perhaps the Thames had swallowed her up and she was now dead – floating lightly without any burdens to weigh her down.

Something rippled against her side, stirring her conscience. Was someone with her? She leaned back into the mass that carefully buoyed her body. Her awareness rose and she suddenly recognized that cool distinction between wet and dry, the feel of liquid pressing upon her and the gentle splashes it made as she moved.

"No." She jerked upright, fully alert, her arms and legs thrashing about as her bottom slid forward and her head almost went down under the surface in her moment of panic.

Something firm wound its way around her and pulled her back, holding her steady in a solid embrace. "Easy now." The low murmur in her ear was wonderfully soothing. "Just lean against me an' relax. Ye're safe now, Regina, but ye need to get warm. We both do."

Swallowing, she forced her brain to focus on Carlton's coaxing voice and on the feel of his body so close to hers, of his arms and legs caging her in. She inhaled again and savored the warmth for a moment before she opened her eyes. They were in his parlor at The Black Swan, submerged in water that filled a large tub. Her back rested on his chest, her head on his shoulder.

He shifted and one of his knees poked out of the water. Regina stared at it until it disappeared once again beneath the surface. But seeing it made her realize what she'd not yet been aware of – what her muddled mind had refused to register. And as she focused her thoughts more fully, she finally had to ask, "Are we naked?"

Her question was met by silence at first. And then, "It's better than catchin' our deaths, wouldn't ye say?"

She wasn't sure she understood what he was talking about. "Why would we do that?" She was naked in a tub of water with Carlton Guthrie. And he was naked as well.

Her cheeks started to burn, and not because of the steam in the air.

"Ye don't remember fallin' into the water?" One of his arms tightened around her middle and pulled her back into his body more firmly. Possessively.

She swallowed and tried to relax in spite of her chagrin. No man had ever seen her undressed and to think that he had, without her permission no less and while she'd been unconscious, caused mortification to sweep through her.

"I need to get up," she said, then thought of something, "and you need to close your eyes."

"They are closed," he murmured.

"But surely you must have seen...um...something. I mean...you—"

"I wasn't really paying attention to yer body, if that's yer concern."

Well. That comment wasn't nearly as uplifting as it should have been. Clearing her throat, she repeated her previous statement. "I need to get up."

"I nearly lost ye," he said, ignoring her comment.

Frowning, she tried to recall what had happened, but her memory was blurry. "I remember you shooting Naughton and then stabbing the man who was helping him stand."

"Aye."

He growled the word in a way that caused shivers to race down Regina's spine. It wasn't unpleasant. Which surprised her somewhat. Should watching him kill a man not repulse her?

Not if he'd done it to save her life, she supposed. Not when the men he'd hurt had been eager to harm young women and girls in the worst ways possible.

"You jumped in the river and saved me?" She suddenly remembered how wet he'd been when he'd gone to face Patrick. And how weak and unstable she'd felt on her legs.

One hand reached up to caress her jaw. His moustache grazed her skin as he lowered his mouth to her ear. "I sure as 'ell wasn't goin' to let ye drown," he told her roughly and pressed a firm kiss to her temple.

"Did I faint?"

"Aye. Hit yer head on the barge deck before I was able to catch ye." He sighed. "I'm sorry about that, Regina. I'm sorry fer all that ye've been through today."

"It wasn't your fault."

"Nevertheless," he grumbled.

Although she hated the water and longed to escape it, she forced herself to relax against Carlton. Nothing would happen to her in this bath. Not as long as he was with her. He'd keep her safe. Of that she was certain. So she closed her eyes and savored the soothing warmth the water offered and the comfort she felt being held in his arms. Did it really matter if they weren't wearing clothes or if he'd undressed her and seen her naked?

No, she decided. This was the man she wanted to be with in every way that mattered. And maybe now, in this intimate state they were in, she would finally make him surrender to what she knew they both wanted.

So she twisted around, causing the water to rise and fall with larger ripples until it splashed over the sides of the tub. "This is rather awkward," she said, not the least bit pleased by the hindrance in movement the narrow space provided.

"What on earth are ye tryin' to do, woman?"

"I want to face you."

"Face me?" His voice was slightly strangled, no doubt because of her knee pushing into his thigh. As if intending to steady her movements, he moved one large hand and brought it up under her bottom.

Regina's eyes widened with immediate surprise. Hovering over him, she saw that he was a little stunned too. Perhaps if she lowered herself...

She brought her face closer to his and he tightened his grip, curling his fingers into her flesh and holding her steady. Yes...this could work... just like one of the pictures she'd seen in his book.

Heart pounding, she pressed her mouth to his and placed one hand on his shoulder. But when she attempted to settle herself in his lap, he fought her downward progress while kissing her back. "I won't let ye make a mistake," he murmured against her lips even as he claimed her mouth with possessive force.

She tried to run her hand between them, to touch him as she so desperately longed for him to touch her, but he pushed her away every time, fighting off her advances until she was overcome by exhaustion. Falling back on her haunches, she braced herself against the opposite end of the tub and stared at him. "Being with you would never be a mistake, Carlton."

His eyes darkened, revealing the need he felt for her too, before returning to their natural shade. "Ye should rest." And as if it were the most natural thing in the world, he stood, offering her a full view of his glorious body.

The blatant display made her feel less confident than she had seconds earlier, so she averted her gaze and waited for him to dry off. Instead, she found herself hauled up into his arms as he lifted her out of the tub. Instinctively, she squealed, earning her a chuckle.

"I'm sorry," he said, "but it's too late fer modesty now." He set her on her feet near the fire and reached for a towel. Moving to stand behind her, he draped it over her shoulders, pressed a soft kiss to the side of her neck and then disappeared into the bedroom.

When he returned, he was wearing a shirt and a pair of breeches. "I brought yer nightgown," he said and promptly dropped the garment over her head.

Caught off guard, Regina swayed to one side and was happy to feel his steadying hand at her elbow. She yawned. Perhaps he was right after all. Today had been rather taxing and rest would no doubt do them both good. "Will you stay with me," she asked, the sudden idea of him leaving her sending a new dart of panic straight through her. "I don't want to be alone right now."

"Of course, luv." He helped her push her arms through the sleeves of the nightgown and lower it over her hips before taking the towel away. "We'll get some rest together."

When Regina woke later, she was uncovered, so she pulled the blanket up over her shoulder, rolled onto her side and reached for Carlton. But the space he'd occupied earlier was now cold and vacant, instilling in her a sense of loss that pushed back the comfort she'd found in his arms and reminded her of the horrid experience she'd had on the barge. She recalled Patrick's men looking their fill, Naughton's greedy expression, the dreadful weight of the water dragging her down.

The recollection brought tears to her eyes. So many men had watched her, stared at her, drooled over what had been poorly hidden beneath the thin veil of the dress she'd been given. And they'd imagined... Those men who had bid on her hadn't reigned in their despicable thoughts. She'd seen it in their eyes, especially in Naughton's. The things he'd been planning made drowning look like a fine experience.

"Oh God."

How would she ever get past the shame?

The creaking of floorboards informed her that someone had entered the room. She swallowed and pressed her face into the pillow, hiding her tears. The mattress dipped and a solid hand settled upon her head, the fingers stroking easily over her hair in a way that made her cry harder. "Patrick sold me, Carlton..." She gasped for air between sobs. "He sold me to Naughton who wanted to... to..." She couldn't make herself say it, the thought of it alone, of what would have happened to her if Carlton hadn't arrived in time so sickening it made her heave.

"It's all right, luv. None of those people will ever harm ye again." Carlton wiped the tears from her eyes with his thumb, then bent to kiss her closed eyelids. "Patrick an' his crew have been rounded up an' hauled off to Newgate."

"But what about you?" she choked out. "Wha — what will happen to you?"

"Because of the men I killed?" She nodded so violently that her forehead made contact with his thigh. His hand stroked down over her neck and across her shoulders. "Agh. I'll be fine. When the magistrate stopped by an hour ago to inquire about the events, I told 'im the truth. As the rational man he is, he accepts that I did what was necessary in order to save the women who'd been taken."

"What about Ida? What about the others?"

"They're all safe."

"And Scarlet?" She clutched at his sleeve as fresh tears spilled down her cheeks.

"She's safe as well, luv. Philipa's takin' care of her."

Regina choked down a sob and then managed to say, "You were right about Reynolds. I can't believe he would be involved with this sort of thing. He always seemed so nice, so amicable and...and decent."

"The worst monsters generally do," he told her grimly, then altered his tone to a brighter one. "I brought ye somethin' to eat an' drink. Can ye sit?"

Regina wasn't quite ready to do so. She liked the position she was in with the blanket keeping her warm, her head nestled close to Carlton and his hand moving over her body like she was a cat he was petting. But she also knew that she needed to replenish her energy and that the best way to do so was with food. So she pushed the blanket aside just enough to let her scoot up against the pillows until she reclined in a partial sitting position. Light from an oil lamp placed on the dresser cast the room in a warm yellow hue. It allowed Regina to see Carlton's face and to see the concern that marred his features.

He held a piece of ham to her mouth and she

bit into it with a sudden hunger that was likely brought on by its smoky smell. "Good girl." The edge of his mouth drew up at one side in what looked like the beginnings of a smile.

Regina swallowed the morsel, then another and a third before he gave her some wine to drink. When she'd had a few sips he gave her some cheese followed by a plum cut into halves and then some more wine.

"Thank you." She held his gaze.

"Ye're welcome." A tumultuous emotion she couldn't put words to appeared on his face. He moved, as if preparing to stand, but Regina reached out. Her hand closed tightly around his wrist, forcing him to stay.

"I didn't like finding you gone."

"I wasn't able to sleep," he confessed.

"Another bad dream?"

He shook his head. "Just a series of unpleasant thoughts."

She knew what he meant as she stared up at him, at this man who had killed in order to save her. "Please don't go." The words were just a soft whisper, easily ignored. But Carlton didn't do so. He set the plate and glass aside on the table next to the bed and turned more fully toward her. Her grip on his wrist went slack and she eased back against the pillows. "Don't leave me alone with mine."

Understanding flashed in his eyes and he said nothing further. He just kicked off his shoes and pulled back the covers so he could climb into the bed beside her. He nudged her gently until she turned, then pulled her back against his chest, giving her warmth and that wonderful sense of security only he could provide.

The rich scent of sandalwood filled her nostrils as she breathed him in. One hand settled on her hip while the other one snuck beneath her, offering her head an extra bit of support. His breath fanned over the back of her neck, heating her insides while his heart beat a steady rhythm that chased all her terrible memories away.

"There's still a few hours until mornin'," he murmured. "Ye should probably try to get some more rest."

"Will you sleep as well?"

"I'm goin' to try."

The low rumble of his voice was remarkably calming. She closed her eyes and attempted to do as he suggested, only to find her thoughts moving back to Patrick, the barge, the young girls who'd been there and the men...those lecherous men with their horrid intentions. And then the water...

On the edge between waking and sleeping, she felt the fear of drowning once more. Her body twitched in response and she gasped.

A firm hand pressed down into her thigh. "Shhh...Ye're all right, Regina. Ye're with me now."

The tension in her body eased in response to his soothing tone. Shifting, she turned toward him until she was on her back and was able to reach for his hand. When she opened her eyes to remind herself she was no longer on the barge, she was met by his darker gaze. The light from the oil lamp revealed flecks of gold that anchored her mind and reminded her that she was safe.

"Carlton." She spoke his name with as much determination as someone who was hanging off a cliff might use to grasp at a rope.

"Regina." He didn't move but held himself utterly still.

Her heart beat loud against her breast. Nerves bundled together in her belly. He'd kissed her before, several times in fact, including in the bath-tub while they'd both been naked. But nothing had ever come of those kisses. He'd always broken it off before either of them could get carried away.

Yet she sensed that if they kissed again now there would be no retreat – no going back. He'd surrender and so would she, and then they'd be bound together forever. Because it would show him that she accepted his actions, that what he'd done was all right and that no matter what, she needed him more than she'd ever need anyone else.

And since this was the absolute truth, there was no choice for her but to do as she wished. So she reached for him with every hope that she had for the future, with every dream she had in her heart, and with all the love that she harbored for this incredible man.

He didn't resist, and then his mouth was on hers, his soft lips moving beneath the moustache, just as perfectly as they always did. He kissed her as if she were some distant star that he hoped to capture forever, as if she was everything he'd ever wanted and a dream he hoped to hold on to.

"Please," she gasped while meeting his mouth with hunger and longing. "I need you."

"Christ, Regina." He deepened the kiss and pulled her closer. With aching slowness, his hand moved over her thigh, bunching her nightgown a little. "I will not take ye," he muttered, so low she barely heard him.

"Not even if I ask you to?"

His only response was a harder kiss than before, both fierce and possessive – the sort that informed her that she was his. At least for this moment in time. So she wound her arms around his neck and allowed her fingers to brush through his hair while his hand crept over her hip.

He paused there, for what felt like forever, until finally, blessedly, he decided to tend to her need. A helpless whimper rose from her throat the moment he touched her, carefully, reverently, with hands that must have been kissed by magic.

"Carlton…"

"Yes, luv?" His voice was low and sensual. "Do ye not like this?"

He found a spot that caused light to flash behind her eyes as pleasure shot through her veins. "No. I mean yes." She clutched at his shirt while sensations that left her in awe rushed through her.

Grinning like the scoundrel he was, Carlton pressed his mouth to hers once again while she, wanton that she apparently was, gave herself up to his ministrations. But when she reached for the placket of his breeches, he pushed her hands away. "I said I wouldn't take yer innocence, Regina, and that's a promise I plan to keep."

"But, Carlton. I want to…"

"No," he told her firmly. And before she was able to argue further, he caught her wrists with his free hand and pinned them against the bed while continuing to use his other to slake her body's wild cravings.

Regina gasped, partly from shock and dismay, but mostly because of the pleasure building inside her. It was more intense than anything else she'd ever known, like flames being stoked into an inferno. And when she cried out his name seconds later while ecstasy claimed her, she knew the experience was one she would cherish forever.

CHAPTER SEVENTEEN

PROPPED ON HIS FOREARM, CARLTON watched the woman who slept in his bed. She'd cracked his chest wide open and left him vulnerable to the worst kind of heartache imaginable. He knew this because of how close he'd come to losing her. In that moment of uncertainty, when the balance could have tipped either way, he'd learned what hell really was: a world without Regina in it.

His heart beat now, slow and steady. It expanded each time her eyelashes fluttered against her cheeks, whenever she muttered something in response to the dream she was having, and as she snuggled closer to where he was resting. This innocent woman, so different from him that she might as well be a mythical creature, had walked into the darkness he'd lived in for twenty years and filled it with sunshine.

Oh, how he wished he could make her his forever.

He sighed in response to the gnawing ache that was building inside him. If Hedgewick hadn't done what he'd done, Carlton could have grown up to court her properly, in a glittering ballroom just like she deserved.

Leaning in, he ignored the tight squeeze of his throat and pressed a kiss to her brow. It wasn't just his life her father had stolen that day twenty years ago, but hers as well. She could have lived up to her parents' expectations and married the heir to a dukedom. She could have married *him*.

But now…

He shook his head to rid himself of such a fanciful notion. Eventually, justice would come to call at his door and when it did, he wanted Regina gone.

In the meantime however, he'd do his best to make sure she never forgot him.

So he kissed her again, waking her gently with sweet caresses until she reached out and drew him closer. "Good mornin', luv." His hand moved between her thighs, giving her all that he could while punishing himself with restraint. The way she responded to him alone, with gasps and moans, was almost enough to make him spend. Hell, his body ached for it in a way it had never ached before.

But he resisted. Even as he watched her give up control and welcome the onslaught of pleasure.

Instead, he withdrew his hand and claimed her mouth. He kissed her with every bit of need bursting through him, showing her exactly what he craved without using words and without any added touch. When he finally broke the kiss and stood, she was as breathless as he, her cheeks flushed and her lips slightly swollen.

Eyes the most perfect shade of sapphire blue gazed back at him in wonder. And then she said the one thing capable of bringing him to his knees. "What about you?"

"I'll be fine," he told her gruffly, his voice like gravel.

"I don't think—"

"There's no need for further discussion."

"But I would like to—"

"No!" Whatever it was she'd like to do, he didn't want to hear it. Just the very idea of her touching him as he'd touched her or... "No," he repeated and turned away, his muscles bunched tight across his shoulders, his hands clenched into a pair of hard fists that would drive the very devil away. He crossed to the parlor and grabbed a half-empty glass of brandy from the night before. Downing the remainder of the liquid, he appreciated the biting effect it had on his tongue and the burn it created in his throat.

Directing his mind toward Hedgewick, to that moment in time when he'd realized he'd lost his father forever, he felt his arousal ease and abate. Christ, the effect Regina had on him... He glanced over his shoulder and saw she was now in the process of dressing. There was something intimate about that, about watching her pull up her stockings and tie her stays. Perhaps because he'd never watched any other woman do so. The women he'd had in the past had always risen after he'd gone downstairs. They'd taken the money he'd left for them on the nightstand and let themselves out without any words of parting.

So this was different. Not only because he would never treat Regina like she was a whore, but because it felt like they were already husband and wife.

He shook himself to banish such a ridiculous notion. But not before he recognized the danger she posed to his heart. Here was a woman with the power to destroy him in ways no one else would ever be able to do.

She turned slightly while pushing her arms through the sleeves. The fabric fell easily over her hips and knees until it reached all the way to her toes. Nimbly, she went to work on the fastenings while he, besotted fool that he was, stood mesmerized.

"I'd like ye with me today," he said, the words escaping his mouth before his brain was finished processing them.

Her eyes met his, the surprise there as great as his. What the devil had he just said?

"Downstairs?" she asked as if needing clarification.

He nodded, his body apparently choosing to act on its own accord. "Ye've been here fer three weeks and until ye receive word from Yates…" He paused when she looked away and mentally kicked himself for his insensitivity. Clearing his throat, he then said, "I think it's time fer us to risk it, unless ye want to stay up here ferever."

"I'd rather not."

"Very well then. It's settled." Part of his brain warned him not to do this, but he ignored it. After almost losing her yesterday, and after showing her what her body was capable of, the bond that had forged between them was too close for him to consider leaving her upstairs alone all day. He wanted her by his side where he could see her. But there was also the chance of her being recognized, and a selfish part of him wondered if that might not be for the best.

There was no doubt in his mind that her discovery would bring about certain events – events he no longer had the strength to put into motion himself. Partly because he was loathe to part with her and partly because he didn't want to see her hurt. But he'd waited twenty years for this chance to seek revenge on behalf of his father and he'd known her less than a month. To dismiss this singular goal for her was something he knew he would live to regret. So he was torn, unable to act, unless the decision to do so was made for him.

Grimly, he decided that he would let fate lead the way.

Regina looked down into the courtyard at the man who had the ability to make the tips of her fingers tingle. The taproom was filled to capacity as usual, mostly with rowdy men eager to recover from a hard day's work. Some had brought their wives but most were there with friends, eating supper and playing either cards or dice. The smell of ale and roast meat hung thick in the air.

Earlier, before coming up here, Regina had seen a couple of Amourette's girls. They'd been lounging lazily in a pair of armchairs that stood toward the front of The Black Swan while waiting for potential clients to make their approach. Of greater interest to Regina, was the fight about to start outside. Although Carlton had told her she mustn't go into the courtyard to watch, he allowed her to view it from the walkway above.

One week. That was how long it had been since he'd rescued her from the barge. In that time, she'd slept with him every night, falling into a blissful slumber after having her wanton needs sated in ways that would once have made her blush. Now she just craved.

Last night had been no different, but although she always insisted he let her reciprocate the favor, he firmly denied her each time. Why, she wasn't sure, but the fact that he kept on doing so made it feel like a lump of lead had been placed in her heart. It detracted from the experience, denying her the chance to show him how deeply she loved him.

For she could not tell him. Her courage did not reach quite that far. Not when she didn't think he loved her in return. Cared for her, yes, but loved her? No. Surely he'd offer to marry her if he did, regardless of what he'd initially told her. But there was no indication that he would even consider making that sort of commitment, so she knew, as much as it pained her, that whatever they had would probably not last forever.

The fight began with one boxer punching the other squarely in the face. The crowd cheered, loving the action. Carlton stood on a platform nearby. Dressed in a navy blue velvet jacket, coffee colored breeches and shiny black boots, he looked more dashing than ever as he kept track of the proceedings and accepted bets. The first boxer to take a punch charged his opponent and pummeled him mercilessly until he collapsed on the ground. The crowd roared and additional bets were placed. Carlton glanced up toward her and touched the brim of his hat, acknowledging her presence for the first time since he'd arrived in the courtyard.

A flutter erupted deep in her belly and rose up inside her until it surrounded her heart with a pulsing awareness that made her feel slightly light-headed. She smiled at him and dipped her chin, holding his gaze for a drawn-out minute until he was forced to turn away and return his attention to the match.

Tonight, she promised herself, she'd find a way to convey her love for him then, even if she had to tie him to the bed. Her lips drew to one side, curling upward. Now there was an intriguing thought. Having Carlton spread out before her like a feast to be savored was even more thrilling than the prospect of what he might do to her next.

It was so inspiring she allowed her mind to focus more fully on the idea for a moment and almost missed the arrival of a new spectator. But the profile, though only briefly glimpsed and now hidden from view, caused her stomach to tighten with unmistakable recognition.

Marcus.

Regina swallowed and gripped the railing in front of her while following him with her eyes. He skirted the edge of the crowd as if searching for something. Dressed in a perfectly tailored jacket that showcased his broad shoulders and solid chest, he was the only man present besides Carlton who looked like he drank from fine crystal glasses and slept with an eiderdown quilt. Which he did.

Regina knew she should turn away, that if she stayed where she was her brother would likely see her. But seeing him, so familiar and yet somehow estranged, was a shock. It froze her in place and stopped her from moving.

His head turned left, right. One of the boxers managed to place a jab under his opponent's chin. The man staggered and fell, eliciting a cry from the crowd. But Marcus didn't seem to notice. He appeared to be focused on something else.

Regina's stomach clenched, the muscles holding on tight while the air in her lungs pressed outward. It wanted to escape but she could not recall how to breathe.

And then Marcus turned, his chin rose toward the sky and his eyes locked with hers. Surprise lit his face while horror sped through her limbs. Time slowed. It felt like she was back underwater, sinking into endless darkness, until she heard her brother's voice calling her name.

Regina regained her mobility and took a step back, watching as confusion overtook the relief she'd just witnessed upon his face.

She shifted her gaze to Carlton and saw that he'd noticed her brother's presence. He gestured to MacNeil and together they approached Marcus. Regina edged closer to the solid stability of a wooden pillar supporting the overhang that covered the walkway. She leaned against it and tried to slow her breaths. Marcus appeared to grow more incensed, eyeing her while he spoke in what looked like a clipped tone, judging from the tight set of his mouth. But then Carlton said something – oh, how she wished the crowd still watching the fight would be quiet so she had a chance of hearing the exchange – and Marcus gave a curt nod before following him inside The Black Swan.

Regina sagged against the pillar and blew out a breath. What had Carlton said? Where were the two of them going?

Heavy steps sounded upon the stairs, and her heart convulsed with anxious uncertainty. She pressed her palm to her belly in a pointless attempt at calming the clamoring nerves that were twisting and turning like a fretful creature. The door to the parlor was only a few steps away. If she hurried, she could retreat there before the person approaching found her standing here. Because whoever it was and whatever they wanted, she instinctively knew it wouldn't be good.

MacNeil turned the corner and came to a halt. "Guthrie would like you to join him in his study."

She shook her head. Marcus would be there and he'd want to take her home. How could she tell him she didn't want to go? How could she face him after all the worry she must have caused him? How could she possibly explain that this was where she now belonged?

"I don't want to," she whispered. "Please don't make me."

Sympathy eased the hard determination in Mac-Neil's dark eyes. "I'm sorry, my lady, but I cannae go against Guthrie's wishes." He gestured toward the stairs. "Please."

"My brother won't leave here without me."

MacNeil stared back at her for a long moment and then he said, "You must have faith that all will turn out as it should. You must believe in Guthrie."

Swallowing, Regina took a sharp breath. Why

hadn't Carlton turned her brother away? He could have done so, but instead he'd invited him in. She didn't understand his reasoning and that only made her more apprehensive. But to stay up here, quaking with fear and unwilling to show her face when he'd asked for her presence, would not only make her a coward, it would also show a lack of trust in the man she loved.

So she cast one last glance at the parlor door beckoning for her to seek refuge, and followed MacNeil downstairs. When she reached Carlton's study, he and her brother both rose from the chairs in which they'd been sitting.

"Regina." Marcus rushed toward her and swept her into a tight embrace. Her arms went around him and although she worried what would happen next, she could not resist the familiar comfort he offered, and hugged him back fiercely. "Thank God, I've finally found you."

"Oh, Marcus. I really wish you hadn't," she said as he set her back on her feet. Somehow, she'd find a way to explain to him that she couldn't come with him.

He looked confused. "What are you talking about?" Holding his gaze, she watched as understanding dawned in the depths of his chestnut colored eyes. Pity followed as he carefully said, "I'm sorry, Regina, but you can't stay here with Guthrie."

"It's where I belong now, Marcus. I cannot go home and face Papa." She took a deep breath. "I'm not the same woman I was before I came here – the sort who'd give up her own happiness just to make a convenient match. Not when my heart wants something else."

Marcus tightened his jaw and glared at Carlton. "You've ruined her, you—" He cut himself off as he glanced at Regina.

"Her innocence remains intact," Carlton told him smoothly.

"You know that's not what I'm talking about." Marcus pulled Regina back into his arms and whispered close to her ear, "Why does it have to be him?" She couldn't give a brief answer, so she remained silent instead. He sighed, gave her a squeeze and then said, "You cannot imagine how terrified I've been these last weeks. Have you any idea what you put me through?"

"I sent a letter to let you know I was safe," she told him as they broke apart.

Marcus frowned, his expression a mixture of incredulity and what could only be described as controlled anger. "The only news Father and I received about you came from him." He pointed at Guthrie while steely disdain darkened his eyes. "The scoundrel wrote that you would find comfort with him in his bed!"

Regina flinched. "What?" She glanced at Carlton with incomprehension, then back at her brother. "No. I don't believe you."

Marcus stared at her, then reached inside his breast pocket and retrieved two rumpled pieces of paper that looked like they had been folded and unfolded thousands of times. Regina took them and read while the beat of her pulse grew increasingly unsteady. Until she reached the end of the second letter. A nervous laugh escaped her. "These are both signed V.S." She handed the letters back to her brother. "Whoever wrote them, it wasn't Guthrie." But if it wasn't him, then who? And what was that bit about her father's past sins? Nothing made any sense.

As if following her line of thought, Marcus stared back at her. "I'm guessing he used the V.S. to throw us off and keep us from finding you sooner. But Guthrie wrote those letters, Regina."

Regina laughed. This was ridiculous. "How can you possibly know that?" Carlton might be capable of hurting those who deserved it, but he'd never use her like this. Not when he cared for her as he did. "How can you be so sure?"

Marcus gazed down at her with endless regret. "Because he just told me."

She shook her head, unwilling to accept what Marcus was saying and turned to Carlton in search of the truth. What she found, was a schooled expression that lacked all emotion. "Yer brother is right."

Unsettling quivers scurried down her spine. "I don't understand. What about the letter I asked you to send to Marcus? What happened to that?"

Carlton glanced at MacNeil who stood with his arms crossed next to the door. His answer was precise. "It's upstairs in my room."

"No." Regina pressed her palm to her forehead. Marcus reached out to steady her, his hand at her elbow as he guided her over to the chair he'd been sitting in before she arrived. She sank down onto the seat then looked at Carlton. "The only thing that mattered to me when I came here was making sure Marcus wouldn't worry. You promised you'd send him that letter and instead…" Instead, he'd sent a taunting threat. And just like that, she grasped hold of the only possible explanation. "You used me to blackmail my father, didn't you?"

He stared back at her as if she were a stranger, as if she meant nothing to him. And the heart that had swelled with increasing love for him shattered in anguish.

"What about the letters I wrote to Fielding and Yates?"

When Carlton kept quiet, MacNeil slowly said, "They were never delivered either."

"But…" She blinked rapidly. "I was told Fielding had no interest in forming an attachment with me because he was already courting another young lady."

"A mere fabrication," MacNeil said.

Dear God. Regina's hand clasped the armrest and held on tight while the world she knew spun out of control. "You never meant to let me leave. Did you? You made me stay by letting me think Marcus knew I was safe, that Fielding wasn't an option for me, and that Yates…" She'd not thought of him in over a week, she'd been so distracted by Carlton. Her eyes began to burn with hot tears as she realized how far he'd gone to deceive her. He'd kissed her, touched her in ways she'd never been touched before and made her feel cherished.

But he didn't rob you of your innocence. Even though he could have.

He made it clear that you wouldn't have a future together.

He told you that there was a lot you did not know about him.

And he seemed to believe it would push you away if

you ever found out.

"What does V.S. stand for?" she asked, feeling numb.

"They're just letters," Carlton told her coolly. "Meant to throw yer family off me scent."

Regina glanced at a granite paperweight sitting on top of his desk and wondered if now would be the appropriate time to throw it at him. She dug her nails into the armrest and tried to stay calm. "What's the connection between you and my father?" In retrospect, he'd seemed to get angry whenever they'd spoken of him. "What sin are you referring to?"

"He knows what he did and that's all that matters. Keepin' ye here an' makin' him squirm is nothin' compared with his own misdeeds." He turned away, giving her his back and infuriating her further.

She stood, rounded the desk and stepped right before him so he had no choice but to face her. "You didn't answer me before when I asked if you were using me to blackmail him."

A nerve ticked at the edge of his mouth. It was the only indication that her words affected him in some way. "Blackmail wasn't my goal." And there was that voice again, soft and different, like that of a man who'd been raised in an affluent home. But then it was gone, hardened by some sort of inner determination when he spoke next. "Torturin' yer father a little before he an' I meet again was what I was aimin' fer. I've no doubt in me mind he'll come find me now, an' when he does, I'll be ready."

"For what?"

He seemed to stare straight through her, his dark eyes piercing her soul. "To take revenge."

Regina gasped, just enough for Carlton to blink. "Why?"

He seemed to focus more fully on her this time and for a brief second, he looked bewildered, like a lost boy uncertain of which way to go. But then he shuttered the expression and said, "Because 'e stole from me, and no one does that without payin' the price."

A shiver raked her body. She'd seen firsthand what he was capable of – the sort of punishment he delivered to those who crossed him. He'd killed men in front of her eyes. But he'd also saved her, cared for and comforted her. Aligning the two men was not so simple. He'd been fair when it came to the men on the barge. She'd believed they deserved what they got, especially because they were guilty of trading in women and children for their own sexual gratification. Monsters. That was what Carlton had killed.

But her father wasn't like that. While he might be misguided where she was concerned, he was still good and kind and would never harm anyone else. "You're wrong," was all she could think to say.

That nerve at the edge of his mouth twitched again. "I wish I was, but I was there when 'e did it. I saw 'im with me own eyes. I..." He gave his attention to Marcus. "Take 'er 'ome. Make sure she's safe. And tell yer father what ye've discovered."

"No." Regina refused to move. She needed answers, but more than anything she needed to breach this hard shell Carlton had chosen to encase himself in. His remoteness was unsettling and… Did she really mean nothing to him?

It didn't seem possible. Not when considering the fear he'd shown when he'd thought he might lose her. Surely that couldn't have been but an act?

She studied him, hoping she'd find the answer in his expression. But the cold detachment she saw there only crushed her spirit more.

"Go," he told her sternly. "I no longer need ye."

The words had the desired effect if what he meant was to hurt her. She took a step back. "Why are you doing this?"

His jaw tightened. "Because I have to. Now get out."

Determined to maintain some sense of dignity, Regina raised her chin and pushed back her shoulders. "Fine." She spun away and crossed to where Marcus stood waiting. Together, they headed for the door, but before she reached it, she turned back to say one last thing. "Know this, Carlton Guthrie, Scoundrel of St. Giles: I love you. No matter what you decide to do."

CHAPTER EIGHTEEN

CARLTON COULDN'T MOVE. HE STARED at the door through which Regina had vanished and did his best to just breathe. Blinking, he struggled to wade through the mess his mind was in. "Did she just say what I think she said?"

"I don't know," MacNeil murmured. "I suppose that depends on what it is you think she said."

Carlton frowned and forced his gaze to MacNeil who was looking at him with what appeared to be innocent uncertainty. But Carlton knew better and his frowned deepened as a result. "I did the right thing," he grumbled, even though his chest felt hollow. The heart Regina had brought back to life had hardened and crumbled within the last hour.

"Of course," MacNeil said.

Carlton eyed him once more. "She'll be better off with her family."

"Mmm...hmm."

"It was nice having her here for a while, but we both knew it couldn't last. I told her that. I made sure she knew right from the start that she'd have to leave me one day."

"Leave you?"

"I mean here. The Black Swan." A horrible ache grasped his lungs and the next breath he drew was more of a wheeze. He coughed and clasped the edge of his desk. "I had a plan, Blayne."

"Plans do occasionally change, Val."

"Not this one." Christ almighty! The effort it took to sound even remotely convincing was draining his energy fast. "And don't call me that."

"Sorry. But it is your name and we are alone." Furrows appeared on Blayne's forehead, drawing his eyebrows together. Silently, he collected the brandy decanter and filled a couple of glasses with the amber liquid. He gave one to Carlton. "Drink. You'll feel better about all of this if you do."

"I seriously doubt that," Carlton murmured. But he set the glass to his lips and did as his friend suggested anyway. "Hedgewick deserves my wrath. I can't let him get away with what he did, not even for her."

Blayne sighed and let his bulk fall into one of the chairs. "Why didn't you tell her the truth?"

"What? That her father's a murderer who deserves to be hung in the street? That he got away with a crime that destroyed my life?" When Blayne just held his gaze with unwavering steadiness, Carlton asked, "What good would that possibly do?"

Blayne shrugged and sipped his drink while Carlton tossed back the remainder of his. "It could have helped her understand your motivation."

"To what end?" Carlton set his glass aside and stared at the last remains of brandy still clinging to the edges. "Even if she understands and chooses to take my side, we still can't have a future together.

Not when I'm going to end up in prison. Or worse, at the end of a rope."

"And you didn't want to cause her that kind of pain." Not a question, but a clear observation.

Carlton raked his fingers through his hair. "No. I can't."

"So then what you're doing now, letting her think you don't care about her at all, that's better?"

"It gives her a chance to put me behind her so she can move on."

Blayne was quiet for a while, and then he said, "You do realize that you love her. Right?"

Carlton gave him a quelling look. "Do I look like an idiot to you? Of course I love her. That's the whole bloody point!"

"Right. So now what?"

Recalling the desperation in Regina's eyes when she'd told him that he was wrong about Hedgewick, made his blood feel like sludge. He hadn't wanted to hurt her and yet he'd managed to do so anyway. Because she had no idea how he felt. She didn't know he was only pushing her away in order to protect her from what was to come. His nerves tightened, partly in anguish and partly in anticipation.

To not think about her was hard, but he made the effort anyway and deliberately focused on what Blayne had asked. "We get the men ready and prepare ourselves for the earl's arrival."

"Will you tell me how you ended up there?" Marcus asked as soon as he'd gotten Regina into a hackney and taken the seat across from her. He didn't sound angry, but rather curious and eager to understand her.

"After speaking with Stokes, I knew it was up to me to prevent an unhappy union between us." She glanced out the window, at other carriages and at the pedestrians. Everything looked so normal, as if nothing had changed. But for Regina, the world she'd once known had vanished and another had taken its place. "So I ran. That morning shortly before the maids began preparing the dining room for breakfast, I snuck out of the house and just..." She made a sweeping motion with her hand.

"You could have come to me," Marcus said. "I would have helped you if you'd asked."

She nodded and turned away from the window, giving him her full attention. "I know. But you're Papa's heir. It would have been wrong of me to make you come with me."

"You wouldn't have been making me do any—"

"And if you'd stayed behind, knowing where I'd gone, chances are Papa would have gotten the truth out of you eventually."

He shook his head and she regretted how hurt he suddenly looked. "I would never have betrayed you."

"You're not a very good liar, Marcus. That's not a bad thing, but it wouldn't have helped me in this instance."

"And yet I still found you."

"Yes. You did." She managed a smile even though it was wobbly. "I've always admired your tenacity. I just...this changes nothing. Papa will find someone else for me to marry now."

"I'm not so certain about that."

Regina frowned. "What do you mean?"

He pursed his lips and then said, "I think he was hell bent on Stokes because he'll be the Duke of Windham one day."

"Of course that's the reason. We already know that he—"

"No. You're mistaking my point, Regina." Marcus leaned slightly forward and held her gaze. "He didn't just want you to marry a future duke. He wanted you to marry *that* future duke, because of the history he had with his predecessor."

"Were they friends or something?"

Marcus nodded. "Until Windham had an affair with Mama."

Shock zigzagged through Regina. "Mama and the last Duke of Windham?" It sounded preposterous. Her mother just wasn't the type. She was far too quiet and demure. Too proper. She wasn't at all the sort of woman who'd sneak about behind her husband's back. The idea of it was one that Regina's brain was intent on rejecting.

"I recently found some letters." Marcus snorted and folded his arms. "Evidence, I suppose, that Papa compiled at the time and never got rid of."

Regina frowned, her mind whirling with possibilities. "Were they dated?"

"Yes. They span a few years. The most recent one was written in 1800." He stretched out his long and slender legs. "I've thought on this a great deal this past week. It didn't make sense to me that Papa would want to attach the family to a name and title he must surely loathe. Until I considered the possibility that installing you as the future duchess was his way of making peace with the past – of seeking some sort of revenge on the man who cuckolded him long ago."

"That sounds really twisted," Regina muttered.

"Agreed. But it does explain his dogged insistence on Stokes and his unwillingness to heed your wishes."

Regina's mouth had gone dry, making it hard for her to form words, so she chose to stay silent while pondering this new information. It didn't have anything to do with the deep resentment Carlton harbored for Hedgewick, which had to be based on something else entirely. One thing the two incidents did have in common, however, was their ability to show her that nothing was as it seemed. And she was now very determined to find out the truth.

But she realized that asking questions and digging into her father's past would have to wait when she stepped through the door of Hedgewick House a short while later.

"Lady Regina," the butler exclaimed so loud it took but a moment before her father arrived in the foyer. He'd been in his study not too far away and was now staring at her as if not quite sure he could trust his own eyes.

"Where have you been?" he eventually asked in a voice that suggested he'd soon lose his temper.

Regina shot her brother a pleading look, and he responded with an apologetic one of his own. "I found her in St. Giles," Marcus said.

Regina groaned. She would have to reconsider giving her brother a gift for Christmas. Although, to be fair, their father deserved to know what had happened however unwilling Regina was to share the information.

"St. Giles?" Hedgewick spat the word as if it tasted sour. "How on earth did you end up there?"

"I believe I turned left onto Oxford Street, took a right and…I'm not sure after that. It's a bit of a blur."

The color in Hedgewick's cheeks turned crimson. "Do you have any idea of the upheaval you have caused? Your mother had no choice but leave the country under the pretense that you had gone with her. Thank God she likes Paris or I'd never hear the end of it." He narrowed his gaze when Regina smiled. "It amuses you, does it? I've been hounding Bow Street every day since you disappeared, ordering them about and insisting they come up with some hint of what might have happened to you." His expression softened as he sighed. "I was worried about you, Regina. We all were."

Stepping forward, she embraced her father and pressed her cheek to his chest. "I'm sorry. I just couldn't go through with that marriage."

There was a pause, and then his hand settled gently against her back. It lasted but a second, but it was enough to inform her that she'd been forgiven and that things would turn out all right. Or at least that was what she thought until Hedgewick said, "St. Giles is not the sort of place I would ever want my daughter to visit. The fact that you stayed there for nearly a month gives me chills." He eased her away and met her gaze for a long solid moment before directing his attention back to Marcus. "Tell me exactly where you found her. I want to know who sent me those letters."

"It was—"

"Nobody," Regina interrupted. She clasped her hands together and fought the tremor that shook her. "I…I mean, I believe someone must have recognized me and taken advantage. I've no idea what—"

"You've always been honest with me." Hedgewick spoke slowly while studying her closely. "But now you're lying. To protect someone, it would seem." His mouth flattened and a pair of tight brackets appeared on either side. "The letters made me think you'd been kidnapped and held against your will, but that's not it at all, is it? You fell for a no good mutt, didn't you? Whoever he was, he was honest when he wrote you'd find comfort with him in his bed. Dear merciful God, I thought he was lying – I prayed that he was – but it's worse than that, isn't it? You gave him your innocence, didn't you?"

His sudden roar of anger startled Regina so much she shrank back and reached out for Marcus to steady her. Uncharacteristic rage burned in Hedgewick's eyes, causing her heart to flutter in panic. "No. I didn't," she gasped. "I swear it."

Hedgewick moved toward her and leaned in close. "Tell me who sent those letters, Regina. Whoever it was did not wish you well."

His comment made sense. The letters Carlton had written had not been with her best interest in mind. She'd been used as a weapon in some strange attack on her father, though the reason for it still puzzled her. And while it hurt, a part of her resisted the urge to give in to anger and pain. For although facts and words ought to make her despise Carlton for what he'd done, her heart urged her to think of the man she'd gotten to know – the man who'd held her in his arms and made her feel safe and cherished. It seemed impossible to her that he'd only pretended to care.

"I'm sorry, Regina, but he did say that I should let Papa know who he was." And then, before Regina could think of some way to stop him, her brother said, "Carlton Guthrie sent the letters."

"No." Regina jerked her head around and stared into her brother's eyes. Her own started pooling with tears. She could not move, let alone speak. All she could do was stand there, mute and motionless.

"You little fool," Hedgewick hissed, his lip curling with disgust. "You ran away from Stokes so you could take up with a villainous scoundrel?" He stared at her as if he scarcely knew who she was anymore. "I ought to have you whipped," he sputtered. "God damn you, Regina! Did you plan this whole thing? Were you secretly sneaking around with Carlton Guthrie when you said you were out visiting friends?"

"No. I only just met him. I—"

"Only just met him and already smitten," Hedgewick sneered. "What exactly did he do to make you forget where your loyalty lies? Did he put his hands up your skirts and—"

"That's enough," Marcus shouted.

Hedgewick seethed. "Yes. It sure as hell is." He glared at her. "Go upstairs this instant and stay in your room. We'll finish this conversation when I return." Without saying another word, he pushed Regina aside and headed toward the front door.

"He'll kill him," she managed to say, her voice so weak she sounded as if she was using her dying breath.

"I won't let that happen," Marcus assured her. Uncertainty marred his handsome features. "I'm sorry, Regina, but we need to figure out what's going on. Perhaps when Papa confronts Guthrie, something will be revealed, and we'll know why he's seeking revenge."

He turned away, intent on following their father. Regina made a desperate grab for his sleeve. "He's not the villain you think him to be, Marcus. In spite of everything, he's a good man, a noble man who protects those who cannot protect themselves. He saved my life, Marcus. You mustn't go after him. Please!"

"I'm sorry." He tugged himself free and looked down at her with sympathy. "It's clear that your judgment has been clouded where he is concerned. Which is only natural if he treated you well and pretended you mattered to him. But I'm not sure you did. The letters he sent us clearly suggest otherwise, as does the fact that he chose not to send me the letter *you* wrote. And as far as saving your life goes… I know that marrying Stokes would have been a terrible fate for you, but it wouldn't have killed you, Regina. You would have found a way to live with it somehow."

"That's not what I mean!"

"I have to go now, if I'm to catch Papa. Get some rest and try not to worry. Everything will work out fine."

He was gone before she had a chance to stop him. "You don't understand," she muttered as she stared at the closed front door. Her cheeks felt damp and when she touched her fingertips to them she realized she was crying. "I wasn't talking about Stokes. I was talking about something much worse than that."

"Perhaps you would like a hot bath?" the butler inquired. "Or something to eat?"

He must have overheard everything, Regina realized. She closed her eyes, not out of shame but because she wanted to block out the world for just one second. Hedgewick was going after Carlton. He had Marcus with him and the pair would probably stop by Bow Street on their way. Hell was about to break loose at The Black Swan; she'd seen the furious determination in Hedgewick's eyes. And although Regina knew that her father would never stand a chance if he took on Carlton alone, she worried the odds would be in his favor if there was a team of runners to help him do it.

She had to warn Carlton. She had to go back to The Black Swan and tell him what to expect. "No thank you," she told the butler. "I'm going out."

"What?" the butler's startled question accompanied her opening of the door. "That isn't wise, my lady. It's late and unsafe. Your father explicitly said that you were to stay in your room. Please. You cannot simply—"

She failed to hear the last of his words as she ran down the street, not caring if anyone saw her. Making a scene or causing a scandal was the last thing that concerned her. What mattered right now was saving Carlton from whatever her father was planning. It was the least she could do after everything he'd done for her. It was also what she *had* to do, because of how much she loved him.

Empty.

That was how he felt.

Like his body had been hollowed out and all that remained was an empty shell. It didn't matter that there were still men in the taproom enjoying their ale, or that MacNeil and Claus had engaged him in cards after Regina left with her brother. Carlton felt her absence acutely and when he eventually dared venture upstairs again to his par-lor, the loneliness he found there echoed through his veins.

Visions of her were everywhere—on the yellow velvet sofa taking a nap, in the armchair working on some mending, crouched on the floor as she studied his books. He could see her with his cat in his lap, sipping sherry while she told him what her dream life would be like.

He crossed to the book case and pulled down those scandalous books she'd been studying. His fingers brushed over the covers where hers had been. A smile pulled at his lips. She'd been morti-fied when he'd addressed her curiosity pertaining to lovemaking. Flames had brightened her cheeks, and yet she hadn't shied away from his questions.

He put the books back and removed his jacket. Crossing to the bedroom, he paused to consider the bed. She'd lain there, her hair fanned out on the pillow while he watched her sleep. This was where she'd comforted him when the past had tormented his dreams. It was also where they'd been intimate and where his feelings for her had expanded tenfold on account of her eager response to his touch.

Aching inside as if someone had parted his ribs and extracted his heart, he turned away and went to the wardrobe. But as he returned his blue jacket, he spotted the purple one that she had worked on. His fingers strayed to the button she'd sewn back on and the muscles in his arms and back shuddered.

She was gone and he missed her like she was a part of him that had been severed and thrown away. The pain in her eyes when they'd parted was something he'd never forget. It would haunt him forever. But it had been necessary. Hurting her was the only way he could think of to make her leave and stay away.

He took a deep breath and held it a moment before letting it go. He'd always known her visit with him would be temporary. And yet he'd allowed himself to get carried away, absorbed and distracted by the fantasy she'd offered of the perfect life that would never be his. Fool that he was, he'd lost his heart in the process. Ironically, he hadn't known he still had one until it had been too late.

Carlton rolled up his shirt sleeves and closed the wardrobe. A fight was coming and when it arrived, he meant to be ready. The pistols he kept in his study had both been prepared and were now placed securely inside his trouser pockets. His men had been told what they could expect. The only thing that remained now was for Hedgewick to show up.

Footsteps, too light to be MacNeil's, sounded in the parlor. Carlton placed one hand on one of his pistols and went to the connecting door. And froze. Because damn it if the woman who'd just been occupying his every thought wasn't standing before him once more.

"How the—"

"I took a hackney and came as quick as I could." She frowned. "MacNeil is paying the driver right now and…Carlton…I…"

The tips of his fingers started to itch with the need to touch her. Instead he gave her his best scowl. "Ye're not supposed to be here."

Her eyes held his with fierce determination. "They're coming for you," she said as she took a step closer to where he stood completely immobile. If he moved he'd likely do something rash, like sweep her off her feet and toss her onto the bed. It wouldn't matter if the whole English army barged through the door. He'd claim her anyway and hang the consequences.

All he could do was nod. "I know."

She paused for a moment. "That's what you want. Isn't it?"

"Yes."

Her approach began once more and he braced himself for the searing heat of her touch. "Why?"

"I cannot tell ye."

"I don't believe that." Her arms wound around his neck and she gazed into his eyes. Her own were intensely dark, like the night sky outside. "I think you are choosing not to."

"I'm just trying to protect ye." This was as honest as he could be with her about his past and about the truth that had bound him to her father for the last twenty years.

"From what?"

Unable to tell her or to keep lying, he pulled her roughly against him and kissed her, certain that this was the last kiss he'd ever share, not just with her, but with anyone. Because after tonight, he would either be dead or arrested for murder.

CHAPTER NINETEEN

THERE WAS NO MISTAKING THE moment when Hedgewick arrived. His voice filled the tavern with so much rage that Carlton glanced up at the ceiling, half expecting to see the plaster crumbling. He placed both hands on Regina's shoulders and allowed himself one more second to imprint every detail of her face on his mind. Then, forcing himself to thwart his instinct, he set her aside and went to the door.

"Stay here," he told her without looking back. He dared not check if she did what he asked as he headed toward the stairs and made his descent. All he could do was hope.

"Where is he?" Hedgewick shouted while Blayne and the rest of Carlton's crew remained as calm as clams in a pool of shallow water. None of them moved, allowing Hedgewick, his son, Lord Seabrook, and the Bow Street runners they'd brought along with them to get a good look around.

Carlton paused on the stairs and met Blayne's gaze. A moment of understanding hovered between them. Leaning one shoulder against the wall, Carlton crossed his ankles and his arms in a casual pose meant to imitate unruffled ease.

"Right 'ere."

All eyes turned toward him, some with interest and some with concern. Hedgewick's, however, were those of a man who had no intention of showing mercy. "You ruined my daughter," he told him icily. "And I intend to make you pay."

Carlton smirked, fully aware the expression would only infuriate Hedgewick further. "On the contrary, me lord, it is I who intends to make *ye* pay."

Hedgewick scoffed. "You and I don't even know each other. We've had no dealings in the past, so whatever it is that you think I have done, you're obviously mistaken." His eyes narrowed and he took a step forward, closer to where Carlton stood. "You, on the other hand, kidnapped my daughter and held her hostage."

A movement at the top of the stairs caught the corner of Carlton's eye, but he chose to ignore it. He couldn't afford to let Regina distract him right now. Not when he was so close to seeing justice served.

He gave his opponent an easy smile. "Would she really be considered a hostage if she was staying with me of her own free will?"

Hedgewick bared his teeth and moved even closer, ignoring his son's words of warning. "You bastard. I'll wring your bloody neck myself if I have to." Moving remarkably fast for his age and size, especially when taking his bad leg into account, Hedgewick lunged at Carlton, who instantly straightened and pulled out one pistol which he pointed at Hedgewick's head.

The earl stopped as if he'd run into a wall, eyes wide and mouth slightly agape. A gasp on the stairs informed Carlton that Regina was near. His heart pulsed with violent disdain, his mind recalling the startled look on his father's face as he lay dying.

Carlton's grip tightened on the pistol, and he smiled with deep satisfaction. The tension in the room had increased tenfold. He could sense the runners approaching and Seabrook trying to figure out how best to help his father. Carlton's crew would be ready to stop them if necessary, so he ignored them.

"Tell me, ye bastard," he drawled with every bit of contempt that he felt for the man now cowering before him, "are ye prepared to pay fer yer sins?"

Hedgwick's left eye twitched. "I…I don't know what you're referring to."

"A reminder then…" Carlton stepped toward Hedgewick until the barrel of his pistol pressed into the other man's chest. Regina said something behind him, but he was too focused on what he was doing to listen. For years, he'd fantasized about this altercation. He'd imagined announcing Hedgewick's crime for the entire world to hear and then planting a lead ball between his eyes. Carlton hesitated, aware that doing so would reveal who he was to his men. It would shatter the illusion he'd crafted and risk the wrath of the people who'd welcomed him into their midst.

And then there was Regina.

He took a deep breath. The least he could do was protect her from the truth. So he deliberately leaned close to Hedgewick's ear and whispered, "I know what ye did, ye murderous scoundrel. I know that yer hands are tainted with the Duke of Windham's blood." He could feel Hedgewick's body go rigid, could hear the sharp little inhale of breath and see the way his throat worked in response to the panic now stealing through him.

"You...you have the wrong man," Hedgewick stammered.

Carlton clenched his jaw and fought to steady his hand. His whole body trembled in response to the rage pouring through him, while the pain he'd harbored for twenty years exploded inside his heart. This was the closest he'd been to Hedgewick since that terrible morning so long ago.

"I don't think so," Carlton hissed. He stepped back so he could appreciate the full effect of the terror in Hedgewick's eyes as he aimed the pistol straight at his forehead.

"No." A gentle hand settled upon his arm, the warmth of it driving away the cold anger and easing the heartache. His arm shook slightly beneath Regina's touch, and then she spoke again, so soft he could not resist listening. "Please don't do this. Whatever my father may have done, he doesn't deserve to die."

Frustration burned behind Carlton's eyes. "I have to finish this," he muttered. "I have no choice."

"Of course you do." Her hand moved to the pistol, the pressure she added there pushing it down and away from her father's forehead. "You'll hang otherwise, and I cannot allow that to happen."

"Regina," Seabrook said, no doubt hoping to

warn his sister against interfering. "You shouldn't have come here."

"Let her be," one of the runners said. "Whatever she's doing, it looks like it's working."

Only because Carlton didn't have the strength to become the man that she would despise forever. He'd thought he could do it but he had been wrong. When it came down to it, saving her from what he'd once suffered himself mattered more than avenging his father. But that didn't make him feel like less of a failure when he finally lowered the pistol completely and accepted defeat. He'd had his chance to put his demons to rest, and he'd walked away because of a woman.

Not just any woman though. The bravest and most remarkable woman in the world.

"You saw him!" Hedgewick shouted as he leapt back. "He just tried to kill me. If he hadn't been stopped, I would be dead right now. And he might yet accomplish his goal when no one is watching. I won't be safe as long as he's free." He turned to the runners. "You must arrest him. For God's sake he's the Scoundrel of St. Giles! Heaven knows he deserves to be locked away behind bars."

"Papa," Regina said, applying a cautious tone. "Nothing happened. You're safe now and—"

"This is your chance to put him away," Hedgewick told the runners. "Let's not forget that he's also guilty of kidnapping, blackmail, and possibly rape!"

Regina gasped and recoiled from the earl. "He's not. I'll vouch for his decency, Papa, for his sense of honor."

"After what just happened? Jesus, Regina, you

are naïve. If you've developed feelings for him then it's only because he manipulated you."

"I have to agree," one of the runners said.

Regina clasped hold of Carlton's hand and squeezed it. "Marcus?"

Seabrook glanced around at the men who protected the law and then at the ones who were loyal to Carlton. He must have realized they weren't going to put up a fight to protect him. He'd given very specific orders so they wouldn't suffer because of his personal vendetta.

"I'm sorry," Seabrook said as he looked back at his sister. He shook his head. "I'm so sorry."

"What did he tell you?"

"What did who tell me?" Hedgewick asked while removing his hat and gloves once they were home.

"Guthrie." Regina had helplessly watched as he'd been accused of kidnapping, issuing threats, and the intention to kill a peer, before being led away by the runners. It hadn't mattered that she'd insisted she'd stayed with him willingly. Her father had simply insisted that Carlton had charmed her into compliance. MacNeil had not interfered, which was something that still baffled Regina.

"A more pertinent question is what were you doing there?" Hedgewick frowned while raising his eyebrows. "You were supposed to stay here. Or are you determined to cause a scandal? As it is we'll be lucky if none of the two dozen men who were at The Black Swan mention your presence."

"You might be dead right now if it wasn't for Regina," Marcus put in. He gave the butler the sort of look that quietly insisted on absolute discretion. Not that he would repeat anything he overheard. His respect for the trust they all placed in him was too great. As evidenced by his blank expression.

Hedgewick gave Regina a considering look. "Maybe." His jaw tightened. "But you still defied me. Again."

"I'm sorry, Papa. Truly."

Hedgewick snorted. "I have to write your mother now and tell her that she must return. And then I will contact Windham to let him know you've changed your mind about Stokes. If we're lucky, you might still marry him and then you'll be his problem to deal with."

"For God's sake," Marcus muttered while Regina stared at her father in disbelief. "You cannot be serious."

"I've never been more so." Hedgewick headed for his study while continuing to speak. "I trust you to make sure she doesn't run off again. Keep an eye on your sister, Marcus. She's already proved herself to be more independent minded than I'd have expected."

Regina bristled. After everything that had happened, she was back to square one with her father still planning to force her into an unhappy marriage. Nothing had changed. And yet...

She followed her father and reached him right before he entered his study. "You didn't answer my question." He gave her an impatient look devoid of the affection he'd always bestowed on her. "What did Guthrie say to you?"

"Nothing of interest. Just threats." He stepped inside the room and closed the door, shutting her out.

Regina frowned. She'd seen her father's face drain of color and fear fill his eyes as Carlton spoke. Whatever he had told Hedgewick, it had terrified him and caused a slight tremor to affect his hands. It wasn't until they'd returned home that he'd seemed to relax and regain his composure.

Pressing her lips together, she turned to find Marcus quietly watching her. "There's something about today's events that doesn't make sense." Casting a quick look at the study door, she moved away from it until she was standing close to her brother. "Guthrie wanted Papa to come find him. He wanted the opportunity to kill him. Which means that Papa must have done something truly awful, or at the very least he must have given Guthrie reason to think he did." She knew this without even having to think about it. "Guthrie would never kill a man unless he believed he was doing the world a favor."

"I worry that you're trying to turn a criminal into a hero, Regina." Marcus's sea blue eyes gazed steadily into hers. "Considering the length of time you spent with him, I would not fault you for developing some sort of attachment to him. Especially not since he helped you and treated you well. But you mustn't—"

"There's something else." Taking her brother by his hand, she led him into the library and closed the door so they could speak more privately. "I don't think Guthrie is who we think him to be."

"What do you mean?"

"I have the feeling he was born into privilege, just like us." He'd told her his father had been an artist and she'd believed him. Although thinking back, he hadn't exactly said that his father wasn't an upstanding member of Society. He'd just steered the conversation away from the topic whenever she'd brought it up again. And then she'd gotten kidnapped and she'd forgotten all about uncovering his true identity. Partly because she'd been too distracted by him. "I saw a miniature of his father whom I judged to be an upper class gentleman based on his garments and the pearl-tipped cravat pin he wore for the portrait."

"That doesn't mean anything. He could have had an affair with a maid, gotten her with child, and sent the pair away, making Guthrie nothing more than a by-blow."

"Yes, I know." Regina crossed to one of the bookcases and let her gaze roam across the colorful leather bound spines on display. "I considered that as well, but there were other things hinting at an upper class upbringing. Like his speech."

Marcus snorted. "I have to disagree with you there, Regina."

"Ordinarily, yes, but there were a few rare moments when he sounded just like you and me or anyone else who'd been taught proper diction." Her fingers trailed over the books, the delicate skin bumping slightly against the embossed gold lettering of the titles. Thinking out loud, she quietly said, "It was almost as if he was wearing a mask."

"Regina." Marcus's voice was solid. "He wouldn't have ended up in St. Giles if his parents were wealthy. He'd have had to have run away in order to do so an—"

"He did." She glanced over her shoulder and saw disbelief etched clearly on Marcus's face. Still she persisted, following the fragmented clues that were at her disposal. "He told me himself that he fled home after his parents died."

"But that makes no sense at all. If what you suggest is true, he would have had a guardian." Marcus shook his head and raised both hands in a gesture of incomprehension. "No child would deliberately choose to leave behind a comfortable home and live on the streets."

"No. They wouldn't." And yet Carlton had. She paused, her hand on a book that she hoped would provide her with answers. Carlton and her father were somehow connected, she just couldn't figure out how, even though she sensed she was awfully close. It felt as if she were missing one piece that remained beyond reach.

"And even if he had been born a peer, that doesn't erase all the terrible things that he's done. The man is a crime lord, Regina, no better than Bartholomew was."

She pulled the book she'd found off the shelf and crossed to a nearby sofa. "You're very wrong about that, Marcus. Bartholomew committed the vilest crimes. He preyed on the innocent for financial gain and there are people out there, eager to do the same." Her jaw clamped tightly at the reminder of what had happened to her and of where she might be right now if Carlton hadn't saved her. "But Guthrie's different. He's righteous and only goes after those who deserve it."

"And who decides who those people are, Regina? Guthrie has taken the liberty of playing judge and executioner when there is a legal process designed to do that for us."

"The authorities don't care if a homeless woman or the child of a whore gets abused or goes missing. But Guthrie does. He'll do what he can to help them, and he'll punish those who deserve it, sometimes by taking their life but...to be honest, after what I've seen, I cannot blame him."

Marcus stared at her in silence so long she was starting to think he'd lost his tongue. But then he muttered, "You're smitten by him." He blinked as if he couldn't quite fathom that realization. "He assured me he hadn't ruined you, that your innocence remains intact, but Regina I have to ask... Did he..."

"No. He told you the truth." She was grateful for the firmness with which she delivered that comment, for although it wasn't a lie, she did not want her brother questioning her further about what had happened between her and Carlton. Eventually, something would betray her, whether it be the look in her eyes or the hitch of her voice or a flush coloring her cheeks.

Marcus let out a long breath and sat down beside her. "Debrett's?" he asked in reference to the book she was cradling in her lap. "Do you honestly think you might find him in there?"

"It's worth a try, isn't it?" When he didn't answer, she flipped the book open and began going through the pages, carefully studying the facts about each individual peer and their children.

"He won't be mentioned if he's a by-blow."

"I know, but..." She thought back on the portrait. "If that were the case, then why would he have his father's miniature?"

"I don't know," Marcus confessed. He came to sit beside her. "I'll admit that it's all very puzzling."

She frowned. "There was something else. A red ribbon that looked like it might belong to a medal."

"And Guthrie had this in his possession?"

"No. It was around his father's neck in the portrait." She looked at Marcus whose brow was now creased in thought.

"Medals aren't worn on red ribbons about the neck, Regina. Only distinguished orders are."

She stared back at her brother. "He's a peer, Marcus. Or at least his father was." Which meant...

"If Guthrie's parents are really dead and it turns out he's not illegitimate," Marcus said, already voicing the thought she was having, "then that could mean he's the heir to a title."

Regina nodded. "How many aristocratic children do we know who've gone missing right after their father died?"

"None that I can think of. And certainly none who'd be Guthrie's age right now."

"No." She tapped her fingers lightly on Debrett's. "Still, he must be in here somewhere."

"Then let's keep looking."

Regina turned the page and then another. Half an hour later, she stopped at a name that jumped out like a flashy headline in the scandal sheets. Unable to speak, she pointed to it while excitement, relief, and foreboding collided inside her.

"Bloody hell," Marcus muttered.

"The initials on those letters you received were V.S., were they not?" She already knew the answer, but she had to hear him say it because she was worried her mind might be playing tricks on her somehow.

"Yes."

She blew out a breath and inhaled once more before managing to say, "So then it is possible for Carlton Guthrie to be Valentine Sterling, the last Duke of Windham's son."

"Windham died in a fire along with a maid. The son's body was never recovered so it was presumed that he perished as well." Marcus pulled the book into his lap and ran his finger down over the text until he reached the list of honors, of which there were several. "Logical reasoning tells me that Guthrie must be an imposter, that he used Valentine's initials to rattle Papa after somehow discovering that he and Windham were close. But my gut tells me that Guthrie and Valentine are one and the same." He met Regina's gaze and stared into her eyes. "How can that possibly be?"

"I don't know. As you say, there must have been an appointed guardian as well as other relatives capable of caring for Valentine after his father died. But instead he ran away, abandoning his heritage, his duty toward the title, and the life of luxury he was accustomed to. Which can only mean that he must have been frightened of something." An unpleasant possibility started to form in her head, and as much as she wished to dismiss it, it clung to her brain with unrelenting determination. "Windham had an affair with Mama."

"What are you getting at?"

"The reason why Guthrie…Valentine…would want Papa dead." She closed Debrett's and clasped its cool leather surface while trying to calm her frantic heart. "He's eight years older than you and would have just turned thirteen when he supposedly died. That puts his death very close to the time when Papa discovered he was being cuckolded by his friend."

"You're not…" Marcus's voice caught and he suddenly stood, his posture tense as he stared down at her. "Are you suggesting that Papa murdered Windham?"

She didn't want to suggest any such thing. The mere idea of it was repellent. And yet she found herself nodding. "Yes, Marcus. Right now it's the one explanation that makes some sense."

He blinked. "Do you have any idea how insane you sound right now? That you would even think to consider Papa capable of such a thing makes me wonder about your rationality. He's our father, for Christ's sake!" A stunned expression crossed his face. "Forgive my language, but I would rather believe that fairies come out to play in our garden at night than that Papa is capable of something so heinous."

"I agree." She stood as well. "Perhaps Papa went to confront him, they argued, and it happened by accident. Perhaps—"

"Stop." Marcus held up a hand. "Not another word."

"Guthrie asked Papa if he was prepared to pay for his sins." She tilted her head. "Remember?"

Marcus's eyebrows dipped while his jaw seemed to tighten. His nostrils flared as he blew out a breath. "He mentioned it in the letter as well. When I questioned Papa about it, he dismissed it as nothing of consequence."

He shoved his hands in his pockets and dropped his gaze to the piece of carpet between them. "But the way he reacted told me the letter had struck a nerve. I just couldn't figure out how." He raised his gaze to hers once more. "That doesn't mean that you're right, though. I refuse to think the worst of Papa without further evidence."

"I agree," Regina said, "which is why I suggest that we find out as much as we can on our own. If I'm wrong, and I really hope that I am, then there must be another explanation for why a duke's son would choose to become someone else. But if I'm right, then Guthrie deserves our help and our father…" She didn't dare think of what he would deserve, so she left the sentence unfinished and went to return Debrett's to the shelf where she'd found it.

It was almost two in the morning and she was exhausted. Yawning, she decided a good night's rest was what she required. Tomorrow, she'd go to Bow Street and speak with Guthrie. If he was honest with her, she hoped the conversation would clarify matters. Because as things stood, there was a chance he'd be condemned to prison for a very long time, and that was something she could not accept. Not when he was the man she wanted to spend the rest of her life with, regardless of whether or not they married. That was the sort of detail that no longer mattered. But the love she felt for him in her heart was like having the sun in her eyes on a hot summer day— bright and blinding and impossible for her to ignore.

CHAPTER TWENTY

IT FELT AS IF HIS head were being split open by an axe. Flat on his back, Carlton stared at the ceiling and groaned. He must have hurled himself into the wall. Rolling onto his side, he placed the palm of his hand on the floor and pushed himself into a sitting position. The same nightmare as usual was to blame, but at least he'd managed to catch Hedgewick this time.

Reaching up, he touched his chin and felt the sting of the graze he'd acquired. Every bone in his body felt like it had been run through a rolling press.

He wiped his hand across his eyes, brushing loose strands of hair aside in the process. Slowly he stood, cursing the slight resistance to his right knee. Once upright, he straightened his back and rolled his shoulders. Every part of him was sore, including his skin. Now that he'd mostly recovered from the jolt of waking up on the floor, he became aware of the tired burn in his eyes and wondered how much he'd slept. Not long, he reckoned. Maybe two to three hours?

A door creaked open further down the hallway and the clicking of numerous footsteps followed.

They grew more distinct as they came closer, then three people turned the corner.

Carlton ignored the Bow Street clerk and Seabrook, his gaze going straight to the woman he couldn't get out of his head.

Regina.

He didn't want her seeing him like this, caged and utterly helpless – a failure in his own eyes.

I love you.

Those words had been spoken with great conviction before she'd watched him threaten her father's life. "Why are ye here?"

She ignored his curt tone and gave him a smile – the sort that forced him to reach for the bars that separated them so he could steady himself. "I have a theory," she began as if she were a scientist with an idea that would change the world.

"Whatever it is, I doubt it will help." His life was over. Hedgewick had won. Angered by the fact that she'd made him abandon his goal, he tightened his hold on the bars and gave her a glare. "Comin' 'ere was a waste of yer time."

"Here's what I think," Regina went on, mercilessly undeterred by his rude attempt to push her away.

He gritted his teeth. "I don't—

"You don't have much choice, I'm afraid," Seabrook drawled. "Your lady is relentless and you're not in a position to run away."

His lady.

It felt like his heart had been clasped and was now being squeezed. She wasn't his lady and yet... His breath shuddered in his throat. As much as he resented her for what she'd forced him to do, he still cared for her, damn it.

"I think," she told him so clearly he could not mistake her words, "that my father killed your father, the Duke of Windham. I think *you* are Valentine Sterling."

Carlton blinked.

What else could he do when faced with such a perfect deduction of facts? He was rendered entirely speechless.

"Um..." he managed after a moment.

"The thing is though," Regina blithely added, "that people don't usually shoot each other without a good reason."

Carlton clutched the cold metal bars and braced himself. She was going to defend her father, and he would be forced to stand there and listen. The ground seemed to move beneath him, so he planted his feet in a wider stance, determined to stay upright while memories flooded his brain.

I was a fool to think you my friend, Windham.

Go home, Hedgewick. You've a lovely wife and two children waiting for you there.

How dare you speak to me of my family? How dare you address me without any hint of remorse as if you have done nothing wrong?

A cracking sound. His father's body landing before him. The stunned look in his father's eyes and the warning not to act but to sit there and watch as he drew his last breath. The shattering of glass and the whiff of smoke curling toward him. His young heart struggling to beat as he'd pulled the Windham signet ring from his father's finger. A whooshing sound as the flames caught hold of the curtains, the creaking of wood as the heat danced over the floor. Tears – enough to last a lifetime – so numerous he couldn't see. The dry burn in his throat as the room filled with smoke and the tight squeeze of his lungs as he inhaled the filthy air.

"Did you know that your father and my mother were lovers?"

The question caught him like a whip, thrusting him back to the present. "What?"

"I believe my father lost his ability to think rationally when he learned that your father was having an affair with my mother. He just grabbed a pistol and went after him."

"No." Carlton shook his head. An unpleasant prickle stirred the nape of his neck. "No. My father was Hedgewick's friend. He would never have done something like that to him."

"And yet he did." She placed her hand over his. "There are letters to prove it."

Carlton clenched his jaw. "Even if what you say is true, your father had no right to do what he did."

"Of course not. That's the whole point." Intense blue eyes filled with determination met his. "It's the reason why we're here."

He shook his head, not sure that he dared understand her meaning. "If you clear my name, you'll be ruining your father's instead."

"I know." Her hand touched his, the warmth of her touch seeping through his skin so wonderfully soothing it made him forget time and place for a second.

"I don't think you fully comprehend the repercussions."

"Carlton, I…" Her voice shook and she took a deep breath before saying, "I know that I took from you the satisfaction you'd find in revenge, and as sorry as I am to have been the one who ruined your plans, the truth is I'd do it again in a heartbeat." Instinctively, he tried to pull away from her, but she only tightened her hold on his hand. "If you'd killed him, I would have lost you as well, and I just couldn't let that happen."

"Regina, I lied to you in order to keep you with me."

"I know," she whispered, so quietly he scarcely heard her. "But I understand why you did it and…I also believe that somewhere along the way, your reason for wanting me to stay with you changed. So if you can forgive me, perhaps the—"

"Forgive you?" He could scarcely believe that this woman who'd come here ready to sacrifice her father's freedom for his was asking him for absolution. Stunned, he gazed at her in disbelief. "You've done nothing wrong, Regina. If anything, it is I who should ask for your forgiveness."

Her lips quirked while her eyes took on a watery shimmer. "There's no need. I understand your actions completely, but I would rather rely on the law where my father's concerned so that you may be free to live the life you deserve."

Carlton struggled to breathe. "You'll forever be known as the daughter of a murderer." He looked at Seabrook. "The Hedgewick title will be dissolved."

"If you think the title matters more to me than bringing the man who murdered your father to justice, then you're mistaken," Seabrook muttered.

"Some things are more important than one's reputation," Regina added with that same degree of tenacity she'd shown when he'd first met her and she'd asked for his help.

Christ, how he loved her.

But now was not the time or place for such a heartfelt declaration. Especially not since there was still one important detail to consider. "I'll have to prove my identity beyond any shadow of a doubt." He looked across at the clerk and tried not to show how much turning back into Valentine Sterling troubled him. The people of St. Giles would resent him, not just for the lies but for being a toff. He'd lose the friendships he'd made over the years and would likely be met by distrust if he ever returned. But what choice did he have? If he was going to regain his freedom, see Hedgewick punished, and find a way to include Regina in his future, then this was what had to be done. "My moustache hides a distinctive scar that I've had since birth. It will be recognized by those who knew me as a child. And then there's this." Reaching inside his jacket pocket, he retrieved the signet ring that he'd removed from his father's finger as he lay dying.

The clerk's eyes widened. "The Windham signet ring."

"You recognize it?" Carlton asked.

The clerk nodded. "How could I not? The question of what might have happened to it has been a great mystery among the runners over the years. Bets were placed and..." He grinned. "I dare say nobody ever suggested that you might have it."

"Well then," Carlton said, "if you're ready, I believe I'd like to make a statement."

"I'll make the necessary preparations right away," the clerk said. "If you'll please come with me, my lord and lady." He started down the hall-way.

Regina withdrew her hand, gave Carlton a meaningful look and followed the clerk. When Seabrook prepared to do the same, Carlton asked him to wait. He then whispered, so low that neither the clerk nor Regina would hear him, "As Guthrie, I did a lot of things that could still result in severe punishment. I've killed people."

Seabrook's eyes darkened. "Did they deserve it?"

Carlton thought of the men who'd raped women and children and shuddered. "They were monsters."

"Does Regina know that you did this?" When Carlton nodded, Seabrook surprised him by saying, "Then don't say a word about it again. There's no proof after all or you would have been arrested a long time ago."

The focus would be on what Hedgewick had done and on the fact that Carlton hadn't actually killed him or abducted his daughter. To punish him for attempting to do either would be impossible once people learned that he was the true Duke of Windham. Bow Street would have no choice but to let him go.

Carlton bowed his head and offered his thanks, upon which Seabrook took his leave.

When the clerk returned, he brought a middle-aged man with a narrow face and thinning hair with him. "This is Mr. Hutchins, a magistrate with the Bow Street offices." The clerk glanced at the official before returning his attention to Carlton. "I've told him who you are, but he needs to hear it from you."

Carlton faced Mr. Hutchins and took a deep breath. This was it. He was about to jump over a cliff and swim to freedom. "My name is Valentine Francis Belvedere Sterling. I was born at Fairlawn Manor in Somerset on July thirteenth, 1787. Carlton Guthrie is the identity I assumed after watching the Earl of Hedgewick kill my father, the Duke of Windham."

CHAPTER TWENTY ONE

SEATED IN THE RECEPTION AREA of the Bow Street Magistrate's Court, Regina waited with Marcus while Carlton provided Mr. Hutchins with his statement. The minutes ticked by, and as information began to circulate through the building, Regina became aware of the glances directed at both her and her brother.

It would only get worse from this point onward, she realized. Society thrived on scandals and this one would be tremendous. Playing a hand in her father's arrest would probably always feel like a sort of betrayal, even though she knew she had done the right thing. It was a choice she would have to live with, no matter what happened or what people said.

"The next few weeks won't be easy," she said as she glanced at Marcus.

He snorted. "I do believe we ought to think in terms of months and years."

The storm that loomed before them darkened, and Regina fought to ease the anxiety coursing through her. "What will you do without your title?"

"A man's title isn't everything, you know." He

reached for her hand and squeezed it, reminding her that they were in this together, that she wasn't the only one who'd urged Carlton to do what was necessary. "Without it, I dare say I might have a chance to follow my own dreams for a change. And you, dear sister, shall be able to marry the man you want."

She didn't manage to question him about what his dreams included before Carlton arrived. His moustache was now gone, which made him look several years younger than before. And in spite of the scar that puckered the upper left side of his lip, Regina decided that the lack of a moustache also made him more handsome

"Are you free to go?" she asked while forcing herself to remain where she was, not to step toward him and fling her arms around his neck in a public display of affection.

Carlton nodded. "Mr. Hutchins believes what I've told him." Orders being issued around them alerted her to the fact that a team of runners was being assembled. Sensing her awareness, Carlton said, "They're preparing for Hedgewick's arrest now."

"I hope you'll let me come with you," Marcus told Hutchins. The magistrate took a moment to consider, then gave a firm nod. Marcus glanced back at Regina. "You should stay here."

"But—"

"He's right," Carlton said. Taking a step toward her, he reached up to tuck a stray strand of hair behind her ear. His fingers brushed her cheek and she instinctively breathed out a small sigh of pleasure. "Things might turn ugly. And since

Hedgewick is your father no matter what, I think it best if you're not there to witness it."

She took a moment to consider and decided that he was right. "Very well. I'll remain here until it's over." The look in his eyes as he thanked her was so familiar it caused a hot blush to color her cheeks.

"Let us be off," Hutchins called.

Carlton held her gaze for one second longer before he turned and strode to the door with Marcus, following the runners out into the street where carriages awaited.

Crossing to the window, Regina watched until the doors closed and the drivers whipped the horses into motion. She then returned to the seat she'd been occupying earlier and prepared to wait. Whatever happened now, it was out of her hands.

"Your allegations are outrageous!" Hedgewick stood with both hands clenched by his sides. His posture was stiff, his eyes blazing so fiercely it looked like they might start spewing fiery sparks. "How dare you come into my home and accuse me of such contemptible actions? I find it down-right offensive, you know." He'd barely spared Carlton a glance, most likely because he'd stayed at the back of the group when they'd filed into Hedgewick's study. The earl had been briefly distracted by Seabrook's presence, but his entire focus was now on Mr. Hutchins and the runners.

"We wouldn't have come here like this if we didn't have proof," Mr. Hutchins told him in a tone so calm he almost sounded as if he were trying to placate an unhappy child.

"Proof? What proof?" Hedgewick glared at the magistrate. "Windham was my friend. I mourned him, damn you, yet here you are, making up stories and wasting your time when the man you ought to be focusing on is that bloody scoundrel from St. Giles. Have you made any progress there? Has a date been set for his trial?"

"No," Mr. Hutchins remarked.

"Good God," Hedgewick blustered. "You are incompetent, aren't you? He's the criminal, not me. I am an upstanding citizen. An earl, for Christ's sake." His face had gone from rose pink to beet red in a matter of seconds. "Why are you here anyway? Who concocted this ludicrous tale about me?" His fist slammed into the top of his desk, rattling everything on it. "I demand to know this instant!"

There was an almost angry moment of silence, like right before an opponent strikes a mighty blow. And then Carlton took a step forward, pinning Hedgewick with every bit of disdain he had for him. "It isn't a ludicrous tale, you puffed up piece of shit. It's the truth."

"What the hell are you doing here?" Hedgewick demanded. His angry voice helped hide the unease that showed in his eyes, though not enough for Carlton to miss it. "Why isn't he behind bars?"

Mr. Hutchins remained seemingly unaffected by Hedgewick's hard tone. "Because it would seem that he doesn't belong there."

"The devil, you say?" A vein began throbbing on Hedgewick's forehead. "You've no idea who he is, do you?" Marcus asked his father with an edge of curiosity.

"Of course I do. He's the bloody bastard who kidnapped my daughter, a renowned criminal who—"

"He's Valentine Sterling," Mr. Hutchins said. "The last Duke of Windham's son."

Hedgewick's eyes widened for a brief second until he regained his composure. "That's impossible. He's obviously lying to you."

"And yet, I have the scar to prove my identity," Carlton said, "not to mention my father's signet ring."

"But tha…that's ridiculous," Hedgewick stammered. "It simply cannot be."

"And yet it is," Carlton said.

Hedgewick stared back him. A vein began throbbing next to Hedgewick's eye. "I want you out of my house."

"That isn't going to happen," Marcus said. "We know you killed Windham and his maid."

Hedgewick bared his teeth in rabid fury while pinning his son with a venomous glare. "Why you treacherous little louse. Have you no sense of where your loyalties lie?"

"Well, they're not with a cold blooded murderer, I'll tell you that much."

Moving with surprising swiftness for a man with a permanent limp, Hedgewick lunged at Seabrook. The viscount, caught off guard, stumbled back before losing his balance completely and falling to the floor. His father landed on top of him, his hands going around his son's neck in a stranglehold that made Seabrook's eyes start to bulge as he struggled to get himself free.

Without even thinking, Carlton landed a blow against Hedgewick's jaw, causing him to loosen his grip long enough for Carlton to shove him away from Seabrook.

"Damn the lot of you," Hedgewick sputtered while Carlton helped Seabrook rise. "You're all a waste of good air, while I am a bloody earl!"

"Not for much longer," Hutchins remarked. With a nod, he ordered a pair of runners to take hold of Hedgewick.

Grabbing him by his arms, they hoisted him to his feet.

Carlton stared at him. Oddly, after all these years of anticipating his enemy's eventual downfall, he did not enjoy destroying the man as much as he'd thought he would. After all, Hedgewick was Regina's father and she would suffer as a result. But that didn't mean he'd show mercy. For his own father's sake, doing so wasn't an option.

"Why did you do it?" When Hedgewick didn't answer, Carlton pressed, "Because my father was having an affair with your wife? Is that what—"

"I was supposed to marry Edwina," Hedgewick spat with explosive force. "Your mother should have been *my* wife! *I* courted her first. Hell, we even began planning our wedding. But then your father decided to steal her away, and since he was the heir to a duke, her parents encouraged her to break off her engagement with me and accept his offer instead." His eyes blazed with deep and violent anger. "She later told me the affection she'd thought she had for me was nothing compared to her feelings for Windham. And then, when she died, the bastard went after Louise! He sneaked around with her behind my back for almost five years until I found out about it by chance."

Hedgewick scoffed. "Friend indeed." His chin tilted up and he met Carlton's gaze with loathing. "Your father was selfish. I suppose his rank made him feel entitled, for he never gave any indication that what he did was wrong. But he ruined my life, damn him. Hell, I don't even know if Marcus is mine or not, though I'm certain of Regina since she was born two years after his death."

A sick feeling crept along Carlton's spine before it was cast aside by immense relief. He'd thank God for that himself. The alternative was too awful to think of, considering his own relationship with her.

With an inward shake, Carlton forced himself to finish what he'd started. "So you killed my father because you hated what he had done to you?"

"He had to be stopped," Hedgewick said. A crazed look appeared in his eyes. "I was so incensed that I went there without a plan." He laughed. "All I knew was that I had to purge him from my life and using a pistol seemed like an excellent way to do so. I suppose the maid must have heard the shot because she was suddenly there and…"

Carlton closed his eyes. The memory of Sarah's scream and the choking sound that had followed had haunted him for years. "You strangled her. An innocent woman."

"I had no choice at that point."

Silence descended over the room as every man present absorbed the horror of what had been done. "How could you live with yourself after what you did? When you thought you'd killed an innocent child?" Christ have mercy, if it had been him, he'd have taken a shot to his own head after that piece of news had surfaced.

"It was extremely difficult to live with."

Carlton stared at him while a fresh wave of anger rose up inside him. Blood rushed through his veins until it became a roar in his ears. His heart beat painfully against his constricting rib-cage, and it took every bit of restraint he possessed not to close the distance between them so he could punch the bastard in the throat.

Instead, Carlton pinched the bridge of his nose and drew in a ragged breath. When he looked at Hedgewick again, the disgust and rage that he felt must have shown on his face, for the earl shrank back against the runners, visibly shaken. "It seems to me that you managed well enough. You went on with your life as if nothing had happened. Until it was time for your daughter to marry." Surprise flickered in Hedgewick's eyes. "Here was your chance to take something that belonged to my father and make it yours. It's why you insisted Regina must marry Stokes, is it not?"

"I don't know what you're getting at," Hedge-wick muttered.

Carlton smirked. "Don't you?" When Hedge-wick said nothing, Carlton said, "Your darling daughter has confided a great deal in me. In fact, you should know that she and I are very well acquainted with each other."

Someone behind him cleared his throat, most likely Marcus, causing Carlton to pause. A month ago, he'd have used Regina to hurt Hedgewick in every conceivable way. Now, he just wanted to go and find her so they could move on with their lives together. And yet, he felt compelled to add one last thing. "She's mine now, Hedgewick, so I suppose you'll get at least one of the things you wanted – a family connection to the Windham title."

CHAPTER TWENTY TWO

IT WAS STRANGE, ARRIVING HOME with the knowledge that Hedgewick was gone and would never return. Regina removed her bonnet and gloves with a numbness that seemed to detach her from the world. The servants moved quietly, not uttering a word unless it was necessary. Marcus had explained everything to her in detail on the carriage ride home from the Bow Street Magistrate's Court. She understood what had transpired and had been given a greater understanding of her father's motivations. Still, nothing could excuse what he'd done. It pained her to think of the hurt and upheaval he'd caused Carlton as a young boy.

It also made her wish that Carlton had come to collect her together with Marcus, but apparently he'd gone back to The Black Swan intent on explaining things to his men. She dared not even wonder how such a discussion might go, for she knew that losing their respect and having them turn against him would be his biggest regret.

"Drink?" Marcus lifted a decanter as he posed the question.

Somehow, they'd arrived in the parlor, though she hadn't registered the small walk they'd taken from the foyer in order to get there. She nodded and went to sit on the sofa. "I feel as if my heart has been grabbed by an iron fist."

Marcus placed a glass before her. "Coming to terms with what Papa did is trying. And it's not over yet, I'm afraid." He lowered himself to the adjacent chair. "We must prepare ourselves for slander. Our reputations have been blackened by this, Regina. I fear there will be no way back to Society."

She set her glass to her lips on that thought and took a long sip. The rich and spicy flavor of the brandy nipped at her tongue and her throat. Heat followed, accompanied by a lethargic relief. "We'll get through it."

"Of course we will," Marcus said as if that went without saying. "We have each other and…I believe we did the right thing – that *you* did the right thing – no matter how hard it might be to accept it."

She appreciated that. It made her decision to save Carlton instead of her father an easier one to bear. Biting her lip, she considered her brother before hesitantly asking, "Do you think you might be Windham's son?"

"I don't know and it doesn't really matter, does it? Whether I'm Windham's son or not makes no difference. You are my family, Regina. You always will be."

They chose to remain in the parlor for supper and were just finishing up when a knock at the parlor door brought the butler into the room. "My lord, my lady, there is a Valentine Sterling here to see you."

Regina almost toppled her tray in her haste to stand. "Please show him in," she gasped with the same giddy voice she'd used as a child whenever she'd shown excitement.

The butler gave a short bow and retreated to the foyer. Marcus smiled and helped Regina set their trays on a side table so they were out of the way. "One thing is for certain," he told her. "Your radiant smile will leave no doubt in Sterling's mind about how happy you are to see him."

And then the man in question arrived. Unlike earlier, he now wore the burgundy velvet jacket on which she'd reattached a button. Beneath, was the black and gold brocade fabric of his waist-coat. His trousers were grey, his boots gleaming black, and the cravat at his neck tied to perfection. Regina stared in wonder at his bare upper lip before raising her gaze to his eyes. A yearning fire burned there, so intense that she caught her breath. Without even thinking, she walked straight into his arms and kissed him, heedless of her brother's presence and of what was proper.

Carlton froze for a second but then he grinned against her lips and kissed her back. "I could get quite used to this sort of welcome from you," he murmured as he pulled back. Gently, he eased her away before she found the words to respond, and stepped past her.

Startled by the swiftness with which she'd been removed from his arms, she spun around and found the man that she loved addressing Marcus with polite respect. "I would like to speak with you in private if you can spare the time."

Regina frowned. "Is that really necessary?"

"Yes," both men told her without hesitation.

Huffing out a breath, Regina waited for them to depart before dropping onto the sofa. She then poured herself another measure of brandy. "Annoying men," she muttered, and knocked the drink back.

It took about half an hour for Carlton to return to the parlor. When he did, he was alone. Regina rose from the spot she'd been occupying on the sofa and faced him. A dark lock had fallen over his left eyebrow, affording him with a slightly roguish look that instantly caused a flutter in the pit of her belly.

The edge of his mouth lifted to form a crooked smile full of promise and mischief. Without removing his gaze from her, he closed the parlor door until it clicked into place, and leaned his shoulder against it.

Regina stared back at him. Her tummy did a little flip, prompting her to speak so she could distract herself from her nerves. "How did your visit to The Black Swan go?"

"Not as badly as I'd feared." His words were soft but precise. "Seems MacNeil was right and I was wrong about how the people there would respond to me being the son of a duke."

Happiness on his behalf bubbled up inside her. "That's wonderful news."

A flicker of appreciation brightened his eyes. "Mr. Hutchins, the magistrate, is going to request an audience with the king. He will explain the intricacies of what has happened, after which the king will decide if I ought to be reinstated as duke." He pushed himself away from the door and straightened his posture. "My situation is unique. On one hand, I'm the rightful heir to the Windham title, but on the other, there's already another duke in place. And to be honest, I'm actually quite content to let him keep the title. After all, I've accumulated enough funds over the years to allow for a comfortable life and…" He shrugged. "I'm really not sure I want the burden of a dukedom."

"Whatever happens, it won't make any difference to me," Regina told him softly.

His eyes brightened, gleaming with hints of gold. "Do you mean that?"

"Of course." She took a step forward, the pull he exerted on her too strong for her to resist. "I knew I wanted to share my life with you before I realized your true identity. When I thought being with you would require living at The Black Swan forever. So I don't care if you're a duke, Valentine Sterling, or Carlton Guthrie, though I would like to know which name you'd prefer me to use."

"I've been Carlton so long that Valentine almost sounds foreign."

She nodded. "Good." Her lips twitched with the beginning of a smile. "I prefer Carlton too. It's what I've gotten used to."

He inhaled deeply, his nostrils flaring as he stared down at her. To think she could have lost him because of her father's determination to be rid of him caused her throat to squeeze so painfully she could barely speak. And yet, she forced out the necessary words even as tears began stinging her eyes.

"I love you. And I'll never stop loving you, no matter what."

His hand settled firmly against her cheek and she felt the rough scrape of his calloused thumb stroking her skin. "I love you too, Regina. You've filled my world with light. My heart, once dead, now beats again." The emotion in his voice caused her heart to flutter. "Like a fairy wielding a magical wand you've sprinkled pieces of joy on my life and I...I don't want to live without you. To be honest, I cannot imagine taking another step without you by my side, Regina. So please..." He blinked and a single tear spilled from the corner of his eye and trickled down over his cheek. "I've spoken to your brother and he has allowed me to ask for your hand."

Regina's legs wobbled a little in response to his declaration. She wanted to grab him by his lapels and pull him closer – she wanted to wind her arms around his neck and drag his mouth to hers for a kiss. It took more restraint than she thought she possessed just to stand there and wait for him to continue. Indeed, she was seconds away from tapping her foot with impatience.

When she could not stand the suspense any longer, she opened her mouth to tell him that she accepted so they could skip past the question.

Only he cut her off by saying, "I'm nothing but a scoundrel without you. Please, do me the honor of being my wife, and I will spend every waking moment ensuring that you are happy and safe. Marry me, Regina, and I promise that I'll never stop trying to be the best man I can be."

She wanted to fling herself at him, she was so

overjoyed, so it took some effort to allow the necessary time required to form an answer. And when she spoke, she was rather surprised that it wasn't with a quick and simple yes.

Instead she said, "On one condition."

He raised an eyebrow. "Name it."

Heat flooded her cheeks. She bit her lip and was close to losing her nerve, but the fierce intensity in his eyes urged her on. "I miss the way you used to speak, so maybe you can revert to that manner?" She cleared her throat and dropped her gaze for a second. "When we're alone?"

He bent his head and whispered close to her ear, "Ye like the uncultured tone do ye?" His breath tickled the side of her neck and a shiver raced through her.

"Yes." Her voice was no more than a gasp – a sound she hardly recognized as her own. With one simple question, spoken like a pirate, he'd almost removed her ability to stand. So she reached for him quickly and felt the hard press of his hand at her back as he steadied her at the same time.

"Yes, ye like the uncultured tone, or yes, ye'll marry me, Regina?"

His low murmur sent the most delicious vibrations through her. "Both," she managed.

He emitted a satisfied growl from somewhere deep in his throat right before he pressed his mouth to hers with the fierceness of a man who'd just conquered the world. It was the most possessive kiss yet, and Regina reveled in it, loving the thrill and the taste and the sounds. She felt as if she were caught in a violent storm with rain beating down from every angle. His hands were somehow everywhere at once, his body a solid wall at her front, and the kiss so hot and intense that it threatened to burn her to cinders.

"My God," he rasped while kissing a path down her neck and toward her neckline. He drew her tighter as if he wanted to somehow consume her.

His breaths cooled the damp spots his kisses created, producing the loveliest frissons on the surface of her skin. Craving more, she thrust her fingers into his hair and directed his mouth back to hers. She led the kiss this time, showing him without words the extent of her desire, the desperation she felt in her heart, and the longing to be with him in the most elemental way possible.

A rap at the door broke the spell and reminded her of where they were. Swallowing, she stepped back and patted her feverish cheeks. When her eyes met Carlton's, she smiled, for he looked just as ravished as she felt. "Yes?" she called to the unwelcome intruder.

Marcus opened the door and glanced at them each in turn. He cleared his throat. "I gather there's a wedding to plan, because if there isn't—"

"Yes," Carlton said. He raked his hand through his hair in a pointless attempt to bring his haphazard locks in order. "She said yes."

"Then I congratulate you both." Marcus went to Regina and gave her a hug. He then shook Carlton's hand. "Shall we decide on a date for the ceremony?"

"I suggest three weeks from today," Carlton said.

Regina's head snapped around and she stared at him without any effort at hiding her shock. "Can we not try to obtain a special license?"

He looked at her with a mixture of love and hunger that had the effect of curling her toes. "I understand that you're eager to marry, and I can assure you that I am as well. However, I would like to know where I stand first since that will determine where we will be living."

"Can we not go back to The Black Swan?"

"No." The word was spoken simultaneously by Carlton and Marcus. The two men shared a look before Carlton returned his attention to Regina. "Your reputation right now is extremely fragile. My mission from this moment on is to preserve it to the best of my abilities. That means planning a wedding that won't raise an eyebrow and giving you a respectable home to move into immediately after. Until then, you will remain here with your brother."

"But that's intolerable," Regina protested, in response to which Carlton grinned. "We've lived together for a month and have even…" The remainder of what she was going to say died on her lips when she saw how uncomfortable Marcus looked. She waved her hand. "You know what I mean."

"Yes," Carlton agreed, "but only a few people know that. The rest believe you were off on a trip to Paris with your mother. And besides, don't you think we should wait for her to return so she can watch you get married?"

Regina sighed. "I suppose…"

Carlton's smile broadened and a twinkle appeared in his eyes. "You won't be the only one to suffer the wait, I assure you. Just remember, anticipation can be a powerful thing."

Marcus cleared his throat. "I can call on the vicar if you like, so you don't have to do so. Lord knows you'll be busy enough in the weeks to come."

"Thank you," Carlton told him. "I appreciate that."

"And don't forget," Marcus told Regina, "that you and Sterling can still spend time together before your wedding."

"Might I suggest that we start with a stroll in the park tomorrow?" Carlton asked.

"If you prefer a ride, you're welcome to borrow my carriage," Marcus said.

Regina could only look at the man she loved. He stood before her with hope in his eyes, as if his every happiness hinged on her saying she'd join him. "A stroll sounds perfect," she said, dismissing the carriage because there was something far more compelling about being seen on his arm.

"Happy?" he asked one week later while they were walking through the Royal Academy of Art.

"Never more so," she replied.

Carlton drew her against his side as they paused to admire a painting of a boy with black hair. He was standing beneath a tree with a greyhound by his side. "I know you think I lied to you about my father."

"It's fine, Carlton. Really." She had no wish to discuss his dishonesty with her. Failing to post the letters she'd written while letting her think that he had had hurt her the most. "I understand your reasoning."

"I'm glad. But you ought to know that I wasn't completely dishonest." He pointed toward the plaque at the bottom of the frame.

Regina leaned forward. "Valentine Sterling by Montgomery Sterling, Fifth Duke of Windham." Going still, she raised her gaze to the boy's face. The likeness had eluded her before, but now it was obvious, especially once she spotted the scar. "This is you?"

"My father painted it when I was ten." The pride in his voice couldn't be missed.

"It's incredible, like a real person trapped on a canvas."

He was smiling at her when she glanced up at him again. "It's not the only painting of his in this gallery. Come, I'll show you." He led her into another room where a group of young ladies were gathered around a Vermeer. They glanced toward Carlton and Regina as they approached and promptly hurried away.

Carlton stilled, his posture tensing. "Does it bother you?"

There was no doubt about what he meant. "Not at all." She glanced up at him, at the handsomest and most considerate man she knew. "You're the best choice I ever made for myself. It only stands to reason that every young lady in London should shy away from me with envy."

"Do you honestly mean that?"

Noting a hint of uncertainty in his dark eyes, she nodded. "Yes, Carlton. I would not live my life without you."

His answering smile was followed by a kiss so

scandalous, Regina was certain it would be mentioned in the Mayfair Chronicle the following morning.

And so it was.

CHAPTER TWENTY THREE

AN OVERABUNDANCE OF JOY COURSED through Regina's body when she woke on the morning of her wedding. She stretched out her arms and savored the weightless bliss she experienced thanks to a good night's rest and a comfortable bed.

After rising, she slipped her feet into her slippers, pulled on her robe and went to open the curtains. Outside, a sheen of morning frost sparkled upon the ground. Reds, yellows, oranges, and greens combined to create a bright combination of autumn foliage.

Eager with anticipation, Regina turned her back on the picturesque scene and rang for her maid. "Are you ready to embark on your new adventure, my lady?" Lillian asked as she combed out her hair.

"More than you can imagine." She'd spent the last three weeks meeting with Carlton almost every day. And during that time, she'd fallen more deeply in love with him. Amidst all the gossip, she'd found strength in his company, and in return she'd done her best to help him adjust to his new position within Society.

Being reinstated as duke was something the king had insisted upon after learning that Carlton was the true heir to the Windham title. Marcus had not been as lucky. He'd had to surrender his honorary title as well as the one he was meant to inherit from Hedgewick. But at least he had managed to keep the house in exchange for a sizeable sum donated to the royal coffers.

Lillian twisted a lock and pinned it in place. "I'm pleased for you, my lady. It appears as though you've found the happily ever after all women dream of."

Regina smiled at her reflection. Lillian was working a miracle with her hair. On the table was the diamond necklace and matching earrings Carlton had given her yesterday.

"He's a good man," Regina murmured. "The very best, I believe." She couldn't imagine sharing her life with anyone else, and when she finally entered the church three hours later and saw him waiting for her at the end of the aisle, it was all she could do not to leave her brother's side and run toward him.

"Shall we?" Marcus asked as the organ began to play. The pews were filled with people who'd come to witness the ceremony, either out of curiosity or because they'd been invited. With a tiny nod Regina took the arm Marcus offered and smiled. Speaking was difficult, if not impossible, the emotion she felt so intense it clogged up her throat.

They started forward together and as they walked, she was pleased to see Claus and Philipa near the back. A tiny bubble of laughter spiraled up through her and made her relax. The idea of lords and ladies occupying the same building as a bawd was outrageously funny. Regina bit her lip to stop the giggles that pressed their way forward.

"What is it?" Marcus asked in a whisper.

"Just a humorous contradiction." She spotted the Duke and Duchess of Coventry, the Duke and Duchess of Huntley, and the Duke and Duchess of Redding. All were gathered to watch the proceedings, regardless of whether they approved of her and Carlton or not. At the front of the church where her mother should have been was an empty seat. The former countess was too ashamed to show her face in public after everything that had happened, so Regina had known for a while that she would be absent. Instead, she was glad that MacNeil was there next to Carlton, his solid body and height silently offering strength and support to his friend.

"I trust you to take good care of her, Windham," Marcus said as he placed her hand in Carlton's.

"Of course." Carlton's eyes were trained on her and her alone. As if no one else existed. His fingers closed around hers before he muttered a hushed, "You look stunning," and turned her to face the vicar.

The next hour passed in a blur. All Regina could concentrate on was how warm Carlton's hand felt against her own. He glanced down at her. A frown creased his brow and the vicar coughed.

"Do you?" Carlton asked in a voice so low only she would hear it.

The sound of it, the change in cadence and tone, snapped her out of her reverie and helped sharpen her focus. "Yes," she whispered, and then a much louder, "Yes. Yes of course."

Smiling up at Carlton, she gave her consent to a few more questions. A wry smile teased his lips as he spoke his vows next, leaving no doubt in her mind that he bound himself to her without any regret.

"May I kiss the bride?" Carlton asked Regina after the ceremony when they were alone in the carriage that would take them to the Berkly residence for a wedding breakfast hosted by Marcus. His arm was around her, pressing her into his side.

In answer, she tipped her head back and turned to face him. A slight nod was all it took for his mouth to find hers in a gentle, unhurried caress. The tenderness opened her heart and laid it bare, forcing her to reveal the extent to which she loved him. The powerful feeling was matched by his own. She could feel it in every touch, each soft and reverent slide of his lips over hers.

With a sigh, she conveyed her appreciation for the tender embrace. She wasn't ready for it to end moments later when the carriage drew to a halt. "We'll have to continue this later," Carlton told her in a low rumble that caused her entire body to quiver. And when he punctuated the statement with a quick kiss to the side of her neck, she felt her skin prick and a rush of heat claim her.

Lord, the patience she would have to endure for the next few hours was likely to kill her. This certainty grew more pronounced with each heated glance Carlton gave her while they mingled with guests in the Berkly parlor. And it only got worse once they were shown into the dining room and took their seats there, for his hand found her thigh beneath the table, after which it became quite trying for her to carry on any conversation.

"You're a terrible scoundrel," she told him as soon as they climbed back into their carriage and set off for Windham House. "I could hardly concentrate on Marcus's speech."

"It was excellent," Carlton told her slyly. "A pity you cannot recall each word."

She slapped his arm but failed to keep a straight face. "At least he had it written down, so there's a chance I'll be able to read it one day as long as he doesn't throw it away."

"I'm sorry. Keepin' me 'ands off ye just wasn't an option."

His change of dialect sent a thrill darting through her. A flutter of anticipation stirred in her belly. She reached for his hand and clasped it tightly. "It was a lovely wedding."

He raised their joined hands and pressed a kiss against hers. "Ye didn't have very much cake though."

She grinned. "I simply couldn't get one more bite down." Perhaps because her belly had been in constant upheaval, fluttering like mad with the expectation of what would happen between them once they were alone. "I did ask Marcus to have some of it sent over to the house tomorrow."

"Not too early, I hope."

"Around noon?"

His eyes glinted like a pair of black diamonds. "I'm not so sure ye'll be out of bed by then, luv."

The promise of sensual pleasure was curled around every word, and Regina's pulse leapt in response. She swallowed and gripped his hand tighter. He answered with a low chuckle and pulled her into his arms for the sort of kiss that threatened to scorch her. It was urgent and unapologetic, almost savage in its roughness. But Regina didn't mind. She savored her husband's desire for her, his fierce display of need, for it easily matched her own.

By the time they reached their house, her breaths were ragged, her heart beating wildly against her breast. A few loose strands dangling over one cheek suggested some hairpins had fallen from her hair. Her gown was also slightly twisted, and Carlton's cravat looked more like a hastily tied rag than a fashionable piece of gentleman's attire. His hair was in such disarray there could be no doubt about what they'd been doing during the ride. Which caused her to blush when the coachman wished them both happy. Too flustered to speak, she nodded her thanks while her husband voiced them on both their behalf.

"Finally," Carlton said as soon as they'd made it inside the house and had shut out the rest of the world. Stepping toward her, he nudged her chin slightly upward with his finger and brushed his lips over hers. Then, before she knew what he planned to do next, he swept her up into his arms. She squealed and instinctively wrapped her arms around his neck. Which only made him chuckle. "Didn't expect that, did ye?"

Her legs swung over the side of his arm while her face settled firmly against his chest. "Um. No. Not really." This only made him laugh louder, which caused a deep rumble to vibrate through him and straight into her. Loving the feel, she pressed herself closer and held on tight while he started up the stairs.

Carlton made a left at the top of the landing and strode straight into the room at the end of the hallway. Carefully, he set her on her feet, but when she moved to step away from him so she could get a better look at the flowers decorating the space and the baskets filled with what looked like baked goods, champagne, and fruit, he held her in place.

"Later," he murmured and set his mouth to the sensitive spot where her neck curved into her shoulder.

With a sigh, she surrendered to his ministrations, the flowers and gift baskets quite forgotten. All she could focus on now was the sweet exploration of his hands and the feather-light kisses rekindling the needy desire she'd felt in the carriage. Her legs grew increasingly weak and a slow burning heat flared up deep inside her, sparking with each expert stroke of his fingers. Each touch made her long for him even more fiercely than ever before, perhaps because things were different now. He was her husband, which meant that there would be no restraint, no walking away from what they both wanted. He'd claim her properly this time, and that piece of knowledge was so inviting it almost made her weep.

Instead, she sighed with relief when he finally undid the buttons at the back of her gown and allowed the garment to fall off her shoulders. His eyes darkened, the black fringe of lashes lowering slightly as he went to work on her stays and chemise. Everything was tossed aside, landing in heaps all over the floor until she was utterly naked.

He swallowed, the cords at this throat straining and flexing in response to the movement. His lips were pressed firmly together and there was an almost angry set to his jaw. It caused her to shudder, though not with fear but with pure excitement, for she knew what she saw in his face was primal – an intense desire to mate that caused every muscle inside him to tense.

"Christ, I've missed ye."

She knew what he meant. They'd had no chance to be intimate since she'd left The Black Swan. "Me too," she whispered.

He inhaled sharply, nostrils flaring, in response to that small confession. Eyes locked on hers, he yanked at his cravat until it came free. He shoved his jacket off his shoulders and tossed it aside. A few buttons on his waistcoat flew through the air as he ripped the garment away from his chest and sent it flying. His shirt followed and then his trousers.

Regina gulped. "No smalls?" she inquired with what sounded like a squeak.

His lips curled with unrepentant roguishness as he straightened his back and allowed her the most perfect view of taught skin drawn over honed muscles. "I didn't want to waste time removin' more clothes," he told her as he kicked off his shoes and bent to peel off his hose. "So I only wore what was absolutely necessary."

She stared, completely taken in by his pure masculinity, by the hard planes sculpting his body with a firmness she lacked. He was magnificent and she was completely enthralled.

Christ!

He was going to make a fool of himself if she didn't quit staring at him like that – as if he were a toy she wanted to play with. So he did the only thing he could think to do and stalked forward. His hands landed firmly on her waist before lifting her up in the air.

She gasped with surprise but he ignored her. "Wrap yer legs around me," he ordered and looped one arm beneath her bottom to hold her in place while he walked them both to the bed. Setting one knee on the mattress, he captured her mouth with a hungry kiss and followed her straight down.

She instantly arched against him and murmured his name like a plea. And as eager as he was to get on with things, he forced himself to remember that she was a novice at this and that he must be gentle. So he took his time making sure she was ready and then distracted her from the pain he caused as he joined his body with her, with a kiss that stole his own breath. She was his, just as he'd hoped she would be. The look in her eyes as he broke off the kiss and gazed down at her lovely face was slightly dazed, her cheeks a charming shade of pink, and her lips…he'd soon kiss them again.

"Are ye all right, luv?" he asked, just to be sure. She nodded and then adjusted her position, bringing him closer and almost breaking the final thread of restraint he possessed as she moved against him.

A hiss tore past his teeth and God help him if she didn't smile, like a vixen who knew exactly what she was doing. "Careful now or I won't be able to control meself any longer."

"I don't think I'm going to break. In fact, I quite like the way this feels already." And then she moved again, threading her fingers through his hair and hooking one foot around his thigh as she did so.

A rush of desire rose up inside him. It was like a wave sweeping over his body and wrecking his fragile control. Driven by instinct he surged forward, both giving and taking in equal measure, all the while conscious of how bloody lucky he was to have met her, to have won her heart and made her his wife, to be here right now in this bed with her gasping and sighing beneath him.

She was more untamed than he'd ever expected and he, scoundrel that he was, totally loved it – the contradiction between proper lady and uninhibited woman so heady it pushed him toward a steep climb made even more powerful by the emotions that she instilled in his heart.

"I love ye," he managed the second before he peaked and started to soar. She joined him a heartbeat later, concentrating the pleasure until it grew so intense he could scarcely think.

"I love you too," she said a while later when they'd both caught their breath. Undone and somewhat shaken by the intensity of the experience, he'd collapsed on his forearms, rolled onto his side and pulled her against him.

He kissed her shoulder in response to her comment and felt his body prepare itself for round two. "Are ye sore?"

"A little," she confessed. Then after a moment, "But that doesn't mean we can't do it again."

This comment earned her a playful nip which in turn made her giggle. "Perhaps we should have a snack first," he said and deliberately pushed himself up and away from her glorious body before he could take advantage. Because no matter how eager she was for more lovemaking or how thrilled he was by her blatant enthusiasm, he believed she needed a rest. So he prepared a couple of plates with some fruit, cheese, and biscuits and poured them each a glass of champagne.

"Will you ever grow your moustache back, do you think?" she asked while they picnicked on the bed.

He shrugged one shoulder. "Only if you want me to."

She considered that for a second and finally shook her head. "I prefer you without it."

"Then it's settled. No more moustaches." She grinned and he could not resist, so he leaned toward her and kissed her deeply, tasting the pear she'd been eating as well as a hint of champagne. "You smell divine, by the way." When he broke the kiss and leaned back, she was so delightfully flushed that he had to kiss her again. "I have somethin' fer ye," he whispered close to her ear.

"But…you've already given me jewelry and—"

"Perhaps I should amend me statement by sayin' I've somethin' fer both of us." Removing their plates, he set them on the dresser and collected one of the books she'd been studying with Philipa. He handed it to Regina and watched her eyes widen and her face turn a bright shade of red. "If ye like, we can start at the very beginnin' and work our way through it."

Without saying a word, she reached for him and pulled him to her, bringing him home. This was where he belonged. With Regina. And fate had shown him the way.

CHAPTER TWENTY FOUR

IT WAS ANOTHER TYPICAL EVENING at Amourette's. The men who came here to enjoy a decadent evening of debauchery included only those with enough coin to afford it. This wasn't the sort of a cheap establishment one might expect in St. Giles, but one that prided itself on quality. This kept the riffraff away and resulted in the occasional peer walking through the doors.

Everything was possible here, every fantasy just one payment away from being realized. Provided no harm came to the girls. They weren't dressed in common clothes but in silk and lace with dozens of ribbons, the occasional feathers, and enough crystal beads to dazzle any man looking to have a good time. Few clients were bachelors. The majority were either betrothed or married, which was why Amourette's was as popular as it was. Because it promised discretion.

Sitting on the floor at the top of the stairs leading up from the wood paneled foyer, Ida Veronica Strong watched as Philipa played the hostess. She paired each man who arrived with one of the available courtesans, who then either escorted her companion into the parlor or upstairs to her bedchamber. None of the men ever spotted Ida. They were much too preoccupied by the courtesans to do so, and in any case, she was sitting away from the steps, on the landing just past the spot where the banister turned.

Her face pressed against the balusters for a better view. She'd recognized the previous man who'd arrived. He was a regular client who came once a week and always asked to see Scarlet. But although Scarlet had returned to Amourette's, she no longer worked, so the man in question was now paired off with other women.

Having spent the last four years of her life in this brothel since her father brought her here at the age of fifteen, Ida viewed the women who lived here as friends. Perhaps even family, though only Philipa knew her real reason for being there. Everyone else believed that she was the daughter of one of Philipa's old acquaintances and that Philipa had assumed guardianship of her after the parent had died. Which was more or less true, although there was more to it than that.

The front door opened again and a new gentleman entered the foyer. Seen from above, it was hard for Ida to gauge his height except by measuring him against the painting that hung immediately to his left. His shoulders appeared to reach the lower part of the frame, making him several inches taller than she. He removed his hat, allowing her to see the top of his head, which was covered by lustrous hair colored in shades of oak and chestnut brown. His build was both imposing yet somehow elegant at the same time. Perhaps because of the authoritative way in which he moved that suggested high social standing and power.

He glanced around and, finding the foyer empty, looked up.

Ida froze. Even though she knew she ought to retreat to her room and hide, she could not seem to move. Her gaze was locked with his, her heart pounding harder with each passing second. Heavens, he was far more handsome than she had expected, perhaps the most handsome man she had ever seen.

Eventually, it was he who spoke. "You there." His voice was not unpleasant, but the arrogance of his tone made Ida tense with irritation. "Will you keep me waiting forever or do you plan on serving me? I haven't all night."

Her curiosity about him turned to immediate dislike. She shifted her gaze to the parlor door and then to the one leading into the music room. Both were shut and Philipa wasn't in sight. Most likely, she'd become distracted by Mr. Greer, an old client of hers who still flirted with her even though he now found his pleasure with some of the younger women.

"It will likely take an hour before one of the women is free and ready to take you," Ida told the newcomer, hoping to send him on his way. "They're all fully occupied at the moment."

"You're not."

The comment was like a slap in the face, even though it ought not to have been. After all, she was a young woman, just nineteen years old, and she did live in a brothel. He wasn't the first man to make assumptions, and yet it still felt like an insult.

"I'm not available," she told him plainly.

He tilted his head and continued to study her. "A pity," he finally murmured.

Deliberately, Ida quashed the surge of appreciation the compliment caused and stood. His gaze followed her every movement as she began descending the stairs and for the first time in her life, she felt her stomach flutter in response to a man's perusal.

She forced herself not to focus on that but on seeing to his satisfaction instead. After all, if he was a peer, as she now believed him to be, he would have influence. One bad word uttered by him against Amourette's and the business Philipa had struggled to build might crumble. Ida couldn't allow that to happen, so she would just have to be helpful and nice to him no matter how much it grated.

"If you're willing to wait, I can have some food brought up from the kitchen – a plate of sandwiches perhaps? There are also newspapers available to help you pass the time."

He nodded, but made no remark.

Moving past him, Ida caught a whiff of something wonderfully rich and enticing, a blend of leather and musk combined with a hint of coffee. She was almost tempted to pause and sniff the air, but resisted the urge and went to the front desk instead. "Name?" she inquired. When he didn't answer immediately, she glanced up and was met by a stony expression. "It doesn't have to be your real name."

He stared at her until she was forced to move on

account of the piercing intensity of his eyes. They were like two glass orbs filled with liquid gold, both bright and unyielding in their command.

"Mr. N. will do," he eventually said.

"Excellent." Ida made a note in the ledger Philipa used to keep track of her clients. "And do you have any particular tastes, Mr. N?"

The pause that followed caused heat to erupt all over Ida's skin like an unpleasant rash. She could feel him staring at her even though she kept her eyes trained on the paper where she'd been writing.

"Why do you need to know that?" he finally asked.

She took a moment to allow a deep breath to calm her. For reasons she could not explain, this man was frazzling her nerves. "Some of the women here specialize in more uncommon modes of…um…gratification." She barely managed to say that last bit without choking on her tongue.

"I see." Another pause, and then, "Does asking her to pretend she's my maid fall into that category?"

Ida's skin grew even hotter. The very idea… "No." She scribbled a note and silently cursed herself for the uneven stroke of her letters.

"How about if…" His voice trailed off and Ida waited once again for him to say the unexpected. But just when she was about to look up and make sure that he meant to continue, he grabbed her wrist and jerked it toward him.

What the..?

"Where did you get this?"

The harshness in his voice sent a tremor down

Ida's spine. She tried to pull her wrist back but he held on too tight and refused to release her. "Let me go," she demanded. If he didn't, she'd scream to alert the two men that Philipa employed for protection.

"Not until you tell me why you're wearing this bracelet."

Ida went utterly still. Fear crept under her skin and knotted her insides. "It was a gift," she whispered. "I...I don't know where it was purchased, if that's what you want to know."

He narrowed his gaze, gave the bracelet one final look and let her wrist go. "It isn't. I already know that part." Ida sucked in a breath and took a step back, dropping the quill in the process. "Matthew Strong ordered it from a jeweler on Bond Street when he returned from France. He said it would make a fine gift for his daughter."

Swallowing past the dryness in her throat, Ida shook her head. "Why would you say that?"

"Because I was there." As if seeing something in the way she reacted to that particular comment, he leaned in closer, his eyes now wide with disbelief. "My God. You're her, aren't you? You're Ida Strong."

And just like that, the safety Ida had known for the past four years was torn from her grasp. If this man knew who she was, others would learn of her existence soon. Word would spread and the men who'd had her father tried for treason would hunt her down and kill her as well.

THANK YOU SO MUCH FOR taking the time to read *The Forgotten Duke*. If you enjoyed this novel and would like to try some of my other books, I suggest giving the Crawfords series a go, starting with *No Ordinary Duke*. This book features a duke who just wants to live a normal life and a woman who despises the aristocracy. When sparks start to fly between them and she then discovers his true identity, compromises must be made if they're to stand a chance of a happily ever after together.

Or if you haven't read the previous books in my *Diamonds In The Rough* series, you might consider starting at the very beginning with *A Most Unlikely Duke* where bare-knuckle boxer, Raphe Matthews, unexpectedly inherits a duke's title. Figuring out how to navigate Society won't be easy, but receiving advice from the lady next door may just be worth it.

You can find out more about my new releases, backlist deals and giveaways by signing up for my newsletter here: *www.sophiebarnes.com*

And don't forget to follow me on Facebook for even more updates and fun book related posts.

Once again, I thank you for your interest in my books. Please take a moment to leave a review since this can help other readers discover my books. And please continue reading for an excerpt from *A Most Unlikely Duke*.

A MOST UNLIKELY DUKE

Diamonds in the Rough
Available now!

CHAPTER ONE

London, 1818

THICK CLOUDS DARKENED TO SHADES of gray as they rolled across the London sky. Beneath them, standing in the middle of the Black Swan courtyard, Raphe Matthews drew back his fist, his muscles bunching tightly together—just long enough for him to assess the angle and speed with which to release all that power. Instinct made it a brief calculation. Less than a second, and then he sent his fist flying.

The punch snapped his opponent's face sideways, producing a spray of spit and blood that painted the air with specks of crimson. A cheer erupted from those who'd come to witness the fight—a motley selection of hardened individuals. This place was not for the weak or the wealthy. It reeked of filth and the daily struggle to survive. This was St. Giles, but it might as well have been the bowels of hell for all the difference it made.

"Come on!" someone shouted.

Raphe's other fist met a hard chest with a *crunch*. His knuckles ached, the force of the punch vibrating through him.

"Matthews, Matthews, Matthews..." The chant shook the air while Raphe shifted his footing, regaining his balance just in time to accept the blows that followed. He didn't mind, for it only revealed his opponent's sudden desperation.

Raising his fists to block the attack, Raphe bobbed to the side, turning away, just out of reach. And yet, he was close—so close he could smell the sweat on the other man's skin, see the fear that shone in his eyes, the beads of moisture clinging to his hair that dripped onto his brow.

More shouts flooded the air, drowning him in a cacophony of unintelligible noise. The wave of encouragement shifted, alerting him that support had changed—no longer in his favor.

Forcing it into the background, Raphe focused on the man he was meant to beat. Today his name was Calvin Butler. Raphe launched himself forward, surrendering to the rage, and let the punches fly, beating back pain and anger until Calvin Butler lay stretched out on the ground, hands covering his face in surrender. A fleeting second of silence passed, just long enough to be sure of the outcome, and then the spectators sent up a roar in response to Raphe's victory.

Exhausted, he stumbled back, a light drizzle dampening his skin. A coat was draped over his shoulders while Butler was helped to his feet—a sorry sight, with his blackened eye and swollen lip distorting an otherwise handsome face.

Turning away, Raphe pushed his way in the direction of the taproom. All he wanted right now was a drink.

Fast.

"Butler ain't lookin' too good," Raphe's friend, Benjamin Thompson, said as he came up beside him. A couple of inches shorter than Raphe, his green eyes were a handsome complement to his ginger hair and freckles. He was without a doubt the kindest and most dependable person Raphe knew, besides his own sisters. Together, they made their way to the bar, where Ben promptly called for a server. "Give us a couple o' pints."

Resting his elbows on the counter, Raphe grunted his response to Ben's question. "He knew what 'e was in fer."

Ben nodded. The beer arrived, and both men took a healthy swig. "Ye could 'ave been gentler, though. The man was done. No need to keep beatin' at him like that."

Stilling, Raphe slid his gaze toward his friend. "I couldn't 'elp it." The rage had burned its way through him, driving him forward and filling his mind with one singular purpose: The need to win. "I don't know 'ow to fight any other way."

"I know," Ben said softly.

No, you don't. You have no bloody idea.

In this, he'd never been completely honest, not even with Ben. "In any case, the blunt's pretty good—lets me keep a roof over me sisters' heads."

"Aye, an' a decent one at that."

Raphe couldn't argue. He'd visited Ben's home once—an overcrowded single room that he shared with his parents and five siblings. By comparison, Raphe and his sisters lived like royalty. "Have ye ever thought of gettin' out of this place? Out of St. Giles?"

Ben shrugged his shoulders. "An' go where?"

"Somewhere better. Christ, Ben, anywhere's better than this. Ye're a likeable man. Ye could probably snatch up a job at one of 'em fancy 'ouses in Mayfair."

His friend snorted. "An' 'ave some nob lookin' down on me, demandin' I polish 'is boots—or worse, empty 'is chamber pot? I'd rather stay by the docks, thank ye very much. At least there I can take some pride in me work."

"Understood. But the pay there's never goin' to afford ye with yer own home. Don't ye wish to marry one day?"

"Sure. But there's a limit to what I'm willing to do for a bit of blunt, Raphe." He took another sip of his beer. "I'll not lose me dignity by workin' for a class o' people I can't abide, nor by lowerin' meself to doin' demeanin' work."

The words speared Raphe to his soul, filling him with shame. "I know," he muttered with admiration. If only he could be more like him, not wanting anything beyond what life had tossed his way. Perhaps, if he didn't have his sisters to consider, he wouldn't care so much.

"Ye fought well today, lad," a man's voice suddenly spoke from directly behind him.

Bristling, Raphe set down his beer on the counter and turned to face his handler, whose attire—a purple velvet jacket and matching top hat—lent an air of flamboyance unmatched by anyone else. And yet, in spite of the fine clothes, there was nothing cultured about this man, a scoundrel who'd gained his wealth through illicit deals and by taking advantage of others. His origins were questionable, but rumor had it he'd killed more than once in pursuit of power. Raphe didn't know what to believe. All he knew was that in spite of his own prejudices, crime in St. Giles had decreased since Carlton Guthrie's arrival eighteen years earlier. Or so he'd been told.

"Mr. Guthrie. Good to see ye." A blatant lie, if ever there was one.

Guthrie's moustache twitched. "Likewise." He sounded jovial, but only a fool would mistake that for kindness. Least of all when his henchman, a scarred boulder of a Scotsman by the name of MacNeil, stood at his right shoulder. Guthrie nodded toward Ben, who returned the salutation.

"Come. Share a drink with me," Guthrie said, addressing Raphe. "We've much to discuss, you 'n I."

"And Thompson?" Raphe asked, not wanting to abandon his friend.

"I'm sure he'll be willin' to wait for ye till ye get back." Reaching into his pocket, he pulled out a gold coin and dropped it in front of Ben. "For yer trouble. What I 'ave to say to Matthews 'ere doesn't concern ye. Understand?"

Raphe glared at Guthrie for a moment before looking at Ben. "I'm sorry. I—"

"No worries," Ben said, pocketing the coin that would keep his family fed for the next few days. "I'll see ye tomorrow at work, aye?"

Nodding, Raphe watched him go.

"Well?" Guthrie's voice drew Raphe's attention back to him. " 'Ow about that drink then?"

Eyeing first Guthrie and then MacNeil, Raphe gave a curt nod. "By all means."

Guthrie's eyes sparkled. "Excellent." His lips

stretched into a smile. "Follow me." Turning away, he led Raphe through the taproom, where tobacco smoke mingled with the smell of roasting meat and beer. Dice rolled across one table in a game of hazard. A hand touched his thigh, inappropriately stroking upward until he pushed it away.

"No' in the mood, luv?" the woman to whom it belonged asked. She was sitting down, her legs spread across the lap of a man who was busily burying his face between her half-exposed breasts.

Pitying the life she'd been dealt, he told her gently, "I've not the time."

"La'er then?" she called as he strode away, not answering her question. Blessedly, his sisters had managed to avoid such a fate.

" 'Ave a seat," Guthrie said moments later as they stepped inside a private room at the end of a hallway. It was sparsely furnished, with just a plain wooden table and four chairs. On top of the table stood a pitcher and a couple of mugs. "Some ale for me champion?" Guthrie asked, indicating the pitcher.

Grabbing a chair, Raphe dropped down onto it and poured himself a drink, while Guthrie claimed the other chair with more finesse. "Will ye 'ave some?" Raphe asked, indicating the same pitcher.

Guthrie beamed. "Don't mind if I do." He waited for Raphe to pour before reaching for the mug and raising it. "To yer victory today."

"To me victory," Raphe muttered, downing the bitter resentment he felt with a brew to match.

"I've 'igh 'opes for ye," Guthrie said, tapping

a finger against his nose. "Unbeaten for the fifteenth time. That's unprecedented, tha' is."

Raphe saw the spark that lit his eyes, like the promise of treasure or some such thing. "Wha' do ye want, Guthrie?"

"So cynical, Matthews." Guthrie's upper lip drew back, revealing his teeth. "Must a man always want some'in? Can't 'e simply enjoy a drink wi' an old friend?"

Old friend?

Hardly.

"Not when 'e's got 'im by the bollocks."

Guthrie's mouth tightened, his eyes darkening just enough to offer a glimpse of his true nature. "Is tha' 'ow ye see our relationship, laddy?"

His demeaning tone made Raphe's muscles flex. He glanced at MacNeil, who stood by the door, running his thumb along the edge of a wicked blade, and was instantly reminded of the punishment he'd suffered the one time when he'd been foolish enough to try and thwart Guthrie's wishes. Shoulders tensing, Raphe returned his gaze to the man who owned him. " 'Ow else should I see it? I'm yer puppet, ain't I?"

Guthrie nodded. "Aye, but ye're me favorite one. Which is why I'd like to offer ye a deal."

Raphe stiffened. "What sor' of deal?"

"The sor' that could set ye free, laddy."

A tempting notion, but surely too good to be true. Still, he couldn't help but ask. "What do ye have in mind?"

Leaning forward, Guthrie placed his elbows on the table, the fingers of his right hand reaching up to stroke his chin. "Ye see, there's goin' to be an opportunity soon—a grand one, at that."

Raphe crossed his arms. "Ye don't say."

The corner of Guthrie's eye flinched. "No need to get cocky, now." Snapping his fingers, he drew MacNeil closer. "Give the laddy 'is earnin's." There was a pause, and then a pouch dropped onto the table with a jangling *thump*. "Naturally, we've kept our share."

A fat 90 percent.

"Naturally," Raphe echoed. He didn't bother to hide his displeasure.

"But..." Guthrie took another sip of his ale. "Word 'as it, the Bull will be comin' to town in a month or so." Raphe straightened in his chair, while Guthrie wiped his mouth with the back of his hand, removing a line of foam. "If ye figh' 'im and ye win, ye'll be debt-free. The winnings are gonna be that huge."

Raphe didn't doubt it. The Bull was, after all, the bare-knuckle boxing world champion—undefeated since beating Tobias Flannigan several years earlier. Since then, he'd crippled several of his opponents. The man was a legend. "I'll do it," Raphe said without blinking.

"But if ye lose..."

"I won't," Raphe assured him.

"But if ye do..."

Grabbing the pouch that still sat on the table, Raphe pocketed his money. "I know the risk, Guthrie, an' I'm willin' to take it."

It was past eleven o'clock in the evening by the time Raphe returned home, his knuckles tender and his body still sore from the fight. Glad to get out of the cold, he closed the door on the rain that now poured from a thunderous sky, shrugged out of his coat and hung it on a hook behind the door just as his sister Amelia entered from an adjoining room that served as a small parlor.

"Good evenin'." She yawned, leaning against the door frame.

Squinting through the darkness, Raphe echoed her salutation. "I thought ye would be asleep by now." Stepping past her, he entered their tiny kitchen and snatched up the tinder box.

"I was," Amelia said, following him into the chilly room.

A threadbare shawl was draped across her shoulders, and as she pulled it tighter with pale and trembling fingers, Raphe felt his heart lurch. This wasn't right. His sister did not deserve to live like this. None of them did.

Pushing aside such fruitless ponderings, he found a candle, struck a flint and held it to the wick until a flame began to bloom, driving the darkness toward the walls where it struggled against the light.

"If it makes any difference, Juliette's safely tucked into bed." Amelia said, referring to their younger sister, whose weaker disposition was a constant cause for unease. When Raphe lifted the lid of a nearby pot and peered inside, Amelia added, "I made soup for dinner."

"Smells delicious," he dutifully told her.

"We both know 'ow untrue that is, bu' I appreciate yer optimism."

Meeting her gaze, Raphe made a deliberate effort to smile. "Per'aps I can manage some meat for us tomorrow." It would certainly be a welcome change from the potatoes and turnips they'd been eating for what seemed like forever. Christ, he was so tired of having a sore belly all the time, and his sisters... they never complained, but he knew they needed better nourishment than what they were getting.

"That'd be nice," Amelia said. Her tone, however, suggested that she doubted his ability to manage such a feat.

Bothered by her lack of faith in him, he grabbed a chunk of bread and tore off a large piece. "A chicken ought to be possible. If we make it last a few days."

Amelia simply nodded. Grabbing a cup, she filled it with water and placed it before him. "I miss the smell of a bustlin' kitchen."

The comment threw him for a second. "Wha'?"

"Meat roastin' on the fire, bread bakin' in the oven." She shook her head wistfully. "It's funny. I can't picture Mama, but I remember Cook— plump cheeks an' a kind smile. I remember bein' 'appy in the kitchen back 'ome."

The sentimental thought made Raphe weary. He didn't bother to point out that she'd only been seven when they'd lost their parents and there'd been nothing left for Raphe to do but turn his back on the house in which they'd spent the early years of their childhoods and walk away, taking his siblings with him. He'd been no more than eight years old and with a mighty burden weighing on his shoulders. "I know this isn't the sor' of life that any of us ever imagined." Feeling his temper begin to rise at the memory of what their parents had done to them all, he added, "Hopefully, in time, things'll get better."

"I'm sure ye're right." *Could she possibly sound any more unconvinced?*

He ate a spoonful of soup, the bland flavor just a touch better than plain hot water. Amelia took a step forward. "The reason I didn't retire with Juliette earlier is 'cause of this letter." She waved a piece of paper in his direction. "It arrived for ye today while ye were out."

Frowning, Raphe stared at her. "Do ye know who sent it?" He couldn't even recall the last time he'd received a letter. Nobody ever wrote to him or his sisters.

"The sender's name's smudged. So's the address. It's a miracle it arrived here at all." Handing the letter to Raphe, she watched as he turned it over and studied the penmanship. Sure enough, the only legible part of the address, which even appeared to have been altered once or twice, was his name: Mister Raphael Matthews.

Curious, he set down his spoon and tore open the seal.

"What's it say?" Amelia eagerly asked.

Reading it slowly to ensure he understood it correctly, Raphe sucked in a breath. He looked up at his sister, blinked, then bowed his head and read the letter again. Silence settled. Amelia's feet shifted, conveying her impatience. It seemed impossible, yet there it was—an extraordinary pronouncement staring him right in the face. Raising his gaze, he leaned back in his seat, the letter rustling between his fingers. "According to this..." He shook his head, unable to fathom the absurdity of it. "I'm the new Duke of Huntley."

The silence that followed was acute. Amelia stared at him, eyes wide with a strange blend of surprise, uncertainty and hope. She looked like she wanted to believe him, and yet... "Really?"

"If what this says is true, then yes."

"But as far as I know, Papa 'ad no title, so I don't—I don't understand."

"I know. It seems inconceivable. Preposterous. But..." He handed her the letter and watched while she read. "Do ye think it might be a hoax?"

Amelia shook her head. "I daren't suppose such a thing. It looks authentic enough with this seal right 'ere and a stamp at the bottom. Squinting, she read the small print that Raphe had missed in his surprise. "Mr. Rupert Etheridge, Solicitor to the Duke of Huntley." Amelia drew a deep breath. Expelled it again. "Bloody hell!"

Raphe quietly nodded. "It's the damnedest thing, don't ye think?" He stared up at Amelia, still trying to process the news.

"Yes. It is. In fact, I wouldn't 'ave thought it possible at all. Not ever."

"Me neither." Amelia handed the letter back to Raphe, He set it on the table next to his bowl of soup and jabbed it with his finger. "But our great grandfather *was* the Sixth Duke of Huntley."

"I'm aware of that. But when 'e died, the title passed to our great uncle an' split off from our side of the family." She hesitated, as if trying to understand. "I thought succession 'ad to be lineal—that it 'ad to go from son to son. So 'ow can it possibly jump to ye?"

"That's just it. Says 'ere that—" leaning forward, he carefully read what had to be the most significant part, "the letters patent generally include a limitation pertainin' to the heirs of the body, but in this instance it 'as been left out. With this taken into consideration, we've looked fer the late duke's nearest kin, and ye, Mr. Matthews, appear to be it."

"Ye're *it*?" Amelie's eyebrows were raised, her lips parted with dumbfounded surprise.

"Apparently so."

"Bloody hell," she said again as she slumped down onto another chair with a dazed expression. "I can't believe 'e 'ad no sons. Don't aristocrats always 'ave an heir an' a spare for these situations?"

"Yes, but accordin' to this, the Eighth Duke of Huntley's sons perished at sea a couple o' months ago. The shock of it was apparently too much for their father. It killed 'im."

"God." Amelia paused for a moment before saying, "So there's nobody else but ye to fill 'is shoes."

"No. Only problem is, I ain't so sure I'll be able to manage it. It's been fifteen years since..." His shoulders stiffened and his chest tightened. He couldn't speak of the event that had plunged them all into destitution. Refused to do so—refused to open the door to the darkness.

Thankfully, Amelia spoke, filling the silence. "Ye can ignore the letter if the thought of being a duke disagrees with ye."

"True." He considered the ramifications of showing up at Huntley House. And then the door to the darkness creaked open, quite unexpectedly, and he was faced with the faith that Bethany had placed in him. She'd believed in his ability to save her. He'd been her older brother, and she'd looked to him for help. Except he'd failed her, and now she was dead.

He slammed the door to the darkness and stared at Amelia. This was it. The chance to do what he wished he could have done for Bethany—a chance to get his surviving sisters out of St. Giles and back to the world where they belonged. "I can't ignore this opportunity. I can't deny ye the things ye deserve." *I can't take the risk of losing you because of my own apprehensions and prejudices.* "Think of it, Amelia. No more 'ungry bellies, or worryin' about money. No more scrapin' to get by."

"No more Mr. Guthrie," she murmured.

The uplifting thought spilled through him, immediately halted by another. "Ye know, we'll never fit in." They'd spent too long amidst the lower classes—could barely recall what it meant to live in a fine house and to have servants. Fox Grove Manor, where they'd grown up, had not been overly large, and most of the servants had been gone at the end, but he had a vague recollection of tin soldiers and the sound of piano music playing while Molly dusted the china. It seemed so peculiar now, the thought of hiring someone to do the simplest task.

He shook his head at the absurdity of it all and wondered if he would be capable of becoming such a person after growing accustomed to the working-class ways. And that was just the beginning. It did not take into account the ridicule they were bound to face with every misstep they made.

Because if there was one thing he knew about the aristocracy, it was their cold, hard censure of those who didn't belong.

"Here at least we 'ave friends." He thought of what Ben had told him earlier. Of Ben, in general. He'd never understand the decision Raphe now considered making. Worse than that, Raphe knew in his gut that claiming the Huntley title would destroy that friendship—that in order for him and his sisters to stand any chance at all of making a life for themselves in Mayfair, they'd have to sever all ties to St. Giles.

"True. There are surely people I'll miss—people who've been kind to us over the years, like Mary-Ellen's family an' the 'aroldsons." She reached for Raphe's hand and squeezed it tight. "But we also 'ave no future 'ere. At least none that I can see."

"I know. It's me greatest regret."

"It's not yer fault."

"No, but I 'ave the chance to change things now." Mind made up, he said, "I'll claim the title an' make things right fer both of ye."

She pressed her lips together and nodded agreement. "It'll be an easier life than the one we 'ave now."

Even though he knew she underestimated the task that stood before them, he didn't argue, happy with the knowledge that his sisters would soon be living the lives to which they'd both been born. But the truth of it was that they faced a daunting struggle—one in which their pride and dignity would be tested at every turn. Steeling himself for the battle ahead, Raphe bid his sister a good night, aware that the dawn would bring turbulence with it.

AUTHOR'S NOTE

Dear Reader,

Since much of *The Forgotten Duke* hinges on Regina running away from an arranged marriage to a fourteen-year-old boy, I'd like to take a moment to address the law that inspired such a plot.

In today's world, it might seem outrageous or even implausible for such a marriage to take place in a country like England. And even during the Regency, it could only have happened with both parties' consent, so forced marriages like the one Regina and Stokes faced were probably not very likely to occur. However, the Hedgewicks and Windhams are powerful people determined to do whatever it takes for their children to wed. Bribing a vicar or resorting to blackmail would eventually have led to this desired result, prompting the idea of having to flee.

As for the law itself:

From 1753 until its repeal in 1823, *An Act for the Better Preventing of Clandestine Marriage,* more commonly known as *Lord Hardwicke's Act*, was the law by which marriage was governed in England. With regard to permissible age of marriage, the act provided that "a marriage by parties at the age of consent (14 for males, 12 for females) was good, though without the consent of parents; and even when contracted before that age, if they did not dissent when they attained it." (*Priestly v Hughes* 909)

That being said, parties under the age of twenty-one (the age of majority, which is different from the age of consent to marry) needed their parents' approval in order to marry by special license – if the marriage was to be considered valid. Regina and Stokes both had this, albeit against their wills.

For those of you wondering about the disease Stokes was diagnosed with, asthenic gout was the first description of rheumatoid arthritis, which was made in 1800 by Augustin Jacob Landré-Beauvais for his medical doctorate.

As for the night terrors (which I've described as nightmares since no other word existed until 1965), these can be a real burden and sometimes even a danger to those who suffer from them. According to the Mayo Clinic, symptoms include: screaming or shouting, staring wide-eyed, sweating, kicking and thrashing, being hard to awaken, being confused if awakened, having no or little memory of the event the next morning, possibly getting out of bed and running around the house or having aggressive behavior if blocked or restrained.

Examples of triggers include anxiety, depression and post-traumatic stress.

I hope you have enjoyed this story! The next Diamond In The Rough novel will feature Ida who finds an unlikely ally in the Earl of Fielding, whom you may remember as Gabriella's unlikeable fiancé in *A Most Unlikely Duke*. But characters can grow with experience, and the Fielding you will encounter in 1821 is not the same man he was in 1818.

Hopefully you're just as eager as I am to discover just how much he has changed.

Until then, I wish you happy reading!

ACKNOWLEDGMENTS

I would like to thank Ellen Brock and the Killion Group for their incredible help with the editing of this book. To my beta readers Maria Rose and Barb Hoffarth, your advice truly helped this story shine. My thanks also go to Chris Cocozza who stepped in and offered his help when he learned that I wanted to match the cover of this book to the previous ones in the series. I think you'll agree that the artwork he has provided is stunning as always. I am also extremely grateful for the help offered to me by the following proof readers: Danielle Hankins, Susan Downs Lucas, Barb Hoffarth, Jennifer Becker and Jacqueline Ang.

And to my friends and family, thank you for your constant support and for believing in me. I would be lost without you!

ABOUT THE AUTHOR

Born in Denmark, Sophie has spent her youth traveling with her parents to wonderful places around the world. She's lived in five different countries, on three different continents, has studied design in Paris and New York, and has a bachelor's degree from Parson's School of Design. But most impressive of all – she's been married to the same man three times, in three different countries and in three different dresses.

While living in Africa, Sophie turned to her lifelong passion – writing.

When she's not busy dreaming up her next romance novel, Sophie enjoys spending time with her family, swimming, cooking, gardening, watching romantic comedies and, of course, reading. She currently lives on the East Coast.

You can contact her through her website at *www.sophiebarnes.com*

And please consider leaving a review for this book.

Every review is greatly appreciated!

CPSIA information can be obtained
at www.ICGtesting.com
Printed in the USA
BVHW031823300421
606227BV00005B/41